NOVELS BY JENIFER LEVIN

WATER DANCER
SNOW

SNOW

JENIFER LEVIN

POSEIDON PRESS
NEW YORK

Copyright © 1983 by Jenifer Levin
All rights reserved
including the right of reproduction
in whole or in part in any form
A Poseidon Press Book
Published by Pocket Books, a Division of Simon & Schuster, Inc.
Simon & Schuster Building
Rockefeller Center
1230 Avenue of the Americas
New York, New York 10020
POSEIDON PRESS is a trademark of Simon & Schuster, Inc.
Designed by Irving Perkins Associates
Manufactured in the United States of America

1 2 3 4 5 6 7 8 9 10

Library of Congress Cataloging in Publication Data
Levin, Jenifer.
Snow.

I. Title.
PS3562.E8896S65 1983   813'.52   83-21117
ISBN 0-671-47314-X

THIS BOOK IS DEDICATED TO HUMPHREY EVANS.

But not yet have we solved the incantation of this whiteness, and learned why it appeals with such power to the soul; and more strange and far more portentous—why, as we have seen, it is at once the most meaning symbol of spiritual things, nay, the very veil of the Christian's Deity; and yet should be as it is, the intensifying agent in things the most appalling to mankind.

HERMAN MELVILLE, MOBY DICK

PROLOGUE

Summer in the Gulf of Eilat. Beastly hot was an understatement. Farther north, you could touch the bleached white stones of Jericho's ruins with a fingertip and get a second- or third-degree burn. But up in Jericho what prevailed was a smell of honeysuckle—divine recompense, he guessed, for suffering through the temperature of hell. Farther south there was no recompense—just the Dead Sea, corpse-still water glimmering in the humid atmosphere. Farther still was the Gulf. Eilat—a nothing town battered by heat, by sand, boasting a little museum with a fantastic collection of mounted sharks, the town's main drawing card. Farther south was Nuweiba, then Dahav, little beach oases where you'd crawl out from under palm fronds each morning to face sleepy-eyed camels, black-robed men kneeling in low tide to pray, facing Mecca. And the last stop, Sharm el Sheikh. Soldiers patrolled sand promontories, stripped to the waist. Some covered their shoulders with white prayer shawls—Not for prayer! they told Pablo emphatically, proud of the national propensity for atheism; not for prayer, but against the sun. They were young men, skin blazing rusty brown. The guns they carried were heavy, and by early morning the olive-green thighs of their army trousers were soaked through with sweat.

He'd gotten a lucky lift via army jeep, arrived there at this southern-most point of a land that—on most maps—was nothing more than a barely visible sliver surrounded by far meatier flesh. He'd arrived with his equipment, taken a few shots of jeering, eagerly posing young soldiers, foul cigarettes

9

smoldering out of the sides of their lips. One morning he recognized a Sephardic face among all the others and introduced himself in Spanish. Soon they were rattling away with each other. The Sephardic kid acted like he'd found his best friend—woke him early the next day to point out over the water. There, he said, look. There are the friends you're waiting for. Pablo saw a definite, gliding parade of fins out there in the Gulf's shimmering air. He thought at first they were traveling in a line which somehow disappeared, then realized they were circling. Circling around some other thing in the water, doing their death dance. The air rippled with heat. In the distance the dark fins wavered, rippled like the air, kept gliding around. He wasn't sure but he thought the circle kept getting smaller. The Sephardic kid chuckled. Please to meet your friends. You see them? They're smiling for you, Pablo. You can't bite with your camera.

He poked around the base that day. Not much to do—things were ghastly hot, lethargic. And he'd been permitted only on the special provision that he would severely limit his photography. Only shots of faces, posed, while on army property. No shots of structures, no shots of interiors, of signs, of any equipment whatsoever. Pablo kept his part of the bargain obediently. He was waiting, anyway. He was waiting for Raina Scott.

That day wilted on, and once in a while Pablo walked out along the shore. The boat she'd arranged for was there, motor idle, waiting empty at the makeshift dock. He'd search for fins, eyes shadowed by a hand. Sometimes he'd see one. Sometimes more. They were like dark, broad-edged daggers, and there was something eerie about the way they appeared, from a distance, to be slowly gliding. The smooth trail of fins poking through water appeared to him to have a subtle grace, and a power that, in its singularity, was close to beauty.

The following day his wait ended. It was early, after a bitter breakfast of tomatoes, bread, some kind of sesame mash, mud coffee. He'd gone out to sit on the beach before heat hit full-force, and when he looked along the shoreline thought he saw a mirage. He looked twice. A group of three walked toward him along the sand, and as they got closer he saw they were laden with backpacks and heavy canisters of some sort; he saw that one was a woman, and that she was carrying archery gear. The incongruity of it—this almost-mirage, appearing to him in a morning haze of the world's worst heat—made him start, laugh. A bow and arrow down here in this modern war zone. The sight made him feel he'd lost all sense of place and time. She—with her bow, her arrows—was more foreign than he'd ever be.

He stood.

He noticed she also carried a medium-sized canvas sack with red seeping *through. She stopped when she saw him, waved. The two men stopped with her, glanced at him in a strange sort of unplanned unison, continued walking when she did as if on cue. Pablo grinned. Raina Scott. Well here she was.*

He went to meet her, hand extended.

"Mr. Photographer."

She smiled. Her eyes were large and very dark. They glimmered a little laughter at him.

"Mr. Photographer. Are you part of this show? Or just sitting with the audience?"

She dropped the sack she'd been carrying, offered her hand, and he shook it.

"Pablo Klemer," he muttered.

"I like that! I like that name." She was dark, dark hair curling thickly against her neck, skin browned by sun. And fairly young—he guessed around his own age, late twenties or so, perhaps a couple of years older—but there were no lines on her face to indicate wear and tear. She was all dark vibrancy. She winked. "We're chumming for hammerheads. Want to come along?"

He noticed the silent men in back of her. One had dropped his gear and lit a harsh-scented cigarette. Egyptian, he thought. And a Greek, maybe. Chumming for hammerheads.

"What's that mean?"

"This is chum, Pablo." She kicked at the sack. It sounded a solid thwack and more red came through.

"For what?"

"Hammerheads."

"Oh." Pablo smiled politely. He felt sweat dribble down his spine. "Hammerheads?"

"Hammerhead sharks. Nice mean ones."

She wore a bathing suit, loose lightweight white trousers, deck sneakers. He fell in step beside her as they entered the base. Her crew was not allowed, and Pablo watched them walk silently to the outboard dock, board the cabin boat waiting for them. He'd heard she was meticulous about arrangements, a good organizer of men and of things. She was checking in with the proper authorities. They'd been informed of her commission from the museum in Eilat. And even in this part of the world, they might have heard something about her. Still, to their way of thinking, she would be just one more crazy American doing one more useless thing, and they'd watch her with a careless sort of interest tinged by both envy and scorn.

Pablo got his own gear together. He noticed his hands were trembling sometimes and wondered why. He set an old white cap carefully on his head—

he didn't want to die of sunstroke—and she nodded approvingly. He found himself avoiding her eyes. He felt shy in her presence, tongue-tied. She was somehow awesome to him. Perhaps it was her abundance of visceral power— a fluidity of motion which comes only with immersion in the environment. It was something he remembered admiring in animals before: that natural, strong, almost predatory look which is a combination of male and female principles of motion and bearing. She scared him a little. It was not just her formidable reputation, or the abrupt, half-teasing way she'd addressed him. She could be a little frightening, he thought.

He began to take pictures.

He followed her down to the dock. She disappeared into the boat's cabin, brought out large wooden shovel-like spoons and a couple of metal ladles. The men—dark, silent—were already on deck, busy with riggings. Pablo felt out of place, an intruder. He was unknowledgeable and physically clumsy in this situation. But each time the shutter clicked it gained him some entrance into their way of being—each time he observed something, captured it, he'd become a part of the strange things going on.

Raina dropped the heavy red-seeping canvas sack on the dock boards. She knelt, untied the sack's neck and began shoveling small mounds of fine-ground pulp into each of several waiting pails.

"Hammerheads." Pulp splatted on metal. "Oh, they put up a nice fight. You'll enjoy it, Pablo."

Pablo sat. He watched what she did gravely, focused on the dripping mush and got a shot. From the deck someone called out to her and she paused, listened, then responded in a language he could not recognize.

She smiled at him. "They've got it rigged. We'll go middle or deep for these bastards. Dead bait."

Pablo just sat there on the dock, watching her ladle out beaten red-dripping meat. He concentrated on the slightly musty smell. His sweat dried in the heat. He clicked, clicked, kept getting shots. Sun washed down without obstruction of a single cloud.

She reached into the bucket suddenly with both bare hands, held them out to him dripping red, grinning for the camera.

"Great shot."

"Oh, I put on a good show. And you're going to—what did they say?"— catapult me into the headlines, aren't you? That's what you want to do, isn't it?"

He took a couple more shots. "Of course."

"Good," she said, satisfied. "I like the sound of that."

The dead sopping meat at the bottom of each pail had been mixed with sea water and now swirled bloodily, like the undiluted ingredients of a thick broth. Stepping up on deck, Pablo deposited his own pack of equipment in a secure corner, felt his feet spring and roll with the rock of the boat.

As they left the dock there was a loud boom—a shot—and he wheeled around to see the Sephardic kid standing on shore with a few buddies, army rifle held high, laughing. That you go with the little angels! he teased from shore. And good luck, my friend. Don't let them chew your camera.

Raina waved to them.

The Greek was steering and she stuck close by him. The men followed her orders immediately; although she spoke with them each in his own language and in a casual, friendly tone, she did not seem to be intimately connected to either one. Pablo watched her move from place to place on deck. The boat's motion had created breeze that relieved heat, rippled the water's dark into churning lines of white behind them. She was a little taller than average and her frame was large-boned, lean. He watched the browned flesh ripple along her back, her arms, watched the full-breasted rise and fall of her chest when she breathed—there was something riveting in her presence and the curious thing about it was that it was not really anything sexual. There was about her a kind of raw physical magnificence more animal than human. He could have looked at her all day in admiration, in fascination—he could have watched a leopard, too, all the lithe strength of its movements. He didn't know her. Not at all. She was merely his subject; this, his best assignment yet. He gently patted the lens guard of the camera swinging around his neck—Alfredo, his favorite camera, a long-time companion of sorts.

Breeze blew now from the northeast. The Egyptian had rigged two rods of varying size, one with lead and bait, and now stood motionless between them, scanning the calm, dark water that whitened in sure lines with the boat's wake. Pablo watched Raina mostly, kept clicking away and used up a couple more rolls. But once in a while something would nudge him uncomfortably, an almost physical sensation. Then he'd look up to see a dark pair of eyes rest on him for a moment before flashing swiftly away. He was being sized up himself.

Raina shut off the motor.

"Let's get rid of that chum." Her eyes twinkled invitation.

"Here you go." She offered him a metal ladle, grabbed one of the chum pails and he followed her to windward. That's right, she encouraged as he hesitantly, instinctively stirred the ladle through slop, that's right. "Now just spoon it over."

Pablo looked at her questioningly.

"Spoon it, Pablo."

He lifted the ladle up and over, dropped its contents toward the water. It settled there, rusty blood-brown against the dark, then began to spread and sink. Raina leaned over to watch. She nodded approval.

"Again."

Pablo ladled some more, easier this time, let it drop over the gunwales until it became another part of the dark liquid trail they'd begun, snaking after the slowly drifting boat. He wondered where all the fins were. He'd seen so many yesterday, and now not a single one. Alfredo flapped, unused, on his stomach.

With the third ladle he was beginning almost to enjoy it, and this time breeze caught the chum, sprayed it against the boat's side, splattered his face and Raina's with dark drops. He looked over and saw her white trousers spattered red. She grinned, shrugged.

Twenty minutes and they'd created a long, spreading, sinking line of slimy broth fanning southwesterly from the drifting boat. Raina turned to the Egyptian. There was discussion. His hands flailed the air in disagreement. She was insistent, though, quietly so, and after a while he nodded, fed one baited line carefully down over the side. Soon the only sound audible was the gentle click-click of the reel feeding line out slowly, floated by a bright yellow cork that showed just where bait had been dropped. So the boat was trailed now by a low, widening, continuous slick of chum, and by a fishing line with wire leader, large slab of dead meat attached to its sunken tip.

Pablo wiped his red hands off on some cloth rag. He looked down to find the lens guard blood-spattered and, cursing, searched through his gear for a replacement.

"You have your choice." Raina's voice goaded along after him. "Participate or observe. The two generally don't mix, Pablo."

He didn't reply. He wondered why she enjoyed knocking his profession so much—especially since it could, as she'd gleefully said, catapult her into the headlines.

Ah, said Raina.

There was silence. It made him pause with a hand in his gear pack. The breeze seemed to still, the boat to stop. He noticed that the click of the reel had ceased.

Fumbling with a new lens guard, glancing up, he saw Raina gazing over into the water. A strange, dark woman surrounded by swarthy men. All of them silent. He aimed, took the shot, reluctantly put Alfredo aside for a second camera with zoom. Another shot. Again. And suddenly there was a mad click-clicking of reel, and he felt the boat being given a sharp tug. There was the quick roll to windward, the roll back upright. And another.

The Egyptian shook coal-black hair from his face. He was fitting on a broad sort of leather belt, fingering the thick handle of one of the rods.

Raina smiled. "We're on."

Pablo stood, camera shooting almost of its own accord. Without looking his way she gestured to him: Come on. Quick.

"Have a look."

Surfacing gently, many yards from the boat, were the dark, pointed dagger tips he'd seen yesterday. Only now he saw them in close-up. He counted two, three. There was a sudden dark bubbling of the surface, a wave-like movement of water, and something broke through it with calm certainty— another fin. Four. He wiped his hands on the seat of his pants. They shook slightly. But he calmed them, aimed, got some shots.

Raina was doing something now with the other spinning gear: attaching more bait, he thought, until he saw differently. She was attaching an arrow, taping the head securely to the line's wire leader, her fingers almost caressing the Fiberglas shaft. The Egyptian laughed quietly. He pointed a dark, slender hand and Pablo followed with his eyes. Another brief oiling of the surface, another glide, another broad-edged blade emerged, darted a little nervously in one direction, returned to the cluster of fins that had begun to circle, then to break aimlessly, then to re-form near the bobbing yellow cork.

"No tooth marks!" Raina scowled at the sight of fins, talked to them, to herself, to Pablo. "I'll choose the best man there and I want him whole. Not in disrepair. Oh, this is going to be tricky." She turned to Pablo, grinned. "They need some diversion, you know. Otherwise they'll eat their own tails. And I want a perfect body to bring back. I'm on commission!"

She laughed almost childishly. She seemed in high spirits, chattered away to herself using terms he could only half understand, kept laughing and was still laughing when—at the stern—the Greek lowered an outboard and she disappeared easily after it, bow over a shoulder, sheathed fiber-glass broad-heads bristling from it like porcupine quills. In a minute she'd motored around to starboard and waved up at them. Pablo got the shot. She half stood in the little boat, reached into a pocket and brought something out in her fist. He squinted to see, then saw her fasten something around her neck. She looked up; the delicate silver necklace flashed briefly in sunlight.

"I almost forgot." She winked—the wink was intended for him, he knew. "Would you like to come along?"

He got that shot, too.

"No, thanks."

She shrugged. "Your choice. Watch, then. You want a great show, don't you? Then watch."

The Egyptian was lowering the other line to her. The arrow she'd attached dangled toward her, lopsided, and she grabbed hold. Pablo made mental notes. Things she was saying. Captions. And he kept taking pictures.

"This—" Raina motioned to him, the gesture flamboyant, the show begun "—is a little unconventional. I don't know anybody else"—she chuckled happily, he was surprised at the light, relaxed tone of her voice—"anybody else who gets out there on the slick with them. Not in a boat this size."

She turned the outboard in the direction of the fins, the cork, the circular turbulence many yards away. The motor made a high, fine-honed sound, like a buzz saw, and the small boat edged out slowly in the direction of drifting chum, line with attached lead and arrow feeding out with her.

Pablo felt sweat sliding down his neck. His fingers shivered on the camera. He wondered why he experienced fear. An odd, subtle kind of fear and he sensed it was born of excitement: his own excitement at what was about to happen. He didn't know what the details might be, but that it would be something the likes of which he hadn't seen before, he knew for a fact—and this funny, savage thrill rumbled through him like background noise, made him tremble with anticipation, made him slightly nauseated. He was no longer conscious of the other men on the boat—they'd become part of the wood, Raina's servants, visible only when they did her bidding. A tunnel connected him to Raina out there in the little boat, and this tunnel was the lens of his camera—Alfredo, hanging around his neck, dearly beloved old friend. Sometimes it was the zoom of the alternate camera, but Pablo used this sparingly. There was some deceit, he felt, in using a zoom. It did not indicate the true position of the photographer. Now he was removed from the action, safe. The zoom would make him—in the eyes of the viewing public— more closely involved. It would make a brave man out of him.

He watched Raina. His camera watched and noticed that as she approached the increasingly tight circle of fins she steered more slowly. She was full-handed, outboard tiller in one hand, arrow and leader in the other. Perfect grace. Perfect sense of balance as she leaned over slightly to get a look. The second rig's reel had spun line out rapidly after her, and now the clicking slowed, almost stopped.

It was nearly noon. Pablo jammed his cap on tighter. White haze of heat over the bobbing surface. He was all sweat, and slippery.

She laughed. The sound echoed back: raw, throaty, a lunatic laugh. He felt it crawl down his skin. His fingers shivered, he re-focused and shot.

Raina held up the arrow. It was a dramatic gesture, for his benefit. The spinning gear clicked, camera clicked. And she was suddenly in motion— small boat swerving into a fast pace, tracing a wide white-rippled circle in the water. Within the large circle she created, the black moving fins also circled. As they began to glide tighter and tighter, edging inward toward the slab of meat waiting for them on the end of a yellow-corked lead, the small outboard with Raina in it made a smaller circle around them. Smaller and smaller still. Until she was very close—almost one of them. He watched through the zoom. She'd slowed, brought the boat to a crawl.

What happened next he wouldn't have believed if he'd heard it. So he was glad, in retrospect, that there were photographs to prove it, and that he'd taken them himself. Raina had stopped circling. He saw a gliding fin pass in front of her—its tip reached taller than the outboard's gunwales. She'd pointed the prow toward the center of the circle. The fins drew invisible lines. She crossed into the middle. The boat inched in and it was moving so slowly now it seemed to glide effortlessly, like the salty surface, the deadly hot air, like the fins themselves. Raina's boat glided into the circle. And out. Turned very slowly and slid in, nosing between passing fins. Pablo focused. He could feel sweat pearl on his fingertips. She looked, through the zoom, to be curious. Nosing over the side of her outboard, half standing, maintaining balance while the boat moved and both her hands were occupied. Did she smile? He wasn't sure.

The boat slid through, hovered, and out again. Now she'd taken it several yards away. Suddenly, she cut the motor. He heard nothing except air. It was filled with a sort of heaviness that was almost like sound. And while Raina sat and fit the arrow she'd been holding to the bow, Pablo aimed again. He aimed and watched her aim. The zoom brought her face close to him, an intimate silhouette. It was a hard, fine, dark face with large female eyes and lips, all focused on the thing ahead. The lower part of the face was blocked by her hand, fingers steady on the string, ready. It was an extravagant bow—custom designed. A forty-pounder. This bow was a recurve. There were no wheels, no cables, just the thing itself, shape modified slightly through centuries but essentially the same. So that the power released through it would be hers. There were no automatic adjustments. Only her strength, technique. Her aim. She'd have to own every mistake she made, have to pay for every one. Or glory—by herself—in every error-free endeavor. It was all hers. He took the picture. And another.

He missed the release. No more than a flicker of fingers.

Suddenly everything was motion. Raina lost in the jetting, speeding, swerving motion of the outboard as she revved it and shot around to the other side of the pandemonium she'd created. Sea splashed skyward in a geyser of foam. There was churning, and the sound was like the crash of a rock through trees—a tearing, booming sound—as a massive tail smacked the water, sent spray sky-high, dove and surfaced to crash again in rage, or agony. Pablo clicked. The ugly, two-edged head roared up and out, the shark spun around in air and flipped over, tail up, before diving down. Somewhere, Pablo caught sight of the arrow dangling from its side near the head; somewhere, a drool of blood and white water. Raina was aiming again, a regular unattached arrow this time. He saw her poised in that crouching stance, string, nock, waiting for the release. The arrow ripped straight away— another shark hit, yards apart from the first. A streak darker than chum colored the water; he saw the second creature submerge in clouds of reddened foam, then take off wildly in the opposite direction. Trailing after the streams of red were other fins. Her diversion. All in a matter of seconds. Pablo breathed. Turning to his side, he saw the Egyptian had maneuvered the rod butt into his gimbal belt and was touching the spinning reel lightly with a thumb. Raina had done her part, now the job was his. Pablo looked out again to the thrashing water, the white tips of surf pinkened by blood, greased with swirling clouds of chum. Beyond the madly twirling fintip of the wounded shark he saw Raina seated calmly in the outboard, gunning the motor. She caught his gaze through the lens, saw him through his camera lens—he could have sworn it—and winked.

The boat tugged gently, rolled, tugged.

Pablo took a picture.

She was angling a wide arc away from trouble now, heading for home.

Pablo leaned over. He was going to be sick. No. Mustn't. He stood, felt his pulse racing against the temples. He took a couple of shots of the Greek, who leaned casually against some coiled starboard rope smoking a cigarette.

He waited for Raina's head to appear near the stern. First her hair. Then face. Then neck. Shoulders. She was hanging over and easing onto the deck. The Greek coped with the outboard while she stretched, arms over head, cat-like.

Pablo took her picture. He noticed she was drenched—blood-spotted trousers soaked through, suit shiny wet—and guessed it was sweat. The thought made her seem suddenly mortal. She'd loosened her bow, set it on the deck. He didn't notice any tremor of movement, though. She was steady.

She grinned for another shot.

"Good show, Pablo?"

"Good show." His voice was hoarse.

She fingered her necklace. "I have a friend, a very close friend, who believes that somewhere there is peace. This friend keeps me safe. And gave me this." She smiled again, a little tiredly. "What about you, Pablo? Do you believe in peace?"

His head throbbed. He thought a moment. "I don't know."

There was a screaming, ripping sound as more line fed through the reel. Out on water, the hammerhead rolled like a sharp-edged blade gone crazy, flipped up and back down spewing white waves, spewing blood.

There were more photos. The fish, a good twelve feet long, was strapped to the side of the boat and gaffed with a sudden, thrusting motion—Raina had struck the initial blow and reserved rights to the final one as well. Blood spilled from the open, twisting mouth, washed the white teeth a clotted red. The clear, shallow fish eyes froze. And the tail twitched in spasms, banged the boat's wood with a vacant sound. The two-edged head hung down.

Another of Raina, standing next to the dead monster on the dock later. It had been hung tail-first. She'd put on a white mesh no-sleeve shirt—she was dark, but even so, she said, even so, glancing at the sun—and snuggled up next to it, bare arm part way around the skin-scraping girth. A dangerous thing to do, she teased Pablo, you never know when they're good for one last bite. Even dead. It's the last reflex to go. And she'd hugged it almost affectionately so blood soaked the front of her white mesh shirt and made it cling, accentuated her breasts. Then she stepped back from it, leaned down so her face was directly parallel to one of the dead eyes.

"You lucky bastard. We gave you a good fight, didn't we? What a way to go. Nothing ignoble about that, now, is there. Is there. Lucky you! Do you know who killed you?"

Pablo said goodbye to the Sephardic boy, then took another rolling jeep trip over sand-spewed roads with Raina, the Egyptian, the Greek, and a couple of soldiers. Wrapped in foul-smelling, chemically treated layers of cloth, secured by ropes and small hooks, the lucky hammerhead was a mummy bouncing in back, weighing down their progress. They drove slowly in the heat.

He kept taking pictures. He'd forgotten to drink enough water and felt dizzy at times, felt himself swooning into the endless brown-white of the desert. He wondered feverishly what it would be like to lay his head on Raina's breasts. They seemed perfectly formed to him now, nipples erect, the white mesh over them crusty with blood. Somewhere along the road he fell asleep.

Eilat. More rolls of film gunning through his cameras. The Greek, the Egyptian, Raina, a couple of research specialists connected to the museum— they'd sat on a beach that night in after-sundown chill drinking brandy, some foul local brand that nevertheless did its trick. She'd gone off somewhere for a while, returned with a few scraps of precious wood. She showed them how to build a fire from practically nothing. By the light of that fire they laughed, drank some more, and a few of them dozed off on straw mats on the sand.

His voice was slurred. "You're pretty amazing, Raina. Pretty bizarre." He laughed.

He opened his eyes to see her standing over him, hands on hips. Firelight gave her face a strange glow—all brown and golden shadows. "Amazing? Of course. You don't understand, Pablo, I'm the embodiment of a lot of things."

Embodiment? he mumbled, half-conscious.

"Oh, yes. Asherah, Hecate, Astarte, Diana, Artemis. Artemis! Something very old, like the moon. Like witches and the moon. Long before." She laughed softly. He tried to raise himself on an elbow but couldn't. Too much lousy brandy. Her face glowed and wavered in shadow, the silver necklace cut a dark line across her partly bared chest. She laughed. "Anath. Artemis. From the people who brought you the moon. And now, ladies and gentlemen— Raina Scott! Poor boy. Don't you know? Don't you know who I am?"

Staring up, he knew that whoever she was she had taken him far away for a while. And when she was no longer in front of his camera, and the camera no longer in front of his eye, he would be face to face with a much-diminished vision: himself, in all his mediocrity. Without a people. Without a god.

I

OUR NEW AMELIA EARHART

A NATION

Before its independence—before taking its hastily set-up seat in the United Nations to learn what such seats are worth—Bellagua was a British colony.

The British had taken it from the French, who had taken it from the Spanish. And the Spanish had taken it from the Bellaguans. This, however, was accomplished with much more ease than the subsequent changes of hand. It was done on a placid, turquoise Atlantic day, the sun tropical, heat steaming from the dense leafy green of the island's interior. The small *escuadra* of ships hovered along the eastern coastal shore and a long boat was rowed in, filled with the most expendable members of the *Bendita's* crew. One, a Sevillan pig farmer who would later be tried for murder and theft, was the first to wet his boots and slog toward sand. He planted the empire's flag. Then he and his companions fired a salute. From the shadows of surrounding jungle foliage they were watched by many pairs of light brown eyes. When the volleys went off, there were cries of terror from the jungle as the Bellaguans—an unwarlike people not partial to loud noises—fled. So the island belonged to the Spanish empire.

The Spaniards, though, did not follow the usual procedures on Bellagua. The desire to do so was there, certainly. They would gladly have raped had there been anyone to rape, gladly pillaged had there been any city or town worth pillaging. But there were at most a few native villages clustered around one point on the eastern shore; this the Spanish named Sagrabél, and set

23

up shop there themselves. They moved in men, and tents, and powder for guns.

They had never seen natives like the Bellaguans—these people were not red or yellow or black, but seemed to be a mixture of everything. Small, delicate-boned people for the most part, they were dusky-skinned and thick-haired, light-brown-eyed with a touch of oriental shape to the eyes and cheeks, small, expressive mouths, thin noses. The Spanish made slaves of them. But even the most hardened *machote* would write home to his family— if he had a home, a family, and the ability to write—that the people here were *encantadores*—enchanting—there was something pretty about them, and also familiar. Whenever you were forced to kill a Bellaguan, well, it tore the walls of any good man's heart.

The island was a large one. The eastern shore was rimmed by sand and was therefore the accessible side of the island, blessed with a large bay where bathing was warm, green-blue and safe, blessed with the conglomeration of palm-strewn native villages which together were renamed Sagrabél. The island's western coast was a rocky, inaccessible, dangerous reef that made boat fishing impossible. The natives who lived there fished from shore and remained relatively untouched by the Spaniards. There was nothing among them of interest to European minds. They were thus allowed to live as they always had.

What interested the Spanish was the country's interior, the vast, untapped central territory of Bellagua. They heard its thick jungle terrain was here and there broken by stretches of grassland. They heard of a mountainous, barren area near its center where there was no life. It was told that the interior was infrequently dotted by small native villages subsisting on hunting and on the small-scale cultivation of a certain ugly green vegetable with an unpronounceable native name. But there was human life in there, and the Spanish were enterprising. Where there was life there could also be material gain. Dark, vast, unknown, the interior spoke one word to every listening European ear: treasure, it said, *tesoro*, if only you can find me. And they tried. They were men of enterprise. It was as simple, they thought, as the building of roads: what was needed were bands of men to be sent in with the proper materials and with slaves. They would have wood, and metal tools. They would supplement the poor quality of the Bellaguan slave force— these natives were frail and constantly dying—with sturdier African slaves. They would have necessary articles sent by ship, courtesy of the empire and of a well-established trading concern in Barcelona. There would be expe-ditions, a good deal of building. And men to lead—men good enough, or driven enough. The lust for *tesoro* ran deep because it rose out of desperation.

Nobility had to be purchased back home. Younger brothers had to be pulled out of debt to save the family honor. Without honor there was no life, something the Bellaguans did not seem to understand: they ran from guns, refused to fight like men even for the honor of a woman, clung to survival and to life as if it were everything. And the longer you were there on that tropical, heat-drenched edge of the world, the less sorry you felt about killing.

Black slaves came, and chains, tools, wood. One by one, expeditions were sent from Sagrabél into the interior. They left, donkeys laden with materials, tails flipping at insects in the heavy, wet heat. One by one these expeditions were sent and swallowed whole, it seemed. Nothing was ever heard of them again. A messenger came back once, many months later, from the expedition of a certain Don Jorge Páquino de la Gracia. The Bellaguans had deserted in fear, he said, and the donkeys had all died. About the others he could not say. Just that it was an infirmity of mind that took over—they all went mad, he was sure. The poor man babbled on. He perspired in a strange sort of fever that everyone hoped was not contagious. *Sueños ambulantes*, he kept muttering. *Walking dreams.* They were dreams that walked toward you on foot. To each man, his own walking dream. Turn in the other direction, and you would meet it still. There was no escape. Your walking dream would find you out inevitably, should you get close enough to the core of the interior; it enveloped you, possessed you, it was an insanity of the jungle and the Bellaguans knew of it, spoke of it to him. Walking dreams, they had called it. And fled the following day. Once you meet the true nature of your dream, then surely the dream will envelop you, surely you will become it. And never return.

This man from the expedition of Don Jorge Páquino de la Gracia expired a few days later in fever and delirium. No other survivors were discovered. If there was treasure in the interior, it remained there for the duration of the Spanish rule—the expense of sending these perpetually ill-fated expeditions into jungle that closed up behind them was being complained of in Barcelona. Soon there was no money available at all, and the men responsible for the idea in the first place were being called back to Madrid. Sagrabél became a chaotic, filthy little port city where ships of every nationality docked, spilled out their worst and picked up whatever they could of value: fruit, miniature stone carvings made by the natives of Bellagua.

Black mixed with native brown mixed with pallid Spanish white; a new sort of *mestizo* became more and more common. In spite of this, by the time of the empire's decline, things had changed little on the island—the Spanish had kept it in a permanent state of decline anyway, and the French, when they took over, brought with them an elaborate bureaucracy. The

English, upon seizing power, maintained both the decline and the bureaucracy in that way they had of upholding any given status quo. The money mixed, languages mixed, colors bled into one another like oils melting toward the center of a palette. One group or another staged a coup every few years. Mercenaries had to be imported each time— the island's natives, despite the extensive mixing of their blood with more warlike temperaments, still showed a distinct lack of the urge to kill. So Bellagua became a sort of haven for soldiers of fortune from every corner of the world. They could meet there, trade off tips there. The black market throbbed with life. They could buy there, change all sorts of money there. Some of them would die there. And the jungle interior remained unexplored, untouched, a dark region too closed for men to penetrate, clotted with green growth that kept out the sun and with slimy unknown things, and with walking dreams.

THE DISTRICT MANAGER

In New York, the District Manager for Royal Hotel Corporation was giving a pep talk.

"A good thing to remember." The District Manager raised a hand. Stop, the hand said. Or: silence. But nobody else was talking. He slicked his hair back with the other hand. He turned to the map spread against the wall, large enough and dark green enough for everybody to be impressed. "This is the interior. It's jungle. I mean real live jungle, you can see that, can't you?" There were a few nervous laughs. He smiled briefly, pleased with himself. "That means nobody steps foot in it. Let me stress that. Nobody. Is that clear?" He went on as if it had not been clear, signaled for silence again and all eyes were attentive in the pale, clean-shaven faces watching him. "Case in point. You all remember the Raina Scott party a couple of years back? There were a dozen of them. These were experts. A couple of them were combat-trained. The point is that they were beyond the norm. They were all of them fit to survive in a variety of impossible situations, and after a few months *one* of them made it back alive. Keep that in mind. I don't want anyone"—and he grinned youthfully, well-controlled features rearranging in an instant—"I don't want anyone playing Boy Scout for a group of tourists who think a safari might be a nice idea." He got quite a laugh on that one. His smooth mouth took on a complacent look. Then he was all business. "International believes the island is rich in natural resources—I mean oil, ore and precious stones—so we're taking the necessary steps toward a scientific exploration of the interior. But let's leave that to the experts, all right? It's a big island. Stick to East Bay and everything will be fine. And tell all clients to do the same. Everywhere else is officially off-limits, anyway—that's a precaution you can be thankful for. We've made arrangements with just this problem in mind. We've made arrangements with the national government of Bellagua and—between you and me—what we request they're usually happy to accommodate. I want you to keep in mind"—he paused, got lost himself gazing at the large spectrum of green spread on the wall before them all—"that you're in business for Royal Hotel Corporation. Not for our clients and not for ourselves, but for the company. Royal is owned by International Communications Enterprises, Incorporated. You know about benefits. I'd say they're the best in the world. And you gentlemen, you've all been selected carefully." He turned to them, smiled. "You all come highly recommended."

The District Manager was a sharp sort of fellow who kept himself up in the best corporate image. Cuffs just so, ties of the finest silk. He wore a three-piece even in summer. Even in the heat, and the city pressing down outside, he was dressed in a way that made you respect him. No pin would pop, he seemed to say, not a solitary button would be undone no matter what the pressure. He had a smile to inspire confidence in more than himself—in the company, the company. It pleased you to look at him. It made you feel you'd gotten yourself into the right organization.

Later, in his office, the District Manager rolled back his chair and leaned full against it. It seemed for a minute as if he'd stick his feet on the well-polished desk surface, but he did not.

The office sheltered a silence that was self-contained. Outside, phones buzzed. There was the tapping and ringing of electronic typewriters, the hum of fluorescent lights and of air conditioners. Down one of the many white-and-tan corridors, the sound of word processors printing out material, the click of high heels on white shining floors, and the sudden hush of paper rustling in carpeted reception rooms. Elevator lights blinked red, arrows pointing up or down. And people talked, meeting each other in these hallways, flapping sheaths of black-bound paper at one another; the conversations, though mostly of a friendly nature and having nothing to do with confidential business matters, were almost whispered in low tones of voice. Eyes met briefly, everyone smiled. In the District Manager's office, though, was silence. He pressed a button and spoke into a phone attachment. His own voice sounded odd to him, echoing in the room's carpeted stillness.

Tell Nash I'll see him now, he said.

He remained poised over the desk a moment later to catch a glimpse of his own face on the polished surface. It glimmered back—whitish, blurred, still young. He felt tired and dissatisfied for one short moment. Then he leaned back again and was filled with an equally brief surge of self-confidence and well-being. For that moment, he was at peace.

The phone buzzed.

Send him in, he said.

And Nash was standing there silently, a little nervous, dressed likewise in a three-piece with hands in pockets sweeping back jacket corners—his attempt at a casual stance. He was white too, solidly, blandly male, well-groomed, nearly young. His glasses were dark-framed and serious, the eyes small behind them and they sparkled with something—what, the District Manager could not quite discern—but it was something other than as-suredness. Perhaps some fear. Perhaps. Why this should be, he'd never known. Still, Nash was competent. Maybe it was that suspected touch of fear that catalyzed his competence—the District Manager thought it might be so, and if so he didn't want to eliminate the fear entirely. You could not know what would most effectively motivate a man, you could only sense it. The mark of good management was this sensitivity. And the District Manager prided himself on sensible, sensitive management. It was his job, after all. He glanced at Nash again, smiled welcome.

"Sit down, Frank."

Smiling back, Nash sat. His hands left his pockets and one went to a lapel, fumbled inside at some clipped pens.

"How are things in your neck of the woods?"

"No complaints," Nash said brightly. "Everything under control."

"Good." The District Manager's voice was warm, almost affectionate. The chair rolled forward, his elbows found the desk. "I want you to know I'm pleased about that. Corporate is pleased. You've been doing a fine job and it hasn't gone unnoticed."

Nash blushed slightly. He stopped unsnapping pens from their clipped vest-pocket position and faced the District Manager, chest unguarded, in a posture of open self-confidence.

"We hold up our end pretty well," he smiled.

"You do! You do, Frank. And I've got a little project I'd like you to handle."

Nash leaned forward now. He noticed the dark, polished edge of the desk just before him and the smudge of a fingerprint there—single, solitary grayish blur along the carefully gleaming desk edge. For a moment, he wanted to laugh and point that out to the District Manager—there was some remarkable sort of irony in it, he thought, though he could not explain why he thought that. And he had another, deeper urge—to place his own sweating fingertips deliberately alongside it, smear and smear in long perspiring lines along the whole dark edge of the desk. He kept his face open, blandly inviting.

The District Manager played with a pencil, bounced it rubber-tip down on the surface. "I've c-c'd a memo to you about Royal Hotel. The new opening on Bellagua—"

Nash nodded.

"Interoffice mail being what it is, you might get it by Friday."

They shared a laugh.

"The original memo was to Royal's Creative Design Department—you're more familiar with the people over there, I think?" He looked at Nash, who nodded again reassuringly. "Well," the District Manager dropped the pencil suddenly, satisfied, "I need a sort of watchdog to keep an eye on them. They've got this tourist brochure project on their heads, and frankly I don't think their heads are large enough for the task. You know what I mean."

Nash muttered of course. Of course, he knew. He waited while the District Manager paused, wondered if the time was ripe for a familiar sort of remark, decided it would have to wait. The District Manager grinned easily.

"I've asked them to get a class photographer out there. And make it known—Corporate can be moved to forgive and forget where budgets are concerned. They've got vested interest, Frank. They'd like a class job on this one. Something nice."

Nash glanced up. He cleared his throat, chose words carefully. "I'm sure that won't be too difficult."

And the District Manager sat back, face brightening. Great! he said. That was great. Just what he liked to hear.

Nash experienced an odd sensation—a surge of devotion to the man across the desk. Something akin to team spirit, what he recalled from junior varsity baseball days. If Corporate thought it was important, what a feather in his cap. And no good District Manager would want to deal directly with Royal's C.D.D.—that department was one of the most slipshod he'd come across. They'd have to go to a free-lance source for photographs, he knew. Probably for design, too. He already had it all mapped out in his head—a good game plan. He looked up smiling.

"I'll take Goldberg to lunch," he offered calmly. "I'll get a memo out to him beforehand with a few suggestions. I can have my girl deliver it to you by hand—"

"Oh." The District Manager stood, and so did Nash. "Don't bother. I can send someone over early next week."

They shook hands. Their bodies were the same, neat and compact in the right clothes. They stood comfortably on the carpeted surface, arms extended over the desk toward one another.

The District Manager skipped lunch. He had one of his girls set up the conference room. He put through a call to Corporate but the head honcho was out and he didn't leave a message. He put through a couple of calls to Zachary Chemical Corporation. He wanted them to be on their toes. Things could happen. Part of good management was an awareness of the potentialities of any given situation. He wanted people over there to prepare for competent action, even if the need for it never arose—there was no benefit to himself, he knew, no benefit at all, if they disappointed Corporate from their end. He would run a neat ship, and do so without ever appearing to overstep his boundaries. It was a true talent, this.

He reread the material he'd used for background information. Sitting alone in the conference room, he closed his eyes to the neat row of crystal-clean ashtrays spaced along the long table's sides. The air conditioning was soothing, the walls carpeted a light, pleasing green and the door sound-proofed. He'd asked for a slide projector from the Video Department, had his girl set up yellow lined pads and several sharpened pencils in front of one empty chair. And he'd asked for coffee; now, a large silver pot of it simmered quietly on a metal table in the corner, near the projection screen. There were napkins, packets of sugar and sugar substitute, powdered creaming agent and small sealed containers of liquid milk substitute.

When the door opened, he stood casually.

The man who closed the door carefully behind was a short man of stocky build, with skin that had a dark, Polynesian-type hue and curly black hair, large dark eyes. His lips were large and soft, African. He was dressed in suit and tie, the material expensive, but the clothes did not seem right on him. His white shirt had crumpled in the heat outside. He looked somehow as if he always appeared this way—well outfitted, crumpled, a little ill at ease. He and the District Manager shook hands.

"Mr. Santigo. My pleasure."

Mine, as well, the dark little man replied. His eyes flashed with a curiously dull glow at the table, the projector. He carried a brown briefcase which he set next to the projector.

"I hope you had a pleasant trip."

"I did, indeed I did."

The District Manager offered coffee. When Santigo accepted he buzzed for one of his girls and she came in, poured them two porcelain cups—black for Santigo, cream and half a packet of sugar substitute for the District Manager. He was a man of particular tastes. One small container of cream, half a packet of the sugar substitute, a napkin. She'd worked for him a long time and knew his habits.

The District Manager sat with a good view of the screen. Sipping coffee every few minutes, Santigo had opened the briefcase and was setting up slides from neatly marked packets on the table. He talked a great deal, the District Manager noticed—coolly and fluidly, for all his slightly disheveled appearance. The District Manager began to appreciate this fluidity, began to think that maybe the people who'd sent him had chosen the right man for the job, after all. He admired that in an organization: choosing the right man for the job. He sipped his coffee, waited. At the risk of seeming abrupt, Santigo explained, he would set things up directly. He did not wish to appear obtrusive but also he did not wish to waste time. There were things here of interest, things that had a direct bearing on the economic and social issues presently facing the nation of Bellagua. And—as any emerging nation would wish to do—his country desired very much to maintain its trade and tourist relations with foreign enterprise. Such as Royal Hotel Corporation. Such as Zachary Chemical. Such as International Communications Enterprises, Incorporated, the organization which owned them both. To be sure, his government wished to maintain an economic, social and political equilibrium in the spirit of a free state—to maintain an ambiance in which trade and mutual profit might flourish. And—as the District Manager no doubt knew—the maintenance of such a mutually profitable status quo was often a two-way street. All parties concerned might, at times, need to contribute a certain effort.

Lights were dimmed at the push of a button. The District Manager watched green fade as the wall carpet vanished to black, then saw the striking white of the projector light aimed blankly at the full-drawn screen. A button clicked, the screen was flooded with green—this green a heavy, dense, natural one of jungle foliage, different in its thick authenticity from the green of wall carpets or of office maps.

"The interior of Bellagua." Santigo's voice echoed in a cool, businesslike way. "This terrain covers nearly four-fifths of the total area of our nation. There are no roads through the interior. Limited accessibility is possible via helicopter"—the projector clicked, and a picture of barren, rocky, near-mountainous terrain flashed on the screen—"in terrain such as this, which occurs near the central area of the jungle"—there was another click, and the District Manager stared at a photo of bleak, yellow grassland, hemmed in at the distant horizon by the dark green of jungle growth—"and terrain such as this, which is found also near the central area."

Click, and the picture changed. Against an ill-lit background of green, a short, lean man stood naked. His body was light, dusky-colored: a reddish brown accentuated by the shadows of lean muscles, the lips were full, the eyes large and oriental; straight black hair fell to his shoulders. A native Bellaguan, the District Manager knew, blood unmixed. This photo had been taken somewhere on the fringes of the interior, he guessed, because natives of unmixed blood were rare along any of the coastal regions and nearly nonexistent in the capital of Sagrabél. Strapped around the man's naked waist was a frond-woven basket containing several long, sharp sticks. Slung over a shoulder, what looked like a crude bow.

"A native of the interior," Santigo said matter-of-factly. "We believe they are few in number. Many of course have never been seen. And they do not know a world exists outside of the jungle. They subsist on a combination of hunting and agriculture, we believe. Of course, they have never been studied scientifically. This has been impossible."

More pictures flew by. West Reef natives and their typical fishing villages. Here, the blood was mixed: European features began to show, along with African. These people looked hungry to the District Manager, the children scrawny, the palm-frond shacks along the coast ramshackle and dirty. Pictures of the island's other coast: East Bay, that haven of tourist sunbathing, of lovely tall palms caught in ocean breeze. He saw pictures of yachts, of fishing parties, the white faces tanned and beaming in honeymoon delight, of chic restaurants and air-conditioned bars along the concentrated high-priced hotel strip. Water skiing, snorkeling. One golden-haired beauty smiled suggestively into the camera, bikini top exposing everything but nipples. He felt the beginnings of an erection and smiled, sipped more coffee.

The pictures changed. Sagrabél, the port capital. It was filthy, crowded chaos for the most part, as far as he could see. The native faces here were more mixed still, darker, bodies taller, cynical resignation born of several generations of urban poverty displayed on the faces of the young. In the narrow streets foreign cars mingled with goats and skinny roosters. Even through the polished blur of Kodacolor, he saw sweat glimmering everywhere.

The slides shifted, pictured a man of light brown skin, dressed simply in white cotton shirt rolled to the elbows and patched, knee-length trousers. He wore metal-rimmed spectacles, face dreamily smiling, unremarkable. Santigo sighed. The District Manager looked his way once, quickly.

"The name of this man is Dr. Tristam Saunderson. That is what he calls himself—a doctor. He was expelled from medical school at Oxford for his subversive political activities. The man"—Santigo paused, selected the proper words carefully—"the man, sir, is a revolutionary. He has been practicing medicine illegally on West Reef for many years—he claims he is one of only two physicians available to the population there. And a movement exists—you'll have to forgive my deliberations here, sir, I am trying to put the matter delicately—a movement exists on West Reef, and now in Sagrabél, among many of our people, claiming him as their savior. They believe he is the incarnation of an old god." Santigo laughed briefly. The District Manager shot him another glance. There was no mirth on the dark, dull face.

The click sounded again, the picture shifted to a tall, broad-hipped, dark-skinned woman. She was grinning strongly into the camera. The large eyes were bold and shone with intelligence.

"His common-law wife," said Santigo, "Dr. Manella Porter. They met at Oxford, although she went on to complete her studies. They have a young son and reside together in a West Reef fishing village"—the ocean came into view, small, domed frond huts and the sand—"which has of late become the center for all sorts of politically subversive activities. They are preaching redistribution of wealth, sir, and a policy of so-called passive resistance to many government policies. One of which they do not approve is our time-honored policy of leaving the doors open for foreign investment and trade. You understand my meaning."

The District Manager nodded.

"This movement of Tristam Saunderson's has been through a certain upheaval, though." Santigo's eyes glittered in the dark. His voice maintained its tone of smooth efficiency; he might have been some sort of professor, delivering an often-rehearsed lecture. "Within the last year and a half. As if Saunderson's own policies were not disruptive enough, there are now several splinter groups from his original group, a few of which advocate violent change. All worship Saunderson as a god, however. We have a good deal of trouble with one of these groups, sir."

The slides had not changed for many minutes. They did now, though, and the District Manager found himself leaning forward because this photograph had been hastily taken and was therefore underexposed, dim, blurred. It showed several shadowy figures moving cautiously through a background of dark green—another interior shot, he guessed—and in their hands some seemed to be holding crude replicas of the hand-made bow he'd already seen, while some held objects of a different shape. Rifles, he supposed, army surplus.

Santigo's voice was quieter now than it had been. "These terrorists—for that is what they are, sir!—have been making it increasingly difficult to carry on exploration of the rich natural resources in the interior. They have caused the violent deaths of several members of the last research team sent in, some months ago."

Click and the picture changed again.

Here the terrain was different from any that had come before, different from the dense impenetrable green, the mountainous wastes, the yellow grassland, the beach areas, the solitary palms. A few whitened stumps of some kind of tree remained here, and the ground itself was littered with a kind of fine, white, grainy substance that was not sand, not desert, not anything the District Manager remembered having seen before.

Santigo's voice didn't change. It was calm and measured, sounding out in the dark. "The remarkable effects of snow."

The image blurred slightly. Santigo refocused it with an expert hand. "Please note that the area here is found on the fringes of the interior's grassland. It was once nearly as densely foliated as much of the rest of the interior, sir—"

The District Manager made a motion with his hand. It was half a motion, actually, nearly a Stop! but did not have the force to make its point. Santigo waited politely but the hand dropped, the District Manager settled back in his chair. After a few seconds Santigo sensed that it would be all right to continue.

"You see," he said softly, "how effective it is in eliminating potential cover for terrorists."

Click, and the picture now was of a Caucasian corpse, head tilted back in an agony of death and body washed with blood.

"The handiwork of terrorists," Santigo said calmly, "from one of the factions of the political movement of Dr. Tristam Saunderson. This group operates in the interior—they are the most troublesome of the lot. This man was a research scientist from a European firm."

Pictures flew by—more white corpses, limbs deeply lacerated, blood streaming everywhere as if its sources were endless. One was penetrated by a crude arrow that apparently had gone too deep to remove—this arrow stuck straight up out of the man's chest, an obscenity. The District Manager examined each shot carefully. It could be shocking, these crude forms of death. Barbarous.

The slide shifted to show a Bellaguan crouching, face hidden, bow still slung over one shoulder and the coppery, naked body doubled with obvious terror. Along the back, the buttocks, along the backs of the thighs and arms, skin seemed to have peeled in long strips. And what replaced the skin were blistered, paste-like streaks of pure white.

"Snow," said Santigo.

The District Manager was silent. He heard the buzz of projector lights and reached for his coffee. He sipped but none was left.

There were more pictures now: Sagrabél, the halls of a beginning industry in the island's capital. Publicity shots of Bellaguan businessmen shaking hands with American and European investors, various companies and their office signs, office doors. Coconut punch and honorary luncheons. It looked well managed, looked somehow appealing.

"You see, sir. Our government is quite eager to cooperate. We welcome the continued development of resources and the pursuit of industrial excellence. It's unfortunate that certain political minorities would stand in the way of this."

The last slide clicked out, the screen went stark white again. Slowly, lights were turned back on, turned higher until the illumination of the room was normal. And for a while the two men sat in silence.

Finally the District Manager spoke.

"I'm impressed," he said, "in many respects."

Again, they were silent.

"You seem to have some good organization going for you," said the District Manager carefully. "You understand, of course, that I have no direct jurisdiction vis-à-vis Corporate affairs—"

"Of course, sir. It was suggested, however, by certain people—you understand—that we speak with you initially—"

"I do." The District Manager leaned forward. The projector had been shut off, and he was aware of the intensity of the green room's silence, the flat, full brown of the face near his own. "Let us be frank, Mr. Santigo. I can only present to my superiors what facts I know. So I'll ask you quite openly—" he paused, searched out the words.

Santigo nodded, waiting.

"What is it you need?"

Santigo sat back. His hands, bland and brown, tapped the surface of the conference table. "Well, sir, to be quite honest—"

The District Manager watched while Santigo struggled. It was gratifying somehow, to see this man struggle here in the perfectly lit, artificially cool room that kept out summer. While he watched, he felt himself regain his sense of power. With it came the familiar flood of well-being, of almost-peace. And he smiled.

Santigo met his eyes. "We have a great many dreams for our nation's commercial potential, sir. Dreams which can be attained only with the aid of mutual cooperation of foreign interests. Impediments on the road to progress, such as political terrorism, cannot be allowed to continue. So, to be honest—" He stopped again. His eyes dropped, hands tapped briefly. He fought something back. Then the words came out anyway.

"To be honest, sir, we need more snow."

The District Manager plucked at the edge of his napkin. Paper came away in pieces with a feathery, ripping noise. Then he realized the napkin was ravaged, white pieces strewn in a small circular area of the table right in front of him. He might have blushed but stopped himself. The way to cover up an error was simply to ignore it. Thus history might also fail to record it—and, in any event, when one pretended dignity or indifference others often assumed that the façade was the genuine article. He shoved the napkin carelessly away, swept the thin pieces to one side. He glanced coolly at Santigo, who was smiling at him now in a sweaty desperate way.

"Well, Mr. Santigo. I will see what I can do about that."

Both men seemed to relax then. They talked briefly of other things that had nothing to do with business. Outside the still, green-walled room, phones buzzed. There was the continual click-click of leather heels down the high-polished, clean white surface of hallway floors.

PABLO GETS A NEW FREE-LANCE JOB

Frank Nash smiled at him. Pablo relaxed. They were, he guessed, somewhere around the same age, but Nash had a sort of perfection about him—each gesture meticulous yet somehow easy, every article of clothing the right color and texture, from a respectable retailer—the sort of perfection that always made Pablo feel a little ill at ease, as if he'd landed on the wrong planet. Maybe it was because Nash had the serious, manicured look of a man with goals. A man who had done the right thing all the way along the line in pursuit of certain ambitions, and therefore looked somehow older next to a guy like Pablo, who was a free lance, and dressed the way he wanted. Maybe that was it. Pablo grinned. The free-lance look was markedly different from the nine-to-five look. The free-lance look gave an impression of borders blurred, distinctions poorly maintained. The corporate look, on the other hand, inspired confidence.

Nash offered a hand before sitting behind his desk. Pablo was careful to press it in an emphatically masculine way. Then he sat in the brown leather chair across the desk from Nash. The window wasn't the kind that opened, and the air conditioner was on so everything had that cool tinge that obliterated all seasons, but through the permanently sealed glass summer sunlight came anyway. It glinted across Nash's glasses, so for a moment Pablo couldn't see his eyes at all—just two sharply gleaming circular pools of golden light.

A secretary had scurried in and out seconds before with coffee, sugar packets, an apologetic air. Pablo had noticed her breasts—which were full and lovely—and felt himself blush.

It wasn't a particularly large office, but the furniture was new and that said something. A man they'd order new furniture for was going places; such a man was merely waiting for the right-sized office to be prepared so he could move into it. At which point he would order even newer desk, chair, and shelf models from the company stockroom. And one day, if he played each card right, he'd be able to skip the stockroom stuff entirely and have his office custom designed.

Nash nodded pleasantly, and behind the glasses eyes appeared again. For some reason he couldn't figure out, Pablo felt embarrassed. He sipped his coffee.

"Mr. Klemer—"

"Pablo!" He wondered, for an instant, if he'd made a mistake. He blushed again. But Nash smiled in a friendly way.

"Of course. Pablo. Pablo, I want you to know how pleased we are to have you on board."

"Thanks."

"Goldberg—Joe Goldberg's told me about your work. Impressive credentials."

Nash's fingers tapped some papers on his desk. Pablo watched the fingers drum; then they paused, pinched the corner of an eight-by-ten glossy and held it up off the desk. The head bent down to examine. Blinding light reflected briefly off the glasses again.

"An extraordinary photograph, Pablo."

"Yes," Pablo said proudly, "it is."

He thought Nash was caught off guard. Maybe it was the note of unmixed pride; it was foreign to Pablo himself. But the eight-by-ten rested once more on the desk surface. Nash cleared his throat and in the stillness of the room the sound seemed to echo. The calm, bland smile appeared again.

"Tell me," Nash said brightly, "you're not originally American?"

"I was born in Lima. Peru, not Ohio."

"I see." He observed Pablo.

Nash could see nothing harmful in the man sitting across his desk: the eyes were pale, clear, honest. Pablo was a short, slender man, dark hair curling over the tops of his ears, and though Nash knew from the memo Goldberg's girl had hand-delivered that morning that Pablo Klemer was thirty-two, he would not have guessed it. He looked so much younger. He had that quality which shows sometimes in slightly built men of good health—that impish, ageless quality, as if the process of physical maturation had stopped for good somewhere in the early twenties. An innocent. Nash gave himself an internal grin. Nothing harmful here. He decided to proceed as planned. Corporate would get their class job this time—good photographer, bordering on artistic, and a swell brochure to make the collateral boys at Royal Hotel purple with envy—good return on all that vested interest, and a nice feather in his own cap to boot. Still, certain things had to be clarified. Even though he'd run a security check through Corporate, it would not hurt to ask. Clarify—it was the mark, he thought, of good management. And Nash was a man of ambition. District Manager—there was a nice title. In his fondest dreams it was his own. His fingers found the glossy corner again, plucked the photograph from the desk and waved it in air.

"Tell me, Pablo"—he nodded toward the photo—"were you close friends?"

"Friends?" Pablo looked startled. "No, no. I photographed her once. On assignment."

"Five years ago."

"I was on assignment for *Century* magazine."

"A wonderful job, too." Nash set the photo on the desk again; his fingers caressed it almost thoughtlessly. He smiled. "Really, it was an impressive accomplishment, I think."

Pablo heard himself with curiosity again. There was that glow in his voice he wasn't accustomed to. "She was an impressive subject, Mr. Nash."

Nash nodded. His smile remained. "Frank."

"Okay. She was amazing! She was pretty amazing."

Again, Nash nodded. He almost knew what Pablo meant. But then, everyone would know. Raina Scott Simmonds—yes, she was amazing. And her disappearance had made the front page of the *Times* three days in a row—no small feat. He guessed nothing the woman had ever done was minor-league stuff. He'd been lower on the corporate ladder then, of course, busy with his own work; still, it was hard to ignore the publicity she'd been able to generate. He remembered specifics even now—the hunting safaris, the archery championships, rock-climbing expeditions that became endurance events and, due to the public interest her name managed to stir up, warranted day-by-day media coverage. The icing on the cake: spear-fishing for sharks. All these bizarre pursuits you wouldn't have heard of or thought much about on your own. It seemed every year she was at it again with something different, something more dangerous, more formidable, more daring than what she'd done before. Reading about it all from time to time, Nash remembered actually chuckling in outright amazement. *Amazing*— yes, that was the word to describe her. He remembered wondering whether

Raina Scott was running toward or away from something and—in any case— what it was that drove her so hard. He remembered that being the last time he'd had such a thought. Looking across the desk at the photographer Goldberg had hired, Nash knew suddenly that Pablo Klemer had never been conscious of such a thought within himself, and—for that reason—knew he was the right man for this job.

He relaxed then. Nash half listened while Pablo spoke lightly about previous assignments, coming back time and again to the photo on the desk. It had been a remarkable assignment, he told Nash, his first real big one from a top monthly and he wouldn't have passed it up for all the Hasselblads in Europe. Raina Scott—bow hunter, adventurer. Adventure*ss*. She was one of those daredevils who went on safaris and climbed mountains just for kicks. One of the Amelia Earhart types who made great press about once a year or so. She was maybe the top-ranked bow hunter in the world. And how many people did what she did, even for kicks? How many women? Or men? She was a survival expert, did things like travel miles in a blizzard and stay out there for days with nothing but her bow and a box of matches. She was—words escaped him—she was pretty extraordinary. She was amazing.

Nash called his girl in and had her serve more coffee. He talked wildlife photography with Pablo—wildlife photography was the way Pablo had started out, after all. He'd garnered quite a nice reputation doing high-quality work for the nature magazines, bounced from field to field taking nice pictures, all of them well paid for. In the panoply of Pablo Klemer's work, only one series of photographs stood out as more than merely nice—the photographs of Raina Scott. They had been praised as art. They'd appeared in hardcover collections displayed on the coffee tables of the wealthy. Some had been hung in museums. And Pablo Klemer—who'd never been particularly good at contemplation, maybe—had continued to take on whatever assignments paid enough. He preferred working in the tropics. He liked having a nice tan year-round. Pablo made a good living.

Nash leaned across the desk.

"Pablo—"

He paused. It had occurred to him that he might not want to stress certain points too much. He might want simply to mention—almost in passing— things the District Manager had mentioned in his own near-casual way. Yes. Mention succinctly, in nearly identical words, the salient features of the problem. Then drop it. That way, your own rear end was safely camouflaged. His hands slid easily along the desk surface, relaxed on a stainless steel paperweight that bore the insignia of Royal Hotel Corporation and, above that, the initials of International Communications Enterprises, Incorporated.

Nash spoke calmly of the sometimes troublesome political situation on Bellagua, the growing power of the military there, the weakness of the present government—which, he said, had all the right intentions but none of the required power to back up those intentions. The general chaos ensuing, constant rumblings about military coups—Bellagua's independence had been marked with one coup after another anyway, and now maybe the military thought it their turn to have a crack. The religious unrest. Catholicism was the official religion. But there were fundamentalist sects there too—old pagan traditions proliferated. And sometimes religious polarities became political on Bellagua. Their latest domestic problem, for instance— Nash smiled in a fatherly way—was the quasi-religious, quasi-political movement headed up by a foreign-educated Bellaguan who called himself Dr. Tristam Saunderson. When Pablo got there, chances were he'd hear quite a bit about this Saunderson. But it was nothing to be alarmed by. The government believed him to be a socialist revolutionary with terrorist connections; still, his movement was a tiny one even though it was loud. All in all, things were pretty much under control. And as for tropical beauty—ah. Nash's own face brightened in a pure and guileless way. For a beautiful vacation, you couldn't beat Bellagua's East Bay. It was the up-and-coming spot, the latest place to be seen. He envied Pablo this assignment—he did. It made him wish he'd chosen a different career himself. It made him wish he was a free-lance man. And sticking to East Bay was the way to enjoy yourself on Bellagua. There was only one city, anyway— Sagrabél, a filthy mess. Aside from that, nothing but jungle. Jungle so inhospitable that even an expedition headed by the likes of Raina Scott— his fingers tapped the eight-by-ten glossy—had disappeared, coughing up but one survivor. No. On the island of Bellagua you would not want to venture off East Bay. It was strongly advised against. It would not be in your best interests.

Nash stood. Pablo took his cue and stood, too. He was inches shorter than Nash. Reaching across the desk to shake hands, he felt much younger too—though he knew he wasn't—and, for a second, a little nervous. But the feeling passed completely, giving way to a kind of blithe expectancy: he'd had a lucky life, he knew, being paid well to do something he enjoyed, setting pretty much his own hours, more often than not getting a nice tan in the bargain.

"Pablo, you come highly recommended."

The words stumbled to Pablo's tongue—*Thanks, Frank!*—but for some reason they would not slide off. So he remained silent, emphatically shaking Nash's hand.

"As I said before, it's good to have you on board."

"Great," said Pablo, embarrassed. "I'm looking forward to it." *Looking forward to it, Frank!* he'd wanted to say, but again could not bring himself to speak the man's name.

As Nash watched him leave, it occurred to him that the name Klemer was of German origin. Nevertheless—although he didn't particularly look like one—Nash was certain Pablo was a Jew, and not just because Goldberg had done the hiring. It was a certainty that came with practice. You got to sense things like that when you'd spent enough time in a city like this one; when you'd spent enough time in Corporate learning the ropes, learning how to sense things like that.

On his way out, Pablo bumped into someone.

He looked up to the hard, broad, handsome face of a big man. Dressed in white and gray—hardly summer colors, but certain colors were actually seasonless—silk-breasted and silver-studded and three-pieced, the man seemed big, like a rugby player or a heavyweight. This initial impression of bigness was supported by the broad chest and powerful shoulders, a thick-thighed appearance. The power was electric. It seemed to make him move slowly under its weight, as if in a hard and heavy, finely wrought coat of mail. Pablo looked up, panicked for a moment—he didn't know why. Two large, dark eyes gazed down at him unblinking. But the voice, when it spoke, was cheery, almost gentle.

"Excuse me."

Pablo stepped back. My fault, he mumbled.

"Not at all. No problem."

The voice was incongruous in its open friendliness, because the man himself looked built for aggression, built to fight somehow. But the dark eyes shifted away from Pablo's, zoomed over his head and focused on someone else. Behind him, Pablo heard the almost silent swinging open of an office door. Then he heard Nash's voice.

"Mr. Connery. Good to see you."

Pablo headed down the hall. He walked quickly, a little unnerved, heard the rubber soles of his shoes, LS Firebirds—he did some jogging—squeaking along the floor's smooth surface. He heard Nash's words echo quietly behind him: *The District Manager is waiting.* Then, the closing of an office door. Walking to the elevators, Pablo passed rows of secretarial desks, phone buttons blinking to indicate incoming calls.

* * *

A few floors down, winding through more white-and-tan corridors with an occasional startling mirror placed at an odd angle along oddly angled walls, the Creative Design Department of Royal Hotel Corporation nested, all but abandoned, poorly budgeted each fiscal year but somehow surviving. Pablo decided on a semi-social visit. He owed Goldberg for the job and, anyway, he liked Goldberg. He wandered past open work bays where graphics people did paste-ups, mechanicals, illustrations, and fluorescent desk lamps hummed over drafting tables. Creative Design Department—C.D.D.— gave the impression of encroaching chaos. Maybe it was the inevitable strewing-about of art supplies. Maybe that, combined with the unspoken knowledge floating almost tangibly through the department air that, of all departments in Royal Hotel Corporation—and of all departments in other companies belonging to International Communications Enterprises, Incorporated—theirs was the one most thickly populated by Jews and homosexuals and, therefore, the one least favored by fiscal management. This unspoken cloak of rejection lent the entire department a somewhat forlorn look, one mingled with a kind of underlying snobbery and clownishness. It was the smartass attitude of the court jester who knows he must perform well in order to survive and who—cast as he is, time and again, at fate's feet—determines that the amusement he serves up will be riddled with the spice of satire—satire which the king, lacking outsider status, can never be aware of, but which makes other court jesters shriek in bitter delight.

Pablo wandered past work bays to the administrative corridor. He knocked a few times on Goldberg's office door but got no answer. Joe around? he asked the temp. Not today, she said, he takes Mondays off. Pablo wrote a note and was about to Scotch-tape it to the door when everything opened in front of him, hinges creaked like a moat bridge lowering, and Goldberg stood there in dismal fluorescent light emitting clouds of smoke. He had a cigarette between his lips, and one stuck behind an ear for safekeeping.

"All right, come on in."

"I thought you took Mondays off."

"Yeah." Goldberg's belly folded over his belt when he bent to flick ash into a loaded tray. "That line keeps the heat away."

As he sat in front of the desk with his shoes lodged comfortably on the blotter, Pablo's hand went protectively to Alfredo, deposited the camera against his crotch for balance. Lens cap on, a good thing with all this smoke. Whenever he was in here he'd get the feeling he was in some cellar with a solitary light bulb swinging overhead. Though well lit, the office gave an impression of darkness. Goldberg's old Shetland wool sweater—his summer protection against air conditioning, he said—had cigarette burns on each sleeve. Like him, both sweater and office appeared comfortably seedy. Every-thing had once been of excellent quality, and had been allowed to fall from grace with time. When you worked for C.D.D. you might work nine to five but were nevertheless allowed to dress with some of the carelessness of a free-lance man.

Goldberg snuffed out his Camel and lit another. He squinted through the first puff's cloud, ran a hand over his hair hoping to find glasses. He gave Pablo a questioning look.

"So?"

"So. I'm leaving town."

"Good." Goldberg sighed. He gave Pablo his best court jester wink. "The little *goy* liked you."

Pablo felt himself blush. "Tell me about Bellagua."

Goldberg picked at some ash on his sweater front. When he sniffed, his sinuses made slurping sounds. Pablo was sort of impressed by the fact that Goldberg was such a slob, something both repelling and intriguing about it. His slobbery was so extreme. And Pablo guessed all extremity was kind of fascinating.

Goldberg shrugged. "Lots of tropical flora and fauna. It's the usual—one place for the tourists, plenty of palm trees and booze, shantytowns for the natives. A lousy political situation. Messy, very messy."

"I got that impression."

"Nash give you his speech? That *schmuck*. Okay, so you know."

"Tell me the real story."

"Messy political situation."

"So you said."

Goldberg found a cigarette and lit up. Watching, Pablo could tell it might be a while—Goldberg took his time telling stories. "Right now nobody would be too surprised if they wound up arresting this guy—one of the native Bellaguans who a lot of the other natives think is the living embod-iment of one of their gods—"

"I thought they were Catholic."

Goldberg glared. "Do you want the scoop or not?"

Pablo sat back passively. He grinned, waited.

"Around the time of the Spanish possession there was a lot of so-called converting that went on. The Bellaguans were never big fans of resistance. Someone in a frock came through and said worship this that or the other thing or I'll kill you, they were completely willing to go along with the idea. The thing was, they just sort of adopted another god. And I guess they figured that if the priests wanted them to gather one day a week and pray to this minor deity named Jesus, they could accommodate. They're polytheistic, you know. They worship plenty of deities and their big two are the Dark God and the White Goddess—a brother and sister team, I think. Their customs never really changed much. They adapted when they could and ran away and died when they couldn't. That's about it." He puffed out circles, broke the rim of white with his fingertip. "Anyway, this guy—I forget his name—has a pretty big following—"

"Dr. Tristam Saunderson, right?"

"Right! That's the name."

"I thought his following was small."

Goldberg glared again. His glare had in it, though, a kind of pity. "You've got to stop listening to everything these corporate *schmucks* tell you, chico. Some day you'll wind up believing Rhode Island is bigger than Texas. Believe me, this Saunderson whatever has a pretty big following. There's plenty of unrest. Enough to threaten the government there, at any rate. Although to tell you the truth, it doesn't take much to threaten that government. Whoever's in power at the moment is there due to the good graces of foreign business interests, if you know what I mean. Like our beloved Royal Hotel, for instance. And governments are a dime a dozen. Especially in that part of the world." Goldberg leaned forward, eyes gleaming. "There's a big dig going on there, too."

Archaeological? Pablo asked.

Goldberg nodded. "It's been going on for about two years now. On the eastern side of the island, partway between Sagrabél—which is a pit but if you want to get some shots of anything besides blue water and white tits you might want to check it out—and East Bay. You'll be staying in East Bay, of course. Royal Hotel tourist country. Lots of other hotels along the strip, restaurants, lots of pretty sunbathing. It's honeymoon land."

"Well?" Pablo said impatiently.

"Well what?"

"What about the dig. You didn't say—"

"The dig." Goldberg nodded gleefully. "They're onto something big, it looks like. They've got all the historians shitting bricks. But there's no doubt about it"—he smacked his lips—"Bellagua's in the right place. They've unearthed one layer of a city and it looks like there's at least a couple more extensive layers underneath. You've heard of Atlantis?"

Sure, Pablo told him. And Goldberg sat back. Well, his expression clearly said, case in point. Pablo laughed, uncapped Alfredo's lens. For the hell of it, he took a shot.

Goldberg briefly examined the dark face in front of him. He'd known

Pablo a few years now, they'd done some minor free-lance stuff together and he knew Pablo was essentially a practical guy. Practical like him; neither one liked to contemplate too much. Goldberg shrugged off a sudden twinge of nerves. Why contemplate, anyway. What the fuck was there to contemplate. Still, there was something irreconcilable about it all to him—Goldberg the would-be historian sitting across his corporate desk from some guy who could have taken great photographs maybe but preferred to skim the surface with vacation brochures. For a decent living, but what about it was all that fucking decent? once in a while, he'd wonder—something irreconcilable about it, like shitting on a grave. At worst, what they both did was rubbish and if Pablo never thought about it, there were times Goldberg did. Maybe that was why he wouldn't meet Pablo's eyes just now. What were they, after all, but minor teeth in the mouth of what Goldberg called *the goyim!*—as if *the goyim!* were a terrorist organization—both of them part of the mechanized mouth, both in their own way, corporate schmucks.

"Thanks," Pablo muttered. But Goldberg avoided responding, so Pablo slapped his shoulder gratefully when he stood, told him he was one hell of an art director and it was good to be working with him again. He told him he'd bring some nice pictures back. Nice honeymoon stuff—he promised.

"Screw yourself, Pablo."

"Listen," said Pablo, "don't think I haven't tried."

Before heading downtown Pablo stopped off at the travel agency to clear up a few details. Then he got restless and decided to walk. It was summer, just before the really deadly heat began to set in, and Alfredo swung around his neck uncased. He didn't like to let opportunities pass. Without that camera bulk around his neck or shoulders, Pablo felt a little naked.

It was after lunch and before rush hour. He liked this time. You didn't have to dodge bodies or shish-kebob vendors. You didn't have to crush up against three-pieced corporate clerks smelling of after-shave and sweat. It was a limbo time of city afternoons, when minutes could be spent under an illusion of leisure. He wandered toward the East Side.

The Schreiber was an odd combination of things—a museum with a split personality. Most of its space was dedicated to archaeological antiquities—a varied assortment, not just the usual Mediterranean Basin vases and statuettes, but artifacts from India too, from African coastal regions, and from the Americas. Fritz Schreiber, archaeologist, radical historian, had been eclectic in pursuit as well as thought. The Nazis didn't much care for him and he'd died at Dachau in the early forties, but by then most of his work was safely stored and itemized in North American museums, and people of influence—*Jews!* Goldberg would have crowed, *Jews of course!*—funneled funding through some corporation grant or other to maintain the museum in his name. By the late sixties a little more of the interior space was devoted to photography. As time went on, it was photography that became the museum's main attraction.

The desk sign gave the title: YOUNG AMERICAN PHOTOGRAPHERS: A RETROSPECTIVE.

It was dimly lit, artificially cool. No one else was in the room he made his way to, and he went right to his section of wall.

The photo Nash had waved across the smudged top of his desk was a smaller version of this. The face gazed back at him in black and white: a woman in her late twenties or thereabouts, full-lipped, haughty mouth. The eyes curved exotically at their outer corners, big eyes, dark, and proud, so proud. The hammerhead hung dead by its tail and it was dripping sea slime and blood, core of its flat, vicious two-pronged head pierced cleanly by one of her specially designed arrows. She'd snuggled up to the monster, had a bare arm around it, bow slung over her opposite shoulder. She was grinning broadly, face all sunshine and openly arrogant. She'd worn a white mesh no-sleeve shirt that accentuated her breasts. The shirt was liberally blood-spattered. The necklace made a fragile line, draped lightly across her collar bones. It was like a barely noticeable gash.

RAINA SCOTT, read the title plaque below, OUR NEW AMELIA EARHART.

Pablo Kelmer, it read, and gave the date.

Pablo smiled gently. This Royal Hotel job was a great one—he'd make plenty on it. "You," he whispered to the picture, "are my lucky charm."

He examined the arrogant lips, and the eyes which were a dark enigma to him, unreadable.

THE INQUIRY

Waiting at the American Consulate in Sagrabél, Lee Simmonds remembered the inquiry, ran through what he'd memorized over and over again. He could see tape recorders, the cool glint of the microphone, the dark-haired, emaciated man speaking into it. At these times he remembered only the words that described what had actually happened. The actual events themselves were locked away somewhere else altogether, known only to the emaciated survivor. Lee guessed he rarely pressed the play switch on those. Or maybe he'd done it once too often, after all—three months after the inquiry, Vince St.-Peters had pointed a loaded .22-caliber Magnum into his mouth and pulled the trigger.

It was somewhere between the sixty-ninth and the seventy-fifth day. The voice rolled clearly from the tape. *That's as close as I could figure it later. Somewhere in there I turned around and she was gone.* Although it was a strong, well-modulated voice—one obviously used to reciting this same script many times before—there was in it a note of awe, and shock.

The Lieutenant's words came next. They were respectful, businesslike. *Would you mind telling us one more time, Mr. St.-Peters, for the record, how you knew it was between the sixty-ninth and the seventy-fifth day of the expedition?*

I knew because Judd Allen died on the sixty-ninth day. I kept a log. She did too. Raina Scott. By day number sixty-nine I was pretty ill but I remember writing in the entry that Judd had died—he was the tenth one to die, a day after Buck Taylor died—so I remember the date—

What was that date?

That was July sixteenth.

And of what significance is day number seventy-five, then?

That's a rough estimate of when I would have started back alone. I'm estimating the time it must have taken me to make it back, considering all the variables of the situation. I was extremely ill, and lost. I know I reached Sagrabél on August twenty-third, so I've estimated—and I believe this is an accurate estimation—that it took me at least a month and a day or two to make it back.

And during that trip back alone, you remember seeing nothing of Raina Scott or noticing any indication that she was alive—

There was nothing! I looked for her—I spent days, I think. You'll have to forgive me here, my perception of time often must have been warped because of the delirium, as I've explained.

Of course, Mr. St.-Peters. The clipped voice was sympathetic. After all, they weren't cross-examining the man. They were just trying to get the story, some picture of what things had been like. And he was the only survivor. That left a vast burden on his shoulders. Listening to the tape, you felt it. As survivor he had to be journalist, poet, painter. He had to somehow describe a cataclysmic reality; for him to have survived was not enough when the world demanded knowledge. And his voice, sometimes betraying the smallest hint of weariness, of boredom almost, held up with great effort under that weight.

Mr. St.-Peters, said the Lieutenant, *what would you say was Raina Scott's condition—her physical condition—on the last day you saw her?*

There was a pause.

Jesus, he said. *Half dead, I guess.*

Can you please elaborate?

She was delirious with fever. We both were. And she'd lost a great deal of weight. I know that her hands shook constantly and we both had trouble walking more than thirty paces at a time. We counted paces, which is how we knew we were making progress. Thirty at a time. I know also that she had trouble focusing visually—I know this because she told me several times, I think, and I was experiencing the same symptom myself—that and auditory hallucinations. There was more silence. The tape clicked in its reel. *That's it,* St.-Peters' voice echoed. *That's about how I would describe her condition.*

And as a professional, sir, with medical knowledge—also as a practiced expert in the field of wilderness survival and a hunter of many years' experience—what would you estimate her chances for survival to be?

St.-Peters didn't reply for quite a while. When he did his voice was subdued with a heavy edge of pain. *I can't give you a statistical estimate.*

No, sir. Of course not.

I'd say her chances were extremely slim. I've often thought—I believe I told you this before, Lieutenant—the only reason I survived so long myself was simply that I didn't die sooner. As you say, I'm an expert in the field, so for whatever that's worth you can bet I wouldn't make such a statement lightly. In my opinion Raina Scott was among the best in the so-called field, too. I give her about the same chances I had of making it. And I know that if I hadn't been able to make it back, then surely I would have been dead within a few days after August twenty-third. A few days at the most.

Thank you, Mr. St.-Peters. I know this is unpleasant for you. We'll try to make it brief—

I appreciate that.

One last time now, would you try to describe as fully as possible everything you remember from the time of Judd Allen's death to August twenty-third of that year?

St.-Peters began. The story was fragmented, an odd counterpoint to the steady, controlled masculine style of the voice. They'd tried to cover the body with some leaves and stalks. They were too weak to dig. And he remembered noting it in his log, he remembered she had noted it in hers as well because as leader she noted everything. Then they walked thirty paces and sat to rest, and they had some water to drink, he thought he remembered—only two swallows each because good water in there was hard to come by, although stagnant, swampy rivulets and slimy mudholes abounded. So they'd agreed to ration water. She'd spoken to him but he could not remember what she said. He remembered she had been delirious and not rational. But certainly she spoke to him; he didn't think he'd hallucinated that. And they continued another thirty paces. When he stopped to rest and turned around, she was gone.

He looked for her. He went in circles, then straight lines back and forth, tried to zig zag the territory as much as he was able, looking for a sign, a body. He had even called her name and it echoed against the green of leaves, the thick entangled foliage that kept out sun. He thought he'd looked for days. He could not be sure. Raina Scott was gone. He guessed she'd crawled off somewhere to die. Maybe she'd lost track of where they were heading—it would have been easy to do. And she'd stopped focusing on him ahead, turned off a different way. But he had looked as best he could, and she was gone.

St.-Peters remembered days melting into the darker nights. He remembered eating bugs. You had to pull off the legs, he said. And tree leeches too, but you had to make sure they were dead first; leeches were known to survive the human digestive system. He remembered bunches of bananas and the longing for one. But he was too weak to climb. And the tree snakes, coiled like green branches, hissing in the humid, muddy dark. The lust for water. It became an obsession. He would squeeze it out of mud and let the filthy water trickle past his lips. He'd slash milky, bitter roots with his knife and suck them dry. And his hands shook, he could barely hold the knife. He couldn't have pulled a trigger, much less release a bow. When the soles of his boots began to come off he ripped up his shirt and tied it around the boots to keep them together. But still they slipped, irritated the bottoms of his feet to blistered scabs. When a scab infected he cut it out with his knife edge and held a lighted match to the area to burn germs away. He remembered wanting to scream but not having the strength. He remembered— oh, he remembered a lot of things. A lot of things.

He was silent.

Could he reiterate, one last time, what the original purpose of the expedition had been?

Yes he could. It was an exploratory sort of hunting expedition. This was tough territory and hadn't been dented yet by so much as one hunting party. Virgin area. They didn't know what to expect so they came prepared for anything. They were experts, all, well versed in wilderness survival of every sort. Each one a hunter. And they were ready for jungle territory; they knew how to survive.

And you yourself, Mr. St.-Peters, how were you armed? Could you describe this one last time?

St.-Peters' sigh rose from the tape. It knew, that sigh, that this would not be the last time. It knew there would never be a last time. But he talked. *Briefly, I carried a custom-designed sporting rifle with Mauser action and a variable illuminator scope. I carried a supply of bullets—I cast my own. I had a sheath knife, an all-purpose knife and a Bear Magnum compound bow with four aluminum broadhead arrows and a backup supply of replaceable blades. There were a couple of other items—do I need to go into anything else or—*

That's fine, Mr. St.-Peters. Thank you. And could you also describe, to the best of your present knowledge, how Raina Scott was armed on the last day you saw her?

She carried a sheath knife and a custom designed recurve bow that sheathed five fixed-blade fiber-glass broadheads. She had a sort of vest she wore—it was similar to a combat vest but had been custom designed for her and made by hand, I know. It was part leather and its compartments had some other items in them, I don't know if I can enumerate them all.

She carried no firearms?

Firearms? St.-Peters laughed a little. It was a sad sound, jumping from the tape in a muted way. No. No, Raina didn't carry guns. She didn't believe in them.

The rock that crashed through the Consulate window was hand-grenade size, so it caused more panic than usual. At first they thought the entire building ought to be evacuated, foreigners scuttled away in waiting embassy cars through the heat of Sagrabél's crowded August streets. But eventually reason prevailed. It was just a rock, in fact—wrapped in a torn piece of white sheet—and after additional security measures had been speedily implemented, the entire staff wound up grouping near windows with a view of the main street. The Bellaguan Civil Guard was restoring order. As usual, their restoration of order was a disruptive process and billy clubs flailed, bodies sweating darkly through light layers of cheap clothing got flung over car hoods, twisted in broken-limbed positions and crumpled to the sludge-running curbs.

It wasn't a large demonstration. There were more Civil Guards than demonstrators. To the Americans flowing out on the Consulate balconies for a better view, there was something not quite serious about it. All this frenetic, bloody action for something that seemed so minor. It was like watching a badly refereed game of indeterminate rules, with players who had little skill and poor coordination. Like Monopoly money, none of the material seemed real—not when you were used to Chicago or Detroit or L.A. The scale was so small.

Across the rock's wrapping of sheet, letters had been scrawled in what looked like real blood—probably chicken blood.

MURDERERS. THE BLOOD OF THE PEOPLE ON YOUR HEADS.

Afternoon settled in with an additional blast of heat. The street below was clear now. At least there was no greater chaos than usual. Just the ordinary mixture of sidewalk vendors hawking flowers, fruit, caged parrots and trinkets, the foreign cars glinting dust and sunlight, windshield wipers jammed with corpses of insects who'd met their death flying against glass.

Women walked by, skin brown or reddish gold, baskets of something or other on their heads or across their shoulders, children with distended bellies clutching their skirts to either side. They were always carrying or balancing straw baskets. They were always accompanied by children. And the occasional chicken strutted by, scrounging food in the gutters. The occasional goat. Mixed with all this were foreign clothes, white skin burning in omnipresent sun. You could tell a newcomer by his sunburn, and by his careful sidestepping of other bodies in the crowded streets. Old-timers walked with eyes straight ahead under hat brims or behind dark glasses.

Inside, the Cultural Attaché settled in his chair and gazed across the desk, and Lee Simmonds looked back at him the way he'd looked at a long line of diplomats across unused desk-tops for the past several months. Dressed casually, Lee looked healthier than the man staring back at him, healthier than the long line of men like this who had come before. There was something pleasant about Lee's face, its gentle bland health, perhaps, that gave him an open, perpetually friendly look. The look of mediator. The look of team captain. Not a likely husband for Raina Scott. But he'd married her young.

He set his ankle on his knee—the foot was encased in the combination scarlet/electric blue of the LS 4000, a cross-country training flat his company was promoting. The 4000 was newest on their line. It had been the LS Firebird and Lady Firebird that first broke the market in a big way—a good middle-distance shoe—and if his college track record had made him famous, it was the franchise that finally made him rich. So Lee Simmonds slipped into his promotional role with ease. It was now a matter of course that he'd wear whatever the latest hot product happened to be. Promoting was as everyday an occurrence to him as brushing his teeth, and he didn't much notice it any more. But these things weren't on his mind now. He was busy with diplomatic red tape and all these people—ciphers, he'd wanted to call them, but his essential good breeding wouldn't allow it— who one by one stood temporarily in the way of finding his wife.

When Connery arrived, he told himself, there'd be no more waiting. Connery would move things along. But he kept this to himself.

Experience had taught him not to be direct at first. Why this should work, he didn't know. Still, all useful tactics were to be adhered to—this he'd learned from track days, and he'd learned it over again in business. Lee smiled pleasantly.

"Quite a demonstration there."

"Oh." The Attaché waved it away with his hand. It was a pale hand, a little flabby. "That's par for the course around here. They're all up in arms now about this Tristam Saunderson thing—you've heard the story on that, haven't you?"

Lee mumbled that maybe he had. He hadn't, of course; there were too many things going on in the world, in business and in his own disrupted life, for him to keep up with everything in some backwater country like Bellagua. Even though it was Bellagua.

"We try to keep our noses clean," said the Attaché. "We try to keep well out of the national government's affairs, you know. They have their own way of handling things here, and it's our policy not to interfere."

Of course, Lee said, he understood.

"But this Saunderson thing has gotten a little out of hand. The government of Bellagua claims he's a revolutionary and guilty of treason. Those demonstrators out there—the ones with the rocks—claim he's the greatest thing since sliced bread, and their savior. At any rate, the government's been arresting followers of his lately and holding them without bail. That's what we know."

He spread his hands, as if to say you see, that's it, that's really it. Watching, Lee knew that wasn't it and never could have been, and despite himself he was a little intrigued.

"What does he say about himself?"

"Who?"

"This man. Saunderson."

The Attaché shrugged. "Not much, really. He spouts off once in a while about human rights and peaceful change, that sort of thing. Still, as I guess you can see, peaceful change isn't the way things get done around here." He chuckled, shook his head in a patronizing manner. "Not on either side."

Lee chuckled sympathetically. He felt no sympathy but guessed it was a good idea to show some anyway. His legs shifted position uneasily—they were long, graceful and corded, the rest of him very lean. Though the days of collegiate triumph were a good fifteen years past, he'd kept himself in what was for him a natural state—that near-emaciated look of the classical top-flight runner. In everyday clothes, though, he was merely slender. And he had a pleasing face and a good handshake. Broach the subject painlessly, that was the key. Still, it was never really easy.

"I've been told to inform you," he said, "of my activities in the area."

The Attaché listened.

"You've probably heard. I intend to find my wife. I've engaged a professional military expert specializing in wilderness survival for that purpose. What I need is a go-ahead from the Bellaguans. I understand the interior is still officially off-limits, that's what everyone keeps telling me anyway."

After a while the Attaché nodded and pursed his lips saying yes, yes, he understood the situation and had, of course—he blushed slightly, because of course everyone had—heard of the rather extraordinary circumstances. He nodded carefully. He'd like to be of help if he could. Yes it was true the interior was off-limits, but roadblocks could be eased aside. What was required was tact. Certain people had to be taken to a nice dinner here and there, they had to be talked to. For gentlemen, anything was possible.

"It might be of interest to you"—Lee paused, tone carefully neutral—"to you and to the government of Bellagua, that my own company is a division of International Communications Enterprises."

"I didn't know."

Yes, Lee nodded, it was true.

They talked about other things. The Attaché slipped immediately into a buddylike way of behaving, reaching across the desk now and then sloppily, as if to slap his shoulder or shake hands on a bet. He'd always been a track fan in college himself, he said, even though he wasn't much of a runner. But Lee Simmonds—well, everybody had heard of Lee Simmonds. The 5,000/10,000-meter man. Sure. Lee listened politely. It was no longer a tireless source of amusement for him, this business of hearing about his old victories. Maybe he'd gotten jaded during the past few years. Maybe it was—as Raina once said—that the sense of immortality you got from a particular triumph lasted such a short time, really. If you wanted to feel it again, you had to pursue something else almost immediately. And whatever you went after next would have to be more difficult. The surmounting of obstacles was like a drug, she claimed. To prove yourself the next time you'd need a larger dose. Go farther. Deeper. And so on. But the ecstasy—ah. She'd smiled; Lee remembered. Ah, that was something. Yes it was.

He stood, a little dazed. They were saying goodbye. The Attaché said he'd be in touch soon. And not to worry. As he'd said, everything was possible if you went about it in the right way. If you acted through the appropriate channels. All it took was a little time. A little patience.

It was hot out there. Lee felt that tropical summer haze settling down in the heavy white sunlight. He tipped some skinny-ribbed, dark-colored kid to find him a cab. He'd head back to East Bay to wait. More waiting. He hoped this would be the last wait until Connery came. Then no more waiting.

Whatever the thing was that had started shivering inside him a long time ago kept moving slightly, still in nervous action. He was thinking of the face of Raina, his wife and best friend. Settling into the vinyl seat, he told the driver in smatterings of bad French which hotel he was heading for.

Lee played another tape in his head. The last discussion with Vince St.-Peters—maybe Lee was the last man he'd spoken to before the .22 had done its job. He'd taped it—at St.-Peters' request—shared the tape with no one but Connery. Then destroyed it. But he remembered each word.

"—so much evil in the world."

"What do you mean by evil?" came his own voice.

"Oh. It comes in different forms. Sometimes they call it a fertilizer."

"A fertilizer?"

"Sure. They'll give it to you. A fertilizer, take this in with you, spread it on a few plants while you're at it and we'll check it out later. Our scientists will, our research specialists will, you see, we all have a vested interest in the success of this new fertilizer. So you do as you're told. Spread it. And the devil has the last laugh. Because—ha-ha!—it's not fertilizer—it's poison—"

Vince St.-Peters had stopped suddenly and the tape rolled on, silent.

"Poison?" Lee heard himself say.

Then more silence. On tape, something rustled. "A liquid. Poison. It comes in special bottles. It looks silver. And it—" the voice stopped itself from sobbing, choked, and struggled. The words came out hoarse: "—turns white upon contact, turns everything white. Jesus Christ." The sobs broke through, long, full.

Lee's voice resumed after a while. The tone attempted to be quiet, soothing, but failed. "Vince, I think you need to tell me about this." Behind his voice the sobs continued. "I think that you need to tell me exactly what happened on Bellagua. But not until you're ready."

"Now. I'm ready now."

There was silence.

"Once you know, Simmonds"—St.-Peters' voice had softened, rang on the tape with a subtle, sly sound—"once you know, make sure they don't find out. They have vested interest. Vested interest."

"I'm not afraid of that, Vince."

"Then you're a fool. But a brave fool. Like Raina. She—now she—wasn't afraid of pain, either. Not like the others. Wasn't afraid of it. But she told me, that last day, she told me why."

"Why what?"

"Oh. Why she wouldn't come back. She stayed behind, you know." The voice had slowed; there was little suffering in it, now, more awe. "Of her own free will."

"Vince." Lee heard himself wait. He remembered that meeting, the pale, desperate look of the man sitting across the room from him, still emaciated, hands quivering uncontrollably. *"That's not what you told them at the inquiry—"*

"The inquiry! The inquiry! They can stuff their fucking inquiries! What do they care, once you've done the job? You've spread their poison for them— what do they care? Their hands are clean."

Remembering his own words, his own failures at insight, Lee wondered why he had doubted him so. He wondered what it had been about the man, the sight of him, his story, that made him so afraid.

He felt his eyes roll back in his head and head tilt back on the cab seat to rest, then he was dozing off and on. He woke once in shock to the imagined sound of a voice leaping louder than other words off slickly rolling tape: *"—Raina! God forgive me!"*

He saw her face and knew why he hadn't fallen apart during the past two years. It was because he had a fundamental belief in her self-sufficiency. It was because he knew that sufficiency to be far superior to his own. She was gone on an extended trip, his heart told him, a lengthy project, one surpassing in length and difficulty all she had attempted before. That was it. He knew also that everything was nothing but a matter of time, anyway. It was not intimate love that gave Lee this knowledge, but the friendship between them—he'd always said it was the one thing that had been there before the feast and the one thing that remained with the leftovers, and now it was what moved him still.

He rolled down a window.

The cab sidled its way through streets. Progress was slow; the city was stifled with sunlit bodies, with the aroma of sweat and fruit rinds, an odor of stewed vegetables, meat in the garbage, chicken feathers, flowers. He leaned back, sweating, closed his eyes to the sunlight that shot in through the windshield, the street talk drifting by in foreign languages.

A sudden gust blew through the window, wild mixture of the streets and hot salt-sweet air. He opened his eyes. They were heading for the country, the single paved highway leading away from Sagrabél's winding, twisted little alleys and toward East Bay. The way stretched flat and sandy, ocean on one side, on the other green palms and sparse scrub that became thicker foliage that became even thicker and then, eventually, the jungle. Sadly, he smiled. He would have liked to tell her something now, to thank her somehow. For what, he didn't quite know. Imagining her brought a sense of great loss, but no erotic visions. It brought little anguish, little arousal; there was only the hard, clear, certain light of her face, the definite illumination of what she was, that came to mind. It was a strong image, one that told no lies.

* * *

Our new Amelia Earhart, they'd called her.

Not that she flew. But she was a daredevil on the ground. Raina Scott, always looking for the next thrill—that's what her detractors had said, nodding in sage psychological analyses of why she did what she did. A *death wish* was the most popular theory among so-called experts. But the public had a different point of view: greatest show on earth. It was the Raina Scott show—every year or so something different. Mountain climbing. Exploring underwater caves. Bow hunting. Endurance treks through deserts, through blizzards. Spear-fishing for Great White Sharks. Et cetera. And if the public found what she did bizarre, or excessive, or crazy, they also found it undeniably fascinating. She was, in fact, a household word. Good press, said the press. Good press. With each new feat she was better and better press. Her climbs, her safaris, her hunting expeditions and all the attendant hype warranted a lot of media coverage. Raina Scott the three-ring circus, some might joke. But the fascination with what she did could be turned into high ratings, wider circulation—the commercial possibilities at times seemed endless. Raina was not oblivious to this. Oh, she wanted to be a household word in her own way. Lee remembered her boasts—tickled pink! she'd exclaim, sure, I'm tickled pink or red or something the way they carry on— and he knew what tickled her most was that no one gave a damn about her motives except the so-called experts. And they could stuff it, she'd said angrily once, when accused yet again of harboring a death wish, stuff it. He guessed she knew her own motives well enough. He guessed at times she had moments of bright and painless clarity, that in those moments she saw herself revealed and in all the nakedness of whatever her desire was she might revel in, might recognize—if only for that brief instant—herself: pure, undiluted, unashamed. Curled into his own tired arms once in a while her head would rest. He'd watch the thick dark hair shine back at him. She was nestled in his arms like a much-loved pet, or child. What he felt for her at those times was an extraordinarily paternal ache, a nostalgia for what things might have been, had they been otherwise—but also it was a yearning to know her better. Surely, he told himself, surely he would soon know what moved her to do the things she did. Knowing that, he might know the most intimate core of her, might know her completely then. And they might again become lovers. Again become husband and wife in the traditional sense—have a home together, share a bed. Children. Lee was a man of unusual accomplishment but, having lived the life of a champion and of an extremely successful business executive, he'd imbued the ordinary with a romantic hue. A house, a lawn, a tricycle in the driveway, a wife's arm reaching to turn off the early morning alarm—these images moved him in a way that was at times erotic. He had a lust for what others considered normality. And the certain knowlege that it would never be his lent a poetic desperation to his imaginings. No. He could not picture such a life with Raina. He could not even honestly picture himself inside such a life. And Lee mourned for what he hadn't ever had.

But he'd committed himself to accepting this state of things, his physical solitude, their living apart. As time went on and he threw himself more and more into matters of business, he found business reaping the benefits of the publicity she stirred up, the endorsements she would occasionally make on behalf of this shoe or that piece of wilderness apparel. She was contracted to the company, and the company to her. They were succeeding—apart and together—and as time went on the finances became high. Until Raina Scott, Our New Amelia Earhart, and Lee Simmonds, America's 5,000/10,000-Meter Golden Boy, were inextricably bound by more than marriage. Their financial destinies were tied. Raina was incorporated. And Lee had the running shoe concern expanded, franchised. Three branches in New York. Boston. Los Angeles. San Francisco. Denver. He was thinking of Fort Lauderdale. He was thinking of a lot of things. The stock expanded: hiking and camping equipment, fishing gear, gear for a variety of field sports. Consistently, their most popular commercial endorsements for these items came from Raina. America's Sweethearts, he sometimes thought bitterly—but the ads worked. Business flourished. Her beyond-the-fringe activities were copyrighted for advertisements; the farther away she went from it all, the more she became big bucks. If she'd permitted it, a toy manufacturer would have produced a line of Raina Scott dolls, replete with bow and arrow. Our New Amelia Earhart. Alone at night for the most part, he wondered if she felt lonely sometimes, or if she had gone too far to feel that at all any more. And sometimes he was comforted by a woman's body next to him—some blonde with friendly enough eyes. He chose a certain type these days, a physical type different from Raina.

Sure, he'd learned to move with the rhythm of a strange marriage. And if that meant separation, big bucks, occasional long phone conversations and the rare meetings for dinner, the even rarer nights spent next to her, communication through agents and lawyers—well, if that was what it meant he thought himself equal to the task. Take things one step at a time. He loved her still; in better moments she was his best friend.

He remembered the last night they'd spent together.

She'd shown up unexpectedly and was suddenly there, leaning casually against the kitchen counter, grinning. She looked tanned and spectacular.

Not that her individual features were anything particularly special, but she was charismatic. And something in him kept wanting to step toward her, touch her fine sun-darkened skin and run fingers through her hair as if he were a child seeking to touch something pleasurable. He hated the way he thought of himself in her presence. It seemed he could conceive of himself in only one of two ways: as wanting child, or as understanding parent. Neither way was satisfactory. He'd want to hit her sometimes. At others, to stroke her the way you would a thoroughbred kitten. She was no kitten, though; Raina was trouble. However it came to you, it would certainly come when you got near her—and for all her genuine fairness of spirit and all her thorough, professional preparations before any new undertaking, she invariably attracted a whirlwind of trouble, and it invariably caught more bodies than hers in its inexorable, swirling mesh.

"I hoped you'd be home tonight!"

"Did you?" He sidled toward her, stopped himself. He took another step forward and kissed her forehead calmly.

She seemed receptive. She would make him dinner, she offered. He noted with appreciation that her voice was quiet, friendly. And he laughed, telling her no. The last time she'd ventured into a kitchen she'd left disaster—burned everything and created some mess in the sink that couldn't even be scoured out. She might find success in the mountains of Tanganyika or Tanzania or wherever, he teased her, but he'd rather she kept away from the stove. He thought for a moment, with surprise, that she was going to be insulted, but she smiled instead and half bowed to him. All right, all right. She'd let him provide. He told her they'd order something. Steak. Fish. Whatever she wanted. They could have it delivered.

"How's Karlen?"

Her smile sparkled back, unperturbed. "Fine," she said.

He told her he had some nice wine around.

They'd sat on the floor, carving tough steak and laughing a little as they warmed to each other all over again. It was always like that—the first stilted meeting, the slow, subtle sinking in to an old familiarity that made him want to tell her all his secrets. She was everything his upbringing had taught him to stay away from in a woman: independent, dark, with a sudden, boisterous laugh. He'd been raised to wed a quiet, bird-like, magazine-pretty, fair-skinned, fair-haired lady of elegant upbringing and stark white tastes. Raina sat loosely on his apartment floor that night, epitome of all the opposite things. She appeared almost Italian, or Greek, the large eyes flashing from her tanned skin like an animal's. Her eyes could be all black sometimes, nearly depthless. They seemed to have no fear in them at all, but rather some old, cold, essential wisdom that could not be described. Maybe the word closest to it was instinct. Yes, Raina had instinct; she lived by instinct; it was quite close to the surface in her. It was what made her exciting to be next to, what made her dangerous. Because maybe she would cut you loose by instinct. If the raft seemed to be sinking. If there was only room for one. Raina had become an expert, he reminded himself, in the field of survival. Certainly, then, there was no limit to what she'd do—at any rate, she succeeded in giving you that impression. The odd thing about it all was that she gave an impression of great tenderness, too. It was a tenderness in the way she could gently examine something, or the way she would, on rare occasion, reach out to brush his shoulder or chest lightly with her fingertips—the touch was always delicate, utterly feminine. It never failed to surprise or stir him.

They discussed an endorsement deal that night, settled the matter in a leisurely way. It was like a contractual handshake between friends, the deal sealed. He knew she'd live up to her part of the bargain. She always did.

"You look good, Raina."

She thanked him.

"You look like you're in love."

Raina blushed. He noticed the sudden gaping openness of her blush—eyes quickly closed to conceal whatever real feeling had flashed through them. He was offended that she chose to conceal it from him. Then he felt glad in a way. After all, he told himself, he didn't want to know in detail about her happiness in the arms of some other—some other whatever. He could still claim himself as the first. In the clinical sense he really had been, and this fact he found himself clinging to bitterly. But all his bitterness passed away in seconds; and he allowed himself a kind of sweet sensation bordering again on nostalgia: happiness for the happiness of Raina, his friend. Because despite everything that had ever gone on between them her joy was infectious. He reveled in it a little, too. He'd always liked to see her smile.

She nodded. Oh, certainly, she said. She was. Yes. It felt like—it felt like it was. *Love.* She didn't want to decipher the term too much.

"To you." He raised his glass but didn't drink.

Some time that night, he remembered, he'd looked down to see her stretched beside him on the floor, her arms gently circling his waist. She ran fingers along his belt, patted his belly comfortably. Old friends. He scratched her head and massaged her temples. They were like two kids playing with teddy bears.

"Why don't you spend the night?"

He hated himself for asking. But he ignored whatever answer she might be about to make, stood and put something on the stereo. Later she asked him to take it off. She stacked up the plates they'd eaten from and carried them into the kitchen. He heard something dropping with a metallic bounce, Raina cursing a little as she bent to pick it up, the dull clatter of things as she set them in the sink. He took off the record and in the room's dull light listened to the silence she'd left behind. He thought of a three-page-ad deal they'd investigated the day before, decision still pending with the account executive assigned him from the agency. He'd have to get on that tomorrow. And other things. Money in dollars. In pounds and lire and drachmas. Francs. Kronor. Money swam around him in a yellow light, without her presence—he understood now why men went to war for money. Understood why armies had no women in them. A fight to the death for something unliving must remain untouched by breasts or soft thighs or lips.

She re-entered the room and the air warmed. He felt a sense of calm overtake him; Lee possessed himself fully again. Whatever decision she might make, he knew he'd be all right. He had been all along. She'd taken his life and the lives of others on a crazy ride, but who was to say that the ride had not been in some sense worthwhile? And no one could claim it had been uninstructive. Seated on the floor, he grinned wryly to himself.

"Lee. I think we should make love. I don't know when I'll see you again."

She sounded dead serious. Was there an uneasy edge of something else to her words? She smiled calmly.

He stayed where he was. It occurred to him that perhaps he'd arrived at that blessed point of maturity he'd always hoped for in times of unshadowed idealism: the moment of selfless love, in which he could love her without wanting her. It seemed that, in wanting her, he would only oppress her with his desire. She did not desire his desire; what she desired of him was familiarity, a platonic, spiritual way of being—perfect friendship. Perhaps he'd be capable of that now. He shook his head, saying he didn't know, he just didn't know whether they ought to. He wasn't sure it was the right thing to do. She grinned easily. Well, she asked in a teasing tone, was it the *wrong* thing to do?

Lee lit candles, an old custom of theirs. They'd done it back in days of studious friendship that led to studious romance, littered each surface, furniture, each empty space of shelf, with candles. Turned off the lights. He did again. He felt himself in a sanctuary of sorts, a chapel. The candles had been Raina's idea in the first place, he remembered, those years ago. A tomb! he'd protested back then before he'd gotten used to the idea. But she'd laughed.

"Hey."

She turned at the sound of his voice.

"Why won't we see each other again soon?"

"Oh, I didn't say that! I said I didn't know."

"Ah."

He let the matter drop. She was Raina Scott, after all. And in his eyes, as well as the eyes of the world, he guessed she'd attained a stature that went beyond the personal—maybe he allowed her things he could not stand for in others. Questions between them might go unanswered. She was Raina Scott, Our New Amelia Earhart. And insofar as matters of life and death were concerned, he was out of the picture. She held all the cards to her own destiny.

Candlelight jumped over their faces. It jumped in yellow strips up and down bookcases, walls, made funny zigzags on the door and shot long flashes into the kitchen's dark.

They stripped quietly, matter-of-factly. When they were together, it never ceased to amaze him how familiar it felt, even though they rarely saw each other naked. As if there were no surprises between them, no sense of awareness now and then when they glanced at each other's bodies. Thinking back, he realized it had always been this way. They'd started out as friends. But there was a curious lack of passion between them, always had been— he couldn't help but be fully aware of himself. In some way, he thanked her for that. Raina always gave you back yourself, when you expected most to lose it. Naked, unaroused, he stood examining her with friendly interest, and though unaroused he was also unafraid. She was—well, full. Things in really nice, strong shape; still, it wasn't by any means the most beautiful body he'd ever seen. Just, in some way, the most complete. She was very strong, and gracious in each motion. There was something royal about her. And she hadn't always had that quality in full force, he knew—only since the time when she had for all intents and purposes ceased to be his wife and become Raina Scott instead, Our New Amelia Earhart, flying into dark things on land instead of in the air. Only since then had she attained this aura of completeness in his eyes. Inimitable. Raina Scott dolls, indeed. He laughed. This fullness—it could be a frightening thing if you didn't know her. She never lost herself. Raina always held a piece of herself in reserve.

Still, they were tied to each other via endorsements, via corporate agreements. They probably couldn't have divorced if they'd wanted to. This gave him some kind of satisfaction. A barren marriage, he told himself, but a marriage nevertheless.

Lee opened his arms to her. "Sorry. I'm not Don Juan tonight."

"Oh, that's really all right. We can cuddle instead, like old friends—"

"Any time."

Stretched out beside her on the carpet, Lee felt himself in the tired grip of that moment he'd been striving for: the time of perfected love, a love lacking only desire. He rubbed her back, her shoulders. She seemed content with that. Well, she had a lover, after all. It couldn't have been for any kind of sexual satisfaction that she'd wanted to make love—it had sounded, instead, as if she was saying goodbye. He couldn't believe she'd meant it that way. She'd promised to be available for some more promo shots and to get things moving on another contract. And he knew Raina never cut out on her part of a deal.

"Where are you off to?"

"Nowhere." She smiled. "Here for now. That's good enough, Lee, isn't it?"

He said he guessed so.

Her eyes got drowsy. He watched with concern.

"Lee. What's the matter?"

"I think I understand how I need to be with you, now."

The eyes widened, roused themselves reluctantly. She waited.

He couldn't have told her the rest of it. He felt complete in her arms for the first time. Without desire he was also without bitterness. And he could love her, truly, perhaps—he could wish her well.

He said nothing and after a while she held his face in both her hands and kissed his nose, his forehead, kissed his eyes to close them. She squeezed the back of his neck with affection. Golden boy, she giggled.

"What?"

"Sun God."

"Me?"

"Sure. Sun God. Moon Goddess. And these"—she gestured around the room, motioning at the multi-flickering shadows of all the candles he'd lit—"these are the stars."

"You're crazy, Raina."

She considered it a moment, then nodded in serious agreement. Her eyes were wide awake now. He wondered what she wanted. Not him, he knew. But he wondered.

They slept, and woke sometimes to hug or gently caress. She snapped awake once suddenly, left breast jumping visibly with her heart's pounding. What is it? he asked. She told him a dream. A recurring dream she'd had of tracking something in the snow.

"Big Foot?" he teased.

She smiled. He stroked her hair to quiet her.

They slept again, calmly. Lee fell in and out of deep sleep—much of the time he was wallowing in half-dream country. In his dreams he was a kid again, trying to make her, back in the days when she'd just begun to be amazing. In his dreams his potency was endless, hard and quick and youthful—he had endless supplies of sperm and an endless desire to rid himself of it, and somewhere along the line all this excess had pointed toward her. Limitless potential, he told her, he felt himself to be limitless. The Cross-Country Championships this year, law school two years down the pike, business and the fulfillment of every dream shortly thereafter. Because he was American, and a modern man—white, Protestant—the world was his oyster. Life would never catch up with him.

Oh, she told him seriously, but it does you know. With everyone.

She knew, he guessed. She was the daughter of classical scholars, world travelers who'd raised her with careful attention to physical and intellectual training, who'd cultivated in her at a young age an appetite for adventure, for knowledge, for the bizarre. Reading all those things from days gone by, she knew intimately the nature of the days that had gone by, knew the causes for their passing. And her studies taught her that all things, indeed, passed on. But he would have glory nonetheless, he told her, have what he wanted and still live a decent life. He believed it possible to do both.

And he remembered the moment: on the floor of the room, ledges with candles, mad flicker on badly painted walls, and the hiss of wax melting on chair arms. She'd explained to him the myth of the centaur. Long, strong-legged, he felt her pinned beneath his heavy thighs, corded calves— his upper body a mere mortal's. And he was brought back to mortality with a shock when she clutched at him, gasped in genuine pain, tried to push him away and off and out of her. Shhh, he told her. No, she said, please. Please. She bit her lip. Then she seemed to give up temporarily; her hands gripping his shoulders were tight but did not move; her eyes closed, and he was something foreign, half-human, swaying above her in a harsh, adoring, insistent motion. He felt how tight she was inside. Resisting. A virgin. There was something horrible in that. Something strangely exciting. He was proud. And afraid.

Outside, he remembered, it was getting on toward winter. He'd looked down at her thighs later, seen half-dried smatterings of blood. He'd wet a tissue and wiped her tenderly, wanted to tell her how sorry he was. But there was a part of him that was so proud instead. So he just propped her head on pillows there on the floor. He told her she'd get used to it after a while. Yes, she said, tears in her eyes, she knew. Yes, she knew. And it would all be all right, she promised him. It would. He remembered her pale, young face. They'd stripped her bed of blankets and covered themselves, gone to sleep there on the floor that night and outside they could hear the wind, would wake sometimes to find another candle dripped to nothing on a table edge, the flame drowned by wax. They'd gone to sleep friends and he had woken up in love, it was as simple as that—in love, in pity, in some kind of terror—as simple as any of that ever is.

Lee opened his eyes. There she was—Raina, his wife. He wanted to ask why she'd come here tonight, what she was after; usually she was open with him about what she needed. He couldn't have suspected, those years ago, the nature of the road she would lead him along. It was not a road so much, he thought, as a series of increasingly complex detours. And no pain he'd ever feel would be as pure as that first, simple pain—he'd felt it in her *no, please*—the irrevocability of it, marked with blood. No more of that between them—no violation or vulnerable pleasures. She was going away somewhere, had come to say goodbye. And whatever way she now went, he could not follow. Lee held her closer for a while. He watched candles drip, destroying the finish on his furniture. She always brought some kind of damage, Raina. Some kind of desolation, for all her fullness and all her strength.

THE MEETING

The meeting was one of a series of monthly meetings at the residence of Dr. Tristam Saunderson, and as always it was crowded. Each month it seemed more people showed. Tonight, bodies packed the small tin and palm-thatched house, spilled down wooden steps. They edged out and around into the village center, milled nervously on the stretch of beach. The tide was low. Some had come from far away—some from as far as Sagrabél. Some had brought children. They let them play in the water's low lapping surf, make sand hut constructions with children of the village. The sun had faded. Above receding horizon light began the first glimmerings of stars. The crowd grew larger. There was some anxiety, some discussion: how would it be possible for everyone to hear? The bodies were different colors, one from the other—African black to dusky brown to almost white. They glowed, mingled in growing dark.

The village was small—a few short rows of similarly thatched little houses facing the sea. To their back, the jungle. In the center of all the rows of houses was a large stone-rimmed fire pit. Every night a fire was lit here when darkness became absolute. Each adult member of the village took turns guarding it. Tonight, a woman struggled her way down the steps of Dr. Tristam Saunderson's house—she was a tall, large-boned woman with dark brown skin and she had eyes that shone with intrinsic intelligence— her face always looked to be on the verge of laughing at some secret but harmless joke. Harmless because the eyes were also kind. And in the intelligence with which they looked out on things, there was a genuine sort of concern. Gazing into these eyes, you might feel that were you to complain of a bruise she'd ask gently to see it. Then she might provide the perfect remedy. And all things, regardless of their scale, would find careful consideration in those eyes. Certainly, you'd know, she was a mother.

Good evening, Doctor! she was greeted. Good evening, Dr. Porter. She nodded back pleasantly. She didn't seem bothered by the proliferation of bodies. Small box in hand, she made her way slowly to the fire pit. She checked the area, quietly requested children to move. She bent over, tossed a dried palm frond in and with perfect aim sent a lit wooden match after it. Orange flared up, tongued over the pit's edge before settling to a steady bright burn. People crowded around. Not for the warmth, because the evening was hot, but for light. Firm and broad-hipped in her place, she guarded it. She talked easily with people. Once in a while her laughter rose above the humming noise. It was giddy, strong laughter, and made you want to echo its enthusiasm. She talked constantly, and when not talking she listened. People gravitated toward her and the fire's light. She'd made a home for herself—a sort of emanating presence of comfort and entirety— she was at home with crowds, inviting them in.

"There he is," someone said.

It spread through the crowd, down to the shoreline. It spread around the fire, caused heads to turn, necks twisting to see. In the entranceway at the top of the steps there was some movement.

Dr. Tristam Saunderson stepped down.

He was a man of medium size, in his late thirties or early forties. He wore the patched knee-length trousers everyone else wore, and an off-white cotton shirt. Against the light color his skin looked darker than it was—it was a light, red-touched brown. His face was unremarkable, his eyes very large behind rimless glasses, dark and dreamy in an absent-minded way. His progress down the steps was slow. With one arm he reached out to touch all the many hands held up to him, one by one. With his other he held a child of about three, a light brown boy with a face that laughed gleefully. The boy's eyes stayed wide with interest, large and brown, dreaming while awake. He was naked, like all the other children. His small buttocks wrinkled slightly under the pressure of his father's arm.

Slowly, certainly, Saunderson progressed toward the fire. The wave of expectation followed him there, bodies turned as if in a carefully controlled line of force to watch where he walked, and soon—without a word being said—people began to sit on the sand, on the steps, along the row of village houses, their expectant bodies swirling out from the center of the fire pit like irregularly shaped octopus arms. He deposited the boy in Dr. Porter's lap. She smiled. She held him there, whispered something into his ear that set him giggling. He played with her fingers, sucking and twisting gently.

Saunderson remained standing. He'd come outside, he said, because there were so many tonight. He'd like discussion afterward, wanted everyone to be able to participate. And he smiled, a little wearily. Their son had been awake all the previous night, he explained, with nightmares. And the nightmares of children were a serious affair. There was one thing clear: only tenderness could stop them. For a child, this came in the form of physical contact. For an adult, likewise, contact ought to be made—but if the physical was not possible there were other modes of communication available. It was the exploration of such modes that constituted their business here tonight.

He'd been asked, he said, to speak of political matters. This he did not feel he could do, except to say that oppositions were a deception. There was, inherent in every thing, more than a shadow of its opposite. He could say freely that the worst oppressors were striving with more desperation than others to oppress their own fear of victimization. So that men of power were beggars in disguise. And their reign was deceptive—it was never long-lasting, never successful, for it was based on unwholesome qualities. When a thing was harmful to the earth, it was never wholesome—by wholesome he meant it was not whole, or complete, it did not have a center to it. There was nothing at the core of an unwholesome, harmful thing—an action that placed the value of money over the value of a man's life, for instance, or, say, a violent action on the part of a government. Every harmful thing was hollow, without a soul. It had no fires inside. It lived a brief, unhappy life in the realm of darkness. So those who were caught up in the pursuit of power ought to be pitied. They were shells of men.

The night cooled. A slight breeze ruffled his off-white shirt sleeves. Saunderson shifted feet in the sand, talked quietly. He had a naturally musical voice which carried a long way.

Any man, he said, who hit a woman, was striking to destroy some part of himself. So it was with a wealthy and powerful oppressor. The wealthy, the powerful, they tried to take more and more because somewhere inside they were empty, and hungry. They tried to fill their own emptiness with the hearts of others. But they could never satiate this emptiness—they could not take enough to complete themselves because the core of their action was without tenderness and, therefore, essentially hollow. In their eternal hunger, they were also to be pitied. All their wealth hid a gaping poverty. Unlike fire—he pointed down into the glowing pit—unlike fire, they consumed endlessly without giving back anything to the world. The mechanism inside, of heat, of warmth and passion—the mechanism that could transform all matter into something different, to be spilled back into the world—this was lacking in them. And it could be understood, by looking at the nature of fire, that the principle of reciprocity rested in great part on the principle of transformation. All things changed. All men. All women. And as they changed, they emitted something different back to the world—the life—that changed them. So it had always been. To *hoard* stopped the mechanism of life. To hoard was to die.

He talked a while longer. Yellow flames glowed on the dark faces turned up to him. He spoke quietly. It was nothing very important that he had to say tonight, he told them. It was nothing they didn't already know, somewhere inside.

The moon was high, cold, almost full.

There was some discussion afterward.

The things said bothered him. There was violence in all the talk. They were talking about children starving, and about guns. The Americans give food to the pigs and cows every season, or they burn food in large pits so the remainder of the crop will bring a high price on the market. And to us they bring not food, but industry. They hire women for pennies a day, to work in factories without light. They sell us poisoned powder to replace the milk of the breast. It's the Americans doing this, the Americans with their business organizations in Sagrabél, and after them the Europeans.

Capitalists, someone else said. It's the work of capitalist imperialists.

The moon glowed down coolly.

What is that? someone asked. There was laughter.

No, said a young man, you're wrong. It is the Jews.

And there was silence.

Do you want power? Saunderson asked, finally. Yes, hissed the response from the young man standing among the others, his body lit by the fire into strange jumping patterns. He looked painted, standing there, in wild swirls of light. Why do you want power? Saunderson challenged. And people became more attentive than usual. There was an edge to his voice not often heard.

The young man shook his head. You and I speak on different levels, Dr. Saunderson. You speak about philosophy. I speak about reality.

And do you think—Saunderson felt himself perspire—do you think that what is philosophically unacceptable can also be politically defensible?

The young man paused. Finally he said no, not always defensible. But sometimes necessary nevertheless. Sometimes. For the survival of a people.

"And you'll have us all in heaven before we get the chance to live, Doctor! Go on thinking philosophy until you drop dead, if you like—but you'll probably drop dead of hunger, remember that. Philosophy never put food into anyone's mouth."

Saunderson spread his arms wide. It was a dramatic gesture, for the benefit of an audience. "Am I in want of food?"

There were murmurings, slight waves of whispers rippling among the crowd. Saunderson was nervous for the first time in months. That the young man could be handled easily, he had no doubt. That he was also of high intelligence—and that there were others, in growing number, like him—could be easily surmised. It made Saunderson anxious, not for himself so much, but for what they might do. And he saw their fate for years to come, etched on the horizon in red—the words were political, the blood real; it was theirs, and his own.

The young man's laugh had a sharp, nasty ring to it. Saunderson noted uneasily that now eyes were shifting to him. The young man seemed to expand in size, arms rose in a strutting motion.

"There are two ways to oppress a people, Doctor. You can oppress them in body—that's already done on Bellagua. And you can oppress them in mind. Who pays you, Tristam Saunderson? Who pays you to poison our minds with pacifism, when real action is what we need? Is it the Americans? Or the Jews?"

What are the Jews? someone asked.

Saunderson took this opportunity to make a joke. It was obvious, he said, gesturing widely again, that he received large sums of money from many sources. Everyone laughed. The laughter was nervous, then more relaxed. In it the young man began to lose face and, physically, to wilt. He began a weak verbal protest—what he said, though, Saunderson could not hear because his words were overridden by the mockings of others. Eventually the young man crept toward the back of the crowd, and sat. And Saunderson eased into more gentle conversation, with less challenging questioners.

Later, when things had settled down and the crowd's attention was largely distracted, he had his men remove this person quietly. Gently, he advised them, but firmly. Saunderson watched them do so out of the corner of his eye. He couldn't risk such things at this point. He must appear to be in control. Otherwise it would hurt the movement.

The moon had drifted in one direction. Saunderson stayed awake after most of those remaining were curled in sand close to the fire, close to each other for warmth.

Dr. Manella Porter sat by the fire, eyes wide. Their son Yosh slept. Once in a while he smacked his lips in sleep. And although Tristam Saunderson sat close to her, they did not touch, or speak.

After a while, he tapped her lightly on the shoulder and stood. She nodded. She turned back to the fire. He stepped silently over sleeping bodies, heard the cries of insects fluttering wings and mating in the night, heard behind him the gentle slush of surf on sand. Saunderson looked carefully around to make sure he wouldn't be seen. He headed behind the last row of little homes facing the ocean, farther still. He held his breath a short while before stepping in. Then, beach and firelight behind, he was walking silently, by instinct, through the near-pitch dark of dense jungle growth.

He walked a long time. His eyes had accustomed themselves to the almost total lack of light. They could perceive, now, that here and there a little moon filtered through, cast a dull, cool glow on the twining leaves and vines before him. He walked until his feet were covered with mud. Soon he came to a small space where the undergrowth was sparser. A single shaft of moonlight shot through here, puddled silver on damp ground. In it he could see bugs dance as if enjoying the moonlight, twirl and soar away. Saunderson stopped. He listened. There was nothing but the sound of insects and, from somewhere far off, a lonely bird cry. It was more like a wail, actually—long, piercing, alone. There was something almost human in the tone. There was a chill to it. And as he listened it came again—longer this time, and closer. Saunderson reached behind to touch the soft bark of a tree. He felt along it for snakes, then leaned carefully against it. He waited, and kept listening.

After a while he spoke quietly.

"Here I am, sister. Come and talk."

He waited. The moonlight drifted down.

The wail came closer—animal, then bird, then faintly recognizable. It haunted at intervals. It became more recognizable still, until it was nearly fully human: a voice of indeterminate sex, wailing from the shadows next to him in a piercing, horrible way.

Saunderson waited. He could feel the trickle of sweat down his chest. The right stem of his glasses had been repaired haphazardly with twine. He touched the knot of twine now, touched it again, as if the touching were a sort of ritual. He focused on the single puddle of moonlit earth. After a while, he became aware of someone breathing from the shadows next to him. He exhaled loudly; there was a second's lapse, then an answering breath to his left and just behind. Saunderson stood quite still. He hesitated before speaking; when he did, the words were carefully chosen.

"Your methods have become too extreme. They may ruin everything, you know."

The whisper was playfully petulant. *Listen, we've been through this before, haven't we? Haven't we been through this at least a dozen times?*

"At least," he sighed.

Follow your own logic, please. Where there is gentleness there is also great violence—right? Oh, something like that, anyway. Your people are a violent people, Doctor.

"Yes," he said softly, regretfully.

And it's a little too late in the game, don't you think? It's a little too late in the game to begin changing tactics. You said so yourself—

"That is true—"

They were silent.

Then, "There is the question of money," he said.

It's being arranged.

"We need money for paper, and clothes. Medical supplies—"

And guns! Of course! The voice had become more overtly mocking; still, there was a kind of gentleness to it. *Don't worry, Doctor. It's being arranged, I believe. Messengers came back just yesterday. I have definite information— I believe it's being arranged—*

"You are sure?"

*As sure as I can be. I have a friend, Doctor, a close friend, who would do anything for me. Anything! I'm quite sure of it! And I—*the voice lost its biting edge completely—*I don't forget what I owe you. Life. I was a goner, Doc.*

Saunderson watched an insect crawl across the white puddle of moonlight. He waited for mockery to return to the voice whispering behind his left shoulder; it always did. But he was never insulted by it—in a certain way, he understood it completely. The whisper hardened behind him:

From Goner to Goddess. Hah! There's a metamorphosis for you.

"Yes," he said gently. "And I owe much to you, I know."

A smile had edged its way into his voice. Saunderson enjoyed these talks despite himself. They caused him to reevaluate. He was in a continual process of reevaluation anyway, and the constant threat he lived with—the threat of imminent arrest, assassination even—was softened by these solitary meetings. At these times he felt himself without a personal identity to uphold; he felt himself a slender, bespectacled, dark-skinned man posing as the Black God of Bellagua for a multitude of good reasons; he felt himself to be unmuddled, simplified, quite alone. And they were both, he reminded himself, playing certain roles for a multitude of good reasons. If he had never approved of her methods, he supposed a number of his followers did—and as long as he remained affiliated with her, they remained affiliated with him. He supposed quarrels vis-à-vis methods had always taken place, even among the gods.

They spoke of other things that night. He was preparing, he said, for certain inevitabilities. The movement was growing in power. The authorities would probably not tolerate it much longer. He was prepared to be arrested— even the incarceration of the Black God had a convenient basis in Bellaguan mythology—prepared to be arrested and imprisoned for a long time, if necessary. In which case his half of power would likely shift onto her shoulders. There was—he smiled, speaking this—there was some mythological basis for that, as well. And he asked that special care be taken in regard to Dr. Manella Porter and the boy, Yosh. A special kind of care. This he asked—he hesitated, but continued—this he asked, not as a leader of political movements, but as a man who had loved. As someone who had also loved, perhaps she would understand his request. He hoped she would.

They were silent again, a nearly comfortable silence during which each could hear the other breathe in darkness. The puddle of moonlight on the jungle floor shifted, changed shape, began to dissipate.

He'd return to find waiting men in national military uniform flapping government documents at him, and guns. The area around the fire pit deserted except for Dr. Manella Porter who—head gravely bowed—held a sleeping boy in her arms. They didn't acknowledge each other.

A MEAN CORNER GAME

There were bars on Bellagua for everyone. Tourist bars, nightclub cafés where bellies of native entertainers glistened sweat and rolled like dark flashing gems in the spotlights. There were bars where businessmen met, shook hands over verbal agreements that would be enacted back in the States, or on the Continent. These men kept their money in billfolds fastened by silver clips. Their wrists, laid firmly on the bar's dark wood surface, glowed sometimes like hair-speckled ivory. They were always buying each other drinks. Alcohol was a main item of import on Bellagua.

There were bars for natives, but these were lost in the back yards of waterfront tourist towns, wood shacks with bug-infested shelves. They served bad rum and cheap beer, ran as long as they could on credit and then folded.

Then there was the new bar, the one especially designed for men on the dig.

Not all the men on the dig were scientists, or experts in any particular field. Most, in fact, were paid corporate labor, overseers and administrators of a minor, petty sort, guards, quasi-military types who had to account to superiors for the well-being of all kinds of materials that meant nothing to them. They were a small, listless army without a war, stationed overseas in this dreary port. They had neither the influence nor the know-how to make it with the tourist set, and native life was closed to them—invisible among the bright lights of East Bay. On West Reef, they heard, villages where old religions were still practiced lined the coastal rim. But West Reef was off limits to all except men with top-priority security cards. So most of the listless army traveled nowhere. When duties were finished for a day, there was little to do. Eventually they set up a bar of their own in Sagrabél—complete with recreation room—materials provided gratis as a fringe benefit from International Communications Enterprises, Incorporated. International was funding the dig.

She stepped lightly inside the door.

She had on a red baseball cap, rim turned to the back. Around her neck and shoulder a leather strap attached to a small hand-tooled leather case. This swayed against one hip in the shape of a miniature stringed instrument, or flattened gourd.

Moving through a few streaks of sunlight, her face was momentarily, diagonally striped, bleached expressionless. Even expressionless, it was a striking face. The chin a perfect oval tip, perfect baby skin, lips open in seeming vulnerability. Eyes large, dark, and she moved with real grace. Not ballet grace, not gymnastic grace, but a natural healthy slender kind of grace that made everyone look up. She wasn't very tall. But she was beautiful.

"Anybody play table tennis?"

It was a challenge.

The voice rang out, light, young, with a slightly husky timbre. Words faded in sudden silence—glasses had been set down on wet bar puddles, mugs allowed to spill over and foam while every guy in the place sat upright, straightened his sweaty shirt front. Everyone stared.

Kaz looked around. A pretty sorry group, for sure. But you made do with the stuff at hand. Her new motto. She was always changing mottos—because circumstance, she said, was constantly changing anyway—and she was always on the lookout for new ones. No *pain*, *no gain* had been a favorite for quite a while, until she'd realized that pain hurt, and that she had no real gut-deep desire to feel it. The next one, *Living well is the best revenge*, lasted until financial matters took a definite turn for the worse. And so on. So making do with whatever was at hand seemed practical right now and, essentially a pragmatist, Kaz was ready. She fingered the hand-tooled case at her hip tenderly, hitched her opposite hand at opposite hip and stood there tapping her foot, the toe of which peeked out through the tattered dark tip of a basketball sneaker.

"Come on, guys. What about it?"

Someone laughed. "Ping-Pong?"

After a minute she moved her head slightly to meet his stare. Just as she'd thought, some beet-faced young scumbag trying to grow a mustache. She didn't bother answering, merely looked until he averted his own eyes and took a nervous gulp of his booze. There were a couple of other guffaws rising now—at his expense, not hers.

We got a pool table somewheres, another voice volunteered.

The basketball sneaker tapped. "Not my game. But if you dig up some real action for me"—she emphasized the *real*, gently patted the hand-tooled case—"I'll shoot a little later on. Everyone chips in"—her eyes paraded along the bar, met each pair gazing back in turn, as if rolling silently down open vertebra—"and winner takes all."

There were a few gruff murmurings and more than a few snickers. Then uneasy silence again. Sun shot in through the one window, streaked the damp floor, the top of a bar stool, her magic face and the fire-engine-red cap perched just above it. From a keg, beer dribbled. You could hear its steady drip-drip. Here was this woman stepping in from nowhere. There was shyness in the air, and a growing sense of male outrage.

Then she heard it to her left, an ugly sound, the kind that had hounded her down big-city streets countless times before. It was that obscene smacking of lips followed by something like *Hey baby*, that always made her think of shoe soles. She'd have one brief, withering vision of herself flattened to spatula width on pavement while the foul male bottom of a shoe descended. Then she'd enjoyed a few castration fantasies. Now, though, only the tightening of her hand on leather showed any anxiety. She'd take care of this bum sooner or later, the sooner the better, and those ugly, slurping sounds were a sort of opening through which—if she played her hand right—she could easily step.

She turned to face him. Ugly as shit. Scruffy week's worth of beard, clear nasty blue eyes and lips that were full, almost feminine. The lips gave him a sadistic appearance.

"What about you?"

Her voice had risen a little but was still composed.

He made a kiss with those lips, blew it to her across the dusty, humid air. Air conditioner was busted again and they'd had to shovel through one of the company warehouses on East Bay for a couple of fans. Which, when cleaned off and plugged in, also didn't work. So the air was filled with men sweating.

He grinned. His thumb pounced questioningly against his chest. Me?

"Yeah, you. Do you play any tennis?"

"The real kind," he sneered. He looked for her breasts.

"Then put it on a table, Joe. Come on. It's a dare."

He laughed, wiped sticky liquor from palms to trouser legs as he got off his stool. He told her his name was Mike. Oh, she said, eyes gleaming coolly, what difference does it make?

They fit two tables together and somebody fished a couple of rusted poles out from somewhere. These she stationed upright between the tables, one at each outer edge. She was industrious, all attention to the endeavor at hand. *Make do with the stuff at hand*, she prided herself silently; not a bad motto, not a bad one at all. She was springing lightly from place to place, bringing a fresh scent and kind of glow to whatever space she occupied. Each step made her leap smoothly ahead—the feet were well-placed, legs flexible and sure of themselves, at home on solid ground. She was asking for old fishing net. Someone scrambled for the rec room where rusty bottle openers and broken dishes got thrown—there'd been some there a while back. There still was. She unraveled the half-rotting roll of net. It would have to do. In the semi-darkness she perspired faintly, damp shining across the smooth breadth of her forehead. Miraculously, there were a couple of unused rackets around, too. So the sucker could choose his weapon. She smiled to herself.

Her jeans were faded, loose-fitting. She wore a hand-stitched vest. Everything was well-traveled but clean. Those basketball shoes. And the backwards red cap. She leaned over the makeshift table, chalking lines. Her naked arms glowed in whatever light there was, and all eyes followed the long, sure lines of those arms as they moved, followed them up to the well-defined shoulder, the slender neck, and down the V-neck of the vest to where her breasts were softly hiding.

Brown hair spilled from the cap's edges. She shook it back. It fell insistently around her face and waved all the way down her neck.

She straightened at one end of the court she'd created.

"Ready?"

Everyone watched. More drinks had been ordered and sounds of swallowing broke the heavy hush. There was something nervous about these sounds. No one knew quite how to take her.

She released snaps on the little leather case. One, two, and with both hands gently removed the racket, spun it around like a wand, tossed it softly and caught it with one hand, fingers fitting the grip perfectly, handle custom-made. It was a carbon-blade, smooth rubber for slams and the flip side pipped.

Come on, the goon was sneering. He flexed his tennis muscles. Come on. A fly buzzed in, and down, and settled on the top of one rusty pole.

Kaz fished through a loose pocket for change. Through another, and came up with the ball. A Nittaku. A quarter flashed briefly in air, the goon won the toss, and they faced each other across two bar tables and a half-rotted net. She tossed the ball to him and it blurred white through air; she was a little reluctant to see him finger it. His goon hands.

She crouched slightly, ready to spring. Her tongue touched out against her upper lip, tip wriggled—it was sensuous, a subtle, celebratory antici-pation of movement.

Then it was spinning back, toward her, for her—the ball. And although it was nothing but a whiz of white to anyone watching, Kaz saw its approach with great clarity. She saw its dimensions, its firm white, delicate roundness. Coming over the net. Nearer. Larger. She focused. Closer. Then back-handed. Too quick for him. She aimed for his Adam's apple and his arms fell all over each other trying to react but never did in time. The ball pinged on the floor, bounced while he sweated, recovered physical composure, glared at her. Easy, she seemed to say, that was easy. Just watch.

He served. He had an all right serve. From clay courts, she guessed—and he'd played this before too, of course. Poised on her feet she could feel it, the minute motion of every part of every toe—she could anticipate the light, springing movement that would radiate up through her from the ground. And the ball was spinning, straight for the center of her. Really it was floating. She felt it rise in a brief arc, begin the well-aimed sink. She saw it clearly, completely. It was a perfect round white part of her that was now returning, that she would fling out again like a weightless tentacle in tenths of a second. Poised, she smiled. She had good reach and, if necessary, could play a mean corner game. There was plenty of time.

Many slams later, ball pinging loudly and whizzing out of the goon's grasp, things were all over. Kaz smiled, a little disappointed. She'd hoped for some good competition. But those slams were fine. Felt good. Real topspinners.

She got some applause and the slob began to look mean. No one else was biting. They set up the pool table. More booze got sold and the day declined, flies buzzed in with more frequency while outside trees swayed, bringing evening.

The pot grew. Everyone chip in—she glared along the bar—everyone. That was the deal. The more booze got sold the bigger the pot became. She was leaning against the pool table, hand on hip. She'd chalked up and held the cue gently in one hand. Her other fingered the recased racket at her side.

"I'm challenging all comers." She grinned. "Winner takes all."

There was plenty of money. Kaz shoveled it into a plastic bag provided by the bar.

To shouts of Whew! and Way to go! she meandered toward the door. She was getting offers for drinks left and right, eyes which had at first explored only the possibility of copping a feel now met hers more honestly, and she was thinking of taking a pair of them up on their offer of a beer when she felt a violating hand along her ass, violent fingers pinch. She wheeled halfway to the goon's nasty wet lips, nasty eyes. She grabbed at the leather-cased racket, with one motion brought it up firmly in hand, and with another slammed it full against his open face. The blow's venom was entirely un-premeditated. She wasn't vengeful now—merely appalled somehow, out-raged, as if witnessing the defilement of a sacred thing. He never knew it. There was wild, spinning pain, then the broken leak of blood against his chin, nose, between the eyes. Blinded with pain and the sudden blood, he reached up for protection but not before she'd slammed him a second time for good measure.

"Creep," she spat. "Nobody treats me like that."

She left him there, wiped her racket case off on the money bag as she headed slowly for the door. She'd have liked to cut out at top speed but made herself slink along at seeming leisure instead, bitterly meeting each astonished pair of eyes with a hard light in her own.

No one touched her. Even though she was moving so slowly, almost invitingly, until you saw her expression. With that near-perfect body and that face which was half madonna, half gun moll. Red baseball cap turned backwards. Shit. She was beautiful.

In the hotel lobby on East Bay she stood out too. Even among the stylishly casual polo shirts, satin shorts and floor-slapping sandals, she was rough-shod. She had that easy sauntering gait, though. No one was going to rush her. She half sprang, half slid up to the desk for her keys, plucked them calmly from the clerk's fingers with a grace that said she was used to all this. There was nothing in her demeanor to indicate the least bit of awe. She prowled the lobby and slipped into the elevator with the subtly bored air of someone who owned the place. It made the desk clerk, watching her, want to look up the list of B.O.D. and major stockholders, try to match her name scrawled carelessly on the sheet in front of him. He'd have been surprised. Instead he watched. The well-worn leather case slapped gently against her hip.

Her room was a good one overlooking the bay. They'd first tried to put her in one with a balcony view of the pool, but she'd nipped that in the bud. The last thing she wanted was to stare down at near-naked bodies slathered with lotions, turning cancerous walnut brown in the sun while a few more paddled clumsily along the chlorinated length of water. It struck her as such a waste. And then she'd get sad, she told them, contemplating it. So she insisted on a view of the bay—there, at least, you could see palms, and the sky's blue clarity, and between long rubber-textured green fronds spot some white expanse of beach, some sparkle of ocean beyond.

It was one of those rooms you stepped into as if onto a mattress. Feet went soft against the carpet, ankles flexed gently on the steps leading down to high-polished table, wicker stools and love seat, and potted palms left tastefully here and there. A discreet side door led to the bedroom—which she'd left dark, shades down, on purpose. All this sunlight could get to you. There had to be one small space, always and wherever you went, that was dark, a pitch dark and secret core of your own making into which you could crawl at will, into which you could not be followed except by a chosen few. And Kaz was picky. One other she'd chosen, one only, to come inside. There wouldn't be any others.

Her backpack lay near the bedroom entrance, disheveled streams of material spilling from its open mouth. It was the old canvas kind with buckles everywhere instead of zippers, and it had been sewn a lot and patched up with those tacky cloth emblems that said things like SAN MIGUEL and ITALIA and PARIS: FRATERNITÉ, EGALITÉ. Each emblem was a little torn, too, dirt smudged solidly between the threads. She toed it gently in passing, went on past the bedroom and out toward sunlight, opened the sliding glass doors and delicate sash drapes onto the balcony. Early evening breeze blew through. It ruffled her hair with tropical bouquet, musky salt on the wind. The brown strands lifted, fluttered thickly against her shoulders.

One hand fished through a pocket. Ball scuffed but good for a few more slams. She touched beneath the ball for something, found it, withdrew it in a careful, tender motion. It was a necklace of dainty silver, the thin, frail-seeming kind that would rest against skin like the outline of a shadow. She'd kept it clean and polished and now, held up to sundown, it had a gentle glow. From the thin silver line hung an object in a distorted kind of triangle. It curved slightly at the tip, ivory white. Each edge a cutting edge. It looked like a fine-honed bone razor, or prehistoric tooth. When Kaz slipped the necklace on, reached back to latch it underneath her hair, the white tooth nestled toward the space between her breasts. It pointed the way.

"Great shot, huh? *National Geographic* stuff."

She turned to her right. A few feet separated one balcony from the next, and there he stood, small and slender, camera slung uncased around his neck.

Five six, she guessed. Black hair curling around the ears. Nice face, not quite American. Large, pale eyes. Questionable side of Christian. A Greek from Brooklyn. Cultivated Cuban of pure Castilian origins, maybe. If all else failed, an Israeli. But he had no accent except an indeterminate American one.

"It's great contrast." He got a couple of shots. Then the camera swung her way. Ah, he said, great. "Hold it."

She gave him the finger.

He took the shot and lowered his camera, sent her an offended look. "What brought that on?"

"You're intrusive."

"Am I?"

She nodded, then smiled slightly to soften the blow. When she stepped off the balcony and out of sight behind wind-fluttered drapes, the movement was deliberate but without malice. I want to be alone, it said. No harm intended. He heard the doors slide shut and latch click.

Pablo waited. He was good at that, waiting. Years before, on his first full-fledged assignment, he'd waited all night in mud-soaked bushes to get a shot. Thick plastic had been layered around his legs, cocoon-like, for protection against the wet, but something trickled in anyway and he'd felt it ooze with slow certainty along his thigh. It had all the slimy menace, there in the dark, of a water moccasin. Still, silently miserable, his fear was of snakes and of fangs aiming a strike at his genitals. Then the thick trickle spread and he understood what it was. Just seeping mud. He almost wallowed in it with relief. He felt intact for the remaining hours of night, extremely strong and immune to all harm.

Now he kept the lens cap off, just in case. Fucking gorgeous face she had, and if he could smoke her out somehow he'd like another shot. The sunburnt sky darkened, sun fled to the island's opposite side now and East Bay turned dull purple. He waited.

Several stories down, hotel patio lights went on. In the sudden hard beams you could see moths dance, multi-legged, many-winged insects of exotic specification dare the glow, fly almost close enough to be singed and then back away. They'd tango a wild flight of fascination around the brilliant, brutal light. Upping the ante. Sporadically, they'd dive straight in.

Pablo waited. After a while he'd gotten sick of it. She was carrying things too far, so he'd made a mistake. But she'd caught him somewhere inside and, pinioned, a part of him was helpless before the vision of her. He didn't want to risk not seeing it again.

He sighed, recapped the lens, and turned back to his own room. He gave one last glance over at her balcony, but the doors remained shut and ocean breezes rapped against them with a flat sound. Great face. And he wouldn't want to suffer the eternal loss of it. No.

Showering, Kaz hung her underwear on the open edge of the bathroom door. Then she noticed a cheap oil painting over the sink—the kind she'd seen plenty of times hawked by sidewalk vendors in places like Miami Beach during the height of the season: putrid blues, pinks and unnatural yellows destroying a perfectly good slab of canvas—attempted depictions of boats, of oceans, of palms and sickly flowers. The square-framed piece of junk glared at her through the thin curtain. She stepped out, dripped her way to the door and grabbed her underwear, hung it carefully to cover as much of the painting as possible. There were two things, two things that galled her most: bad art and bad champagne. With everything else, there was always room for improvement.

The warm water poured, heated quickly, steamed out around her. It cut through dirt and sweat and cut through something else, too, so she was vulnerable for a moment and allowed the cold, clear edge of private desperation to show its head inside. Then it was gone. She breathed in with relief, clean, calmed, and whistled almost happily at the image of her underwear, sprawled bat-like above the bathroom sink.

Naked, she rummaged through her backpack and came up with a pair of metal hand grips—high-tension springs—and a couple of bottles of Dos Equis. Casually, she began to work the grips.

He was knocking reluctantly. Reluctantly because now he would have to go to her hat in hand, and apologizing put him at a disadvantage. Still he proceeded, convinced that the worst would not happen. Bad planning, he knew, to operate under that assumption—but it had never let him down so far. The worst had, in fact, never happened to him. So Pablo had lived most of his life with the half-fleeting sensation that he'd gotten away with something—what, he didn't quite know—but somehow, he knew, he'd beat the rap and at times this gave him an intangibly sly, childish look. He had that little-boy look to him anyway. Always, when he smiled, it was the grin of a bad boy who'd returned to the fold, spurred on by the certainty that, no matter what, he would be accepted back.

Pablo kept knocking.

"Can't you read?" It was a slightly plaintive female growl, sounding from behind the door.

Pablo glanced at the knob. The sign swung, DO NOT DISTURB facing out. Having blundered again though, he couldn't back down. Only thing was to continue relentlessly, rack up the blunders until they totaled some kind of asset.

"Sorry," he said. He kept knocking.

There was a pause. Then, "Beat it," she said.

"Can't we talk?"

"Who do you think you are, Joe?"

"My name's Pablo. Can't we?"

"What do you want?"

"To talk. To apologize."

There was more silence. He stopped knocking for a second, allowed himself some glimmering of hope. The whole lush hallway stretched well-lit to either side of him, couples swaggering by in summer evening attire, dinner coats white and low-cut white dresses revealing tans set off by gem bouquets at the necklines. Pablo stood there hoping.

"I forgive you," she called out finally. "Go away."

He paused. "Thank you. Let me buy you a drink."

Behind the door there was laughter. He heard it rise and become louder, voice higher, lighter, a lovely musical female voice with the slightest throaty edge to it. He felt a little miffed, despite the loveliness of the sound. He wanted to make himself smaller still, and crawl under that slight crack between door and carpet. He'd whip his cape around him. Behold, I am here. But the only place he was was out in the hallway, while fresh-spruced white couples went purposefully by under the white lights of a Bellagua evening and a woman's laughter floated through a closed door, directed at him. There was another silence, this one longer. He waited.

Then she was standing there in jeans more faded than the last pair, busted black basketball sneakers and a bright scarlet cotton shirt with white block letters across the front: CINCINNATI, and the number 12. She had on that red old-style baseball cap, rim turned to the back. A silver necklace strung through a white chip of bone, or tooth of some sort. His eyes caught at that space between her breasts. But he stopped himself. He glanced at the worn leather strap around her neck and shoulder, the flat gourd-like case at her hip. He met her eyes. They were dark brown but if you looked closely enough you'd see flecks of green. Not just hazel but real green, extraordinary, offset by the near black of the rest. He nodded at the leather.

"Is that your weapon?"

Kaz hitched her hand on the opposite hip. That toe-tapping started, she held his gaze and smiled back blandly. It was a look that stayed intentionally shallow, gave nothing away, and if he had a brain in his head would light no spark of hope.

"Sure," she said. She pointed down through several floors of hotel. "There's a bar. Something standard. Moët, but only if they've got a decent bottle. You can swing that, can't you?"

Somewhere behind curtains, a band was playing. It wasn't quite a normal woodwind/brass/percussion band and it wasn't one of those native steel bands either, but a combination of different sounds: steel drums pattered softly like gentle sleet underneath the surface of other instruments—a flute, a high-pitched tambourine, and more than one guitar. In the bar, a few couples were dancing. Most looked a little out of step somehow, although this couldn't be defined as lack of grace on their part. The rhythm, part reggae, part samba, part Bellagua hybrid, defied facile footwork. It demanded that you dance with torso and hips and arms too, with the head—it demanded that the whole body shiver in rhythm, that each part of the body maintain its own separate rhythm as well so there was at once a liquid flow, a sudden catch, a syncopated entirety of motion.

The place was packed. There was silk everywhere, tailored cotton, gold shimmered from wrists and fingers in the cool protected dark. And everywhere, ice in alcohol tinkling against the sides of chilled glasses. There was a strong scent of perfume, cologne, flowers and liqueur.

"Pablo Klemer." He offered his right hand while the left traveled instinctively to his abdomen, searching for Alfredo. But he'd left it locked away upstairs—a breach of his standard regulations. He guessed she was worth it. A price paid: view of her face in exchange for the absence of a camera to record it.

They shook hands.

The champagne arrived, towel-wrapped, stashed at an angle in a wooden ice bucket. The waiter displayed it proudly. The waiter grinned and white teeth beamed across the dark. His hands twisting the corkscrew were brown and, like the face, oddly impersonal. Pablo watched the handsome, impersonal face with appreciation, the strong neck, fluid hands. But he was any East Bay waiter, serving tourists, fading facelessly into the background.

Kaz examined the bottle, noted the year, nodded. A few drops were poured and Pablo took the glass to taste it, then grinned and shrugged casually, handed it to her. She tasted, waited a while to let it settle. It would do.

The glasses were fully poured.

"Well?" said Pablo.

She questioned with her eyes.

"Are you going to tell me what your name is?" he pressed, amused and annoyed. "Or should I guess?"

"Oh, you'd never guess. Then she got a teasing look. "It starts with Z."

"Come on!"

"Karlen." She extended her own hand. The gesture was almost solemn, he thought, nothing frivolous about it, and for that reason he made sure to press her palm firmly with his own. He was careful that the pressure be friendly—for now anyway—and not seductive. Otherwise he'd lose everything. He told her he was pleased to meet her again.

"This isn't bad." She nodded toward her glass. "You ought to give it a try."

He examined the white letters of CINCINNATI spread across her chest. Pablo was confused. He'd been waiting for her to begin asking him questions. A woman invariably did. All it took was a few words followed by a question mark—What brings you here? or: Tell me about your work!—and he'd be off and running, regaling her with descriptions of various assignments, his theories of the relationship of photography to traditional art forms, his background, the languages he spoke. He could go on all night. And he was used to the sight of a pretty female face across the table all night, too, sweetly attentive, listening.

But she seemed not at all concerned with him, or knowing anything more than she already did—which was nothing. Her focus, he realized, was the glass of champagne in her hand—she was tasting every wet speck of it, relishing the taste with a look on her face of subtle, private enjoyment. He felt like an intruder. He felt stupid as hell.

"So." He cleared his throat. She looked up distractedly. "What are you doing on Bellagua?" The sound of his voice came cloddishly back to him.

"So far, not much," she said, and smiled. She took another sip.

He gulped some himself. Not used to the taste, his throat rebuffed him and he nearly choked. Great going, Pablo, he told himself. Just terrific. Then he got angry at himself, at how he was coming off like a prize jerk, and he got angry at her too for somehow working things this way. So he set down his glass. He leaned forward, hands firmly on the table, just so.

He looked at his own hands. Not bad. They were good hands, strong and firm, masculine hands. Seeing them, he felt more self-confident.

"Look. I'm just trying to be friendly. What is it exactly that you'd like me to say?"

She seemed surprised. "Nothing," she said.

Then she noticed the vague desperation on his face and took pity. It was a sweet face, really. And she owed him nothing, but—she sipped again—there wasn't any need to be cruel. He was doing his best. That his best would never be good enough she did not tell him. It was neither his fault nor her own. And he'd bought her some halfway decent champagne in the bargain.

Kaz smiled again, more open this time. "Relax, Pablo. Why don't you tell me about yourself? That's what you want, isn't it?"

He felt revealed, and immediately resentful. Then he met her gaze, which was honest, direct, disinterested. And he felt suddenly grateful—he didn't know why.

Halfway through the second bottle he went on a quiet laughing jag. She got a little giggly then. He liked that, the foolishness of the sound. It made her more accessible. And he talked on and on through a soft, very expensive haze of champagne. His past. His camera. Told her about the exhibit at the Schreiber. She said next time she was in New York she'd check it out.

"Ever been here before, Karlen?"

She paused, then shook her head. She poured herself another glass.

"Then let me tell you something about Bellagua. All this crap here, this wealth and glory—do you know what's behind it all? I mean, do you know what's in the backyard of the mansion?" He paused for effect, and because he was getting drunk. Something about the waiter striding by caught his eye and held it, for a second, in inebriated fascination—the white rose hitched carefully in the neat-pressed lapel of his waiter's jacket, shining like a single snowball on a stretch of blacktop pavement. Pablo turned back to her. Through the half-emptied bottle he saw her naked neck, silver hung around it, and that funny ivory-colored tooth-like thing hung from the silver. He reached for the bottle, poured more. "What's behind all this crap is a lot of rot, that's what. Have you ever been to any of the shacks out there, back there"—he gestured wildly, then caught himself and dropped hands to the table—"where all the second-class citizens live? All the people who live here, I mean really, really live here, the ones who are native to the island? Do you have any idea"—his finger stabbed air—"what's being done to their culture?"

She sighed. She hoped he wouldn't go off on one of those oh-so-liberal diatribes, bemoaning the foundations of the luxury he himself had no qualms about enjoying. She was sick of that kind of stuff. What she knew about systems and the management of them she kept to herself. One thing she knew for sure, though—nothing was ever as simple as people like him made it sound. That was one of the problems: things could be clear-cut in a moral sense at times, at other times not. And there was never any way to explain this to someone who was content with a simplified version of the world and its various interconnecting factors. She knew wrong when she saw it—she'd have told him that if she'd thought he might listen, or if she'd cared enough. Neither was the case. Sure, she knew wrong when she saw it and had her own ideas of how to put a stop to it. But she'd come to Bellagua for a different purpose.

"Do you know what they want from me?" He gave her a sly smile. That finger was waving the air again. She didn't like it, too pedantic. But she listened—champagne was making her less harsh. He leaned forward, spoke conspiratorially. "They want *nice* pictures. Tropical paradise type of stuff. I mean, they want photos of weird-looking birds, and fish, stuff like that. Okay. I said to them, okay, you've got it. And to myself I said, Pablo, listen, this is the chance to really do something now. To really expose something that doesn't get much mention in all the tourist pamphlets."

He rattled on. She listened once in a while, at other times she clicked him off. He was on assignment from Royal Hotel Corporation. Small world. She laughed to herself. Oh, he said, sure there was the assignment—take pictures of the new hotel, pictures of the surroundings, and make them tropical and pretty, pretty please, but *he*—his thumb poked his forehead sagely—he was going off in his spare time and fulfilling an assignment of his own. Shantytowns, the poor, the crippled, the ones who were paid in pennies each day. He was going to document life in the backyard of the mansion. That's what. He wanted to blow it wide open. Publish a tourist brochure of his own. She drifted off again. The bottles displayed so tastefully behind the bar made a sort of rainbow collage. It was nice, that blending of dark-lit colors, as if a bright bird had fanned its tail out full and held it there, preening, in the bar's shadowy light. But she was called back to meeting his eyes. He'd asked her a direct question.

"What, Pablo?" She kept her yawn down.

"Do you think it really is there?"

"Do I think what is really there?"

"Atlantis!" His palm slapped the table, met a champagne puddle and sloshed. "Do you think they'll find it?"

The dig. He was talking about that dig. She shrugged. "I don't know. Maybe. Is that what they're looking for?"

Well, he told her, that's what they say they're looking for.

He was off somewhere in his own reverie. She was thankful for this. He'd nearly forgotten her presence, she guessed—she'd become, as she had known she would in this situation, a blank board for him to bounce words off. Just now Kaz didn't mind. She could listen in or ignore at will. And he wouldn't notice, just so long as the flow of his words went uninterrupted. But suddenly he was speaking again, face pressured and intent as he pushed toward her from across the table, and his voice had that conspiratorial tone.

"Do you know where I'd really like to go? The interior. You've heard about what happened a couple of years ago? That expedition?"

She sipped slowly. No, she said, she didn't remember hearing about any expedition.

"You're kidding. It was a pretty hot news item for a while. There was a party of twelve—all of them men except there was one woman, Raina Scott, and she was the leader of this group. See, they were all experts of some sort, marksmen and mountain climbers and survivalists. They were adventurers. You know? Kind of like daredevils, but they didn't always just do it for the kicks, this time they were exploring. These are people, mind you"—his finger stabbed toward her—"who'd been in just about every conceivable situation and come out alive, you know what I mean? They were experienced. You've heard of her, I'm sure. Raina Scott. You've heard the name? She made the front page of the *Times* and everything—she was pretty extraordinary. I'm sure you've heard of her."

Kaz traced the chilled dribblings of the glass. "Maybe I have," she said. "The name sounds familiar."

"Yeah. Well out of the twelve who went in there only one came back alive. This guy, Vince St.-Peters, blew his brains out just a little while afterwards. Anyway, he said that ten of the others had dropped dead in there, one by one, for sure. Disease. Injury. You name it. They were way the hell in there for months. And he didn't know his own name, practically, by the time he found his way back. He said he guessed she—Raina Scott— was dead too. He couldn't say for sure. He only knew that somewhere in there she'd just disappeared, and he was the only other one alive at the time and delirious anyway, but there was no way, in his estimation, she could have survived because they were all so sick toward the end. It was pretty dramatic, he got a lot of press—"

"Yes," said Kaz, "I remember."

"There!" His finger stopped wagging. It tapped against his wrist, foolishly, he wanted to detach his fingers and put them in his pocket right now for safekeeping so they'd do no more foolish things tonight. Around them, the bar had settled down to less than capacity. It was getting late. "Do you know what I sometimes think about?" he said softly. "I think sometimes, what if she's still alive? In there somewhere, I mean. Wouldn't that be outrageous? Just imagine this woman in there, alive for a couple of years now. That's pretty bizarre to think about, isn't it?"

Kaz finished her glass. She looked at him and nodded.

"Raina Scott," he said. "I took her picture once." And he glanced up proudly.

"No kidding, Pablo."

"No kidding. Five years ago, it was in the southern part of the Gulf of Eilat. She was on commission from the museum there to bring in a hammerhead for stuffing and display. And that"—he chuckled in awe, blinked hazily toward her—"that is exactly what she did. I was on assignment. I got some nice shots. She went out in a tiny outboard off the big boat, all by herself. And I'm telling you, it was crazy out there. I mean, there were fins galore and these fish were just about crawling up the sides of the boat. Do you know what she used?"

"Tell me," Kaz urged.

"Bow and arrow! That's how she got her hammerhead! With a bow and fucking arrow! I couldn't believe it." He shook his head. Tired, tired Pablo, he told himself. Pablo go to sleep. But he couldn't stop now, he felt driven to talk. "Out there in this little boat all alone. Jesus."

Kaz watched the empty glass sadly. She patted the leather case at her side. "Did you talk with her?"

He smiled regretfully. "A little. She was amazing. Jesus Christ. Pretty amazing, all right." Then he was silent. And whatever he meant by that *amazing*, he couldn't or wouldn't say. Or maybe didn't know. Watching him, she saw he seemed to be reaching for something, some mode of description, and was failing. He reached more, mouth opened as if to speak but then he shrugged, gave up and lost concentration. Kaz guessed it was time to turn in. She told him so.

On the way up in the elevator he remembered those spots of bright green in her eyes. Then he remembered he'd had lustful visions, too, and remembering brought some of them back. He wanted to lunge across the elevator, bend slightly to kiss the CINCINNATI spread over her breasts like armor. She looked so loose standing there, yawning her way to the eighth floor, hands at her sides and the rest of her lithe and open. One thumb hitched protectively around that strange leather case she'd slung on. Pablo held himself back with difficulty. He'd walk her to her room. Walk her there and that would be all for tonight.

Others sped by them in the hall. Or anyway they seemed to be speeding—Pablo glanced at her occasionally and saw that she was floating too, keeping slow time alongside him. He let himself admire the smooth spring of her walk—even mellowed by plenty of champagne she looked as if you couldn't put anything past her. He tried anyway. He moved toward her slightly at the door to her room, one of his hands plastered against the wall for support, and half shut his eyes, hoping for a kiss. A small one, token of hope. More would not be necessary. But she turned her head slightly. It was a barely noticeable motion, and there was no malice in it. She'd simply conveyed refusal. He leaned back against the wall then and she smiled benignly, a little drunkenly, tousled his hair as if they were locker-room pals. She offered a hand.

"Thanks."

Her lips looked moist. He wanted to trap her hands and hold them against him. "Let's do something tomorrow," he said.

"Do you play volleyball, Pablo?"

"Volleyball, for Christ's sake?"

"Tomorrow." She grinned and pointed down through the floors again. "We can get them to set up a net. One on one. Winner takes all."

She was gone, door closed softly. DO NOT DISTURB swung cleanly before him.

Around three Kaz woke up. Air came through the open balcony doors. She didn't remember opening them. She was sacked out on the floor, head propped by her backpack. She'd just lain there to check out the ceiling for a couple of minutes, and opened her eyes hours later.

"Is that you?"

She stared toward the balcony.

She stood, steadied herself. The basketball sneakers felt like damp grass when she walked. Kaz stepped outside, the pre-morning air enveloping her with fresh heat and all its darkness. She gazed out at the nothing time of night. She flexed fingers on the balcony railing, smoothed them over its coating of dew.

"Is that you?"

She paused. Some reply might come from some invisible space she was not yet conscious enough to ascertain, and if it did she wanted to be open to it, and waiting. But nothing came—not to her ears, not through her fingertips. And when she spoke her whispers held a soft, regretful note of reprimand.

"You really went ahead and did it this time. Now look what's happened. I told you. I hate to say I told you so but I told you so. Didn't I say don't, please? Didn't I say that—don't, don't, it's the thing that's one thing too much, too far and too deep? I did, didn't I? And now look."

She paused to let it sink in. There was a wounded look on her face, lips pulled down. When she spoke again her tone had changed—no longer reprimand, but a plea.

"Okay, you win. You win again. Look, it's all right. Don't worry, it's all right. It was a mistake. That's all it was. You're entitled to mistakes now and then, you too. I know. But honey, listen: things can get dangerous. They can get dangerous in ways you don't know about." The whispers got lost in dark. They were cajoling, convincing. They rose with the light husky timbre of her voice and they were slightly off key, a sad kind of song. "People, other people, might suspect. They do already. What if there's a whole army of them about ready to tear down things looking? What if I don't make it to you first, then what? If I don't get there first?"

Kaz was silent for a while. She closed her eyes, seemed to listen. She was all stretched out and raw, standing and listening, and soon her hands, sliding in dew on the balcony railing, began to tremble with strain. The fingers arched, knuckles wrinkled tensely.

When she relaxed it was sudden. It was as if she'd been a puppet, and the strings—held so long and so tautly by a hard-driving manipulator from above—had been let loose with no warning. She seemed, for a second, to weave dangerously, on the brink of falling. But her hands tightened over the damp railing, eyes opened. She breathed again. Body back, she was herself, and complete.

She smiled. And her voice, when it sounded, was purely tender.

"Don't worry. I'll make it. I know you and you know me, that's the real story. It's going to be all right anyway. Don't cry. Honey don't you cry. I feel you." She pointed to her center. The tooth hung straight down toward the same spot, glowing whitely, a crooked sort of arrow.

I feel you, she whispered, and the whisper was gone. It was taken up, softly stolen, hushed away in the dark.

SOUL STEALING

The several days following would coalesce in Pablo's memory into one long one—a sort of sunlit blur, mornings cutting across the clear dark of the ocean bay in sharp, preliminary stabs of heat. He'd remember the bitter taste of native-ground coffee, fresh sting of fruit against the tongue. Tanning on a pink sand beach he'd catch a sideways glimpse of her, the distinguishable droplets of sweat along her skin like small marbles, or bits of tear-shaped glass.

The feeling born out of this hot, bright haze was unmitigated desire. Because the worst had never happened to Pablo. So he had that sort of license—the one belonging to children, and to naive adolescents—that allowed his desire to roam free and undisciplined through the world of daydreams, untouched by any shadow of reality. She seemed content to let things go on this way indefinitely—beating the crap out of him at volleyball so he was forced to buy every breakfast, mild, comfortable companionship at the beach. She seemed to be in a sort of limbo, to be waiting, almost. He couldn't tell for what. She was friendly in a flatly platonic way, not given to talking much about her feelings, rarely about her past.

He seized at straws. Sensing, somehow, that his first real move on her would also be his last, Pablo drifted miserably with the tide of things: casual companionship. His hopes hung on nothing but fantasy. Still, that was enough to keep them breathing. He didn't know why she was so out of reach—it had always been easy enough for him in the past. Calm, mock casual kiss to start things off. Clutching for a knee under the table, tickle of thumb in palm, or else you could always talk a woman into submission. But Karlen didn't care—she was far from the grasp of things like that. And Pablo found himself all undone. Once, during another long sand-strewn afternoon, she'd let a few things drop: she was an only child, she told him, and spoiled as they come. Close to her family until they disowned her. *Disowned*, he'd rushed in, you mean people still do that? And she nodded matter-of-factly. When he asked why, she told him in vague terms only: an affair she'd had, of which they did not approve. And she shrugged. Well, she'd gotten on without them, then. So much for that. He wanted to know more, ask more, but didn't dare. He was too afraid she'd disappear.

Karlen, he said into his pillow some nights. Like a kid with his first crush. Just her name—the odd, flat sound of it—was erotic, filled him with a crazy cloud of naked imaginings. She so obviously didn't care at all.

This morning was one of those when things seemed hopeless—his wanting her brought him face to face with his own self-imposed mediocrity. He didn't feel good enough for Karlen. No. He didn't feel good enough for himself. Waking, he'd slung Alfredo over a shoulder, sat on the ruined bedsheets, taken some photos out. OUR NEW AMELIA EARHART and others from that series. He'd seen them with a sort of shock. They seemed utterly apart from him. He could not imagine himself taking photos like these. Could not imagine what it had felt like to be behind the camera, to be the one responsible for shutters clicking, for the careful darkroom blend of chemicals. Someone else had sweated sleepishly in the dark. Someone else had risen on that hot Middle Eastern morning, long ago, and followed Raina Scott out into the Gulf of Eilat with a camera. He almost pinched himself to make sure of his own consciousness. And what filled him then was a leaden vacuity—he was bleak inside. All the photos he'd taken since to earn a good living wage trotted out before his mind's eye in a taunting way: the bullshit, the palm trees, the honeymooners and blue-tinted water, the bullshit, the bullshit. Pablo was too sick of himself for tears. No, he mumbled, he wasn't worthy of tears either.

The patio made a good place for breakfast. There was a clear view of one of the East Bay beaches. Bright-colored canvas umbrellas shaded each table; waiters sweated in the early sun, grinned perpetually, served croissants with elegant eggs, bloody marys, and too-sweet rum concoctions. On Bellagua, drinking was—like the sun—a day-long proposition.

"Your serve's getting better, Pablo."

She poured herself more coffee.

His volleyball, he told her, was better these days than his photography.

Alfredo rested coldly in his lap. Sometimes he'd imagine the straps gaining a life of their own. At which time they would wrap around his neck to throttle him—rightfully so—and he'd feel the strong, leathery tug crushing down against the windpipe, leathery arms twining around and around until he looked like a member of one of those African tribes who consider elongated necks a sign of beauty. He'd be crushed, extended. Mediocre as ever. And dead.

Karlen reached across the table to slap his arm gently. The motion bothered him—still that locker-room pal routine, the last thing on earth he wanted from her—and at the same time he felt a slight spark of exhilaration that she'd touched him. He glanced up quickly.

"Hey Pablo. What's the matter?"

He shrugged. How could he explain to her? They were volleyball partners, nothing more. And he was supposed to be as tough as possible, he told himself—even though her serve had decimated him on any number of occasions. He considered it a point of pride to appear happy-go-lucky and competent.

But he was remembering long ago now, and the memory troubled him. The face of Raina Scott, adventuress. Face captured by him, turned into a piece of art, acclaimed and awarded and, finally, exhibited. Maybe that was when death came to you: when you found your work exhibited, made into an artifact along with porcelain vases from dynasties fallen centuries before. He looked Karlen full in the face, and what showed across his own was a kind of melancholy she wasn't used to. His lips sounded the same:

"Raina Scott."

She paled just slightly—if he hadn't been looking full at her, he'd have missed it. What, she said quietly. Her voice sounded a little hoarse.

He pulled himself together, sipped dully at the coffee. "I was thinking of Raina Scott. You remember—you said you remembered hearing about her. There was a big photo essay in *Century* magazine, and also in the *Times* magazine section once—they ran an article on her called 'Our New Amelia Earhart.' Did you ever see it?" He looked but she gave no indication, no change of expression. "Well, I took those shots." Sticking a fingertip into his coffee, he burned himself. He sucked at the finger miserably. "And that was the last time I've done any real work. The rest of it is all shit."

He glanced up, seeking her eyes. He'd revealed himself. And he was a sort of beggar in relation to her, anyway. He saw she wasn't looking at him, though, but past him—to the patio's edge and the hotel's restaurant entrance. A few people had just come in. He followed her gaze and saw the man she was staring at. A medium-tall, very slender man, blond hair thinning slightly, pleasant face. The guy hadn't noticed them. For a second Pablo thought maybe he'd seen him before. He wasn't sure. The tan said he'd been on Bellagua a while. But no, he didn't know the guy. He wondered how she did.

He turned back to her and faced an empty seat. A half-finished croissant crumbled on her plate. Creamed coffee, a light brown color, glistened messily along the edges of her saucer.

Pablo was angry. He'd arranged for a photo session that morning with one of the Royal Hotel head chefs. It would be a perfect set-up for the kind of crap he'd been assigned: white-toothed, beaming black man in white cap and apron proudly displaying a brochette flaming orange and blue. The head cook was a borderline prima donna, so the match was not made in heaven. But the two of them were alone in one of the long, utensil-ridden kitchens, and the meat—which was supposed to burst obligingly into flame— had burnt to black twisted remnants on the steel that speared it. Pablo tried for an interesting angle. One of those long, tunnel effect shots—the way you'd feel looking down an aisle. Then he gave up. Not what the customer wanted. They'd want it clear, sharp, and gaudy. Bright contrast. Red meat bursting into sudden flame on a stick, surrounded by darkness so it seemed a torch in the night, and the brown man smiling whitely, inviting you to have a hunk of this one.

To get things running a little more smoothly, Pablo decided to adopt his ingratiating puppy-dog style. He started to smile a lot. Ask for something from the man—win his condescension and, thus, his cooperation.

"I'm looking to take some pictures of *real* life here on Bellagua." He grinned brightly. "Any ideas where to start?"

For a while, it was as if he hadn't been heard. Then he thought he could sense the chef examining him somehow, reevaluating him with each glance.

The chef paused delicately, reached for another brochette. "Man, I tell you something now."

Pablo wondered where the hell she'd gone off to.

"I tell you something. Want to take a nice little picture?" He flashed a smile. "Go to West Reef. Lots of nice pictures."

The bitch, Pablo sighed under his breath.

"Lots of nice ones." The smile stayed but it was not in the voice. "They got babies there, dying. Lots of babies dying. Lots of babies getting born there in a funny way."

Alfredo dropped against his belly. The words echoed oddly—*babies dying*—they did not match the smile or fussy attitude of the man in front of him. Instinctively he remained silent and listened.

"I heard stories. Babies there getting born with their eyeballs out. Lots of babies getting born and they got no legs. Some no hands. I heard stories, man." He held the brochette up, and with his other hand made a hush motion, finger pressed significantly against his lips before he smiled broadly again at Pablo. Cheeeeeezzzzzze. He blinked. "You want to take some nice pictures, you go there maybe. Listen." He hoisted the brochette higher, held a long unlit match near it. "You don't tell no one about this. No. Don't tell no one I said these things."

Pablo aimed. The brochette was suddenly in flame. He took the shot. Then a couple more.

He lowered the camera. Something pounded in his chest, louder than the heart. Puzzled, he kept going by instinct.

"Okay," he said.

The chef nodded.

Naked waist-up, he spent hours on different beaches. He was looking for her, and as he walked he could feel the heat spreading across his shoulders and chest, feel himself dehydrate slowly. He wished the hell she would like him back, wished she wasn't so unreachable, unpredictable—so crazy in a vague sort of way. Because she was, he decided. A little crazy. There was something bizarre about her, from that Ping-Pong paddle—*racket*, she'd correct him—she insisted on carrying everywhere, to the stupid old clothes that made her look even more beautiful, absurdly feminine, in contrast. She'd played a good game of table tennis once, she told him. Kept it sort of as a memento. A *weapon*, she'd joked, *the only one I need*; mouth curved in a mock sadistic grin. Pablo wondered who she was really hooked up with, after all—had to be someone. Who is he? he'd wanted to ask any number of times, but always stopped himself and kept on being Mr. Nice Guy. He'd play volleyball with her day after endless day, sure. Carry her towels down to the beach. But today he told himself no. No more. He was through with this unrequited love shit. Women usually found him adorable in certain ways, he knew—nice face, nice body even though it was small, interesting background, so-called glamorous profession, so-called creative—women were easy for him. Had been in the past, anyway. And he was through with this one. What the fuck was her problem?

Pablo kept looking.

Sweat marked his skin, dribbled against Alfredo's straps. He went from pink sand to black sand to white. Nothing but tourists lining the beaches even though the real season was months away. Still he didn't see her. He let his eyes tick past every face, searching around and along and behind.

He found her at the site of the dig, a healthy walk from the edge of East Bay. She was leaning against some wire fence with a lot of other tourists, gazing into the pit where digging progressed, into the wired-off compound beyond. THIS PROJECT IS FUNDED BY A GRANT FROM ZACHARY CHEMICAL CORPORATION, A DIVISION OF INTERNATIONAL COMMUNICATIONS ENTERPRISES, INCORPORATED. It was not a major tourist draw—there was little spectacular about the sight of men on hands and knees in a dusty excavation ditch—but every once in a while some tour group would wind up here, cameras flashing at nothing in particular, hearing about the project and the myth of Atlantis and the major discoveries predicted here. And if you looked closely enough, you could see something for sure: beginning outlines of some sort of architectural structure emerging from the dirt.

She moved away from a tour group listening to a lecture in French. He followed behind, made straight for her.

"Karlen."

She turned, surprised him completely by pushing hard against him, head cowed on his chest. He felt the canvas rim of her baseball cap rub his skin. There was the rapid beat of his heart, smell of his own sweat, heat—the unexpected feel of her, wrapped in his arms. Alfredo flapped between them. Pablo pushed the camera to one side to hold her more securely. He could feel her shaking.

"What is it?"

"Pablo, if you—"

She stopped, and he waited. Her hands had spread gently, trembling, against his lower back. They were cold—he felt that with surprise—cold, for all the heat.

"If you loved somebody—"

He nodded encouragingly, his cheek brushing the top of her head.

"—and they were in trouble and no one else knew it but you, wouldn't you go to them? You'd try to go to them."

Sure, he murmured. Sure I would.

"You'd want to get there. I mean, you'd make sure you got there, it wouldn't matter how you did it."

She was so strange. Pablo felt puzzled, and in bliss. He stroked her back, her hair. She shook, birdlike, in his arms. He wanted to see her face, because it was lovely—everything he'd ever wanted to photograph, he knew, would be there in her face and her body if only he could look long enough, hard enough. He would take the time to find her, if she let him.

She pulled back abruptly.

"Good," she said softly. Then her tone changed, hands dropped and, reluctantly, he released her. "Let's go snorkeling."

"*Snorkeling?*"

"Sure. We can rent the gear—"

"Hey!"

She looked at him, a little apologetic.

"What was it? You took off like I don't know what."

He saw her pause, could almost see the shades slowly drawn behind her eyes, the temporary closeness she'd allowed him become, again, forbidden. Oh, she told him, she thought she'd seen someone she knew once but it turned out not to be. Still, it had shocked her a little. And she laughed now, her voice no longer shaking. "Old ghosts, Pablo."

"I don't believe you."

She shrugged, then turned away, began a steady walk back toward East Bay. Furiously, he followed.

He refused the snorkeling idea—a resolve which left him proud for much of the afternoon, and miserable. She went herself, found him on the beach's white glare of sand later and let flippers, mask, and bendable tube drop in wet spatters next to him. She looked cheery now, wearing a very businesslike racing suit that revealed a lot less than he would have hoped for. He wondered why she had to be so secretive about her body. It wasn't secretive, exactly—it was more an insistence on comfort. He guessed the things that teased, that revealed, might be a little uncomfortable to wear. No matter. Her refusal to be revealing was all the more moving—the beauty underneath was apparent somehow, radiated from her face. You could imagine the near perfection of that body simply by looking. And the great ease she had in movement. Aroused, in misery, he rolled quickly onto his stomach.

"Great fish out there." More drops fell on him as she sat. "There are these little ones—they swim in groups of four or five, I think. They look like they're on fire. It was great. They have blue underbellies, and the rest is orange."

She was silent then, noticed his black mood and felt confused. Things always got to be a mess once you began to know someone. She'd promised herself she would not get involved. But she realized, too, that there was no way she could really become deeply involved with this man—it was beyond his resources to move her and it was beyond her, for good, to be moved. Still, she didn't want to hurt him—she was tired of pain. And he was harmless. That in itself made him somewhat special in her eyes.

"Pablo."

He looked up.

"Am I being a creep?"

"I don't know."

"Come on, Joe. I can take it."

He shook his head, returned to bury his face in the darkness of the blanket. He was so sun-hot he felt cold. When she reached to pat his shoulder he felt a sick lurch of despair. There was nothing in the touch which gave any indication of intimacy, or of hopes for future intimacy. He felt that clearly. And maybe it was because he was so hopeless, and sick as any lovesick boy could ever be, that he felt there were no holds barred. Maybe he'd talk—to her, because she happened to be here—tell her everything.

He couldn't see her while he talked, couldn't measure her reaction at all. But that, he guessed, didn't matter either.

"I'm no hot-shot, Karlen."

He felt her listening.

He told her some things. Background stuff. Born in Peru, parents ran there from Germany back in the thirties. Dark, hairy little Jews, all of them. He grinned, half bitterly. Maybe they figured they'd mix in well with the natives. But no go. So on to the U.S. And he felt alienated from them, anyway, and from their background, the fear which made them conservative. No, he didn't keep in touch.

He felt her hesitate. Then her voice. It was softer than it had been before—he liked to hear its softness. "You're the youngest, I'll bet."

"How'd you know?"

"You have a kid-brother attitude."

He didn't know whether or not to take offense. But he grimaced into the blanket. Told her about his brother Gabriel—the oldest, the tallest. Muscle builder. Self-defense expert at an early age, filled with paranoid delusions. Oh, yes, he snickered, Gabriel. Angel Gabriel. Gabriel was—he laughed—a *Zionist* with a capital Z. Big macho paranoid Jew.

"He lives in Israel now. We don't talk. I mean, ever."

"Why not?"

"Oh. Some things that happened. We used to fight all the time about ideals, you know—back when it was chic to have ideals. About Vietnam, mostly. He was such a fucking militarist. And I was going around waving peace symbols at everyone."

She laughed. "You're just the flip side of him, kiddo. And vice versa."

"Huh?"

"Put the two of you together, you'll probably wind up with someone tolerable."

Who asked you? he said, but his voice lightened a little and he felt some of the misery ease off. So he told her about taking pictures. *Pictures,* he called them, still—that was always what he'd felt most comfortable calling the work he did: taking pictures. It was so perfect a description, he said, because things in nature, among people, formed pictures. Formed hundreds of potential pictures in the space of a minute. And when you sealed a second's segment of motion on film—well, you had taken the picture that was there, seized it, made off with it. He laughed. "You know, some Arab sects have this superstition. Or maybe it's Hindi, I'm not sure. Anyway they believe that if you photograph them you're stealing their soul. It's like pointing the evil eye right in their direction, whoever takes the picture is a soul robber. So for protection they'll put a curse on you." The job was to make off with a picture that was already formed. But—and he paused—your point of view, choice of angle, things like that, well, it could irrevocably change the picture in translation. Because, in making off with what was there, you became part of the process—the process of stealing. And the thing you stole could not be the same. It had been taken from place, and from time.

"Like the ones of Raina Scott. Now she's gone, you know what pictures they'll use in history books fifty years from now? The ones I took. See, what happens is this"—he turned to face her, saw her sun-darkened features staring fixedly down—"the picture starts to represent the thing itself. That's how people think of the thing from then on—as the picture of it. Same with her. The pictures I took—they *are* Raina Scott. Because who knows what she was really like?"

"You must have." Her tone was sharp.

Not really, he said.

"Tell me, Pablo. Tell me what she was like." Her expression gentled, she looked down at him apologetically. "Maybe you know." And he detected now, in her voice, a note almost of longing.

Pablo talked. He told her a little, told her a lot. Oh, it wasn't much. Just impressions. Raina Scott, chumming for hammerheads in the Gulf of Eilat. Little Pablo Klemer trying to steal souls—getting his own stolen in the process, maybe.

The sun burned down. Karlen was stretched out beside him and he could smell her hair, the damp, sweet scent of flesh. She hadn't said a word herself. Now he saw her face soften. There was something sad about it. His fingers traced a star on her bare shoulder.

"You know what I'd like?"

"What?" she said quietly.

"I'd like to just fuck the hell out of you."

He was surprised to see no sign of resentment on her face. She smiled a little instead. He could hear splashing in the background, more honey-mooners headed for water. Her snorkeling gear had dried in the sun.

She shook her head slightly. "Sex with a man. I've just about forgotten what that's like."

"Well, what have you been having sex with? Volleyballs?"

She turned to face him, an odd light in her eyes. "You know, Pablo, for a photographer you're pretty blind."

"What?"

"Forget it."

He shrugged. He was amazed at himself, felt dried out and shallow. It came, he guessed, from his all-pervasive sense that there was nothing to lose. "Anyway, if you've forgotten, I'd love to remind you."

They were quiet then. He didn't look at her. He could hear laughter from the bay, and somewhere the faint hum of an outboard motor.

"You're on," she said.

She stood. He sat and looked up to her, astonished. Asking did she mean it? Sure, she told him, but her voice seemed dulled. He thought, for a moment, that the sorrow in her face had crept to her eyes and was there, gazing down at him. Little specks of green sadness caught in all the brown.

She insisted on a bottle of something. Wine. Booze. It could be cheap, she said. Looking at her, he saw she meant it.

She walked ahead of him in the lobby, said nothing in the elevator going up. She walked ahead to her room and didn't pause unlocking her door, just strode in and he followed behind.

She sat, facing him. He picked a chair nearby and set himself on the edge of it—she was making him nervous now—and met her eyes. She gave a small, pale grin. "It won't mean anything, you know."

"How can you be so sure?"

She sighed. She asked him to get some ice, anyway. There were glasses around somewhere. But they needed plenty of ice. Pablo took his ice bucket and stepped into the hall again. He had the feeling that this was not quite real. Still, it was happening. He could pinch himself and, yes, there would be pain. And he would find her out. Whatever her problem, whoever she was. He'd take the time. Tell her he adored her. Because she was beautiful.

"I hope you like bourbon, Pablo. On the rocks."

He took his drink but didn't sip. He settled back in his chair, examining her face which was turned toward the glass she held. The doors to the balcony had been closed and curtains drawn so little light came through. Despite the air conditioning he felt stifled, smelled his own sweat, toed the sand in his shoes.

"Cheers."

She gulped half of it down.

"Are you all right?"

"Oh." She grinned again, vaguely. "Conflict of interests here. I'm not sure I can go through with this, Pablo. I might like you too much."

Hope stabbed his chest. "What's so terrible about that happening, Karlen?"

She saw he'd misunderstood. "I mean," she said softly, "I might like you too much right now to do this to you. Does that make sense?"

Not at all, he told her, sighing. He sat back, resigned to whatever would happen. He was drained by the sun, anyway, and by the fervor of the past few days. He set his drink on the rug. No more drifting out of this world, Pablo. No more. You have had enough.

She finished the bourbon in her glass and poured some more. A hearty helping. She asked would he like to hear something funny? Pablo just looked at her. He examined the lines of her face, the still-young mouth and cheeks. Her skin was lovely, tanned, creamy smooth. He wondered what it was like to be beautiful—it was, he guessed, a different way of being. The obstacles were not the same. Your place in the world was a strange one: you were a different race of human being. Haunted, perhaps, by the sense that others would always seek you regardless of your other treasures or lack thereof. It was probably like having money. Or any sort of real power.

"I haven't told you a lot about me, Pablo."

He nodded. That was true.

"Maybe I lied a little."

He crouched before her, arms crossed over her knees. He looked to see what was in her face. Whatever it is, he wanted to say, whatever it is it's all right. Tell me. *Dígame.* And he smiled to himself. He'd had a Spanish thought for the first time in years.

She finished her second drink. He set Alfredo on the coffee table.

He was on his knees on the rug, hand cupped around her neck, underneath her hair. He let his fingers twine themselves in the dark strands. Her ear was small, damp. He kissed a particle of sand. He kissed her cheek, her chin, her cheek and neck. Lifted her by the waist and slid her to the rug beside him. He felt a kind of unwillingness in her but no physical resistance. He pulled her gently down to lie beside him and offered a cushion for her head. "What is it?" he whispered. He could smell bourbon, see the bright dampness of her lips, the sad eyes. *Dígame.*

"I don't want to hurt you."

"How?"

"I'm afraid."

His own eyes asked her how, and why, asked what was it. I'm afraid, she repeated.

"Afraid? Of me?"

She shook her head.

"Of what, then?"

She smiled flatly. Drunk, he guessed. Maybe it would be easier this way. Like all those high school clichés: get her drunk, have her jerk you off. Whatever. But the booze hadn't been his idea and now, caressing her face, he felt a kind of resignation again to the failure of all this. He pulled away from her, leaned on an elbow and looked down. "What are you afraid of?"

"Oh, things. There are things happening, Pablo. Every day. Sometimes they get dangerous."

"You're pretty weird, Karlen. Do you want to go to sleep?"

She said something that made him stop, stare at her more fully. Then she repeated it: *I knew her.*

"I knew her, Pablo. I mean"—she chuckled—"I knew her."

"What? Who the hell did you know?"

She shook her head, lips pouted petulantly and she glared up at him in a childlike kind of anger. "Oh, never mind. Just do it. Just do it, will you?" She gave him a resentful look. If she was drunk, her voice didn't show it. "Come on and fuck the hell out of me, Joe. That's what you said you wanted. Come on." She sat, reached for the bourbon and her glass, tossed in a couple more ice cubes. She shook her hand and it sprayed wet against the rug, against his face. "I dare you."

Pablo reached for his own glass. The ice had melted, liquor swam crystalline brown before him. Air conditioning buzzed. He was dried out now, all vacant inside. "What is this?" he asked quietly. "Another bet? Winner takes all?"

"Screw you, buddy. It wasn't my idea."

She was right, Pablo thought. She was right about that. He gulped bourbon. It numbed his tongue bitterly, swirled quicker than he'd thought possible to his head and he was glad for it. He couldn't stop the deterioration of things. Something bad was happening now, and he felt powerless to halt it. Wait, he wanted to tell her, please wait. He sipped some more.

Karlen crossed her arms and leaned against a chair. She raised a glass. "I invite you, cordially, to fuck the hell out of me. But no kissing here"— she touched her lips—"or here"—her breasts—"or here"—between her thighs. "Because I have a lover, understand? And if you come while you're in, I'll kill you."

Pablo finished his bourbon. He glanced at her and she was not the same. No, he told himself, definitely not the same person he'd spent the past few days with. Not the woman who had introduced herself as Karlen. This was somebody else he didn't know, someone hard. Beautiful, yes. Very. But hard.

He stood.

"No, thanks. No." He stopped to grab Alfredo on his way to the door. "Some other time maybe."

Mud spun aimlessly inside him. Humiliation, and pain. When he heard her sob he wheeled around and rushed back, sat beside her on the rug and held her head against his chest, stroked her hair like the big brother he had never been, or lover, or friend.

Who? he whispered. Tell me.

Against him, her laugh was muffled. A god, she laughed, no, a goddess. The moon. "Raina."

He pulled back a little and tilted her face up to his, thumb under her chin. Tears dribbled along his thumb, his hand. His arm was streaked with her tears.

She told him a story.

THE MIRROR

They'd met that most banal of ways: at a party. Come on, said the host, I want you to meet someone amazing. In the center of the storm of bodies, beer spills, and shoes tossed on bedroom floors Raina stood silent for a moment, grinning, quite alone. Later she placed the scrap of matchbook cover deliberately in Karlen's pocket. Then she turned and went into a bedroom, and she was searching for something, kicking up some kind of a fuss so her voice sounded out with that husky musical quality it had—its music, Karlen figured, the reason why you forgave its loudness—she was complaining about something or other.

Karlen had had plenty too many, herself. She reeled against a wall stubbornly, pouted. No one to talk to.

And Raina rummaged through the other room complaining. It was after three but there were still plenty of people milling around—more actually seemed to be coming in and few leaving. Karlen stayed crushed against the wall. Don't move, she told herself. Don't. Keep the head in one place. Right. So she stayed. Immobility had always struck her as being preferable to disintegration. One of her problems, Raina would point out later. Oh, she'd say lots of things later. She was a talker. A talker of epic proportions—Raina turned talking into a heightened form of art. Like the best art, it made you see something different each time; like art, it was a universe unto itself that drew liberally from everything around it; like art, it hung there and would not go away. Her complaints sounded, nearly incomprehensible among all the other noise—a coat, she was looking for some coat—and Karlen heard sounds but little specific content. Maybe a piece of her tapped lightly over crowded heads in the hallway and flew through the bedroom door in some kind of drunken fascination, beckoned, beckoned. What? she said.

Raina wove back and forth in front of her. No, Karlen knew, *she* was the one doing the weaving—Raina was holding out a coat ready to slip on her. Gallantly. A crown prince could not have posed with better form. I borrowed a car, she said.

Karlen laughed. "I'll throw up all over the seat."

"I don't care."

She obviously meant it. Going for broke, Karlen could see; even drunk, she could see. Especially drunk. Well, she knew a come-on. She was used to come-ons. From men, from women, from dogs, for Christ's sake. She was beautiful and therefore used to it. But this one made her nervous— she wasn't quite sure why. Maybe because Raina was crazy, and aggressive, and would do anything. She was a dangerous creature somehow. Because she *would* do anything—even without knowing her worth a damn Karlen intuitively knew that about her—anything for kicks. No, not kicks exactly, but to prove something. What, Karlen didn't know. Some *thing*. It hung there very heavily with her presence, a high bright soundless electric pressure that lit the air around her and went all up and down your backbone when you faced her, and it could make you afraid, this thing that she was driven to prove. She gave Karlen a broad smile, childlike. Come on, it said, let's go.

"Get lost."

Raina's face crumbled. As if she'd slapped a baby, Karlen saw everything grow pale, shocked, openly hurting and innocent. Jesus. She wanted to cry. She wanted that face never, ever to look that way again, and something told her silently she would do anything to make sure it never did. Anything. She swore it to herself, barely conscious of doing so. But then she was barely conscious, anyway. Still it was odd, she thought, looking out at Raina's face to see her own hands there touching both cheeks lightly, feeling nothing but a great horror that she'd had the power to hurt so much and had unthinkingly used it. Horror and the inebriated oddness of all this. No, she heard herself saying, no no no, no. I'm sorry. Please. I'm sorry. Telling her she had basketball practice tomorrow anyway—which was true—and the only place she could rightfully go was home.

People spilled in. Out. She shut her eyes. Someone was bitching, bitching. Someone urging Raina: Come on, let's go, huh? There were a number of voices urging her and Karlen wondered briefly what they'd do when they left. She knew they wouldn't just go home and to sleep, no, too tame. But what? And where? Drive top-speed in borrowed cars the wrong way down one-way streets? Dive off bridge rafters? Break into leopard cages at the zoo, into piranha tanks? The thing Raina had to prove was hanging there, buzzing, calling all moths to its lantern core of light. There was to her a strange sense of—what was the word? Karlen shook her head, drunk—*finality*. Unafraid, audacious. And out of her mind.

The thing called and she heard it in a stupor, quiet pocket of silence between the two of them while noise swirled around. She opened her eyes and the face before her had healed. It was pretty in a strange, ebullient sort of way. Looking at it, you'd never guess what she did for a living. She was going off for a while, Raina told her, on some business. Bali, or Java, some place like that—later, Karlen wouldn't remember. Raina removed both hands from her face, held one, palm up, and very gently kissed the palm. When Karlen opened her eyes again she'd gone.

She'd taken a number of people with her, it seemed, because after that things quieted down. And the bodies filtering out were more numerous than those filtering in. Coupled with the generalized atmosphere of late night/early morning relief and exhaustion there was an underlying sense of emptiness, of things grown somehow dim. Wasted green Heineken bottles clanked hollowly against each other in the kitchen doorway. Someone was mouthing off at the host for something or other. Cat shit all over his new sweater. Cat shit, for Christ's sake.

"All alone. Crazy lady."

Karlen left on the arm of some guy she vaguely knew. She wound up dumping him in a cab to pass out and took the subway herself. Vomit spewed all over the seat in one car, stench rising, bloody-edged bottle shards rolled against the tips of her basketball sneakers. She clung to a pole and stood swaying, then remembered the torn matchbook cover and tapped her pocket thankfully. Somehow, she felt grateful. Funny. The hand-worked leather case swung by her side, old familiar feel of her own most comforting weapon.

Twenty dozen anonymous roses arrived at nine the next morning. All over the goddamned living room. All blood-red and rich perfume. She spent the morning sick in the bathroom and called her grandfather to ask a few things about the trust fund payments. Then force-fed herself and looked miserably at those flowers. There was something taunting about them. They were so fucking red. And beautiful. Threatening. She went to basketball practice anyway.

There was the time, a month later, she woke in nervous panic, thighs trembling. Something called silently and she lifted the curtain, saw someone standing across the street near the park—a still, alone figure that was not a man, face turned up but everything dark. Just standing there, waiting. It was after 2 A.M. and Karlen knew where the shadowed face was looking. After a while, the figure waved. She stayed at the window a little longer, waiting for something herself, while Raina waited—an easy thing for her, Karlen thought, to be waiting and alone. Raina was used to things like that. When she let the curtain drop and lay back down the sheets felt clammy. She kept touching her thighs to calm them. They were out of control, jumping. They were jumping all over the place. Nerves.

Two weeks later it was snowing. The first snow, an early one. Karlen stood in the entrance lobby to Raina's building, and the Austrian-sounding doorman examined her with a pinched, gray expression. She had not planned on being here. Ever. Something about the snow, she thought; it kept coming down, southeasterly wind they said on the radio. She didn't have a cap. She was no cold weather fan anyway. And she found herself veering away from the park. Going west. Then suddenly the street—Raina's street—and the number she'd scribbled on the torn matchbook cover and shoved into Karlen's pocket, winking, that night of the party with all her crazy friends.

"Number twelve," she told the doorman. She shook snow from her hair. She gave him her name, and he was speaking into the slick metal intercom in his little booth. Karlen stood there, still undecided. She didn't know why the hell she'd come. Going up in the elevator, she felt slightly bitter.

Everything had hushed around her. It was because of the snow, she knew. There was that insulated feeling to things now—hallway lights like shielded torches, the muted squeaking of her soles on the dark, high-polished floor. Number twelve. It made sense. End of the circle. The twelve tribes, twelve houses of an astrological mandala. The witching hour. Apartment twelve. It was the end of things. You'd jump off the edge of the world into Number twelve. Then she laughed to herself. Moon in Pisces—it always brought out the mystical.

"A good surprise! Oh, not really. I thought maybe you'd come by some time. I thought tomorrow, though—I had a dream about you, you know."

Karlen looked at the figure standing in front of an open door at the hall's end. Raina was half in shadow. But she was smiling, and the voice smiled too. Karlen felt the intended power of her act, in coming here unexpected, dribble away. It was no longer hers alone—it had been dreamt, intuited. One hell of a nerve. When she spoke her voice was slightly caustic.

"I was passing by."

Raina beamed.

"And thought—"

"And thought you'd drop in. That's good! I can't tell you how good it is—I can try though—just listen long enough."

The words were cheerfully self-mocking, and Karlen felt herself relax. There was nothing dangerous here. Maybe it had all been a drunkenly hallucinated sensation, there at the party. That figure waving at night from the park, an illusion. Of course. She began to feel better about having done this. She advanced to the hallway's end shadows and reached out with only a hint of reluctance, offered her hand. Raina pressed it warmly. Come in, she invited, and Karlen followed.

It was cavernous. No, den-like. Both. It was a large, carpeted space with a few short steps here and there leading to other dark rooms. Mahogany shelves cluttered with various extraordinary things: African death masks carved of stone. Hand-carved wooden trinkets, pagan gods jeering from the shelves in contorted postures. Wall tapestries. Some shelves were littered with books. She saw the classics—all hard-bound, with that dusty, musty-looking black or burgundy of old book covers and the titles in raised black or age-speckled gold—one after another. Classics and translations of classics. Texts in languages she could not identify.

Her eyes paused at the mounted shark head, protruding between two bookcases. It was enormous, glassy eyes sightless dark half-mirrors, and teeth jutting whitely from the open mouth like the jagged tips of a much used handsaw. A tiger shark. Karlen looked from the head to Raina, back again, looked to Raina filled with question marks.

"Yes." Raina grinned. "I did. My first with a spear gun—oh, I was a little crazy in those days, I guess. It was off the Great Barrier Reef. I went right out into the chum slick. Right into it. I saw him coming"—she'd crouched slightly, eyes intent and hands open, ready for something—"and *he* saw *me*. So I did a quick dive. I came up just under him. Oh, I was lucky all right." She stood calmly now, shook her head, chuckling. "I was lucky."

The hush went up Karlen's spine, shuddered at her neck. She wandered across to the mounted head and stood staring. The eyes were glass—dead, unseeing. She could not get the feeling from them—the feeling of what it would be like to see them alive and heading coldly for you, razor-edged jaws wide. It would be facing a death that was impersonal, irrevocable. What was life like in those moments facing a death? Facing a potential death repeatedly—your own—did you feel it inside? Was it the limbo area between living and dying? A bright, hot, high-pitched extremity of motion, and of feeling?

She looked back to Raina.

"How do you contain it?"

"What?"

"The feeling. It must be immense."

Raina laughed, delighted. "Oh, I'm abnormal you know. Honestly, I believe it about myself—somewhere fundamentally, I'm mad, stark raving. Certainly, certainly. Don't you know that crazy people don't have to contain anything? They're excused—I hold myself excused from the repressive burden of normalcy."

"Normalcy," Karlen repeated. She caressed a book cover, pulled it from the shelf and felt herself settling comfortably into a vast leather armchair, leg slung over the side as if she'd lived there a long time. Her coat slid off, long folds curling on the rug.

She opened to Chapter Ninety-three, examined the old, dark print without reading. "Normalcy's not the same as sanity, Raina."

It was the first time either had addressed the other by name. The strangeness echoed between them. She lost her temporary feeling of comfort and sat upright suddenly, snapped the book shut.

Long sash drapes were partially drawn over the room's bay window. Raina stood there looking out. It was coming down hard now, the outside all moving white and Raina dark against it.

"You're right," she said.

"I know I'm right."

"Absolutely right," said Raina. "Absolutely."

They were silent for a while.

Karlen noticed how tanned she was. It seemed out of place and time, the burnished quality of her skin and thick dark hair, the dark eyes, set quietly against all the pallor of early winter. She glanced down at her own hands, which were long and thin, very pale on the worn red book cover. Maybe it was not Raina who was out of place, after all. Maybe it was the snow instead, and winter. Here she was colored by sun, by warm winds and tides. She stood against the bleached winter with assurance. No doubt, her stance said, no doubt who was in the right here. Karlen shivered slightly.

"Are you cold?" Raina had the flicker of a grin. It was nearly kind, excitable, almost teasing.

"Cold?" Karlen echoed. She didn't know, she said. She did not know what exactly she was feeling—unease, she said, yes, definite unease and a great insecurity that stemmed in part from not understanding exactly why it was she'd come here in the first place. But Raina was watching her now with those fixed dark eyes. So she leaned forward in the chair. She set the book on her knees, her fingers tapped along it and she heard each thump-thump as if it were coming from inside her body—a pulse beat, perhaps, a lightly pounding heart. She'd have to say something definite now, she knew. Something to clear the air—for herself, if not for Raina. Then she had the words and felt rather daring, brutally sure of herself for the first time all day. "Listen, maybe we can be friends. I think that's what I want. You should know something—I'm not here for anything else at all. I've been with women before and it's not my cup of tea."

Did the torso tense, fine features freeze, for just one second while she watched? Karlen thought they might have but wasn't sure. In any case, the second flew by and Raina looked at her calmly, grinned for real and in a friendly way. "Fine," she said. "We'll be friends. That's good!" The voice was open, genuinely encouraging. There was no hurt in it. Karlen leaned back with relief and the book slid against her stomach. "Something to drink?" asked Raina. Karlen shook her head.

"Married?"

"What?"

"Are you married?" She had that nearly gentle, teasing half-smile again.

"No!"

Raina laughed. "That was emphatic." She crossed to one of the shelves, began rummaging through some objects there. "Well, I *am* married, and here"—she held up a photograph, black and white, set in a wood frame—"here's my husband Lee. A representation of him, anyway. Why so surprised? Categories, maybe—categories. Sure. Don't be insulted, we all have them, but don't be surprised either. Categories are like normalcy, you know, stifling—"

"I agree," she said softly.

"I'm glad you do. I am glad. This picture is of a good man. I know! I love this man. He's my best friend." She headed across the carpet, mounted photo held out in front of her like a gift. Karlen reached for it. "There. My husband. Oh, don't get the wrong idea—we don't live together most of the time. Sometimes I don't know where he is and vice versa. But we're in touch. It's good. It's a good marriage, because we feel each other."

The face smiling back at Karlen was a mild, blandly handsome Protestant face. Fair. Blue blood. It reminded her of the kind of man her father would have wanted her to marry—if only. If only. She could not connect the face to Raina. So she looked up again, eyebrows raised in unhidden surprise.

"Maybe *he's* your cup of tea?" Raina teased. But she seemed half serious. "Take a good look, that's right. Oh, maybe. He'd like that—I want that for him—someone beautiful."

Karlen made sure her eyes dropped back to the photo before what she was feeling showed—because she felt immediately stung. It was a sensation, she realized, akin to jealousy. Not anger at being speculated about in the abstract; no, that would at least have been justified. It was instead a sort of hurt, a sense of injury that Raina could be so quick to let her go, or to toss a vision of her into somebody else's arms.

"No," she said after a while, her voice a little stiff. "I don't think so."

Raina was at the window again, gesturing out, seemed to have forgotten the offering. "It's fantastic. I mean the snow. Let's take a walk."

In the elevator Karlen felt a yearning that surprised her. It was a sense of regret at leaving that large, dimly lit, artifact-cluttered cave of an apartment behind. She'd felt safe and in near hibernation stuck away there in the armchair. But a white, swirling place was outside and, thick coat strung around her, Raina looked ready for it, eager. Raina was talking several miles a minute. Shark hunting off the Great Barrier Reef. Near Montauk. Styles of rigs and baiting techniques. Karlen relaxed completely with the first outside flurry of snow. No burden here—it had been lifted and eased from her by her own long coat, by the snow, by this woman talking relentlessly. So she could be beautiful in and of herself and no expectations would be attached to that beauty. Tomboy, foul-mouth, intellect. Scared. Aesthetically pleasing. Yes. She could be all these things in a white, easy silence: admired and unmolested. Maybe that was why she'd come today. She walked quickly to keep up with Raina. Talking, talking. Karlen listened. They went toward the park.

Raina laughed. She'd ungloved a hand and held it out now, palm up. The flakes dissolved on its surface and she winked at Karlen. "See. Nothing at all. An illusion."

"Not quite. A metamorphosis."

Raina smiled.

They were in the park now, heading south along the road that looped around, and to the east, to the north, back down. The concrete was made slick by an increasingly thick film of white. A solitary jogger passed them. It seemed late to Karlen—was it? She'd forgotten her watch. But everything had that evening feel: the reduction of activity, the insulation given them by these fragmented white curtains of snow, the sensation she had that they were moving against something relentless. She felt a slight touch of panic. She found herself sidling closer to Raina as they walked, trying to match steps. Raina had a way of moving that inspired confidence. She stepped quietly but each stride covered a lot of ground—there was a great self-assurance in her walk. You looked, and felt that the person possessed of this body was an agent to be reckoned with. You couldn't pinpoint why; feature by feature, she was fine-looking but not spectacular. But she was calmly prowling. Better to prowl with her, Karlen guessed, side by side, than to be the thing she stalked.

"Why do you think it's white?"

"What?" Karlen glanced at her. They'd stopped again, Raina stooping to shake some onto her gloved fingers, blow it off into scattering air.

"Snow. Oh, I'm not talking about the physical properties—I'm wondering what you think, what you can make of this. Only because"—she paused, examined Karlen with that teasing look of hers which, Karlen noted with surprise, was now coupled with a certain respect—"because you've got a brain behind your eyes, that's obvious. And I have this desire"—she blushed and the tan darkened—"this desire to be entertained. If you please. Tell me what you think about white things. Clouds. Polar bears. Albino whales—"

"You saw what I was reading."

"I did! White things like the moon. Artemis. Sure! Tell me what you think, why don't you, about oblivion? That's what it all is, anyway. But tell me what you think."

Karlen watched her closely. Mad, she told herself. Quite mad. Still there was some odd strand of sense running through all this, if she could only grab hold of it. Something in Raina was fundamentally cogent at its core. Karlen felt snow trickle on her neck. She was afraid.

"What I think?"

Raina nodded, teasing look gone. Karlen wanted to do something now. Reach out, perhaps. Or run. Why she should be afraid, she didn't know. Still the fear was there. So was an unsettled longing, deep inside. The flakes dropped silently around them and she shrugged, felt them slide unsteadily in a lump of white weight from her shoulders. The word fell out, off her tongue—it wasn't anything she had thought of or intended.

"Somewhere—"

Raina cocked her head, listening.

"I think somewhere there's peace."

The snow had gotten thicker. No one jogged by anymore. They were alone in the park, whole white winter territory deserted and waiting to engulf. There. She sighed relief. She'd pinpointed the source of her fear. Not Raina at all.

Raina smiled. There was a tenderness to her now, a softness of expression and voice that Karlen found momentarily disconcerting. "Is that what you think." Raina nodded some sort of acknowledgment. "You sounded wonderful when you said that. As if you really do believe it. Oh, it's a pretty lie. I don't believe it. But when you say it like that, I want to believe it—or you, maybe. Of course." She shook her head. "No," she said sadly. "No, no."

She walked a few steps away, back turned. Karlen considered following. But she kept her distance. She'd found herself intrigued and—reluctantly—attracted. The other side of all this madness, she guessed, brief flickerings of genuine femininity. Or else a softness that, in anyone, always passed for such.

"Raina."

The dark figure in the snow ahead didn't turn. Karlen wondered if she was humiliated somehow, or ashamed. If she too had recognized the softness as an unintentional revelation of vulnerability.

"Raina, let's go. Let's go drink coffee or something."

Her own voice sounded flat. She was treading unsafe ground. The invitation she'd extended opened *her* up in some way. Still, she had power now. She felt it. Karlen realized she was making a vow of sorts to herself: to use it wisely this time. Proceed with care. She still didn't really know what on earth she wanted out of all this—no, she told herself, she didn't know.

Raina turned. "Coffee?"

"Sure."

"Champagne," said Raina. "Champagne. I've got some—we can chill it on the window ledge. Nice and precarious. Would you like that?" She came closer. Her face was, again, composed and smiling. "You would, wouldn't you? Precarious. I thought so." The sky had darkened. They both looked up. Late afternoon. "I thought—from the dream, you know—I thought, maybe, that you would."

They left the park the way they'd entered. The flakes had built up underfoot by now, there was a soft crunching of boot soles against it and, above, the sky's deepening gray hushed with white. Behind them, trees reached up. They were sharp, twisted things, like hands with too many crippled fingers. Leafless, they pointed aimlessly, caught the sinking snow.

There must have been lights. It was the West Side, near evening—certainly, they must have passed stores with lights blinking a premature Christmas, restaurants edged with well-lit glass and windows steamed by cooking food. Looking back, though, Karlen wouldn't remember lights.

What she'd remember was the hush of snow, the growing darkness. As a child she'd been whisked away to warm climates at the first hint of winter, and even now found any chill difficult to absorb—Florida, she joked to Raina, give me Florida. They shared a laugh but her misery was real, and Raina, sensing it, took her arm casually and began to steer her along at a faster pace. *Once up in Manitoba*, she said, *once*. But she never finished the thought—it drifted away like the last of the day's light—and Karlen would later remember the exact words, would fill in the rest of the sentence herself: Once up in Manitoba so-and-so lost three fingers to frostbite, that's how cold it was. And so-and-so lost his nose. Oh, we had to send so-and-so back with part of an ear gone. It was *cold*. She'd finish the picture in a joyous imitation of Raina—*but we persevered, that's the point!*—and recoil, herself, from the reality it described.

She let herself be steered gently along streets she knew perfectly well. She was giving something now, she thought, by allowing herself to be guided. She glanced once in a while at the dark, hard-cut face moving next to her. No, she decided, she hadn't been attracted after all. She was, in fact, a little repelled. But there was to this sense of repulsion something fascinating, too, intriguing. That was it. Something in this woman she would have to get to know. A walk in the snow, some coffee or a drink afterwards and good conversation. Prelude to friendship. She was relieved, filled with a pleasant sort of anticipation—Raina, after all, was a remarkable woman. Certainly they'd be friends. Karlen had always thrown around the saying that friendship was more valuable in the long run than romance— she guessed she was getting old enough to believe it herself. But no more of this queer stuff. It was not for her. Not her cup of tea. Snow melted on her hair, soaked through to her neck. There was no one in this world who was her cup of tea. That realization came to her with a silent, painful internal thud. No man. No woman.

But they were in the lit lobby, shaking off snow that disappeared on the carpeted hallway floor. They were passing by the doorman's disapproving Teutonic eyes, Raina nodding pleasantly, laughing, chattering away again about something or other—they were in the elevator, going up. Karlen watched lights blink the floors by. She had the irrational feeling that the rest of the world had dropped away.

"Feeling better?" Raina grinned. She'd shaken her head back with one abrupt, regal motion. Dampness flew, thick hair even darker around her face. Karlen managed a half-thawed smile in return. The elevator stopped. And she saw the hallway lights float by. They were heading for Number twelve at a sure, even pace.

Some women have an intimate way of speaking among each other. Karlen emphatically did not. Her way was boisterous and tomboyish, or else it was sardonically intelligent commentary—all methods that slammed the door in the face of potential intimacy. Certainly she was used to many modes of being with women. Basketball. Volleyball. But with Raina she found herself forced into a different mode. Not intimacy, exactly. But she was forced by Raina's abruptness into a thoughtful pause before each phrase. She guessed the pause was a defense of sorts, because Raina's words could seem disconcerting even when they were not. And Raina's way—oh, it wasn't intimate so much as intense. Karlen fell back into the armchair, coat heaped casually on the couch across the room, boots drying by the door. She felt warmer now. Her hand idled by her side. Then she knew what she'd been missing all day—her racket. She'd left it on the bed at home, ventured out totally alone, not a weapon to her name.

"Hungry?"

She shook her head.

Champagne chilled on a window ledge. Raina moved around in the kitchen, the bedroom. She seemed terribly busy—Karlen didn't know with what—and the enervation of the day, the walking, the cold, blurred her with a pleasing sense of near-exhaustion that gave her a full, warm feeling.

It was evening. She realized she'd spent a good part of the day with this woman, had returned to this apartment of her own free will. Something uncomfortable knocked around inside her, but the pervasive, increasing warmth and sense of well-being was overpowering. She'd left the thick, burgundy-bound classic on the carpet before, picked it up now and set it on her lap. Karlen closed her eyes. She played a game: let the book fall open where it would. Like shuffling the tarot and picking out a card at random. Open the eyes. She did.

She smiled. No magic, this. The chapter must have been a big favorite, book opened to this place many times before. She saw the tops of pages creased, some passages underlined in black ink and, in the margin, things written in a rapid, intense scrawl, words miniature and probably illegible. She didn't try deciphering them—it seemed like an invasion of privacy. Ideas you chose to emphasize to yourself and the feelings evoked were highly personal. And while she knew herself to be no expert at all on matters of passion, she'd always harbored a healthy respect for the world of ideas—a world she felt at home in. Karlen decided not to intrude. The underlined passages, though, were less private and she scrutinized them curiously. She nodded once in a while—sure, she'd have plucked that one from the heap herself. Light leaping out of darkness. In all its manifestations.

"Are you still chasing white whales?"

She glanced up and Raina had come around to the side of the armchair, glass offered. She'd wrapped the champagne bottle in a towel, held it unopened under one arm.

Karlen took the glass. She laughed. "No thanks. I'll stick to basketball." She slid a quick look at the mounted head, the unmoving, opened jaw. "What about you?"

"Always."

It was seriously spoken, quick, assured. The champagne bottle got opened easily. Raina did that well, with a flair—Karlen thought her father would have approved and grinned to herself. Style. She liked it. Good champagne. Mist rose from the bottle neck, the liquid made sharp bubbling sounds as it poured. And Raina was talking again. The first time she'd hunted. She told Karlen about it, the story came in bits and snatches, interrupted by her perpetual commentary. Listening, Karlen realized that Raina was the leading critical theorist of her own life. No experience existed in and of itself. It would, in her hands, be fitted to the mold she sought—the thing she needed to prove. Each accomplishment must signify that she had proven it again. And again. Always, there was the haunting sense that more could somehow be done; the thing, whatever it was, could be proven more definitively. The glory for Raina was not in the rainbow that bloomed at the end of each suffering voyage—it was, rather, the defiance of making each voyage in the first place. It was not for the kicks or the sense of adventure, of discovery. Not even for publicity. No. Raina had a great need to suffer.

Listening, Karlen understood this about her. Understanding made the small edge of dread she'd been harboring fall away. She felt somehow closer, much friendlier. Yes, friendship would definitely be possible. She was glad. Seated comfortably in the armchair, Raina on a nearby leather hassock, Karlen listened more. The story of the hunt. And the next hunt. How it had all started: her parents classical scholars, world travelers treasured for their thoroughness in research. They'd reared her with a taste for the unusual. Reared her to archery championships and rock-climbing trips; she'd quickly learned that the only acceptable status quo was an extraordinary one. Then the first hunt. And something inside her had changed then, she knew, something—she stopped, struggled. And gave up; maybe there were no words for the something. But she'd changed. Yes! And all transformation was—wasn't it irrevocable? Oh, it was. Not a reversible thing, it was like some intimation of a thing beyond yourself, transformation. You could look into the void and see it, waiting there. Sure. Just step off the well-beaten path and you'd find it, and then you had effectively joined the universe because everything alive was constantly changing—from life into more life into dying and then into death, out of some womb, toward something final, larger than all the rest of it, something dark. Or white. She smiled. Yes, or white.

"What about you?"

The question was abrupt. Karlen thought a while. Raina grinned in a friendly way—they'd gone more than halfway through the champagne and it was a nice, bubbly, light taste that warmed her now. She didn't feel drunk, just warmer. And she was glad for Raina's sudden shift of focus because it brought a stop to all the intensity of her ramblings, slammed the door in a face of further understanding—which would have bordered dangerously on intimacy.

Karlen laughed. "What about me."

"Well? What do you say?"

"I say"—she let the last swallow mellow her tongue, rolled it down—"I'm rich. I'm a rich bitch, sister."

Raina watched.

"I live on trust funds. What lovers don't buy for me, my father will. When he won't buy it, I go to Grandpa." She laughed again, somewhat bitterly; she didn't know why. She was being snide commentator, reducing her own life to a series of oversimplifications. It made her feel a little removed, isolated, and terribly cold. "But I avoid pulling strings when I can. I live in a lousy neighborhood and take subways and hitch out of town. That way—" She snickered. "That way I'm incognito."

They were silent for a while. Raina poured her more champagne. "But what do you love?"

"Oh, volleyball. Basketball." That's right, she told herself, snide, snappy answers. They would pave the road away from all this. She avoided Raina's eyes and smiled coolly. "Because I like to sweat. I like the way it feels, and how it smells—I think I like that better than anything. It makes me feel real."

Oh, Raina said, of course. Because it's sensuous. Turns you on, as the saying goes, and when you turn the light bulb on then the light is real.

Karlen shook her head. It was all so easy for Raina; Raina was a woman in close and constant touch with her own passions. No, she told her, not exactly. She swallowed more champagne, tapped her crotch carelessly. "To turn this part on—I'll be very honest—just about anything will do. But here"—she patted her left breast—"and here"—her forehead—"it's just not too simple. Up here, and here, I'm pretty unmoved. Frigid, I guess." She shrugged. "One out of three's not bad, right?"

When Raina looked up her face was heated. Karlen leaned back a little in surprise. "Everything so separated. Then what's the good of it? If you feel that way. "*I*"— her chin tilted proudly—"I am *always* in love. Always. It's wanting someone—or something—wanting, oh—satisfaction isn't the ticket so much, it's the wanting you feel inside, you know, *before* you get there—"

"Well, I've never felt it." It came out angry. Karlen was a little ashamed. She hadn't meant to argue, or expose herself at all.

Raina stood slowly, made her way to the drawn curtains over the bay window, turned her back and Karlen was grateful to be unseen right now. Delicate, she thought, it was delicate of Raina to know that. She'd returned her to some vestige of power. And Raina seemed, now, to have forgotten what had just happened. Plucking a length of drape aside, she whistled loud and long, laughed. "It's a blizzard. That's what it is—you ought to see!"

Karlen stood. A little unsteady on the feet there. She focused on an invisible straight line and, glass held daintily out before her, walked precariously toward Raina. The window invited; she pressed her nose flat against it, breathed, traced a monster face in the cloud. Outside snow came at a slant, furious flakes of it, limitless. Lights blinked vaguely from cars on the street below, the glow of lamps in apartment windows across the way shone through the obscuring white pelting down. She wondered, again, what time it was.

She finished her champagne. No more.

"What if I stayed here tonight, Raina? Slept here? What do you think—would it be all right or not? I mean, just to sleep you know, I don't want anything to happen." She turned to face Raina, her own chin tilted now with a little defiance, met the eyes that were staring at her curiously. "Can I do that? And nothing will happen?"

Raina's eyes gave little away. Karlen saw the beginnings of a smile there, just a hint. Then Raina turned and slid softly across the carpet to the bookshelf. She began gently knocking her head against it.

"Hey, stop that." Karlen followed unsteadily but quickly. Somehow the empty glass got deposited on a piece of shelf, her arms swung free and then around Raina from behind and she hugged, giggled, hugged harder and felt the flexible solidity of the body beneath the clothes. Sure. Raina was strong. Karlen made her arms stay there, even though doing this terrified her in some way, and while the moments went by Raina began to laugh, too. She stopped butting the shelf and just stayed there laughing.

"You silly lady. Chicken feed! That's what you are. Oh, I won't molest you. You can stay and even sleep if you want." Her laugh got louder, ribs pressing out against Karlen's arms. "Rest easy! Your virtue's safe with me."

So they sat facing each other on the floor, still laughing, friendly and separate. And Karlen relaxed completely. She opened up, got to really talking about things. Her life. Times she'd hitched from St. Pete on up to East Lansing—how many states spanned?—she forgot. Life and inheriting money and all her non-loves. She had no qualms about excusing herself later, Raina pointing the way to the bedroom. Maybe she was still drunk. Or just exhausted. Whatever, she felt herself floating easily past everything. The bedroom, light dimmed to a pleasant shadowy gold, made her feel she was stepping into a sanctuary. It told a tale different from the one told by the mounted shark's head, the sturdy-bound texts, all that mahogany and leather. The bed was enormous, soft looking, covered with an off-white quilt— some kind of fur, she thought, though she didn't touch it. Lots of pillows. She scrutinized things in the bathroom. A wide variety of carefully selected creams, conditioners. Towels that felt almost velvet, inscribed with the right initials in a flowing, female script. A woman of vanity. Karlen wondered about her clothes closet but decided not to look. Too much discovery for one day. And she was tired.

She peeled off socks, pants, crawled onto the bed and when she felt the thick, lush, furry softness of the quilt ran hands over it, ran her face all over it. She unbuttoned her blouse, then pulled it off, dropped it over the side of the bed onto her socks and trousers. She nestled into the fur's strange, wonderfully soft off-white. Fur of what? She smiled and slid under it, nearly naked. It wrapped around, folds tangling out and covering her, all-encompassing in a perfect, cloud-soft warmth. To be covered by this, by white, to be covered by snow. That's what she wanted. That's what she'd wanted out there today in the park, allowed herself the experience of terror instead to hide the vastness of a childhood desire: to be covered by snow, taken utterly, to nestle in and find the warmth at the core of the snow and curl up there, caress it, suck at it, sleep.

Peace. She had said it herself. Somewhere. Somewhere there's peace. It was the surrounding white that had evoked it in her then, the surrounding off-white that made her feel it now—peace, peace, the approaching oblivion of sleep. Somewhere water was running. Door opening softly. A shower. Her head guarded by folds of fur, and by marvelous pillows. Pillows, she mumbled, pillows, polar bears, peace. She might have been mumbling out loud when Raina slid onto the bed's other side because Raina paused, listened, examined the lovely, half-shut eyes and smiled. Chicken feed, she whispered. And softly laughed.

When she lifted the quilt, though, she paused again because she saw

Karlen was mostly unclothed. She hadn't expected that. So she stopped in perplexity, then eased tentatively under the quilt with plenty of space between them, robe on, quickly turned her back.

"Raina, hey."

"Chicken feed."

A tired hand touched the robe's silk at her shoulder. "Please, Raina. Be my friend."

Oh, Raina whispered, of course. She turned to face her, smiled back at the almost sleeping features. The lips pouted fully, opened, formed a word. Raina listened. *Please*, they said. So she touched the lips gently, said of course they would be friends. She half-heartedly tousled Karlen's hair. That's what you did with friends. Wasn't it. Chicken feed. The quilt covered them both. Affectionately, they laced fingers.

Raina slept.

She was, for all her open veneer, a woman whose nerves often ached at that pitch-point of extremity which leads some to ulcers, some to fine-tuned perception. So slogging through semi-consciousness on the way toward deep sleep was usually a long process for her, one which required total effort. Watching, you might have thought her in the midst of some blood-and-bones struggle during which she'd spent just about every physical resource. Now, near the end of the line, the struggle still worked up a violent twitch or two, an effort toward motion that kept her entire body febrile and shuddering. She'd never particularly welcomed sleep—had the options all been hers, she'd have chosen round-the-clock consciousness. *Sleep caught me*, say the Greeks. As if it were something to run from. But self-esteem dictated that—despite the inevitable outcome—you ought to give it a run for its money. With this, Raina was in complete agreement. Heading reluctantly toward sleep, undistracted by things frenetic or modern, she'd feel herself poised on the brink of some special timeless space, feel her essential self to be old, very old, in the world.

Karlen felt the fingers struggle between hers, sometimes would open her eyes to see Raina's face frown and contract in the dark, mouth move and shoulders twitch, ankles flex. After a while the fight subsided. Karlen was in her own limbo land, not quite awake. Now and then she watched Raina sleep.

Gently, she detached her hands and moved away, fully awake now. She was aware of Raina's sleeping—the eyelids sliding quietly, occasional gasping sounds that grew out of dreams—and, thieflike, she edged a little more of the quilt away. She sat silently. The bed supported her without a creak. Raina's robe was dark, velvety. It moved with each breath.

Karlen examined her as she slept. Raina was turned on her side, face half hidden by pillows, so there was only a partial silhouette apparent; the hard, clear cut of her features obscured, she was nearly faceless. Her hands moved, pressed together. One arm reached a little, nearly touched Karlen's knee in its reach but fell just short on the off-white fur, hand outspread. It was a large, well-shaped hand; still, there was something incongruous about it now, stretching out against the quilt—it seemed detached from the rest of Raina. The long, strong fingers. The palm that no doubt had a fantastic grip, could sense the slightest change of pressure, thumb manipulate for perfect aim. Eyes perceived—hands did the killing work. Pulling bowstrings. Pressing triggers to release a spear. Raina's hands were a potent force in and of themselves. She bent closer to get a better look. The flesh was tight, smooth. She could barely make out the gentle flow of veins beneath skin, the dark mounds that were knuckles. Her wrist was hidden by the velvet robe. Karlen followed the arm's line upward, stopped at the shoulder. The robe flap had fallen open slightly and the shoulder was revealed: smooth, defined. The partly exposed neck twisted toward pillows. Karlen imagined veins along the neck. Pulsing. Core of Raina's life. The thought of her as filled with blood, vulnerable now in sleep, was a little shocking. Her own sense of power was doubly reinforced—Raina's life was in her hands now. Yes. In these moments of unconsciousness. *Raina, you are safe with me.* She felt regal in the flow of her own benevolence. Then the superiority left her and she pulled the quilt tighter around. She would hide in it. Obscure her own face. Raina, at least, knew what she wanted.

What would her body look like, without the robe? Well, she'd been with women before—a bored, rich kid trying something else out for kicks, doing her share of *experimenting,* she said. It had not particularly interested her then. But she wondered, now, about Raina's body. Strong, it would be— would have to be. And darker than her own. She shoved her wonderings aside nervously. Bodies. Everyone always expected so much from bodies— theirs, and the bodies of others. Minor variations were to be found, she told herself, major similarities, acknowledged. Whatever it was she wanted now would not be found in a body. The body was a vehicle—a sad vehicle, at best. It had to be tended to constantly, more often than one of her father's cars. All that to keep something intangible sheltered—spirit?—she didn't know. Raina's body would be different from hers, she decided, and, mostly, the same. Without the robe she'd be a reflection of sorts. In every difference, every similarity, Karlen would see herself in bold relief or see herself blend in gently—there would be no dramatic surge of difference, no disintegration. There would, instead, be a feeling of participation, of recognition. All discovery would hold the promise of being mutual.

She looked down at Raina. Thoughtless, emotionless. A body sleeping. Karlen searched for something that would light a spark. She would like to want something, to feel that *wanting* before attainment, that spark of desire. She felt the need, an open yearning. Desire for desire? Something. So she kept looking. Please, Raina, make me feel it. Pretty please.

Raina slept. Sitting beside her, Karlen was motionless. And time passed.

She could hear it pass in the slow, subtle cessation of wind against windows, wondered whether or not there was still snow falling. She could feel time pass in the silence of the dark, her shoulders vaguely ache with a day-long weariness and temples begin to throb, dully, from too much champagne.

The time she now spent with Raina was different in quality from the rest of the day. It was time invested with her own examinations, her own creations. She was recreating Raina from the still, dark form before her, imbuing Raina with everything she might ever have wanted. Because Raina was strong enough, she thought, to bear that weight. Raina was extraordinary enough. And Karlen had always known, somewhere inside, that whoever she chose for whatever the reason, would have to be exceptional. She was picky, after all. Picky. And spoiled. A rich bitch looking for kicks.

She laughed silently, a little bitterly. What she was thinking was crazy. There was no hope for this—for her. A sort of despair settled heavily along her back. She dozed gently. And woke sweating against the soft, white fur with something like a stifled cry in her throat—despair for more than herself, a despair for Raina, and her self-inflicted sufferings. Out to prove something impossible, dangerous. Raina was doomed. As surely as a torch tossed into the sea. Lost. And beautiful.

The sleeping face turned toward her for the first time all night, eyes still shut, an almost-smile on the lips. Karlen leaned over the face, looking. Her own shadow doubled the darkness, obscured Raina's features even more— but Raina was beautiful, the whole long, dark length of her. She had to be. Karlen had spent so much time with her, alone. Had been nearly smothered by all her colors—then had an opportunity to strip the canvas, repaint it with colors of her own.

Desire. She thought about it. The wanting of something. Someone. The ability to desire led to pursuit and in the pursuit was born a certain ingenuity, a creativity of spirit that led to attainment, climax, to something nicknamed love that in turn drove you on to further attainment, further creativity, ultimately to some sort of—what was it?—oblivion, yes, sure. Maybe the wanting of something, in the first place, was all it took. Please. Please, Raina. Pretty please. She moved closer, reaching to lightly touch her eyelids. *Pretty please. Raina, please.*

Raina woke. She started, then smiled. Her robe was opened. Karlen's hands hovered, hesitant, above her. Then they lowered to rest on the flesh. They were cool, their coolness a gentle shock against her sleep-warmed skin.

"Please, Raina. Be my friend."

"Is this how?"

Karlen nodded. *Pretty please. Touch me.*

Raina smiled up at the eyes—they were large, glittering in the dark, specked by cat color. Brown with dots of emerald. She slid from the bed and brushed Karlen's hair with her fingertips once, barely touching. "Wait."

She crossed to a dresser, opened drawers. Karlen watched her figure move in shadow, shadow bending, reaching, straightening in a constant animal flow of motion. When Raina returned she carried something round and flat, platter-like, under one arm, and held a small vase-shaped bottle in her hand.

"Here."

Karlen reached for the platter-like object. It was the size of a flattened basketball, a dark, opaque surface on one side. She turned it over and caught the shadow of her own reflection. A mirror.

Light flared just behind her, to the side of the bed; the candle Raina had lit gave off an immediate, subtle aroma—of herbs, she thought, or fresh-crushed leaves. The contours of her face were starkly apparent now before her, dark flickering over the features, the light sifting, changing.

"Watch," Raina whispered gently, and in the mirror her shadow loomed behind Karlen. "Just watch. You can see the change. Like magic."

Karlen closed her eyes.

The smell that came to her now was more pungent. It was a musk—heavy, sweet. A quiet shock as oil oozed across her shoulders, down her spine. The aroma deepened and she felt long, light fingers rubbing it softly over her skin. She was warm where the fingers touched. She looked to see her own face in the mirror, a mask of twisted light, and Raina the shadow behind her.

"Karlen Addams Zachary." Raina said it contemplatively. "That's your name, isn't it. It's a funny name. Full of heritage. Full of your father's lineage." She chuckled softly. "Too mortal. You need a new name."

Do I? she wanted to say, but made no sound. The constant, gentle, oiled motion on her back and shoulders was too soothing, musk spreading over to her breasts, flicker of candle across her own pleasing features and a protective figure in darkness just behind. Too soothing for words, she didn't want to interrupt what was happening. A new name. Well, that was all right. Maybe the one she had now was too much of a burden, after all.

"K," said Raina. "A. Z." She laughed. "Your initials. That's it, then. *Kaz*. Between you and me."

Raina set the bottle down at bedside and stretched out beside her.

Karlen stared at herself—her reflection alone now, Raina's gone. There was nothing behind her but candlelight washing the bedroom wall. The scent of oil all around.

Kaz. She liked it. There was something fresh about it, jaunty, utterly new. Kaz. Her name. She would be it, then, would be this creature. A woman she could create again from scratch—no burden of heritage, of money, of particular sexuality. The only baggage she would retain would be this reflection, she thought, this face, this body glimmering oil, newly anointed in the half-light. An unknown world opened before her, blank but for the colors she chose to put there. And Raina had forced it open by mere gesture, mere fancy: giving her this nickname, indicating softly through the feel of fingertips oiling skin that there was easily, yes, a different way of being.

Raina watched.

Karlen looked at the mirror. She looked a long time. Until the candle flickered more savagely, hissed, choked on liquid wax and with a gray puff went out. Then she was staring at a darkness.

Quietly, she reached over the side of the bed, set the mirror on the carpet. When she returned to sit there was only her own shadow next to the shadow of Raina, who lay there, watching. In the silence, Karlen imagined hearing the brush of snow on windowpanes. Something invisible moved along her skin, chilling at the same time it was arousing—a spirit? She laughed softly—no one was touching her. Madness, she thought. All this is crazy, and doomed before it begins. But it was Karlen who'd had those thoughts, a woman burdened by heritage and by all the precepts of her father's world— a world created by his own father, and all the fathers who came before. This, she reminded herself, was a new world. New kicks. New bag of tricks. She lifted the quilt folds up around her, turned to face Raina and curved over her with the white quilt as a cape, her arms outspread.

Crazy, she said. She was afraid.

Then the chill crept over her skin again, tingling, teasing. She looked down at Raina's face in shadow. The eyes glowed up at hers. She backed away.

The quilt folds moved silently, re-formed. She was wanting something now, desperately, and tried to find it in Raina. Something she could have and claim. But she felt frozen, motionless in a kind of fear. Snow. Was that it? The white of it, being swallowed whole by a white blanket, warmth under the cold, fully possessed. To attain something you would give up a part of yourself to it—therein lay the transformation. The metamorphosis. Desire to have what Raina knew. Have that, she wanted that. Her own mode of creation. Raina's strange power—or madness, her unafraid way of being—she wanted a taste of that. And to be close to uncompromised desire. See what she'd been missing all these years. Still, she couldn't move. Could only ask.

Touch me.

Raina's reach was instinctual. But she paused mid-reach, looked up sharply. She would not act on whim alone—Karlen's whim—would not stand another rejection. "Only if you want it. Be sure now. Be sure."

"Please."

Raina reached.

The hands along her back, her breasts, searching her out, were long, long and feathery light. Karlen leaned into the hands, leaned down to them and cupped them together in her own. She held them to her face, smelled the oil scent on them, scent of musk and candle wax, her own scent too. She let go and the hands hovered there against her neck. The fingers teased softly. Tomorrow, said Raina. I thought tomorrow. From the dream, you know. But it *is* tomorrow. Listen. Still snowing—you can hear it.

Pretty please.

Raina stroked her face.

"You're very beautiful."

"That night you stood outside, what did you want?"

"Oh. I was waiting."

Karlen shut her eyes, pushed closer still. She was moving in a sort of rhythm, ducked under the quilt into darkness. If you listened you could hear it here, too: the snow. Here, though, was warmth. Eye of the storm. Raina caused trouble, she knew—she was letting herself in for big trouble and knew, too, that she would not stop herself. Because here she was somehow protected from all the trouble she had let herself in for—here was Raina. She reached out, arms slid around Raina beneath the silk of the robe. She could hear it outside. The snow. And they were covered by white. Karlen shook some quilt from her shoulders, emerged as Kaz, closed her eyes again and her eyelids were being kissed. The word pressed its shape silently on her lips again: *Please*. Oblivion, well, Raina could have all that. She would have Raina.

Kneeling, Pablo stuck a hand in the ice bucket and tossed a couple of dripping cubes into his glass. He poured bourbon, careful to leave a little in the bottle for her.

Outside the afternoon light had dulled to sunset shade. He could feel the air conditioning whip through him, dry him. Pablo lay on the floor. He'd bundled his shirt up and used it as a pillow. He set the glass on his chest, watched it balance there, water beads drip down the sides and spread to his nipples. He wondered whether to believe her. But there were so many details there—hard to discount everything. Still, you could not be sure. She was weird. She'd lie about a lot of things, he bet. Never trust an intelligent woman. He passed a cold, wet hand over his forehead.

He believed her. Poor baby. Drunk, his compassion knew no bounds.

Karlen sat just out of reach, jiggling a glass in her hands. Did you love her? he wanted to ask. Because she hadn't spoken of love at all, and he wanted to believe that—somewhere, somehow—she was capable of feeling it. But maybe her actions spoke for her. She was here for a reason. She'd come to Bellagua, and the reason had to do with Raina. For him, she might be nothing but a tease. A woman of beauty, rich girl jaded in her attitude toward life, looking for the next kick; for Raina she'd transformed herself, become someone with a new name, a creature of pretty extravagance and matching intellect. So he ought to say, not *did* you, but *why*? Why Raina, when the world was yours for the taking? Why do things the hard way? Why hitchhike through all the long southern states when a phone call, the flash of a credit card, would suffice for first class flight? Or sway crazily on subways at 3 A.M. when you could have a private limo? Forsake the trust fund for hard knocks, get disowned by your selection of a mate. Choose a woman—when you could have any man. The hard way. He grinned to himself, weakly. He guessed that was the way she liked it.

"Why did you love her?"

"Good question, Pablo." She lifted her glass in toast. "Maybe the answer's easier than we think."

"Well?"

"Because she's so extreme."

He propped himself on an elbow and things washed dizzily before him. He closed his eyes; it was worse. "What do you mean by extreme?"

"Oh, I don't know, I don't know, really it's indescribable. She's different."

"Different?" He'd be sick soon, he felt it.

"She's remarkable. Raina doesn't care about pain, you know. She just doesn't. She'll do anything, I think she'll do anything to feel that sort of— that sort of *flying* sensation. She will just go out and do something that makes everybody else afraid. Now, a lot of people"—her voice slurred and became angry, young mother lioness warning prowlers away from her cub— "say she's insane, I'm aware of that. But they don't know what they're talking about because they just don't *know*."

Know what? he heard himself say. His voice was argumentative. He felt vaguely angry.

Something rustled along the rug. Her hand, caressing the carpet strands gently as if they were tender flesh. "Oh," she said softly, "know about life and what it feels like to be—to be alive really, you have to walk a borderline a lot of the time I guess. Raina does that. She laughs about it. Just so full, it fills you up, seeing her, because she dares to do that, to be alive."

"Well she's dead now," he said brutally. "I guess that's that." He took another sip.

Karlen laughed, a mocking sound. He glanced furiously at her and her face wasn't bitter so much as defiant. It was the same look he'd seen other times—when she'd challenge you to something one on one, winner take all. She smiled. "You're wrong, Pablo. Surprise."

"What do you mean?"

"I'm going to find her."

He shrugged, drank some more. "You're nuts."

"Maybe. So I ought to fit right in, shouldn't I? With the rest of this crazy mess." She giggled suddenly. "Oh, it's a real mess, Pablo. You'd be surprised."

He didn't know what she was talking about and lay back down, pawed Alfredo with one hand and clutched his half-finished drink with the other. He ought to go now. Really. Get back to his own room and throw up. But he couldn't move. Too drunk, too dried out and without heart.

She was talking about Raina again. Saying yes, she guessed after several years she could say she really knew a lot of what there was to Raina Scott, Our New Amelia Earhart, for all the press and all the hoopla, the celebration of agonies and adventures and deprivations she'd put herself through in order to retain her stature and glory. What ran through Raina deeper than bone was a thick-rooted coil of extravagance. Thorough, fine-tuned, spartan as she could be, for every pull-up, every minute of target practice, there existed some bright and undisciplined private desire. With swift emphasis she strapped these lusts down firmly in a secret place—a place to which few had the key. Discipline. She would be disciplined. And all the fever of every unmet luxury was channeled into this discipline, itself simply a means toward yet another goal. She would be the perfect shot. Have perfect aim, be the perfect stalker, endurer, adventurer, would display perfect courage in the mythical sense, in the ideal—she must become the very best. There was no other way. Because Raina knew, somewhere inside, that the end of something which could begin almost as a game—the end and the primordial origin—was real blood spinning around you. So everything done was immutably serious. There were no more games. There would never be any more games, not for her, and this knowledge made her search deep down through layers of desperation to where, heartlike, the real pulse of her beat cool and unruffled, timeless, self-assured, an enduring core of strength. You know what people say about you, of course, she'd been told in whispers. They say you're mad to do what you do. Quite, quite mad. And so she was. It wasn't a psychological madness, though, but a madness of the heart—the madness that comes with transformation—not hysteria, but brain fever. She'd been blessed with the opportunity to see close up, and in living color, the cold-eyed embodiment of what she feared. Having seen it, she knew it. She set about to study it. She set about to encounter it, to put herself closer to it. The ability to do this—to set yourself face to face with each obstacle that might destroy you—ah, said Karlen, it was the mark of greatness. And Raina had come to the place, eventually, where books would not help her and knowledge was no solace, where social ties were meaningless, where love did not matter and there was no tenderness. In this place she found, time and again, only herself for sustenance. It was herself in the knowledgeless, elemental sense—her physical, instinctive being, out there utterly alone, without a name. When returned from there she felt herself stripped, fell into a lover's arms and curled there, stayed there silently for long periods of time, feeding on the sound of another heart beating and feeding on tenderness, on the presence of beauty, with the insistence of a hungry child. The arms she fell into would have to be soft. Yes. She'd arranged it that way. Each time she recovered she behaved with an easily assumed dominance which many called arrogant and Karlen called divine. But then Raina didn't care who thought her arrogant. She'd seen what it was like to cause blood to spurt through water, known what it was like to freeze, to bake, to thirst and starve and then to survive, seen open mouths rush for her, and seen her own end. And she was no longer afraid.

Pablo slept and had bad dreams. He opened his mouth to yell but no sounds came. The bourbon took over utterly and he just slept. It was blank, white sleep, cured of images.

WEST REEF

Dígame, chica. Dígame.

What was it he wanted her to tell him?

Pablo blinked against a sudden intrusion of light. The scent of fresh hot air blew across his face, dissipated the dry, drained sensation and brought with it a touch of nausea. He kept his eyes shut. The smell of air was lovely, though. If he concentrated he could remember things he thought he'd forgotten long ago, could block out where he might be and why, could imagine the flowers from which such scents would flow and their color, texture. Natural life devoid of hotel strips. He had a brief vision of himself as a child: running somewhere, it was summer. The season's lushness whispered from every side—tree shade, hot scented air, and he could feel his own smallness in the physical scale of things. For a moment he wanted to cry.

"Boy, were you sick."

He kept his eyes closed. The voice was soft, throaty, with a kind of tenderness he half remembered. And when she chuckled there was no mockery in it. He wondered whether this would be his fate: to be sick drunk in the company of a beautiful woman who did not want him. Then he gave himself a tiny grin. At least, not wanting him, she wouldn't be disappointed.

"Sick?" he mumbled. "Was I?"

"All over."

"Oh no." He considered opening his eyes but didn't.

"You don't remember."

"Nothing."

"Well, that's probably the best way." She giggled. "Don't you want to open your eyes?"

He did and she was the first thing he saw, crystal-sharp image framed by daylight that spilled in from the balcony with fresh open air. Brown hair curled all down the sides of her face and strands washed softly onto her neck, lapped over on the breastbones. Her face was dominated by eyes; the eyes ruled by their green, cat-like spots of light. Everything else was classically sculpted: elegant cheek bones, oval chin, the long, thin nose—all but the lips, which were full and soft and seemed, at first sight, to demand kisses. He reached for her hand without stopping to think what he must look like himself, or to wonder how she looked so good after drinking just as much as he did. He was surprised when she cradled his hand gently in hers, tugged almost playfully at his fingers.

He squinted at her.

"I understand"—she smiled—"you're dying to get to West Reef. There are some great pictures waiting there."

"What else did I say?"

"Not much."

He thought back. Snatches of yesterday came to him. He remembered some of their conversation and the way she'd sounded. But he did not believe it. Bullshit, that's what it was. Drunken fantasies. He had one hell of a headache.

She told him a few details and he blushed. Sick all over. Shit. When was the last time that had happened? And she'd cleaned up, cleaned *him* up, for Christ's sake. Given him a bath, then put him back in his underwear and bundled him off to sleep on the couch, like a good little kid. He was too hung over and wiped out now to feel the humiliation of that.

"West Reef is off limits."

"I heard." She shrugged. "Where there's a will, you know, there's more than one way, Pablo. And anyway, listen to this: there are no blockades or anything. I mean, it's illegal if you're caught. But say you had an official-looking vehicle for the day. That's like having carte blanche, you know."

"What do you mean?"

"Oh, I've been busy. Let's say I've been using my charm this morning. Or my prowess. Or"—she winked—"my influence."

Snatches of the past day and night's conversation came to him, confusing. He doubted whether much of it had happened at all now. He'd been too

drunk, too lost in his own wanting. Still, he examined her face with a good
deal of puzzlement, wondering who she really was and what had happened
between them. Her fingers, sheltering his hand, were cool with a light
touch.

"Why are you doing this?" he blurted. "All this—I mean, all this using
your charm? For me?"

She shrugged. "I like you, Joe. I just do. I like you and I owe you."

"Owe me?"

"Sure. That was good Moët, that first night. I always return a favor."

A good policy, he whispered. He was feeling suddenly shy. Maybe he
owed her something himself. "Karlen. I guess I was sort of a pig yesterday,
huh?"

"You bet. But nobody was on their best behavior, Pablo. So let's forget
it." She squeezed his hand. "Friends?"

Okay, he nodded, friends.

He wondered if she was anxious to make friends so that he really would
forget it—forget everything that happened, and particularly everything that
was said, even more completely than he already had. Looking at her face
he thought maybe there was something else she had to say. She seemed to
hesitate, to shift under the weight of some burden. But the eyes became
visibly less open. There was a shrewdness that settled there in the place of
vulnerability Whatever she'd considered telling him had been locked away
for the time being. And he was covered by a thin blanket on the sofa in
her room, with a wretched hangover and warm breeze blowing across his
skin, stripped and cleaned and all washed out like a hairy, overgrown baby.
The day stretched ahead vaguely: there were pictures to be taken. Portraits
being formed somewhere on the island's other side. Accessibility was suddenly possible, due to her: her charm, she'd said. Prowess. Or—what was
it?—influence. Yes, her influence.

The car was light brown, police sedan model. She was in the driver's
seat and as he stepped in he noticed the side windows in the rear were
opaque, blocked off by some sort of vinyl-like substance. Privacy for whoever
rode in back. Across the glove compartment chrome letters had been inscribed. PROPERTY OF ZACHARY CHEMICAL CORPORATION. He traced the
letters with a thumb and turned to her.

She grinned. "Want to know how I got this thing?"

"I'd love to know."

"That archaeological dig they've got going, Pablo. It's funded by this
corporation"—she nodded toward the glove compartment—"and the guys

who work the dig have a lot of time on their hands. So I challenged a couple of them—"

"One on one?"

"Exactly. And the grand prize was car for a day."

"Volleyball?"

"Table tennis."

She tapped the racket at her side. He noticed it again for the first time in days—it was so much a part of her, he'd forgotten all about it. But now he noted the worn leather case, the stitches that lined it like thick embroidery. It seemed, suddenly, the one part of her that he wouldn't have dared touch under any circumstances—her most sacred, most private part. He set his canvas equipment bag on the floor, patted Alfredo in his lap.

"Congratulations, I guess."

She fed gas and they were off, weaving away from the hotel, past palms and the strip of beach and other hotels. They were traveling along the coastal shore, on one side water and sparkling beaches of multicolored sands. This was the one highway Bellagua boasted. He noticed the soft smoothness of the ride—a good car, internal air conditioning fended off blazing midday sun. He hadn't eaten anything since yesterday. And though he'd cleaned, shaved, changed clothes, he felt light-headed. There was a floating, unreal sense to all this—being driven to an off-limits area in a semi-stolen car by a woman he really didn't know. Pablo glanced cautiously at her. She looked fantastic. Tanned, lovely. Things from last night were coming back to him now with more clarity.

"Karlen." He said it hesitantly. But she immediately turned to him, then back to the road.

"I hope," he said, "that you know where we're going."

She grinned easily. Saying oh, she'd checked around. She had a few ideas.

He noticed she'd put on that necklace of hers, dainty silver, with the curved ivory sliver hanging toward her breasts. He could see the line of the tooth sitting on her chest. It rose up and down as she breathed.

They drove past villages where children skinny as sticks rushed toward the car, stringbean arms waving. The people he saw looked malnourished. Their faces were different shades of color: red-brown to nearly black. Once in a while he caught sight of a small, delicate-boned physique in passing—the skin dark rusty tones, eyes oriental in shape and black hair falling near shoulder length. A Bellaguan of unmixed lineage. There weren't many left.

What about here? he'd say, when they passed another cluster of shacks.

But she shook her head. She seemed to be silently calculating, and to know where they were. Finally, she slowed and stopped. He got out when she did and saw this was the end of the road. Before them stretched more rocky beach. To one side, thickening foliage and beyond it the jungle. To the other side, ocean.

Later, it would come to him as half-realized dream visions: the day, what they'd done. Walking along the sand into sundown. She'd taken the car keys and the sound of their jangling became a steady constant, along with the sound of surf, of warm wind blowing in off the ocean and rustling thick dark green tropical leaves. The smell that mixed with salt spray was an overwhelming one of vegetation growing and rotting. There was the feel of his shoe bottoms crunching into sand. He could hear her crunching footsteps, too. Beyond that was a great silence. Removed from bright restaurant lights and calm bays where white people splashed or laughed or drank, where yachts glided by on the placid surface, this place was left to its own devices—it would grow or rot as it pleased. It would do so in silence, broken rarely by the sound of a human voice. And he noticed another smell eventually, one so pervasive he had at first not sensed it at all. It was the stink of fish spoiling. Looking toward the shoreline, he saw the corpses of many fish cluttering the rocks.

Pablo remembered the village they came to. Seemed they'd walked a long time. It was twilight, the sky a fading rose color. The naked children who came running to meet them pointed, giggled, exclaimed in a language he didn't understand. Somehow, though—by gestures, smiles—she made them understand something; after a while he followed her along a sandy path through the ramshackle row of palm-frond shacks. He noticed there were several small fire pits dug along the path, fires blazing in each. He wondered why they'd lit fires in daylight.

She spoke to people. He wouldn't remember, though, who she'd spoken with; only that they were people of the village. Brief segments of her stilted conversations drifted through to him. She was asking strange questions. When had the fish begun to die? The fruit, did it have a different taste? Had anyone traveled into the interior in recent months? If so, did they bring back stories of odd occurrences? Leaves of plants that changed color for no reason? Leaves that withered, or burned to the touch? He concentrated on the steps ahead. Because in there, he knew, were pictures. His for the stealing.

Last snatches of light spread dully through the hut's frond roof onto the sagging floor, onto straw mats littering the floor, and the mat where a woman crouched over a tiny body wrapped in cloth. Pablo stepped nearer. He could feel the floor sag beneath his feet. Karlen was behind him at the door, still talking. He shut out the words.

He bent over the tiny infant's body. It gurgled softly, made fretful baby noises and the mother's hand, laid on the cloth covering it, helped hush these sounds. Pablo squinted to see. At first he thought the child was bald, turned face down on the straw pallet. But he realized he was looking at a face, after all. He made out the tiny nose, dark lips, the soft dark chin. And then, for a minute, he wanted to cry. He'd never seen a face without eyes before.

How did you know? he asked. In the dark, she was only a dull silhouette. She steered along the flat, sandy stretch of road. Wind whipped by the open windows.

"How many pictures did you get, Pablo?"

"You didn't answer my question."

"Tit for tat."

He sighed. "Plenty. Do you want to know how many rolls?"

She shook her head. No, she told him, as long as there were plenty. As long as he did the right thing with whatever he had. Showed them to people back in the States. People of influence. He told her he didn't understand. He didn't understand what he'd just seen, nor her reasons for bringing him here. He didn't understand her, either. Not at all.

She peered through the windshield at the road ahead, bright headlights searching along its smooth darkness.

"Look, Pablo. It's not so important for you to understand me. What's important is those pictures. You show them to someone, okay? Show them to medical people when you get back home. There are reasons for birth deformities."

"All I know is I saw two kids today, Karlen, and one of them's got no hands or feet and the other doesn't have an eyeball to his name. You're telling me the same thing caused it all?"

She shrugged stiffly. "Maybe."

"Come on."

"Pablo." Her voice grew soft. He watched the dim outline of her lips move, struggling to speak. "If I knew for sure what was going on, I'd tell you. Please believe me. I don't. I only know what I think—"

"Well what are you saving it for?"

"All right! This is what I think. I think those people are being poisoned by something."

He was silent. The pictures. He had them. He reached tentatively, caressed her shoulder in a friendly way.

"Okay," he said quietly. "Okay. We'll find out. I'll print these up and we'll find out."

She removed a hand from the steering wheel to grab his fingers, squeeze them thankfully.

He remembered yesterday all of a sudden, and everything she'd said. He had to know. "All that stuff you said yesterday. About Raina." He watched her silhouette for some reaction but could discern none. "Is it true?"

She laughed uneasily, eyes fixed on the road. "Oh, no. That's all bullshit. I lie a lot."

"I don't believe you."

"Okay." She breathed, exasperated and, he thought, more than a little nervous. "It's true. Every bit of it. Okay?"

"You're nuts."

"You asked."

He sat back, silent.

He must have dozed. The sight of lights, sounds of music and glasses clinking and the low, soft swish of night boats cruising the bay seemed suddenly to surround him. She left him near the Royal Hotel pool area and said she had to return the car. He didn't bother saying good night. He told himself he was shut off to her for good. And it was too late—or early. He figured about 2 A.M., because things were settling down in the bar area and the restaurant but weren't yet dead. He went to his room.

When Pablo stepped in he realized he'd been expecting something to be different. It wasn't. Relieved, he checked the glass doors to the balcony. Locked. The bathroom light flicked on easily and he found himself, like an idiot, pulling the curtain aside to glance in the shower. Everything vacant. He stepped out, faced the closet. An alarm of some sort was ringing in his head. He told himself he was an ass and stepped toward the closet doors, grabbed the knobs and pulled wide. A dark, gaping emptiness greeted him.

Pablo laughed. He stripped and crawled into bed with his underwear on. Then he was out of bed again, rummaging through his equipment bag. He got out the rolls he'd shot that day and stashed them, one by one, in the pillow case. Then he lay down again. Christ, but he was exhausted. Crazy paranoid bitch. Nuts. She'd made him a little nuts, too.

He turned off the light.

It was a wail. A long, lonely high-pitched bird call that sounded like the upper range of a child's voice. He sat immediately, panting. Had he been asleep? Yes, maybe. But his eyes were still shut. Everything dark.

The sound came again, closer this time. He could have sworn it was ringing shrilly just over his bed. He could have sworn he heard the whoosh of air as if a projectile were streaking past him, the beat of wings while that cry still echoed in a desolate, lonely way.

Pablo woke and jumped out of bed, soaked with sweat. He looked around wildly—there was nothing in the room with him. Just rumpled bedsheets and shadowy moonlight drifting in from the balcony, puddling the carpet and his feet. He felt his legs shiver. Then he heard insistent rapping at his door, desperate low tones asking to be let in.

He crossed to the door and when he heard her clearly he opened it. Karlen looked past him. He saw her suddenly pale, eyes searching beyond him to the darkness of his room.

"What is that?" he whispered.

She moved in past him. He locked the door behind, flicked on a dull lamp but she'd gone to the balcony already and opened the filmy drapes, unlatched the doors and stepped out. He could hear small snatches of her voice. Pablo crossed over to the balcony, hovered tentatively in the door frame. Her back was to him. He noticed her shoulders tense to the point of trembling and suddenly drop, and he jumped forward to keep her from falling. She didn't resist when he held her firmly, half pulled her inside. He slid the glass doors shut, locked them, and drew the curtains. In dull lamplight she looked suddenly older, utterly exhausted.

He leaned down to examine her face. "Karlen?"

She nodded.

"Are you all right?"

She touched his arms lightly. She said she was all right, just give her a few minutes. He brought her a glass of lukewarm water. She drank a little and he could see the flush of health and overlying tan return to her skin, eyes regain that glow they had. When her lips curved slightly in an almost flippant look, he knew she'd recovered.

"What the hell is going on?"

She smiled. Her eyes, searching his, seemed briefly to ask for something. "Do you believe in extrasensory perception, Pablo?"

"I don't know. I never thought about it much."

She laughed gently, grabbed his hand and pressed it. "I'm glad. I'm glad you don't think about the things you don't think about. Look, Pablo, I think somebody's been in my room."

Funny, he wanted to tell her, I had the same feeling when I stepped in here myself tonight. But he didn't say anything. He watched her face—he'd almost forgotten how pretty she was.

"Want me to call security?"

She shook her head emphatically.

"Well," he cracked, "if you feel safe enough around me, you can spend the night." And he watched her face again, felt curiously tender. What he said next he meant seriously. "Free of charge."

He was surprised when she told him yes.

She seemed fragile, lying beside him in the almost-dark. He didn't touch her for a long time, then laid a hand on her side and just let it stay there. He wanted to tell her he was sorry for everything. Not that it was necessarily his fault but nevertheless he was sorry about the way things had gone between them. Beneath his palm he could feel her breathe steadily. She was awake and blinked tiredly, patted his hand comfortably.

"Do you miss your brother?"

He tensed, looked at her in surprise. He told her he didn't much think about it. Why?

"I don't know, I guess because I would. If I had a brother I'd miss him no matter what. I'm an only child."

"It's no thrill just having a brother."

"No?"

"No. It's like being tied to a certain way of being—*or else*. In the sense that there are footsteps laid out for you all along the way, you know what I mean? Like religion. Who needs it?"

She grinned sleepily. The night was silent now, no fears, no wild bird-calls. She told him she thought maybe he was wrong about that. Religion, she meant. She thought everyone needed something like it, somewhere deep inside. Though not necessarily the religions in power today but something older instead, more elemental. "Like the old pagan matriarchies. Worship of fertility, worship of the seasons, healing and giving back to the earth what you take from it. A religion of reciprocity, Pablo. It used to be pretty widespread, you know."

"I didn't. Never heard of it."

She laughed. "Older than the hills, kiddo. Older than you or I. So old"—her smile faded—"they don't bother to put it in the history books."

"Bullshit."

She was wide awake now. "It's true!"

"Then how come I've never heard of it?"

Maybe there are a few things, she teased gently, that you haven't heard of. "And anyway, it's suppressed information." She met his questioning, exasperated look. "All your churches and synagogues have a lot at stake. What if everyone found out and then went around worshipping *women* instead of men? Or what if—just what if—ripping the earth apart to get at something for so-called profit was against everyone's religion? That would put a lot of corporations and a whole lot of governments out of business, Joe."

"Right," he said, resigned and not listening any more. "Bring back the matriarchy. That will solve everything."

She propped herself on an elbow. He was surprised at the patience of her tone—she still spoke gently without being patronizing. It made him listen again. No, she said, a little sadly, no. Maybe things are too far gone for anything to be solved. And she was quiet for a long time, eyes flickering over his face but looking somewhere else instead. "You're a Jew, Pablo—"

"By birth only. I feel pretty disassociated—"

"Sure, I know. But according to Hitler you'd be a Jew, right? No matter what you considered yourself to be."

He nodded reluctantly.

"How many Jews got wiped out in the death camps? Five million?"

"Six," he said. He was appalled that he knew the figure so well, had ingested it as thoroughly as any painful childhood memory.

"Six million people. Sure, that's the figure. You know that one, don't you? As if it were the only holocaust ever in history! But what if I told you that more witches and goddess worshippers have been slaughtered down through history than Jews—"

"That's ridiculous," he said bitterly.

"It's the truth." He could see the small, lovely specks of green in her eyes glow, like glitter, like lightning bugs. "Do you know what witches were, Pablo? They were wise women. They were healers. They were all bound up in the worship of earth and the moon, and the seasons, and reciprocity in nature. In the tradition of Astarte, or the cult of Diana. Or Hecate. Or Artemis."

He smiled. She wasn't the only one here who knew about mythology. He knew a little. Sure. "What's so healing about any of that? You're talking about some bloodthirsty goddess running around shooting things with bows and arrows."

"Well," she said coolly, "look what she was up against. Maybe she did it in self-defense."

They were quiet for a while, both fully awake. He reached over and flicked out the lamp. He touched her forehead softly. "Do you really want me to forget it?"

"What?"

"Yesterday. Everything you said."

"Yes."

"Really?"

"I told you I lie a lot. Why do you keep asking?"

He petted her hair. His hands were quiet, undemanding. It was the way he wanted it, for once. "I don't know. Just that I thought—oh, I thought if you really were—" he stopped, changed his mind "—if you really did know her, the way you said you did—" she smiled at him as he struggled and the smile gave nothing away"—I thought maybe you'd be pretty lonely."

Her fingertips drew lines along his cheeks. She said nothing for a while. Then, "Pablo," she said, "you're very sweet."

He grimaced. "Thanks."

"I mean it. You are gentle. Don't let them screw you too badly."

"What are you talking about? Who?"

"Oh, the same people who screw everything up. First they did it to the witches. Once that was out of the way they could pretty much do as they pleased with everything else that threatened them. With all the other cultures that traditionally breed creativity. Jews. Blacks. Homosexuals."

The rolls of film in his pillow case lumped uncomfortably under his neck. He sighed. "No one's going to screw me any more for being a Jew, Karlen. That's past history."

"Then they'll screw you for being gentle. Or for taking pictures." When she smiled again he could feel the tension ease from her. Her fingers touched his chin calmly.

He breathed mock relief. "At least they can't touch me for being black. Or queer."

"Oh, I don't know about that." She laughed. "You've got a little *queer* in you, Pablo. Admit it."

He could feel his hand freeze against her shoulder. What the hell do you mean by that? he wanted to ask. Then he didn't—maybe she'd respond. And he guessed he didn't want to know what she meant.

He told her she was crazy. She smiled gently.

"Pablo."

"Yeah?" he muttered tiredly.

"You know the subway station at 96th and Broadway? When you get back to the city, check it out. There's some great graffiti there."

Graffiti, for Christ's sake. He shut his eyes. "You're nuts," he murmured. "Nuts."

Calmly, she nodded. She said they ought to sleep, anyway. And they did. Sometime in the night he woke to find himself pressed against her desperately, thrusting forward with hips and thighs and angrily willing an erection that would not materialize. Shhh, she said. She held him gently by the hips. Shhh. You have no conquests to make, soldier. Just rest. Rest.

After a while he did, curled against her like a child. He felt himself falling into sleep. But there were tears in his eyes. He didn't know why.

He took pictures of her the next day. Rolls and rolls.

He was surprised she let him. Posing on the beach, sun gleaming off the gentle curves of her arms and the lithe, slim length of her, brown hair curling down to the shoulders. He got a few close-ups. The eyes glowed pockets of green. They were sad, so sad. He wondered why he'd never seen their sadness before.

Something inside him was a little broken. He thought maybe she felt the same; there was a kind of resignation in whatever sorrow she had now. But they'd pulled closer to each other in a significant way. He felt that, too. So it might be worth it, after all, this sense of being broken inside.

After a late breakfast she changed into the same old jeans and crimson shirt he'd first seen her in, same cap, same basketball shoes, racket—he kept calling it a paddle and she'd scowl disapprovingly—and gave him a small kiss on the cheek. He noticed she'd strapped on two canteens and a small pouch of something or other. She carried a leather vest under one arm.

"Let's go check out the dig."

"Why? You think they've struck gold?"

Unearthed treasure, she told him, smiling. But he was willing to go along for the ride. His assignment was just about wrapped up, anyway—he had plenty of fun-in-the-sun shots, grinning doorman shots, magnificent twilight-over-the-ocean shots. And the illicit photos taken on West Reef—those rolls of film he kept in the canvas bag slung over his shoulder, close to him. Thinking of it made him breathe faster.

You could reach the dig site just by following East Bay's line of beaches. The sand was miraculous to him—some of it white, some a shade of pink, some black. She took off her shoes and they waded along sometimes by the shoreline. Once she caught at his hand, held it for a while. Do you think they'll find Atlantis? she teased. He told her he hoped so.

They walked silently. He was beginning to feel a lingering sense of loss. Maybe it was the sadness of her eyes today.

The dig site was a thick finger of sand jutting out into surf. Behind it, more sand. Behind that, the highway. Then plant life and sparse vegetation began on the highway's other side; slowly, deceptively, it grew thicker. Weedy grass grew, taller the further into it you went. And the plants grew up and around, became everything there was, became the jungle.

Pablo glanced sideways and saw her looking across the highway. He saw her lips move. She was muttering something silently. For the first time since meeting her, he admitted to himself the great likelihood of her being crazy. A self-confessed liar with—what would that shrink he'd seen once have called it?—*inappropriate affect.* Which meant you'd do weird things at the wrong time.

His fingers tapped along Alfredo's lens, caressed the camera affectionately.

She offered him water from one of the canteens. He sipped gratefully. "Good idea."

"Want to get a look at Atlantis?"

They trudged up from shore, feet drying quickly to burn on the sand. Soon they were at that familiar tourist location. Pablo leaned back against one of the sharp, granite-hewn boulders littering the area and his legs burned; he stepped forward to lean against the prohibitive fence with posted signs, had to remove his hands. The heat was searing. He stood, arms crossed, looking down into the pit and the compound beyond. Same as usual. Men digging. The barely recognizable outlines of what seemed to be a wall emerging from earth. He was surprised they hadn't hit water yet, this close to the shore.

She tapped his shoulder, about to say something. They were moved aside a little in a sudden group of tourists rushing forward. Looking up to the highway he saw they'd come by bus. The bus baked there in sun, uniformed driver sitting wearily on the vehicle's steps. He tried to hear what she was saying but lost it. She waved a little—no matter, the wave said. Later. He smiled and turned back to the dig. She had a habit of grabbing her leather-suited racket by the handle and thwacking it gently against her thigh. He heard the rhythmic sound of that now amidst all the sudden chatter. It was comforting in a way. He concentrated. There was maybe a shot or two to be had now. He uncupped Alfredo and aimed, took a couple. He moved closer and took a couple more. The heat seemed to envelop him; he felt lost in it.

When he looked up and around he didn't see her. He turned from the fence. He scanned the different outfits milling around. No CINCINNATI. He stepped back toward one of the rocks, looked behind it and then scrambled to the top.

She was nowhere in the area.

"Karlen?" He called her name tentatively.

He looked up to the bus. Then to the side of the bus, the highway. And beyond the occasional car whizzing by, he thought he saw something move through the long grass there: a red baseball cap. Almost by instinct he glanced through the lens and focused. Got the shot. Then he was off the rock, running barefoot as fast as he could along blazing sand, to the road.

"Hey!" He shouted her name at the top of his lungs, looked across the highway to where tall grass rippled with whatever breeze there was. No sign of her now. No red cap. No nothing. Cars shot by. He set a foot on the pavement and tears welled in his eyes from the blasting heat of it. He yelled for her again. Pablo took a deep breath and looked for cars. None. He raced across the blacktopped highway and could feel skin tearing and blisters swell underneath. He reached the other side, eyes shut in pain. He called her name. But she was gone. There was only the grass that swayed in front of him, nearly as tall as he, and beyond that more, and beyond that the interior.

Pablo pounded a fist onto the desk. The desk clerk did not seem to understand. He was a white man, imported from the States. And he couldn't make head or tail out of what Pablo was saying.

Pablo gave the room number. And her first name—he colored with embarrassment, realizing that he couldn't remember her last. But he was certain of the room number, and of her description. It was the room next to his own, damn it.

The desk clerk blinked apologetically. I'm sorry, Mr. Klemer. Our records show that room has been vacant for three weeks. Prior to that it was occupied by a Mr. Such-and-such. You must be mistaken.

"You're out of your mind. She was in that room. Right next to mine."

The desk clerk shook his head.

So Pablo wound up banging the desk with a fist, saying he would go up there right this minute and call security. She'd left her stuff in the room, he knew. And they'd see, he said angrily, they'd see then what kind of a *mistake* had been made.

The elevator seemed to inch its way up. He shoved past someone without stopping to excuse himself, tore down the hall and felt baked skin chill in the modulated cool, ruined feet pound numbly on the carpet. He slammed one against the door to her room, kicked it open. It wasn't locked.

The front of the suite looked freshly vacuumed, coffee tables polished. His soles made imprints on the rug as he crossed over to the bedroom. He poked inside. Bed freshly made. Lights off. Everything that could gleam gleamed with a newly dusted look. And there was not a trace of inhabitation. Pablo stood at the room's threshold and something beat dully inside him. He looked around again.

Curtains were drawn away from the closed balcony doors. Sunlight filtered emptily in.

He paused on his way out, looked back at everything. Wiped clean. But she'd had her things all over the place just yesterday. And she hadn't been carrying much at all when they'd trekked from beach to beach. He ought to call security. Some kind of film settled over his eyes, coupled with rising panic. He wouldn't call security.

Those bastards. That thought drifted through him; he didn't know how to place it.

Fumbling for the keys to his own room he was aware of someone close by and wheeled around to face a fairly tall, thin man knocking at the door to Karlen's room. His blondish hair was beginning to thin a little, Pablo saw. And in the near-scarecrow form of chest and arms, the fair, placid features, he recognized the man he'd seen that day down at the outdoor restaurant area, and beyond that recognized someone else, someone he'd known of before. But he could not place him.

The man turned to him. "Excuse me. I'm looking for Miss Zachary?"

It had come out a question, and Pablo didn't respond. He merely gazed back, realized there was a mildly confused smile on his lips.

The man reddened. "The young woman who's been in this room. I thought—they told me at the desk yesterday—" and he shrugged. "Maybe I was given the wrong number. Sorry to bother you."

Pablo watched him go.

He'd seen the man before. A photograph somewhere. Newspaper. Magazine. Sports magazine. Yes, he was certain of it.

He turned back to the door and keys slipped from his hand, fell to the hallway carpet silently. He leaned against the wall for a minute, could feel the unsupported quivering of his knees as something seemed to fly across the blank screen his stomach had become: some black birdlike thing of emptiness, or of fear.

DEATH OF THE VILLAGE

On the side of the island where tourists didn't go, fish were dying. It wasn't the most unusual occurrence. Some remembered that this had happened in other years, the bright-colored fish stinking belly-up, belly-bloated, in tepid shoreline sand. Those years it had been due to a disease that spread the island's circumference, caused minute red insect larvae to sprout like moss on the dead belly-up bodies, caused Portuguese man-of-war to steer clear of the shallow coastal shelf even in August.

This time, though, was different. Poking at the fish-cluttered shoreline with a stick, Dr. Manella Porter couldn't have said why, only that she knew these fish weren't diseased—the disease didn't come from inside of them, at any rate. It came from something foul in the Atlantic itself, something foreign. And now, poking at gasping sick fish with the stick tip, she was reminded of the woman from a coastline village farther south who'd walked several days to reach her. Because of her sister's child, she'd said, voice dulled with fatigue, a son born two days before. This child was without fingers or toes. There weren't even stumps where the digits should be— just smooth club-like paws. No one had seen anything like it. All of their village was in mourning.

She wrapped fruit and bread in a palm leaf, placed it in her hand basket. Then she told the woman to rest and set out herself along the sand in the right direction, walking most of the day until late evening. She avoided the interior, stuck to the coast and the lapping waves. Sometimes her feet crushed with nauseating softness against fish, the dead, the dying. Once a king crab, tail eaten away as if by acid and legs straight out in the air when it rolled over in poisoned agony, seemed to make a high-pitched sighing sound. But Manella told herself it was all like a walking dream. It came from solitude, she knew—men lost in the interior sometimes wandered back to the coast days later, physically unharmed but with mad light in their eyes. And they'd gasp continually in panic, even though nothing was chasing them. Some forgot how to speak. All from walking dreams—anyone who walked far enough alone could become mired in the middle of one, perhaps never emerge. Sometimes she'd find herself almost believing it could happen. So she traveled quickly. She was careful not to stop too long, or listen too closely to the sounds of her own voice.

The day was damp, searing heat intensified on the one side by palms that gave way rapidly to black jungle foliage, on the other lightened by a slow ocean breeze and the open freshness of air blowing freely across an expanse that was nothing but sea and wind, no land, and beyond the openness more breeze, more ocean. By dark of the fourth day she'd reached the village. The remaining fruit and bread she had no stomach for, so left it as a present, basket and all. She'd remember it later like some image recalled after black magic sleep—the fires small and glowing sadly in front of each shack and sharp-pointed sticks leading the way along an inexorable path toward one where a woman had given birth to this monster. In the dark, spattered orange by occasional flame, she heard worms slither down the sides of shacks, bug wings rattle. It was night and as she eased slowly, tiredly up creaking steps to what waited, she knew there would be nothing she could do and knew this was no dream. Dark clubs of hands flailed out at her, tiny clubs of toeless feet waved smoothly, obscenely, from a mattress. And just as she'd think of the child later as she poked among dead fish, so she thought then of the dead fish and her mind sprouted a bridge between them.

"They're killing children."

She spoke to herself. The words echoed in stillness.

"It's come to this, they're killing children."

Who they were, she didn't know. Still she knew they existed. Just as surely as she knew that, although no children had been killed yet, eventually it would happen. First the deformities, then stillborn monsters. She knew, not from medical texts, but from some elemental wisdom of the heart.

And in a different village altogether, they told her, a child had been born last month without toes or fingers and without eyes.

When she heard this Manella knew she had to return. It wasn't any more than that—some inkling which reason couldn't have accounted for, and it told her to go home. The vision came to her of Yosh, constructing shell houses in the sand. His belly protruded, firm and round. He was laughing and when he glanced up his eyes were large, dreamy—they were Tristam's eyes. She felt caught in a web of sudden inextricable fear and left immediately, accepting nothing from the unhappy relatives except a brief warming by their fire, and a new basket of food which they pressed on her for the journey back. Later she was hungry and ate it—the fruit made hard lumps inside, like small remnants of some internal shield she'd tried to construct since her husband's arrest—an attempted warding off of uncontrolled terror. The new basket of fruit rinds and mostly eaten bread crusts hung from one hand, scratched her palm raw with its swinging motion. It was hot and she perspired, smelled herself in the dark air, and something tickled against her memory. Meat. She'd have liked a hunk of cured fish meat now, swallowed with melon and plenty of fresh water. But there weren't any fish this year, only poisoned crabs. Only babies born, eyes and digits ripped out before birth and the empty skin shining dark, very dark, and smooth in the light of mourning fires. The doctor swallowed dryness down her throat. She walked into the night, slept badly on the sand. She woke before dawn and kept walking.

Dr. Porter neared her own village.

Sun glinted off the ocean surface. It was late afternoon. The sky was subtly darker and gentler now, an all-encompassing sheet of unclouded blue. Maybe it was the sudden bulletlike streak of sunlight that shot into her eyes when she turned west; maybe the heavy green stillness at her back. She wouldn't remember, later, what form the warning took. But she stopped suddenly. The narrow coastal shoreline strip curved rockily ahead. Beyond the granite promontory was a free stretch of sand, and a quarter mile along the beach their village, stark and brown, backed against the jungle. Warning stabbed up her spine so for a moment she froze quietly. The surf rolled in, slipped back. The air was silent except for insects humming. She stopped, and nothing had changed. Still something was different.

You're quite right not to continue, she heard, *you don't want to see.*

She heard it—but whether it was a voice speaking the words to her or she'd spoken them silently to herself, she didn't know. She'd headed instinctively toward the foaming surf at a run, basket dropped. But something slid quickly over her head, something pulled tight, and her arms were pinned around behind. She felt the drag of her heels along sand. Then the abrupt, scratching drag of damp earth, then of foliage, and feeling close to suffocation against the heavy material blinding her, she thought of Yosh and began to really struggle. But the grip tightened, the dense silence hushed every thrash. Without sight, she could sense that the sky had gone and was now hidden by a heavy overhead mat of dark leaves. She was being dragged farther away from sky now, into the interior. She stiffened with blind confusion, then grew faint struggling for breath. Then she sagged down, heels passing quickly over the wet ends of crushed roots. Terror came coupled with her son's laughing face, but she had no strength to fight now. Things were darker than before. She seemed, almost, to sleep.

Don't worry. They think you've left the country.
Something was hard against her back. She felt tired and nearly dozed again, sitting there. Damp soaked into her legs. She recognized the voice and relief drifted through every limb, and though she could feel her fingers quiver there was no panic. Her head was covered. Inside the dark covering, she smiled. That voice. She knew it.
Sorry to treat you badly. It was the only way.
The doctor reached out, touched nothing.
Your boy's safe. I had to go in for him at night. Him and your supplies. It was a lot to handle, all at once. I'm glad you didn't see. It's not too pleasant. They tore the place apart looking for you.
Her hands dropped. She cradled them, one in the other, breathed the musty odor of cloth. She listened dizzily.
Just rest awhile. Then we'll get going. I'll see that you get there—don't worry. Call it repaying an old debt. Certainly, I will see to it.
She felt herself moan slightly. This was insane, to be sitting here listening with her head cloaked like a skittish horse. She moved to peel off the sack, fingers fumbled at the rope tied around her neck.
A hand gripped both of hers with hard, cool strength. The firmness of the hold was amazing—it was so sure, and smooth, and had the quality of a vise. She felt her own hands—not weak by any means—wilt immediately. She didn't try to fight.
No. Sorry, but no. You don't want to see all this, anyway. It's just dark here. Sometimes a little sun gets through. Mostly not. That's all right. It takes a while to get used to, though, and I don't want you going crazy on me, all right? I mean it. As they say, there are walking dreams to consider— you don't want that to happen, now, not before you see your boy. Think this way: think where we're going and imagine every detail. You can do that, can't you? You've got nothing else to look at. So imagine your boy. Then you'll see what you imagined soon, all there in front of you, every detail

before your eyes. And you'll be glad you waited. It's easy. Voilà! Magic!
The voice laughed softly again. *You'll see how it is. Don't worry, whatever you do. I'm just sorry about this. I really am sorry to treat you badly!*

She drifted, dizzy with sudden fatigue and that odd, floating sensation she still hadn't shaken. She tried to focus on symptoms. No loss of breath. Center of balance distorted. But she could hear perfectly well. And the voice talked on, softly, comforting and at the same time utterly unnerving— the words logical, calming, openly friendly—the fact that they were being spoken at all a burst of illogic across the blank dark sky which was her only vision.

Actually I prefer you have no idea of where we're going, Dr. Porter. It's better for you that way. This method—oh, it's probably not ideal—but it was the best that could be managed. The village—I'm sorry about the village. There was nothing to be done. It seemed some choice had to be made. You and the boy, or everybody else.

She felt herself sob, sack moving into the vacuum of her open mouth.

The voice went on, tone hushed and regretful.

I saw what would probably happen. It was a matter of making some quick decisions. Maybe if I'd left the boy, they wouldn't have done what they did. They'd have taken him instead. And you. They were waiting. I—oh, I can read their small minds by now, I knew what they were thinking. They like to desecrate. You understand. I saved what I could. That's all I could do. It's all anyone can ever do, although sometimes, sometimes you might think you are extraordinary enough to do more. Vanity! Swollen magpies. Bloated delusions of heroism and grandeur. No, no more. The real mark of greatness is a hands-on comprehension of one's limitations. I feel badly about the village. You wouldn't want to see it. I just did my best, Dr. Porter. I saved what I could.

The doctor was shaking all over. Shock, she told herself. Secondary. Traumatic. A mild case. She was cold. She felt the arms lifting her—they were long, hard arms, and miraculously gentle. They were half carrying her to a different place, setting her down on a surface that seemed dry and warm.

GABRIEL

Pablo looked through the zoom.

It was Gabriel all right. His face had that stony look of dull arrogance Pablo'd come to identify as the Israeli soldier look. Gabriel had a great tan—better than his. It was the kind of pervasive dark glow fashioned in the skin over a period of months, or years. Maybe he'd been living down on that settlement of his in the desert. Pablo forgot the name.

Gabriel sat on a crumbling wedge of freshly exposed rock where, just a few seconds ago, a group of camera-toting tourists had sprawled for a bird's eye view of the rest of the dig. The rock overlooked a large, shallow pit of sorts, surrounded by meshed wire, posts, and signs warning you not to go beyond a certain point. In the pit itself men crawled, brushing the earth with small tools and with toothbrushes, pushed wheelbarrows filled with heaps of rock and artifacts. Beyond the pit, a military-appearing compound stretched toward an off-limits section of beach. This was also guarded by wire, but the wire here was thicker and higher, and the men rushing back and forth within the compound, although they were scientists, researchers, and laborers dressed casually in shorts and short sleeves, had an official, military air to them.

THE ATLANTIS PROJECT, read a sign.

ARCHAEOLOGICAL STUDY IN PROGRESS.

And beneath that:

THIS PROJECT IS FUNDED BY A GRANT FROM ZACHARY CHEMICAL CORPORATION, A DIVISION OF INTERNATIONAL COMMUNICATIONS ENTERPRISES, INC.

Gabriel sat silently. He was almost motionless. Pablo determined the direction of his gaze. It was not at the dig, but at the compound beyond. Leave it to Gabriel to chuck culture for barbed wire. Scenes like this reminded Pablo of the old days, childhood days. Or adolescence, when he'd find Gabriel lifting weights, reading military history, morosely clipping items from the paper that dealt with anti-Semitic regimes in South America or the American Nazi Party. And little Pablo rolling by on skates, giggling, snapping pictures with the baby Kodak his mother'd given him, falling, skinning knees, crying while Gabriel looked on without expression.

Focusing in, background color blurred, he waited. He wondered what in hell Gabriel was doing here. Maybe he could just get the shots and leave, make believe he'd never seen him. No use pretending fraternal warmth where there was none. Maybe he'd just leave.

Pablo stepped through another group of tourists. He let Alfredo swing loose around his neck, moved forward reluctantly. He would come up behind. Pablo grinned. A good tactic. It should put him at an immediate advantage and then, when the dust had settled, they'd be able to determine what misfortune had brought them to the exact same time and place.

"How are you, Pablo?" He didn't even turn around.

Pablo paused, stung, disappointed, then angry. The sight of Gabriel, he realized, always made him angry. He spoke to the back of his brother's head.

"All right. What are you doing here?"

Gabriel turned. His eyes flickered over Pablo, face didn't crack an inch. But Pablo thought he could see a quick, teasing sparkle in the eyes. Maybe he was giving the guy too much credit. Pale eyes, almost blue, they shared that between them. Gabriel yawned. "I'm a tourist today. I'm worshipping sun."

"I'll bet."

"Sure," said Gabriel, "it's true. It's true, *hermano, seguro que sí.*"

And Gabriel's eyes left him briefly, as he turned back to the pit where archaeologists dusted diligently. When he faced Pablo again there was something else flickering in the eyes, some note of concern perhaps, or even worry.

* * *

"I can help you, sirs?"

The waiter was brown-skinned, quite stiffly adept, white jacket tight over shirt layers through which sweat didn't show. Pablo ordered a frappé and was interrupted by Gabriel, who gave explicit, rapid directives in some dialect he couldn't for the life of him identify. He turned to Gabriel, a little offended. The waiter was off across the sun-bright patio, and soon would appear balancing a tray cluttered with full glasses.

"What did you ask for? Arsenic for the gentleman?"

Gabriel laughed. "I'm a language specialist now. One of my duties."

"I thought you were off duty."

Gabriel shrugged. He grinned. The grin infuriated Pablo—it was that competent, big brother grin that had always managed to rain on his parade. There were different languages being spoken at each surrounding table, echoing up to the tent-like awning that provided shade. No love lost between the two of them but still, Pablo figured, they were noticeably brothers. Gabriel taller, broader through the chest and arms, more physically secure in his movements, somehow more steady. Pablo leaned across the table.

"Look, Gabriel, let's cut this horseshit. What the hell are you doing on Bellagua?"

"Visiting. I'm working in the area."

Flies buzzed to the table's edge, one madly humping the other. Pablo watched. The male shimmered blue, enormous eyes dull red in the shade, wings flat along its back. He thought about knocking them off with an easy napkin swipe, but pity overtook him and he decided against it.

"Working?" he said. "Military stuff?"

When Gabriel smiled it was with less formality, more like the old inviting personable Gabriel he'd been once upon a time—before politics and wars and Jews and ideologies tore his sensibilities to shreds—and Pablo felt almost drawn toward him then. Sometimes he could feel a dangerous softening inside himself when it came to Gabriel—a little-brother propensity to adore, to eagerly learn more. Maybe that was the underside, he thought, to all the bitterness. But Gabriel changed the subject.

"I'm married now. Her name is Yael."

"No kidding!"

"We live in Jerusalem. She's a Sephardic girl." He smiled again, with real satisfaction. "We speak Spanish."

Congratulations, Pablo told him. He meant it. He even reached across the table to slap Gabriel's shoulder. Married—that was something.

The waiter arrived. He set napkins on the table and with perfect grace deposited a frappé directly in the center of each napkin. He set down more napkins, two empty wine glasses and then with one hand popped open a full chilled bottle of some Italian white wine. Pablo shot Gabriel a surprised glance. "What's the occasion?"

"We can talk. It's good we met. I was going to find you later today."

"How'd you know I was here?"

Gabriel took the bottle from the waiter and poured. When Pablo looked up the waiter had hurried off in the direction of some German command. "To your health." Gabriel raised his glass. "And long life."

Karlen swam through his head, an open hurt. Maybe that's why he gave Gabriel a look of bitterness. Gabriel's eyebrows arched in surprise.

"What is it, Pablo?"

"What the hell"—he leaned across the table, nearly knocking over the bottle—"are you doing on Bellagua, Gabriel?"

"Don't talk so loud," came back calmly, quietly. "It's important, Pablo. Sit down now. You don't want to be so loud." Gabriel's eyes roamed, took in everything. Pablo would have almost bet they could see in back, too. Swivel vision. His hand rested on Alfredo protectively. He settled in his seat, head still bright with the thought of her, and with pain. And Gabriel was connected somehow now, if for no other reason than that he sat at the table before him, tanned and happily married.

Gabriel sipped. He forced himself to swallow and set the glass down, finally stared back at this man, his brother, who sat across the table from him and whom he did not particularly like. "Are you all right now? Just sit. You don't want people to notice. We'll talk later but now just sit. Drink. That's right."

Pablo gulped wine quickly and spilled some on his trousers. Gabriel's seriousness had impressed him into obedience. He lifted his glass, noticed weariness settling in faint tan lines around his brother's eyes, understood something which he immediately forgot, then let go of his private pain. What took its place was a quick, clear stab of fear. He looked at Gabriel's eyes, which were tired and watching him.

"Cheers," said Pablo.

Gabriel nodded.

The afternoon wilted on. It was one of those endless, pointless days that happen in the tropics during August, days when sweat doesn't dry. Or when dog paws stick to stone, melting, and if you had imagination you could smell burnt animal flesh. If you were quick enough you could see mangy flashes of tail whipping around corners, the usually joyous motion stilted to an agonized scuttle. This heat had deadened bird calls. It forced shops to close. Pablo figured any tourist with a brain had sacked out for the afternoon, crawled onto neatly pressed cool sheets and turned the air conditioner on full blast. He'd just about gone through the entire bottle. Another half glass and he would have gotten pretty drowsy himself, maybe a little maudlin, had the person sitting across from him been anyone but Gabriel. He realized, though, that drinking booze Gabriel had paid for probably forced at least a temporary—albeit uneasy—truce.

"When will you leave Bellagua?"

"I'm staying," Pablo said belligerently. "I can cash in my plane ticket. I've got another advance coming."

Gabriel poured him the last of the bottle. The glittering, clear liquid splashed against the glass and glowed with an ivory tinge. Gabriel had taken only a couple of sips. He didn't like alcohol.

"You should leave tonight, Pablo. I mean it."

That concern was there in the eyes again. Pablo laughed curiously. He finished his glass.

Gabriel ordered another bottle, had it opened and recorked and they left the patio area, headed down for the beach. It was so hot there weren't even a lot of sunbathers around. Wandering along the shoreline, heading from one carefully planted grove of palms to the other at the beach's opposite end, Pablo felt the heat. He felt how bright the sun made everything, how bare the beach was without tourist bodies cluttering it, how naked and how exposed. *An easy mark*—that thought paddled into the mess in his head and stayed a second before scurrying away. He chuckled. All this marksman shit. All these adventurers and daredevil fucking women and wild survivors of catastrophes—it had gotten to him. And he was drunk.

"It's okay now," Gabriel said quietly. "We can talk."

"I don't get it."

"Here." Gabriel tossed the cork away. "Drink. This kills pain."

Pablo did. Pain killer. Just what he needed, but how did Gabriel know.

He listened. Or tried to, anyway, but the words kept drifting in and out of focus. They walked, slowly, slowly, beneath deadening white heat, while to their left bay water glistened warm green, the temperature of a hotel-drawn bath. I'll tell you some things, Gabriel was saying, things it's not so good to know, maybe. Because you must understand. And then leave tonight. This you have to do.

Pablo concentrated. He listened.

"Your girlfriend." Gabriel took his arm. They walked. Sweat slid between them. "Karlen."

Pablo clutched for his sleeve, gave up. Too drunk. He wanted to cry. "What do you know about her, damn it? And how?"

"Shhh. Listen. Just listen. Her name is Karlen Addams Zachary. Very full of heritage. Do you know that last name?"

Pablo shook his head.

"Do you know about stockholders? About major stockholders—"

"Oh for Christ's sake. I'm not a goddamned idiot, you know."

"Good. Her father is a major stockholder in several corporations. He's a very powerful man in your country"—Gabriel emphasized the *your*—"and also of course in the world, I suppose. One of his companies, the most profitable of them in fact, is owned by a group called International Communications Enterprises."

Pablo blinked. Sunlight was red against his eyelids, then dark, then bright white again. "Yeah? They're funding that dig, right? So what?" Did Gabriel think he was going to shock him with one of those conglomerate theories? So corporations owned corporations and plenty of wealth was intricately connected and conspiracies abounded. So what. Everybody with half a brain knew that. It was part of modern life. So she came from wealth. He'd figured as much from the start.

"This company manufactures chemicals." Gabriel looked sideways at Pablo, saw he wasn't getting through. He scanned the stretch of beach carefully. He looked back at his brother. "Never mind about this, Pablo." His voice was almost gentle. "I'll show you all about it later. But you have to leave Bellagua. You have to leave tonight."

"Shit, I'm not going anywhere. You tell me, Gabriel. You tell me what you know."

Pablo realized how much he was sweating, front of his shirt soaked through, and then for some reason he wanted to cry. He wondered how it would be, leaving tonight on a cool, smooth-riding plane while down below you could hear Bellagua whimper with heat and the whimpers become fainter and fainter, then nothing at all. He wondered what it would be like, leaving without knowing what happened to her. Goddamned island. It was a goddamned lousy island, world's worst tourist trap, and there was something about the heat right now, combined with wine and his own exhaustion, that was breaking his heart. He grabbed for Gabriel's arm, tried to keep his feet. He grabbed for some part of his brother's body as if it were salvation.

* * *

Walking up stairs, he could tell this was the really elite section of Sagrabél—more exclusive than the hotel strip. These apartments were all foreign-owned. There was that clean, spacious European look to things here. But his head was mud. Gabriel jangled keys, held the door open for him.

"The bathroom's there."

His voice was touched with pity. It would have made Pablo angrier, but then there was wine. And heat. The bathroom door was polished wood, hand-carved. It looked baroque and out of place, probably imported during some previous decade when severe classicism had been unstylish. He didn't even slam it behind him. The bathroom was king-sized. The tub followed Roman baroque in design, too: enormous, with delicately curled edges and small, ornate gilded legs. The toilet was at the top of two steps. Some kind of altar. He headed up there. Later he washed his face carefully and felt less hazy. He peeled off his shirt, washed his chest and arms until he'd stopped perspiring. You could just about sleep in the sink. He looked at the mirror. Those green-specked eyes. Then he was reeling out the bathroom door yelling for Gabriel.

Gabriel had opened the window wide and was looking down. From somewhere came the faint sound of sirens. Pablo hung out the door, one hand savagely twisting its gilded knob, and when Gabriel heard him he turned.

"I still want an answer," Pablo spat.

Gabriel sounded uninterested. "An answer to what, *hermano?*"

"Her, her." He realized how drunk he was. "What do you know about her, Gabriel?"

"Pablo, go to sleep now."

"Go fuck yourself."

"Go to *sleep.*"

It was a command. Gabriel had pulled himself up, so for a second he seemed to tower over Pablo, strength more apparent, far more capable. His eyes were usually congenial simply because they usually weren't aroused. Now, though, Pablo spotted them growing wider and a little darker. Maybe Gabriel would even slug him one. Pablo wanted him to. He hung there leering, he was asking for it—some kind of explosion, some answer to all the questions, anything.

But Gabriel turned back to the window. "Pablo, you're tired. There's the couch. You can see it, can't you?"

Standing there, Pablo felt vaguely regretful. It was regret for this almost-enmity between them. Like most private enmity, it had come about between two people who once had great regard for each other, and thus had become tinged with the bitterness of disappointment. He remembered when he'd admired his brother; the man still fascinated him.

There was the sofa. Pablo had the good grace to make it that far. It was, for some reason, wool-upholstered. Baroque taste would have demanded velvet, at least velveteen. But he grabbed two cushions and held them passionately against his chest and belly. Drunk, Pablo, he told himself. Pretty drunk, buddy. His mouth still tasted like sun-staled wine. Far away in the background he heard Gabriel moving around, water running somewhere. Then the sound of voices, a door closing softly, latch turning. And he thought of what she'd have looked like naked.

He panicked, wanted to vomit. He felt himself falling instead. He grabbed the sofa's edge. It was the wine, he told himself, and the heat. He wondered what Raina looked like without that white mesh sleeveless shirt. Maybe wonderful. Must be. Strong and wonderful, she fills you up. That's what Karlen said. Fills you up just looking. Raina alive. Somewhere in there. He guessed sometimes she got lonely, for all her strength and all her splendor. Wanted something human, when all was said and done. Something mortal. A lover.

Jesus, he said into the cushion, Jesus. And fell asleep.

Through the open window sirens blasted, closer this time. And from far away came the staccato blasts of machine-gun fire.

He woke once with a strangling in his throat, a tight throbbing, like a scream. He woke with her full name in his mouth. It spilled out in whispers, and he understood the terror freezing him: maybe she was lost for good now. Maybe he would not find her.

Pablo rolled over. Afternoon sun splashed his face, made him cover it in sudden bright pain. He reached for a pillow. There. He pressed it to his forehead, which ached nastily.

He tuned in to Gabriel's voice. "—tonight," and the phone receiver clicked to rest. Then feet slid over the carpet, paused to one side of him, continued on their way.

"Here's coffee," he heard. "Black. Let's talk, Pablo."

The hot cup handle found his fingers. Pablo opened his eyes and what he saw near the sofa were suitcases—his own, and a few of the things from his hotel room. He almost spilled the coffee. He looked up to Gabriel.

Gabriel held Alfredo up by a strap.

Pablo slung the camera over his shoulder. Somehow, he'd stood and made it to the table, and now Gabriel was sitting across from him, casually sipping coffee of his own, watching. The scent rose to Pablo now, muddy, bitter, offering some kind of relief. He sipped painfully.

Short, sharp explosions of gunfire bounced faintly through the window, loud enough to jab insistently against his ears.

"What in hell is going on?"

Gabriel stood. He crossed to the window and shut it. "I'll show you something." He was rummaging through stacks of old newspapers in a corner. He spread a thick layer of them across the table, then went into another room. When he returned he was holding a small metal box with handle attached. He set the box, just so, on the table. He took from it several green twigs on which different species of fresh young leaves had sprouted, shook them out of sealed plastic envelopes and laid them side by side on the paper-layered table. He reached into the box and took out gloves. Pablo recognized them as the type you'd handle Bunsen burners with. Gabriel put them on. Then he reached into the box again, this time brought out in his gloved fingertips a small brown bottle, numbers scrawled across its midriff label, and a sterile eyedropper—both sealed in plastic.

Pablo gulped coffee. It seared his throat but getting hurt felt good to him, made him feel more awake.

"Here," said Gabriel. "Now, watch."

Pablo's head felt like a drum's insides. Still, the coffee's bitter black taste kept his vision clear, and green buds occupied his focus as he watched. Gabriel had taken the bottle and the eyedropper from their plastic cases, was opening the bottle top slowly, methodically.

"Put the coffee somewhere else, Pablo. And keep your hands off the table. Please."

Pablo gulped the rest and set the empty cup on the floor, then dutifully rested both hands in his lap. Gabriel twisted the cap quietly from the bottle, set it to one side. The bottle's tiny brown neck gaped. Inside, a sort of liquid glimmered.

Gently, Gabriel dipped the eyedropper in. He held it steadily there until it filled. The liquid was almost clear but had a cool, silver tinge.

"Watch."

Gabriel removed the eyedropper. He held it over the first leafy twig he'd set on layers of paper. Then, softly, a single drop hit a leaf. The eyedropper poised above, waiting. Pablo ticked off seconds in his head. He got to thirty. Nothing happened. He kept watching. Forty-five. Pablo kept watching and got past sixty. The seconds dragged until he lost them. He glanced up questioningly at Gabriel.

"Watch!"

His eyes slid immediately back to the paper, the twig, its single dampened leaf.

Something was happening.

He saw without noticing at first. It was simply that the leaf seemed to change color slightly in the area where the drop had fallen—seemed to lose some of its green, fade just a little and take on a yellowish hue. The hue spread, fanning out from that central spot like widening octopus arms, yellow lightened until it was white. The whole leaf was becoming white. And Pablo heard a sort of sigh. It was nearly inaudible—such a delicate, high-pitched hiss, like the last puff of steam from a teakettle, a faint dying sigh that came from the leaf. It grew stark white. Then it began to curl inward toward that first dampened spot, edges reached around themselves rolling in, shriveling, and the leaf wasn't a leaf anymore but just a white shriveled coil, clinging to the twig by a pale thread.

Pablo glanced toward Gabriel, looking for answers. His brother gave him a motion: Not now, the shake of the head said, keep watching. So Pablo did.

Gabriel moved to the second twig. He placed a single drop on one of the leaves. Then slowly, almost casually, a single drop on the twig itself.

Gradually the leaf was changing, discoloring. It was shriveling like the first one, in exactly the same pattern. But what was remarkable to him was the state of the twig from which the leaf sprang—its bark was beginning to dissolve in long, whitening strips. Then he heard it again, louder this time: that sigh. Suddenly he remembered the sound from somewhere else, and knew it—sitting around a fire long, long ago he'd heard it—the hissing sigh of damp wood succumbing to flame.

Gabriel had repacked everything in sterile plastic envelopes. He'd remembered to remove the gloves with care, to put them back in the box before locking it. He'd latched the metal box and taken it to the other room.

Now they sat across the table from each other again. Between them the layers of newspaper were still there, and on top of it all, the several twigs in a row, in varying twisted white, lifeless shapes.

Gabriel had opened the window again. A strange, heavy silence drifted through, sirens and gunshots muted. Outside, the sun crawled west. There was no ocean breeze, no distinct relief from the day's unyielding heat. But the prospect of approaching darkness seemed to color things a cooler shade.

"What is it?" he asked finally.

Gabriel leaned back in his chair. He seemed relaxed now, pleased with himself. "Snow," he said. He gave Pablo a half smile. "After the Yom

Kippur War we found something funny had happened on one of our settlements up north. The trees—well, of course most of the trees were destroyed, burned, or they were rammed with tanks—but some of these trees looked different. The leaves and smaller branches—like this." He spanned the shriveled remains with one hand. "And in the fishpond there also, the fish died rapidly. Not of shock, but of some disease. We couldn't isolate it. There was a connection somehow, of that everyone seemed sure. We kept all this, you understand, out of the press. It wouldn't do to demoralize the public in such a manner. The coup d'etat—" Gabriel grinned bitterly. In his eyes Pablo saw the tip of a cold sadness. "The coup d'etat occurred, really, within the next two years. You see, on this settlement a startling thing began to happen. There were monster babies being born in great number. An amazing statistic, a high minority percentage. The deformities followed a certain pattern—limbs and digits missing, sensory organs sometimes missing, too. So it became apparent, you see, that poison had been planted. This was chemical warfare of a type we were not equipped to deal with. You know, don't you, that settlements in our high priority zones are fully equipped with protective devices against most standard forms of chemical warfare—"

Pablo blinked. "*Standard?* That stuff's illegal."

Gabriel's laugh was a hearty belly laugh, mocking but somehow inoffensive. Gabriel looked at him, amused. Pablo could almost have sworn there was a dim light of affection in the eyes. "Pablo, a lot of illegal things go on in wars. Or haven't you heard? Yes, these settlements are equipped with protective devices, and most of the protective provisions are made with children in mind. There are underground nurseries in camouflage, there are—well, I won't bother you with details, *hermano*. Understand that the problem before us was this poison. We were attempting to isolate a chemical defoliant that as a side effect was lethal to fish. We knew some of its components must have a fair-sized half-life, because of the human birth defects occurring so long afterwards. And we could not for the life of us isolate it. So the next step"—he spread his hands in air—"was to determine where they had got this chemical from in the first place. Because we knew, we knew they didn't have the scientific sophistication to produce it themselves. So they must have bought it, or been given it. And if we could trace where the substance came from, the next logical step was to obtain some ourselves." He smiled almost happily. "To steal some, if necessary. Without understanding the cause of a disease, you can't really work effectively on the antidote. Or effect the proper military counter-measures." He leaned forward, voice darkened. "Understand, Pablo, these are security matters.

All this is between you and me—I've used my discretion here, there are no rules breached. But they have been stretched. You understand that?"

Pablo nodded.

Gabriel settled back and continued. "After a period of several years—this brings us to the present—we successfully traced the creator of the defoliant. It was produced and sold by Zachary Chemical Corporation, which is a division of International Communications Enterprises and of which your girlfriend's father is the Chairman of the Board of Directors and the chief stockholder—do you understand?"

"Don't do that," Pablo said dully. "Don't call her my girlfriend."

Gabriel paused. "Excuse me. I'm trying to tell you as briefly as possible. There's no need to get trapped in a lot of details."

"Of course."

"Very well. I suggest to you that there's more going on in that compound there, that area near the dig, than just evaluation of archaeological artifacts. You see, this defoliant has been through a long, careful process of testing and refinement over a period of years. And our settlement was little more than an initial sort of test. We believe that the next full-scale test will be a larger one and that it will take place here, Pablo, on Bellagua, and if I were sure I would suggest to you that perhaps it's already begun."

Pablo shook his head. His hands wrapped around each other between his thighs, palms clammy, nervous. He looked to Gabriel for something else. Why, he was saying, how, I don't understand. Gabriel talked some more. He talked about defoliants and their various wartime uses. And how, for a defoliant of this nature, the ideal environment to test its full potential would be a large area of jungle terrain. Because only there would the actual extent of its potency be realized. Pablo was shaking his head again saying no, no, I don't understand. What's the purpose of this? If they defoliate some of that jungle, then what? He looked at Gabriel unbelievingly.

"Is all this really supposed to be top secret? And if it is, how in hell is it supposed to be *kept* that way, for Christ's sake? I mean, do they expect they can just strip a wide area of foliage and that it will go completely unnoticed or something?"

"Not unnoticed, necessarily. Although they do have the rationale behind them"—Gabriel smiled—"that there are organized groups of armed terrorists based in the interior, so that's some sort of justification for proceeding in case they need to justify things later. Not unnoticed, Pablo. Only un*pro-tested*. A crucial difference, as history would show you."

Pablo felt sun on his neck, his hair. He was perspiring heavily again, shirt soaked under the arms and down the chest. "What about the govern-

ment here? I mean, I'm assuming this would all be news to them, right?—
Saying it's true. Then what? Are you going to tip them off or what?"

"That's problematical."

"What the fuck does that mean?"

Gabriel sighed. "Zachary Chemical is an American corporation, *hermano. American.* You can assume that this kind of research—if it's not
government sponsored, is somewhere being government condoned."

"Yeah—so? These are the same fucks who crippled your goddamned
children." His voice was loud, too loud. He didn't care. "Don't you owe
them a shaft in the back? Or doesn't that fall under the realm of Zionism?"

"Listen to me, Pablo." His tone was quieter now, and darker. His whole
face had darkened, in fact; the mouth, the eyes. Maybe it was just the first
beginnings of evening shadow, maybe he needed a shave. But the darkness
was there, a lurking kind of threat, or sorrow. "Listen. Yes they sold this
weapon to an enemy. Yes. And the government condoning them—their
own government, and yours—also sells many weapons to *us.* Do you understand?" His voice had gotten angry now for the first time, bordering on
out of control. "Do you understand that?"

They were silent a long while.

"Tell me, Gabi." Something caught in his chest. It was that childhood
name, one he'd used so often in baby chants it had become imbedded in
the recesses of his memory. "What about Bellagua? What happens to them
here?" He paused. "The babies, I mean."

He caught his brother's sigh again. It was a long, low sigh. It was the
bottom part of the chord sounded by those dying twigs. And Gabriel was
searching the air now, not meeting his eyes. He was looking for words.
Finally he had them. "I'll always be sorry," he said quietly, "for the people
of Bellagua." And he struggled some more. He was forcing these words
out—they were of his own making, and he'd always hate them and hate
what they made of him, too. But own them he did. "My responsibility is
to my own people, Pablo. That's all. My own people and there aren't so
many left. Still they're mine. You, for instance." He smiled. "Even you."

"No thanks," Pablo said bitterly.

"It's true," Gabriel whispered.

Then Pablo said nothing. After a while he just nodded.

"She's disowned, you know." Pablo blurted it suddenly, senselessly. He
was sorry as soon as the words were out.

"Who? You mean your—you mean Karlen?"

"Yeah. Her father's disowned her." *Because,* he wanted to say, and then
tell Gabriel the reason, the private, personal reason that faded to stupidity

and insignificance in the face of all this. But he kept things to himself. Top secret. Top priority. Right, Pablo. He kept his lips buttoned and, facing Gabriel, he was proud.

"Still," Gabriel smiled tiredly, "she's an only child. Perhaps she's not so totally disowned as you think."

Then Pablo had it. It shot up through him with a vicious, awful taste, and froze him a minute. So he was unable to speak, contemplating it, contemplating the possibility of her knowledge—contemplating the possibility of her disappearance as an act of mission, a crazy act. Or maybe not so crazy. Would anyone have done it? For a lover? Maybe not crazy, for her. Maybe merely an act of defiance, and of love. He kept his face straight, looked fully at Gabriel. "Do you think she knows?"

Gabriel seemed to consider this seriously, and for the first time. Then he discounted it—Pablo saw it leave his consideration almost immediately—and shrugged. "I suppose there's that possibility. I don't know that it matters though. And if she knew, why would she go near the interior, Pablo?"

Evening was coming down with the odd, heavy silence carried over from late afternoon. Sitting there, he watched Gabriel clean everything away—the white twigs, the paper. Sometimes it occurred to him to ask questions: how did you get that stuff? How did you steal it?—Or: how did you know about her? And me? But he never voiced these questions. Some snatch of a phrase flew through him again bleakly—*certain things can be done easily, you know*—he wondered where he was getting these phrases from. Had he heard them elsewhere or did they come from some internal file previously untapped? Then Pablo laughed to himself. The answer was obvious: movies, Pablo, movies. You still think life is a motion picture and you're getting all this crap from old gangster flicks. For a second he felt better. Then the reality of things hit him full force, and sitting there he felt unable to move.

"You have reservations on a plane leaving tonight," said Gabriel. "In three hours. I'll see that you get to the airport."

"I still don't get it. Why should I leave?"

Gabriel had come around behind him. His hand fell on Pablo's shoulder, fingered the leather strap attached to Alfredo. "You don't understand Pablo, do you?"

"No. That's right. I don't understand."

"The pictures." His hand tapped heavily, a slap more than a caress. "You've taken certain pictures on West Reef?" Beneath his hand Pablo's neck grew tight. Beyond that there was no response. Gabriel touched more gently now. He reminded himself that much of what he touched was flesh like his—they were of the same family, same blood. The same people. And he squeezed his brother's shoulder with affection. The pictures, he told him, the pictures, Pablo. Do you understand now why you have to leave?

Pablo turned, looked up to his brother. "What about her?"

Gabriel bent down so they were facing each other. He set a hand on each of Pablo's shoulders. "Listen, *hermano*. What about her? Let me tell you the official line. She doesn't exist. That's what. Do you understand?"

Pablo did. "Fuck you," he said quietly. "I've got pictures of her, too."

"Good. Then the best thing is to keep them safe. That's the best thing for you. And for her."

Pablo shrugged Gabriel's hand off miserably. Three hours. He had a crazy urge to get up and walk out. He and Alfredo. Come on buddy, we can do it. Just up and leave with no spare clothes, no passport, no money and no name—he and his camera. What was stopping him, he wondered. Maybe fear of what would happen—Gabriel's intimations had sent him into a silent sort of panic, and there were those threatening snatches of half-remembered lines swimming through his head. But he realized now it wasn't fear of physical harm. No. That didn't seem real to him—he'd never experienced it really—so he couldn't fully fear it. The terror was of leaving all his identification behind, all the material things that bound him to the planet, gave him a number, clothes, a passport, a suitcase. A way of signing his name. A brother. And he couldn't walk out on all that now. Couldn't do what Karlen had done—just step into the unknown with nothing but her body and a single laughable weapon and a certain unshakeable desire. Or belief. No he couldn't. Not for money. Not for love. She was a better man than he. Pablo laughed. And for a minute he hated himself. He felt his own hands clammy one on the other, useless hands.

"Check your suitcase," said Gabriel. "Make sure you know what's there. Remember to lock it, too."

Pablo wouldn't know, later, what it was exactly that made him do it. He'd never done it before—against his policy to waste good film. But there he was, retreating to the bathroom with Alfredo, opening the camera in the dark while he sat on the mammoth tub's edge. He rolled the film with still a quarter of it unused. He took a fresh roll from his pocket and put it in, snapped the case shut, clicked and clicked, advancing unused film until half the roll had been advanced and wasted. The roll he'd removed he wrapped in toilet paper.

He unbuckled his belt and the pants slid down. There in close humid dark with no one else around, Pablo felt his vulnerability acutely, as if the invisible mirror had eyes to measure him. He grabbed the stretch band of his underwear and reached in. The tissue-wrapped roll was deposited carefully, lodged as an irritating lump against his balls.

The elastic waistband snapped back in place. Pablo pulled his pants up, heard faint belt buckle sounds in the dark. He slung Alfredo on again, patted the camera bulk gently, almost tenderly, as it hung against his abdomen. *Mi amigo.* Alfredo, old friend. He sat again on the curled lip of the tub and felt them in his pants—photographs. He waited until all the sweat subsided and he was breathing normally. The souls he'd stolen were in his safe-keeping. You'd have to kick his nuts off to get to them.

ANOTHER MILITARY COUP

When he followed Gabriel out the door, down those Grecian steps to the street, he was packed. He wasn't surprised to see a newly polished car waiting. Mercedes. Not a hint of decay on the chrome.

He'd made several trips to the bathroom before leaving—the wine, he'd said apologetically, and then the coffee, Gabi—and he stashed a few more rolls down in the underwear. Now, he bulged uncomfortably between the thighs. But not noticeably. Jesus. What if he got hard? There was always that possibility. He thought of all the comic potential of that situation and despite himself he laughed. No, Pablo, no. Keep it in your pants this time. Then he felt sober, bitter, and afraid. Sweat dribbled down his back. Was there a sort of acrid odor to him now? What you always read about in crap thrillers—what was it?—the *smell of fear*. Sure. Maybe he smelled that way.

Whoever was driving didn't get out. Gabriel held the door open. Pablo settled on the seat, sliding in damp heat. He looked at the back of the chauffeur's head. Black. A brown man. Would the face turn around, smile? Would it be someone he recognized? Suddenly, that thought seemed horrifying. A baby face. No eyes. He shivered against the sweating seat, patted the bulge in his trousers.

"Are you all right, Pablo?"

He turned to Gabriel saying yes, sure, why? Because you were making strange sounds now, Gabriel told him. Little sudden sounds, like a bird.

Pablo made himself grin. Gabriel forced a smile too and the chauffeur nodded as if in silent agreement to something. The car started.

It slid through Sagrabél's only quiet streets—the streets of foreign-owned residences, streets of privilege. Pablo saw it all slip by under the occasional street lamp: carefully tended palms lining the curbs, high fences grown over with tropical hanging plants, the rare sight of a tended flower garden or a front yard fountain of imported marble. The buildings themselves were a pastiche of different styles and sensibilities. European neo-classical. Swiss chalet style. Some American's vision of a suitable driftwood-type abode. Somebody else's version of rococo. Spanish stucco. It went on and on, each place true to its own word and, in its own self-contained universe, in impeccable taste; taken together, the neighborhood was an atrocity of bad planning. And the street lamps themselves glowed dimly, seemed to melt, disintegrate. He noticed they were surrounded by flying things, moths and insects weaving in vast numbers around each light, wisp-like bodies flitting across the bright background.

A corner was turned, and another. Approaching the embassy district. Things should be shut down for the night. Pablo was surprised to see military vehicles parked here and there, an olive drab truck stopped carelessly half on, half off a sidewalk, headlights on and uniformed men spilling out the sides, stalking along the curbs, rifles ready and held down by their sides. Many of the faces were white. He realized this with a shock: white men in Bellaguan military dress, many white faces sprinkled even among the uniforms of the Civil Guard, both uniforms blending brown-streaked shades into one another as the lines of men shuffled, moved, prowled in seeming disorganization along the streets.

He thought they were nearing the American Embassy, and it popped into his head that maybe he ought to say Stop. Maybe he ought to tell them Wait a minute, let me out here. And he'd just sit on the steps of the American Embassy and wait until morning, and when the first person showed up for work he'd explain, tell them he must speak with the Ambassador. Or with somebody of influence. Yes, *influence*. He'd explain the situation. About the pictures. About Karlen, what she'd said and how she might be roaming around there in the goddamned jungle and had to be saved. He'd tell them what he knew.

Pablo ran a hand over his face, breathed out in exasperation at his own terror. He didn't know why he was so afraid, just that terror had struck and carried him away on its dark cutting edge. He told himself it was all fantasy. He was a man traveling back to the States. An American returning from a business trip. A photographer, on assignment. He was legitimate, damn it.

Legitimate. And no one would hurt him. Why would they want to? He was a harmless man. Gentle. She'd said so herself.

The car slowed, stopped. Flashlights glared against the windshield, military faces peered in and Gabriel was speaking quietly to one of them, showing some papers. Then they were waved on ahead and accelerated along the avenue.

The streets were suddenly narrower. It was as simple as the turning of a few more corners—they were in a different world of smells, people, noise. A scrawny, feather-thin chicken clucked across the road in front of them, causing the driver to curse and mutter something in another language. Pablo closed his eyes and breathed everything in: sweat, his own and that of a thousand other bodies parading aimlessly through city streets on a hot summer night in the tropics. The food they ate, rotting vegetable skins. An occasional bloody package of spoiled meat. The odor of rum, cheap beer. The noisy clutter of many languages. Skin colors darker than his, darker than his brother's.

He opened his eyes and saw that the bloody package of meat he was staring at along the curb was an article of clothing. A shirt maybe, crumpled and blood-saturated. The noise was not one of spoken languages but of panic, feet running, and he heard the sound of sirens again, from far away the blast of guns. The little brother inside of him wanted to yell out then: Gabi, Gabi, help. Tell me what is happening Gabi. *Dígame, dígame. Por favor.*

Gabriel reached to roll Pablo's window shut. He leaned forward to speak to the driver; soon they were turning more corners still and the real Sagrabél was behind them. They were cutting clear of the city altogether, rolling silently onto the small highway—Bellagua's pride and joy—that led to the airport. Along this road more green trucks were haphazardly stationed, more soldiers wandering around waving firearms. They were stopped once and Pablo sank further down against the seat, stiffened silently. Again, the low mutterings of conversation between Gabriel and another military face, the presentation of certain papers, the waving on. Acceleration along the smooth-rolling highway.

Pablo saw Gabriel check through the rear window occasionally. The swivel-view eyes never stopped moving. When they weren't scrutinizing the rear they were searching ahead, to the sides.

"Almost there, *hermano.*"

Pablo saw the large, bright-colored signs they were approaching—directions to the airport in Spanish, French, English, German. He was an American businessman going to the airport, he told himself. That was all.

He would be sure to have a pleasant flight. The geometric array of lights ahead glowed gently, invitingly. The closer they got, the clearer was the ripping sound of planes overhead. He thought that among the jets he could hear the put-putting whirr of helicopter blades, but he wasn't sure.

The small airport did remarkable business in season. Linked so closely with foreign trade, it was the one extension of the Bellaguan government that worked efficiently, processing the necessary papers and shuffling people through lines with a minimum of delay. Customs was notoriously lax. Officials posed behind their counters like the doormen along the East Bay hotel strip: beaming, pleasant, carefully instructed that they were the first representatives of their nation, the first welcome to sun-hungry tourists who expected dark people to be always serving them, smiling.

The terminal building loomed larger and brighter as they drew close. Glass doors and wide windows of glass exposed the internal ticket counters, information booths, car rental offices, people milling around; and if it was not the height of the season, business was still brisk. The added presence of armed Civil Guard at each counter, each corner, did not seem to interfere with the flow of movement. The dark-skinned men in uniform; the white-skinned in casual attire or business dress, dangling attaché cases along with flight bags, the newlyweds who'd come off-season, the lovers who on the spur of the moment decided it was a better deal, round-trip from Miami, than Grand Cayman.

Gabriel shoved a ticket envelope into his hand.

"You have time until your flight. We'll be in touch."

Pablo stepped out of the car and air smacked him with a sickening hot thump. He set his suitcase down. Alfredo tapped his belly. He looked at the ticket in his hand. He felt calmer now, mind set. He didn't watch the car as it drove off. All that fear of his, it had been brought on by too much wine, too much intensity, the oddness of things. He was going to beat this rap, too. Another military coup for the nation of Bellagua—that's what it looked like—and he, for one, would get out while the getting was good. He picked up his luggage and walked into the terminal. The sudden calculated cool of the place was nearly sensual.

He stood at the end of a line. It wasn't too long. Get to the head of the line and you'd check your baggage, receive a slip with number stamped on it. You'd tell them whether you wanted to sit in the smoking section or not, whether you wanted an aisle or a window seat. It was all so simple. He felt a sudden rush of gratitude for this, the certainty of his knowledge. It reattached him to earth. He found himself silently counting off the few minutes it took each person in line to arrange things with the people behind the counter. Just a few minutes. They were pretty efficient. And he was feeling better all the time.

No smoking, he told the dark-faced man. He ignored the Civil Guard stationed just to his right, the soldier's eyes dully examining. He ignored the dull face and the smell of the gun. A window seat, please. Something inside him froze momentarily at the thought that window seats were claustrophobic, left you less opportunity to escape. Escape from what? He told himself he was full of shit. Proudly, he didn't change his mind. He weighed and checked his suitcase—no customs clearance of luggage necessary on this end. They'd tear things apart in Miami, maybe, but Bellagua didn't care what you were taking out of the country. Maybe they were used to things constantly being taken, so they no longer bothered to look. He grinned happily. Convenience. Such a pleasure. Got his baggage check, got his ticket torn and stamped. Only fifteen minutes to go before boarding. He made sure of the flight number and gate. There weren't many gates. It was, after all, a small country. Civil Guard everywhere. He kept Alfredo and his small bag of equipment. His mouth was dry, tongue grating against his teeth.

Pablo headed for customs.

He stood in line again. As he got closer to the desk something went off in his head. That alarm. He heard the ringing. It kept blaring through him, became louder when he approached the desk, gazed at the flat, fluorescence-dulled face of the official sitting there and presented his passport. He sweated again, though it was a little chilly. Now, he thought, now. No. Please. But the official smiled pleasantly. He stamped a page in the passport booklet routinely, closed it and handed it back to Pablo. The alarm died. Pablo breathed with ease and a smile began to curve his lips. For all his so-called intuition, everything was smooth as cake. And now he was just about free. Through with all of this madness. No more panic, he warned himself. No more.

He wandered casually toward the gate, picked up his boarding pass. He realized how much his testicles hurt. A constant, sore, pinched sensation; well, he'd have to bear with it. At least until he could get into the toilet after take-off, give himself a breather.

The thought flicked across his mind like the nagging end of a miniature whip: what the hell had she meant by saying he had a little queer in him? Was it some way he had? A way of moving, maybe? There was that old saying about how one could spot another one. He didn't know how true stuff like that was; still, it made him a little uneasy. The bitch. And suddenly he felt a gaping hole where his guts should be. Karlen. She was gone, the bitch, gone—lost—he didn't know. And he would not see her again, that face of hers, in the flesh.

When someone brushed his arm by mistake, Pablo intentionally looked away. The feeling against his arm had been a brief, hard one. The last person he'd really touched had been her.

The door was opening, sign lighting. The flight number, and the words BOARDING NOW. He shuffled out the door with the rest of the crowd. Heat slammed into him again when he stepped out of the terminal. He saw the waiting plane, accordion-like steps attached for boarding, attendants standing at the bottom of those steps to tear tickets, take boarding passes, smile stewardess greetings. No military here. He was home free. He felt his feet on the paved ground. His soles squeaked. It seemed to Pablo that he heard the squeaking as a single, isolated sound; that everything else had dropped to a lower pitch around him and he was in a partially insulated tunnel, moving with careful slow symmetry toward this beckoning goal. The steps, the plane. Safe passage. He licked his lips. They had the texture of cracked paper.

"Pablo?"

Yes, he replied, though it was not a voice he recognized.

He saw that his feet were departing from the shuffling line of boarding passengers. He was veering away from the crowd's bulk, away from the plane, toward some corner of the building. A hangar. He realized there was an insistent, firm pressure on his left shoulder, another on his right. Glancing down he saw the pair of boots marching calmly next to him.

They stopped out of sight of the plane. He kept his gaze turned down, saw a shadow fall darker than the evening across his shoes. Then he looked up to his right.

It wasn't an extraordinary face he saw. It was a bland face. But it was white, and this shocked him, shot a chill through him so that he wanted to exclaim loudly but made no sound. And he could have sworn he saw something like a smile—a nearly gentle one—flicker across the bland white face.

Pablo thought of speaking. But all that sounded was a soft whisper.

"Don't," he said.

It came suddenly. He didn't feel it. Still he was on his back on the ground and there was a numb, shattered sensation along his left side. He blinked up at the other man and in a sudden flash of light he couldn't understand he saw that this man was full-lipped, blue-eyed. He was raising his leg, boot poised, just so. Pablo saw it happen slowly. Plenty of time, he thought.

Plenty. Then something tore and he was all doubled up. He looked once more to see the young, bleak-faced goon who was kicking him apart.

Someone screamed, a sudden, short agony that ended abruptly. He moved his lips to see if he'd made that sound, but his lips moved against sharp pieces of metal, half a lens, a broken strap. There was another scream, this one longer. Someone moaning. Oh God, he thought, oh *Dios* oh *Dios* no no no. No. *Por favor* no. *Por favor* make this stop *por favor*. Stop it please, please make this stop now.

He'd been staring up unseeing at a white face, then another, and one by one they seemed to burst into blood in front of him, eyes roll into their heads before they slumped away.

Running feet scraped on cement. He heard the ragged, scratching sound. And there was light, plenty of it, cutting through shadow. Another man towered over things now, straddling him. As the fingers bent closer he saw the dirt-stained, red-smeared face of Gabriel. Gabriel reaching tentatively to touch his forehead, wipe something away with a motion bordering on tender.

"*Las fotografías, Pablo. ¿Dónde son?*"

Pablo felt a hand slide down his thigh. His own hand. Must be. He grabbed his crotch and squeezed. *Aquí, Gabi.* His eyelids slipped shut.

AMBERGRIS

Through trees, Kaz walked. She felt hanging strands of moss brush her shoulders. There was a gentle, sad kind of sucking sound each time a sole touched the ground's wet green fungus. At hip height, the hand-stitched leather case was worn, brown; it had been caressed, had absorbed sweat, resin, spilled ketchup, baby oil, shampoo and perfume, bad beer, good champagne, even blood.

Two men walked in front of her. One brought up the rear. They were slight, quick-moving men whose skins were varying dark shades. Each wore dreary, beaten green khaki trousers stuffed into the tops of outmoded combat boots cracking with wear, each wore a colorless shirt and carried rifles as out of date as the boots. Their teeth were all rotting away, gums diseased—it was the first thing she'd noticed when one of them had stepped out from the trees at the designated spot, smiled and introduced himself in hesitating English as Captain something-or-other of the Army of the People of Bellagua—she'd forgotten his name, and now was too embarrassed to ask. Too embarrassed? Sometimes Kaz surprised herself. Not often, but sometimes.

Closer.

She could reach out to feel darkness drip; it was there on every leaf's underside. Bugs glimmered and slithered across the tops of boots. When she reached for a canteen top, leeches settled contentedly on her fingers. She opened a hand and the palm was dotted with baby leeches. In the unmoving air she could smell the men; she could smell herself, and underneath the stale flatness of sweat many days old could smell leaves around them, the trees, stems bursting with a milky bitter substance and a stench of perpetual decay. Kaz moved in silence broken by the suck of each footstep, the occasional whispers of men she didn't know.

Usually, they ate on the move—dried strands of something they handed to her, she in turn would reach into a pouch of the leather vest she wore, come out with four dried strands of something else and with green-toothed grins they'd share it—they slept for brief periods and one would remain awake, always on guard. They never slept long enough to dream. So after a few days of this Kaz began to feel disoriented, slightly off balance. In fact, it wasn't so; she was in the best shape of her life, knew she wouldn't have come here any other way. The feelings of continual irritability and vertigo were illusory, she knew, as were the moments when everything seemed to stretch blankly colorless all around. Inside herself, at these times, she was smooth and clean and dark, a lightless expanse against which nothing could be differentiated. She'd blink, snap to dizzily; dark hands would wave dead-smelling strips of stiff jerky in front of her and she'd nod, take the time to run a dirty sleeve over her eyes to wipe off sweat, hold the jerky in one numb hand and bite, untasting. *Closer*, she told herself. *Closer*.

It had become a voice in her head. She spoke to it. She listened for bird cries but none came. And the rest of the time Kaz walked in silence.

"'When suddenly from out the very heart of this plague,'" she whispered.

She glanced up guiltily. Three dark pairs of eyes had fixed themselves on her.

"'There stole a faint stream of perfume,'" she said. She smiled at them all, a little apologetically. She nodded, shrugged. Okay, she whispered, I'm okay. After a while they continued—don't mind me, she said to Captain something-or-other, I am all right, not sick really—and when her whispers mumbled out to fill the sucking, pulling dark silence they ignored her this time, and the next, and the next. Polite of them, she thought. She was grateful for such good manners.

"'Which flowed through the tide of bad smells,'" she said, "'without being absorbed by it.'"

Someone waved a canteen in front of her face. She squinted to see. Thankfully she drank, and calmly continued walking.

"'As one river will flow into and then along with another,'" she said. Suck. Pluck. Step down again into fungus.

"'Without at all blending with it for a time.'"

Long, long ago, Raina had told her, before recorded history, the most significant power was the power to bear children. Think how difficult it was to perpetuate such a frail species back then! A hostile environment—every other species far better adapted than human beings—and all they had going for them was the ability to make the crudest of rudimentary implements, thumbs for grasping, head-on as well as peripheral vision—oh, things were rough, Kaz. We don't know how rough they were. Take it for granted that they would not have drawn the conceptual connection between sexual intercourse and pregnancy. So-called primitive cultures today invariably fail to make the connection. The power to bear children was synonymous with the power of creation itself! Pregnancy was a miracle. Magic. A woman had the gift of magic. Creation. Destruction. So along with matrilineage you get a goddess of creation—love? of course—and of destruction—war, the Huntress—because every society fashions its most powerful gods after the most powerful members of the society itself. For all the thousands of centuries before recorded history, just think Kaz, gods were female. Mother Sun. Mother Sky. Mother Moon. Mother Harvest. Mother Blood. Mother Sea. Mother of the Universe. The oldest layers of some of the Middle Eastern excavation sites prove it—goddess statuettes everywhere you turn. You fought the wars, gorgeous. You married the male children off with dowries. You owned all the stocks and bonds.

"Yeah?" Kaz challenged. "And I still do."

Raina had paused then, grinned slyly, teasingly. "Courtesy of the patriarchy."

"*C'est vrai.* But I told you, my father's nuts. Really, it's more than neurosis with him. You can say all you want about the sociohistorical reasons but the fact remains, Raina, he's nuts, and I'll bet you any amount of money the private reasons are more outstanding than all the sociohistorical ones—"

"You'll bet me?"

Betcha.

Ah, Raina said quietly, *but I don't want your money.*

Poor Kaz. What, then, could she bet? One-on-one volleyball, maybe, or basketball. But Raina won every time. The only thing Raina could not ever master, it seemed, was table tennis. And Kaz was a wizard, no doubt about it; she took comfort in the fact that this was also the one game to utterly elude Babe Didrickson Zaharias. She'd practice sometimes with extra venom—those topspinners felt good—take *that*, Babe. And *that.*

Betcha. Get over here right now, Goddess. Look at this, see this necklace? purchased with the medium of patriarchal exchange—do you like it? For safekeeping. Do goddesses need protection? Tell me, do they accept it from mere mortals? Turn around. Lift up your hair—that's right—there you go.

I touched it all over. To keep you safe. Sometimes I hate all this adventuring stuff, Raina. I think about the things you do and it makes me a nervous wreck.

But she liked it, too. Something in her yearned for it. They'd kept quiet a long time, separate, looking calmly at one another, and while they looked this knowledge passed between them. Half smiling, Raina fingered the softly glittering silver chain around her neck.

Occasionally, Raina told her, a goddess would mate with a brother or son. Note Astarte and Baal. Centuries later, Apollo and Artemis. Inherent—Raina stated proudly—inherent in the worship of primarily female divinities was the practice of polytheism. Women knew then, too—and sensed even now, although the instinct had been systematically suppressed throughout centuries—woman had always known that survival was a social event. Even among the gods. Raina winked at Kaz then; she'd anticipated a question: why not monotheism around *Her*, too. Because, because. No being is an island, Kazzy. Not even a superior being. And the coming of all these male gods brought with it a different sort of hierarchy, a pantheon in which supremacy was attained by the actual murder of other gods, or goddesses. Under the rule of the Goddess, there's been plenty of divine quarrels, of course. Plenty of blood-letting, plenty of leading the human hordes into and through battle. But murder among gods? Rarely. And then Kaz understood what Raina was getting at: Raina believed it was the Goddess Herself who had been hunted down time and again and, as weapons became iron and fields were tilled for profit instead of subsistence, time and again She was slain.

Normally, Kaz was not a person who'd thought about much outside of herself. Not that she was all that careless about others; one on one, she knew how to share. But she did not often contemplate the world. Rich, and beautiful, she'd grown up devoid of history.

Even with Raina, her initial urge was to forget about all this history stuff. One on one—that was the way Kaz liked things best; but when she lay beside Raina she was forced to embrace an imagination that spanned the globe, conceived of great possibilities and then set out to make them physical reality. To feel *reality* as she conceived of it in the ideal, Raina would risk her life, shake an ancient, insufficient weapon defiantly in the face of the void out there, dance on the brink of things with no balancing pole. Embracing her, Kaz embraced the world and began to see it for the first time. She had no choice in the matter. Raina rarely rested, even in sleep; she fought through her dreams, and Kaz would lie awake watching. Raina had great ideas, expansive plans, endless self-confidence; she'd been everywhere, spoke every language, touched the Goddess in dusty sun-baked excavation pits with her own hands, knew all of history, knew every good champagne, played every game but Ping-Pong. Restless, she was also relentless—relentless in her intellect, in her knowledge, endlessly questioning, testing, dragging herself and anyone else who happened to be around through many hells and many heavens; she was childish, threw tantrums; she was a great bully when it came to getting her way. You took or left her—Kaz realized that from the start—but you would not change her. She might compromise superficially at times, but there was something fixed and unchanging about her. So you'd put up, grow to accept this about her, and finally you must also learn to adore it—sure, Kaz realized all that from the start. Because one on one was, after all, her favorite game, and even if she had a certain disdain for the world she was nobody's fool. Take it or leave it. Kaz might pout sometimes, throw her own tantrums, make her own threats. But she never seriously considered leaving. The possibility of it seemed more terrifying, somehow, than life with Raina could ever be, even though life with Raina could be terrifying. Raina was a sort of high, something giddily exhilarating, and very, very precarious. *Nice and precarious.* Kaz couldn't go back to what she'd been before—change was indeed irrevocable. Life without Raina would no longer satisfy. She was hooked; she had fallen; she would not find her feet again because the old pair of feet had vanished in the wave of transformation she'd brought upon herself; old diversions would not suffice. No more blasé. Kaz was in love. She had it bad.

There was no choice but to keep going—never mind that the way was no longer safe, or easy. Life without Raina would be so much less. And if Raina was exhausting, Kaz had stepped in close enough to see that Raina exhausted herself above all. The thing Raina had to endure, to prove she was equal to time and again—that thing was Raina. Raina must endure Raina; she must forever set herself out to do battle with Raina: she must caress and defy and ultimately survive Raina; and she must come through at the other end whole, and sane, and walk on the earth again, again be Raina; no warrior now, but a lover.

From the void, she brought back an ivory tooth, and a thin chain of silver to string it on. Beaming, almost shy, she handed it to Kaz. Spoils of battle.

Emerging from quilt folds of white fur she opened both arms. *Peekaboo.* Her embrace was gentle, very delicate—Kaz had been surprised at first—but sometimes what sparked through her fingertips was a strange urgency. *I see you,* Kaz teased. *Shhh,* Raina whispered, *stay. Stay with me. Will you? Stay awhile.*

"Your father wants to see me." She'd tossed a letter on the table.

"My father? You're joking."

"No. He says right here—this is his handwriting, isn't it—"

"Don't go." Kaz panicked. She was gripped with a feeling of horror—for Raina, for herself. The world she'd never much thought of before loomed suddenly large, and against it she saw them both, suddenly small. But Raina teased with her look, stuck out a tongue.

"Oh, why not?"

"Oh, *why?* He hates your guts, honey. He thinks you've corrupted me—"

"And he's right!"

"Shut up!" She laughed, forced to despite her fear—Raina had a way of doing that. But the laugh stopped, Kaz was afraid and it was serious. "Look, Raina, he's nuts, I told you. The man is definitely—look, I just don't want you to get hurt."

"Hurt?" *Who*, Raina's eyes said, *me?* She looked a little incredulous.

"Don't go. Just don't go. He's disowned me, anyway. Not that it matters, I still own about a third of him—"

"How thrilling."

"Sure. Just don't. Don't even write back." She reached across the table for Raina's hand. She tugged the thumb, and each finger, and covered it with her own. "He's got—he thinks you took me away from him."

Raina was silent awhile. The dark eyes narrowed slightly, examining, and when she spoke, she spoke quietly. Something in her tone of voice was a little frightening. "He's got what, Kaz?"

"Nothing."

"What's he got?"

"Money, okay? Money, honey, now let's drop it."

"What's he got, Kaz? Heads of cattle? T.B.? A dose of clap? Tell me. His own private army? Three football teams?" She grinned a little. Beginning to feel relief, Kaz did too. "Fourteen mansions?" Raina smiled. "Seventeen wives? Twelve chests of gold? Fifty hotels? A hundred cars and a thousand chauffeurs? A motion picture company? Twenty-five newspapers? What's he got, Kazzy, tell me. Something to scare you?" The smile faded, hands moved around on the table to hold Kaz's between them. "Tell me all about it. When did he? Did he try to touch you?"

"No," Kaz said faintly, "no. Once." She looked away, crying.

There was no great scandal to report. It had been such a small thing: a kiss on the cheek one hot afternoon; no one in the whole big house but them, Daddy and Daddy's Little Girl, Ping-Pong table set up in the expansive rec-reation-room-cool of a converted basement, Pepsi Cola getting lukewarm in cans along the table's rim. Outside was western Florida—a clear, white-hot sky, occasional bird shrieking by overhead, the egg-shaped pool limpid blue, surface unbroken by any breeze. A kiss on the cheek. He'd watched her practice serves all morning. Could she have told by the pressure of his lips, then, that he'd try to turn it into something more? Later, she'd question whether he'd known himself; and, if he had, question whether she had also known and simply hidden the immediate knowledge from herself. But suddenly the kiss had crept down to her neck, suddenly hands were there too, playing lightly at her hips. She plucked them nervously away but they returned, and while she was instantly repelled there was also something about it all that fascinated her— some attraction? Some attraction to the edge of horror? Undeniably, it was an attraction to *repulsion*—but undeniably an *attraction*. He was her father, hair graying at the sides. She knew this could not be happening. He was her father, encouraging little Karlen the tomboy, rearing her to be bold and agile and unafraid—her father pressing repugnantly close to her—those fingers at her blouse fumbling with buttons were her father's fingers. She heard a far-off gull cry sadly, and for a moment thought the air in the room had changed—a draft had swept in, some tiny black speck inside her sighed no, no, please, no. This could not be. The racket dropped to her side; her hand clenched its stem. No Daddy. Don't. Those were her father's fingers gently touching her nipples; those thick, wet lips at her neck were her father's lips. And the little black speck inside broke loose, grew suddenly bigger—that's how she'd felt it then, that's how she would tell it later to her lover—it was the black speck that possessed her hand, made it quiver strongly on the racket stem, made the racket lift, draw back, come down and around to the side. It slammed his arms, his shoulders, the side of his face. Came down again on his hands, crushing them against his chest in pain and surprise, again, to the side of his face gone suddenly red, then black and blue. The speck ballooned, possessed her completely for that instant: it was a great black balloon of outrage, of nausea, fascination, guilt and love. When he stepped back, blinking, she held the racket out in front of her like a crucifix to a vampire while her other hand held together the folds of her unbuttoned blouse—no longer little Karlen, but a woman who owned stocks and bonds, who would draw her own father's blood. He turned quickly and left. After a while she heard the faint sound of water running through pipes. A shower. She'd gone outside to sit by the pool, stretched fully on the lounge chair, racket clutched to cover her breasts. She'd fallen asleep, woken up with slight sunburn, she remembered. The subject would not be broached again in word or deed.

Breakfast getting cold, table deserted, Kaz sat in the big leather chair she'd first sat in upon entering Number Twelve, long ago. She shared the chair with Raina; it was big enough for them both.

—*But I'm okay now. It's okay.*

This sounded stupid, coming out that way—stupid, yet somehow necessary. After all, she *was* okay. It hadn't been much of anything; more of a blur in her memory now, an attempted violation that, thankfully, had gone unfulfilled. Why then did it feel like violation?

Pressed close to her, Raina cried.

Kaz had never seen her cry before. And she was surprised at the nature of these tears because they weren't what she might have expected—not rage, or frustration. The sound was a gentle kind of sorrow. It was the way you wept when something you loved had been wounded—helplessly, painfully. It was the way women wept.

Feverish, slogging through mossy mud and dodging strands of hanging fungus, Kaz kept walking in line with these soldiers from the Army of the People of Bellagua. Did they know enough about the workings of things, to know that she owned them? That she'd paid for their outmoded combat boots, their illegal automatic rifles? Maybe they knew. They stopped once in a while, attentively; they had strict orders to bring her in alive. But did they know that she was one of the prime financiers of their revolution? And if they knew, could they possibly have known why?

Kaz had reverted to her former identity for a while, for as long as was necessary to complete a few transactions, and Karlen Addams Zachary had taken care of things, sold off some stocks, cashed in some of her daddy's bonds. And she'd made contact with people underground—that vast reservoir of the unseen, the hunted, who with disguises and new passports and old facelifts and self-inflicted scars stalk the land of false identity, always turning to look over a haunted shoulder—all it had taken was a little time. Everything could be done, she knew, with money.

It was the thought of Raina that kept her walking. It was the memory of desire. Desire. Once she had been close to it. But she could not get to that place again, not by herself. Raina pressed close, hovering over her, watching, gently, carefully. *Does it feel good? Does it? Do you feel good now? Now? There. Ah. There. What is it you want. Kazzy? Is this it—this what you wanted? I'll give it to you, all of it, everything. I will give you the core of things, all time, and space. Give you me. Here. Do you like it? The wanting? Lover.*

What was she to do with her beautiful, dominant, arrogant, brilliant Raina? What would she do without her?

The dark, sweating men walking through Bellagua's interior could not know it, but Kaz owned them. She'd bought them all out in order to find her lover, had purchased herself a revolution. Oh, there was nothing she wouldn't finance, no strings she would not pull, no place she would not go, to touch the promise of it again, to quiver once more on the edge of the core of things, one step ahead of the galloping white god that could cover them all, make all things vanish. She was one step ahead, yes. She would step quickly then, keep walking, until she arrived at the edge where Raina waved her spear, waved an arrow, danced. She would keep walking until she got there, then balance on the edge, look down into the void there and see what it was she sought—some sort of finality—Raina.

The men were attentive. They stopped often to give her water, conferred in whispers among themselves. They walked more slowly to accommodate her painful, dizzy pace, and when she fainted they carried her.

THE HELICOPTER

The moon was new, so except for starlight there was darkness. In the air between jungle and stars near-absolute silence was broken by a soft, continual sort of hum. Once in a while a black shape, like a cloud, passed between trees and stars.

The helicopter had shut off its search and landing lights. Its propellors moved with soft speed, a power that, on land, scattered dirt and underbrush. For a while it paused, hovered, then began its gentle descent in one slow, birdlike swoop. As it drifted downward something scattered from its underside: a thick spray of delicate silver-touched drops. In the black air they were almost white. They glowed. When they hit leaves the sound was a hushed, timid sound, like rain.

The helicopter rose again and its liquid emission slowed until there was no more. It swerved, curved an arc in air, headed west. Soon the dark jungle mass below gave way to thin stretches of beach, to rock-lined coast, to the ocean.

Descending rapidly, the chopper hovered over waves a good distance from shore. Silvery, glowing drops leaked from its underside again, briefly. Then ascent began—a swift, abrupt climb nearly straight up, as if scaling a sharp cliff wall. It spun slowly, headed along the coast at a steady, humming clip. After a while its lights went on. They were many-colored, and from the ground the helicopter looked like a sort of pear-shaped insect, its organs glowing pinpoints in the dark.

Over the jungle of the interior was starlit black. The jungle itself made a thicker blackness, untouched by light of any kind; from above, it looked like a vast, sleeping brain, all dark lumps and coils. Until one small area deep in the interior seemed to give a sigh up to the waiting air, a nearly crackling sound, a gentle hissing, like raindrops falling into fire. And then, gradually, this one section of the vast silent brain began to change. It was as if some of the coils had shriveled, lumps melted away. What took its place was a tattered, fibrous hole that glowed in contrast to the surrounding thick darkness. It glowed because it was white. White like foam, or like ash, like fog.

II
OVERTIME

THE TREES

From the air they looked like brown caterpillars crawling methodically along Bellagua's sole highway. The caravan of trucks would slow sometimes, each truck a separate link in the chain inching past Sagrabél toward West Reef. The supply trucks were largest, canvas-shrouded, flaps of the mud-colored canvas slapping up and down with sharp, staccato incessancy in the continuing wind. Here and there the links of supply trucks were broken by a series of smaller links: open-backed convoys swarming with bodies in uniform. Soldiers sat in the trucks, rifles at rest against their shoulders pointing to the sky. Sometimes a bayonette tip glinted in sunlight. Long white kerchiefs flowed out from under helmets. It was the worst of Bellagua's hottest season, a steaming heat that could render all things hopeless.

Sometimes the caterpillar links were smaller still. These were jeeps; in each jeep, mud-brown helmets were occasionally replaced by an officer's hat.

From the ground, explosions could be heard mingled with sudden bursts of machine-gun fire. These seemed to come every few hours. Nothing further could be heard or seen. There was only the tensely pitched tone of machine guns, and sometimes a blasting sound that made it seem as if the air was being torn apart. From the sky, there was only the continual spinning of helicopter propellors. Like giant insects or a flock of clumsy birds, the helicopters would cluster and inch along through air, following the progress of the moving brown chain below. Sometimes they'd fan out slowly, spread across more of the sky like dark clots of cloud.

All this marked the first day of a massive strategic advance. The National Army of Bellagua was moving in on the country's interior. The official purpose: to obliterate terrorism. These terrorists, they had determined, originally derived from one of the splinter groups of the religious movement of Dr. Tristam Saunderson—who was still in protective custody—and now used the interior as their base of operations, calling themselves the Army of the People of Bellagua. Furthermore, the official statement had proclaimed over national radio, furthermore it was a certainty that these terrorists—a disaffected minority—received considerable aid from foreign sources. Otherwise they could never have sustained themselves so long; otherwise they would never dare to mount even the threat of counterattack. And not only were they supplied by foreign sources; it was believed that a great many were foreigners to begin with—mercenaries, criminals from other nations.

The country wasn't officially at war; government statements termed it a civilian action. The government was the military now; all military actions were government actions. The government had a civilian mouthpiece for radio announcements, too, a man named Santigo whom no one could recall seeing photos of in the national press, even before the coup. And there was no national television. But, Santigo explained patiently via radio, let no one be mistaken; this was no state of war—merely a search for criminals, to be followed by the necessary punishment of those who stood in the way of national progress and the well-being of the majority.

Every Bellaguan, though, creeping cautiously once again into the streets of Sagrabél to resume business as usual, knew in his heart what he wouldn't say even over the breakfast table—if, indeed, he owned a table, or had enough food for breakfast—that war was war, and the country was at war. The National Army of Bellagua was at war with the Army of the People of Bellagua. Bellagua was at war with itself.

Edging into the jungle slowly, each boot sole was in search. Perhaps in some hearts a barely understood memory stirred: the awe, the terror of a long-ago Spanish ancestor who had tapped the fly-speckled back of his mule with a stick, wiped sweat from a sunburnt white forehead as he and his conquistador boots, his mule, supplies, slaves, all, drifted into and under a shelter of leaves so green they were nearly black, watched the last gleamings of sunlight vanish behind until the sunlight of Córdoba was less than memory, until the light faded completely from Mediterranean eyes that were homeless without it, and skin paled, hair fell out, flesh hung desiccated from weakening bone and everything crumbled to a rot no longer human; animals ate away the dead flesh and insects the underlying tissue, plants grew over whatever remained and brought it all back, gently, into the earth. Not a sudden death, but a subtle corruption of the body preceded by a breaking of spirit. The slaves had had a name for this time of the spirit crumbling: the time of walking dreams. Wise in the way of those who knew their limitations, they would run back along the trail leading to sunlight before they came face to face with this time, deserting their white masters to the slow, erosive process of dying. The body swayed by minor increments; it inclined toward an inevitable end.

This was not a death such men would expect. They came from the world of empires, where death was dealt in swift, powerful thrusts as an act of will, and blood spilled suddenly. There was no tragedy in this other manner of dying, no honor. It was a death by compilations of tiny erosions, tiny and continual deprivations, until actual death came as one more small step in the process—a female death, dealt by the vast terrain itself which in its denseness, its dampness, was female terrain. It was a terrain foreign to conquistadors. It rose up gently, closed in with the softness of encircling arms. Slowly, slowly, it would urge you down inside of it.

Maybe it was this half-memory that moved them, sometimes, to call out in their sleep. The soldiers of the National Army of Bellagua had never fought a war before. With no comprehension, then, of what was before them, they fell back on dimly remembered cultural truths, and basic training could be lost completely in an instant of real terror. The white men—foreigners all—who moved with them, couldn't understand why for no reason a Bellaguan soldier would drop to the ground, rocking back and forth on his knees, gun tossed down and face hidden by dark brown hands. The words mumbled in singsong chants were babblings; they seemed to be no language at all. One of the American mercenaries swore, the first time it happened, that the guy was speaking in tongues. The second or third time, though—the fourth time, the hundredth time—he understood it as the language of panic and a great, undisguised disgust began to grow inside him. The other white men reacted similarly. In bars back in Sagrabél, the fighting prowess of the National Army had quickly become the subject of endless jokes.

What's black and brown on the outside and yellow through and through?
Answer 1: *A brown egg.*
Answer 2: *Bellaguan.*
Or:

What's yellow on the outside and brown on the inside?
Answer: A *Bellaguan blown inside out.*
Or: *What's black and brown and cold all over?*
A *dead Bellaguan.*
And so on.

Gun sounds ricocheted all the way back to Sagrabél. If there'd been hills, you could have stood at the top of one and seen, far off toward the interior, an occasional burst of smoke pirouetting skyward, the ever-present helicopters begin a clumsy swoop down; heard the rapid drilling report of more gunfire.

Helicopters blasted away at unseen regions of trees. Smoke flares went up to signal a suspected enemy location but always, always, their calculations were a little off. This was an enemy hanging from trees, waiting. They'd strike, unseen, with a few weak rifle shots; still unseen, they would disappear into the trees that hid them before return fire could be effectively made. They seemed content with this pot-shotting: a couple of casualties here, a few more there. These weren't devastating attacks—merely disheartening. Because the snipers couldn't be seen or heard. There was only this perpetual ambush, pathetic sniping from above or from the dense, dark surroundings, the rustle of foliage as if all the jungle had taken its leaves up and rattled them, rattled, whispering hush rising up and out to the waiting tropical air above, the sun, dissipating like a released choir of antiphonal voices. In the midst of such a murmur, who could hear feet running? It was more as if the foliage itself had taken the pot-shots, then curled back into itself with a hiss of laughter. And it was clear to the men, who did it all free-lance, for good pay, that these brown-uniformed, brown-skinned men trained by foreigners in the ways of conventional European warfare were no match for the dark leaves of jungle trees. They simply could not fight. Only be wounded, or die, or fear dying so much that they'd fall to their knees mumbling in tongues. It was quite clear to them that the enemy did not really exist in human form. The enemy was the physical circumstance itself: the foliage, the surrounding darkness. Green, living things kept out sunlight and the waiting return fire of men. The green must be gotten rid of. The trees, which swallowed phantom terrorists back into the interior unharmed, would have to die.

Several weeks into the undeclared war, a National Army patrol disappeared.

Patrols had been ambushed before. It was becoming a common occurrence, even though the war was merely weeks old. Having penetrated some short distance into the interior from the new military operations base on West Reef, a unit would claim the advance, set up camp. From each camp issued daily patrols heading farther inland. The object of these patrols: *to sweep the area for terrorists.* Or, as days turned to weeks: *to sweep the area for rebels.* And as the weeks went on: *to sweep the area for soldiers of the People's Army.* It was common for patrols to lose a man or two. Usually, though, the corpse would be found; there'd be a volley of shots, screams, the unheard thud of bodies collapsing to moss-sheltered earth to lie there in shock, agony, or death. And bugs would crawl immediately into open wounds, worms slither over the wet blood on crushed plant fronds. Little snakes, the Bellaguans called worms, and though they weren't dangerous the soldiers had a superstitious dread of them, coupled with natural disgust at the idea of something like living slime crawling into your flesh. The wounded were transported back from each ambush as quickly as possible— which, in the dense terrain, was often not quickly enough. They were carried back screaming, or muted by terror. The next day another patrol would be sent out, often along the same freshly cut path. The phantom snipers learned where to wait, when to expect a patrol, when to shoot and vanish. So each advance could be measured in yards or meters and also in blood, but more important, it could be measured in terms of fear instilled. Each small advance was met with another dip in troop morale. Two weeks into the undeclared war, the first series of desertions occurred from units all along the West Reef area. And a short time later, there was the combat patrol that disappeared.

The disappearance of this patrol left nothing behind except a mud-brown helmet, later discovered by a search patrol that also suffered ambush and minor casualties. A single helmet, turned up in overgrown mud as if to catch raindrops, proliferation of soft-bodied bugs crawling around and inside it. There was no trace remaining of the man who'd left it behind. No spatterings of blood on leaf. Not a single footprint.

The patrol had covered an already traveled path, stopped at the point where a previous group had been ambushed just the day before, combed the area in pairs. Nothing lurked in trees. Nothing waited behind mats of leafy vine—only the insects, leeches that attached themselves to boots and remained until burnt off. The mercenary accompanying this patrol in his official role of advisor tried not to look too long at the mouths of some of the Bellaguan soldiers; many of their teeth were a moldy, brownish green, attacked by the same fungus that grew with ease between everyone's toes, around the armpits, the genitals—any hot, wet, protected place. The lone white man felt vaguely disgusted, somehow above it all. But he was here to do a job. And do it he would, despite the material at hand—a sorry bunch, he had to admit. He'd seen soldiers with poorer training before but never with poorer heart.

They'd progressed farther than yesterday's line. Through the trees he thought he could hear the whirring of helicopters. One night he'd woken in total blackness and thought he heard the buzz of a chopper flying past. But he'd told himself it couldn't be. He knew what was going on as well as anyone and better than many, knew there were no authorized night operations yet. An advance by night would have to be massive, well-planned and organized with great efficiency—all requirements which the Bellaguans couldn't handle. He'd gone back to sleep.

Now, this whirring of multiple propellors was a dim sort of comfort in the dull green shadows; it meant that up above there was daylight. This terrain was half lit, changing from dark to darker and then to an absolute vacuum which even the lightless time of night couldn't penetrate. It was a land that never spoke of hours, or days; a dense place where, once inside, you seemed to have left the whole world behind.

He thought he heard a bird cry far off. He signaled to stop.

Behind him, the Bellaguans froze single-file. Someone breathed heavily. He heard it with disgust, knew that he had only to look around and he'd see the sweat of fear streaming down every brown face. If he looked long enough someone would give him that *Howdy, Boss!* grin and display a row of rotting green teeth. The white man didn't turn. He listened. Now the air had resumed its insect buzz, an occasional stir of leaves when a tree snake slid up or down. He signaled for them to continue.

The patrol pressed on quietly, following the white man. He was a Britisher, some said, some said an Australian. He had a name no one knew— the name he went by was false. It was the same with all of these white men; they were code-named, true identity unknown. Perhaps each true identity had been so obscured that it no longer existed. The patrol of frightened men moved on as silently as possible through the jungle, each boot crushing moss that had never been stepped on before, fresh leeches clinging thickly to the dangling ends of every clumsily tied lace. The white man moved cautiously, but with grace. His patrol had come farther than any before it, was on the verge of claiming a new line of advance. And there was exhilaration in that knowledge, despite the fact that he prided himself on lack of emotional involvement with his profession—plenty of exhilaration, along with brief stabs of terror. Because even he wasn't immune to terror. He simply controlled his terror with great facility, the essence of success in his chosen field.

Glancing up, he imagined a touch of sky peeking through green darkness. He brushed the image roughly away, no time for distractions. He heard the breathing of men behind him, each breath verging on panic. So far, so good. He'd told them hours before that anyone turning to run would be shot—a personal, off-the-record promise from yours truly, he'd said. They believed him, and he credited their faith in the veracity of his threats with keeping them in line up to this point. A useful tool, fear, if you knew how to wield it.

The patrol continued. It was afternoon by his watch—past midday by the measurements of the world out there—but in here minutes were measured by imprints of boot soles on naked leaves, imprints that would be covered by fresh undergrowth the following day. History had no meaning in here. Its traces were too easily obliterated.

The white man shook his head suddenly as if stung. He signaled to stop and behind him the single file froze again. He listened.

It had sounded like a bird.

He was sure—no, he was *almost* sure—that what he'd heard was a single bird cry coming from far away. Just like the last one he thought he'd heard. But it seemed to be nearly a hallucination; he couldn't remember what direction the sound came from. Unprofessional. He grunted. Wait and see. He wasn't used to his senses letting him down like that.

For a second, he wanted to turn and glance fully at each dark face staring ahead in single-file misery. His glance would have been evaluative—he'd have noted again the film of terror washing every feature with perspiration until each face had the stiff, near-vacant look of traumatic shock—and his glance would also have been slightly questioning. He was filled with the desire to have someone capable at his side right now. A white man who'd understand his questioning look, a good soldier. One who'd have some answers, maybe. Behind him were nothing but the brown faces of normal men in an agony of fear—fool world, he knew, that put normal men in soldiers' uniforms—and for this reason he forced himself to remain standing, listening. He didn't turn around.

No more bird sounds.

He relaxed, signaled again. They continued.

Insects chorused in a rapid click-click-clicking like crickets or cicadas. Each overhanging vine had to be shoved aside with the barrel end of his automatic. The snakes in here were well camouflaged. Touch green vines with one careless hand and a tiny fanged head, eyes like black pinpoints, could curl around it, tongue flicking delicate poison drops. Reach up for a banana and living coils of yellow might suddenly wrap around your wrist. Back in Sagrabél bars he'd been warned with raised eyebrows, half-nasty jests from the mouths of other white men: *When you piss, mate, don't take it out of your pants!* —Although Sagrabél was no bastion of cleanliness, either, and keeping it in your pants was a good idea no matter where you were on Bellagua. He'd been in the business long enough to know diseased pussy when he came near it. In most of the places where he'd conducted business, pussy was usually diseased. And you stayed away from butt fucks— from that above all—unless you wanted gangrene of the prick and a hundred forms of previously unheard-of venereal diseases. He looked around cautiously, squinted ahead to leafy shadows and the uninterrupted click-click-clicking of bugs. He could smell crushed moss bleeding out against the soles of his boots—it rose up, a rotting, damp odor. Keep it in your pants: a good rule. Once in a while, though, he'd make them open their mouths and he'd check for boils on the lips or tongue, disease along the gums. Reasonably clean teeth would do. No teeth at all was better. Sometimes they had to be forcibly persuaded. And he always paid up as agreed. So their sullen brown faces rarely cracked an expression; he was a little rough, but really no bother. And he himself was meticulously clean.

Blue sky. He thought maybe he'd seen it.

Glancing up, he shook his head again. Keep the brain clear, boy. He felt a brief flash of panic. Blue sky. There was not a trace of sky above— only the dense, vegetable darkness. He unsnapped his watch case to check, heard the tiny popping sound as if it was echoing very close to his eardrum. It was nearly evening. Something trickled down his chest; more sweat, he thought at first. But it wasn't that, it was a sort of chill instead. Then the sensation rippling through him was one he'd never felt before, as if a small cluster of buzzing insects had crawled up his spinal cord, rattled around in his head. Blue sky. He looked up longingly.

Boy, you've gone too far.

He didn't know where that thought had come from.

Gone too far this time.

He signaled for a halt and glanced down at the uncapped watch again. It was even later than he'd thought just a few seconds ago—how could that be? Hours later. And no assuring whirr of propellors sounded faintly through the leaves of trees any longer. It was evening, he knew, and the darkness in here was now matched by darkness of the other world outside. So in both lands, sky and earth, it was night, and in the world of sky the only light would be the moon's, gleaming icily down before first shimmerings of starlight. He stared at the face of his watch, and in the dark it began to glow.

The white man turned around. What stared back at him was emptiness, unbroken by frozen brown faces or the sounds of men breathing. He was alone.

The chirping of bugs had grown louder, steadier, all around. He smiled faintly.

"Niggers."

Something slid by underfoot. He heard it go across moss, mud, through leaves. He stared back at the long line of emptiness, once inhabited by frightened faces.

"I'll get you for this."

Standing there, he ran a hand briefly over the pouch compartments of his combat vest. Pistol pouch, above it pistol magazines; his toy, he called it, Little Titty, and it was always there just in case. Six thirty-round magazine pouches, .223. Radio pouch. Radio. He thought vaguely to radio a message back. No. Too risky. An odd languor washed over him; he didn't really want to message back, when all was said and done, did he? Didn't really want anyone to know where he was right now. Compass pouch. He didn't unsnap the flap. He didn't want to know himself how far he'd come, or which was the way back. He felt encased in a soft, bubble-like silence: just him and the dark. He fingered Little Titty, fingered the vest, the utility pouch, three-knife pouch, two pouches side by side for extra ammo magazines. Extra utility sack attached with light-weight clips, filled with scope mounts. No need of scopes here, but he liked to pack them along. Everyone had his professional idiosyncracies. Blue sky. He looked up and thought he saw it—clear, free, open blue sky, beckoning down with a wafting rush of fresh air. Something dribbled quietly from the corner of his eye, joined the sweat beaded along his chin. For a second he thought he'd seen the sky. He felt a quick stab of happiness. He could feel it surge through him, up and up until his tongue rolled sweetly in brief happiness. The uncapped watch cover flapped against his wrist. Blue sky. He was alone. He stood there: a white man, torso encircled by weapons and with ammunition, automatic held in the crook of one arm, canteen slung over one shoulder to rest on the opposite hip, medical kit and rudimentary food supplies strapped in another small pack to his broad, strong back. All these things spoke of survival. All these things were formidable; he was a walking fortress, crushing easily through the soft dankness of green territory.

He went forward two more steps. Ground sucked up at his feet.

A bird cry came again, long, piercing; there was something horrible in the loneliness of it.

He crouched immediately and froze into position, automatic ready. He unsnapped a magazine pouch. But the sound echoed, echo faded. When its last waverings had vanished into the leaves of the trees that absorbed everything here, bugs resumed chirping. Still he was silent and unmoving, crouched in the dark, ready for action.

Blue sky. Too far this time, boy.

By the face of his wristwatch, hours had passed. It felt like seconds to him; it felt like no time at all. His knees locked, thighs stiffened. He wasn't himself, he knew, to remain here without risking a look-see—not himself to have come so far, so absent-mindedly, in the first place. What had happened to time? And how had he lost track of it so completely, almost willingly? The line of black men who'd followed him and then, when he was bound up in an illusory vision of open sky, deserted in perfect silence— the memory of them seemed like another illusion. It was the sky, he told himself, that clear, shining spot of blue he thought he'd seen through treetops today, that had done the mischief: beckoned to him, made him lose concentration. So now he was deep in the unending lightlessness of a territory more foreign than what he'd known before, leaves folding over one another like hot, foul-smelling lips to keep out the sun.

Seconds passed. Minutes circled through an hour. Jungle grew over his footprints.

It was the dead middle of night by his watch when he rose, legs quivering. Dead middle of the night, so when his helmet rolled off and turned upside down on the ground even his pale face and fair hair did not gleam in contrast—everything, including him, had become utterly black. Each movement eased pain from stiff limbs; he moved in a sort of trance, ignored his fallen helmet and went forward through the trees.

Sometimes he stopped, listening. What he listened for were the sounds of his own breathing. If he listened closely, he could hear the delicate pings of sweat falling against his boots, the ground.

A bird cry came again, shrill, desolate, cracked the perpetual buzz of the jungle and, in the sudden suspension of all sound which it had brought about, he thought he could hear someone whispering close to his ear. He thought he could hear the hushed tapping of bare feet along the limbs of trees. The shriek came again, split everything apart with its sadness. It sounded above this time, directly over his head.

He knelt suddenly, automatic cradled in both arms. Things soaked through the wet legs of his khakis, over and into his boots, and the cry echoed. He leaned forward until his cheek brushed something hard. He let his cheek rest there against the sliding damp bark of a tree. Above him something hovered, waiting. He didn't look up.

Blue sky, boy. You've come too far.

The white man nodded gently. Good, he thought dimly, good feeling this, to nod against the fungus-covered sides of trees. His arms relaxed, weapon slipped away until his hands curled around to seize nothing. Eyelids closed over twin mirrors of blue sky. He slept.

Blinking, he thought it was the sun that had woken him. Hand-held torches flared instead—to him, though, it was sunlight, and against the background of sun a strange form towered above, looking down. The bird, he thought vaguely. Even though it did not appear to be a bird, there was something about the crouching, strutting motion of this body towering over him that seemed birdlike; an enormous green-and-white striped bird from whose face peeked sharp, curious dark eyes.

Hello, soldier.

The strange bird stooped slightly, turned in half-profile so it was no longer bird but woman, then stood full height again and was no longer woman but a man, striped hands on hips, staring down.

What do you see? Two suns? A double Thebes?

The voice laughed; it was musical, riveting, neither male nor female but a compelling cross between the two, and hearing it he was suddenly over-whelmed by a feeling of tenderness.

Double walls with seven gates? What do you see? Tell me, soldier.

In sunlight, he smiled. The male had changed to female again, taken on the aspect of a strong predatory bird. Darkness in the perfect diagonals of green that spun along the body, perfect light from the stripes of white. What did he see? He grinned feverishly. He felt tears in his eyes; he was suddenly, irrevocably happy. Things twirled around, again around, and he knew then that he was in the presence of something divine.

The goddess bent lower, leaning forward gracefully until the savage striped mask was quite close to his face.

Oh, maybe I'll tell you. You see as you should see. Sometimes that happens—consider yourself lucky. The gift of insight. Written so long ago but still it's true.

The mask moved to tower far, far above. Something bubbled from his nose. He lifted a curious hand and liquid gurgled down his fingers, touched his lips with a thick, faintly salty taste. He moved the fingers down along his chest. At the center of his body something stopped them. He touched curiously, hand circled around to grip the stiff wooden rod that stuck straight out of him, and he knew then why everything seemed so far away and fading, and knew what had woken him. He wanted to say that he knew he'd come too far this time. That he had finally understood it, and was sorry.

When the mouth stopped making its gurgling, gasping sounds, his eyes froze suddenly and were still.

Torches swayed in moving hands.

Several green-painted hands reached down to lift the corpse, tie its ankles and wrists together. It would be carried like a heavy, sack-like sling, swinging from the ends of ropes.

One by one, the torches passed through dark air, vanished into darkness ahead, and from each green-painted face eyes glittered in torchlight. These faces blended into leaves and then disappeared. The line of bodies moved deeper inland, moved constantly, silently ahead into the interior and night-time's end. They faded into leaves; the trees swallowed them up.

What would appear godlike to an ant?

Dr. Manella Porter often wondered.

Knowing what she knew of recorded history, sensing what she might of all the history gone before which hadn't been recorded, time and again she'd come up with the answer: a large beetle. Because men had created many images of gods, all patterned after their own physical shapes but conceptually much bigger; the explanation had then been that man was created in the image of his god, never the other way around. So maybe an ant would recognize something of its own outline in the enormity of a lurking beetle shell, and through the ant's dim mind would flash the kernel of an idea: this was the great being from which all bugs sprang; ants would build hills in imitation of this divine thing; they'd spend lifetimes working to propagate the race of ants that worshipped such magnitude.

Actually, ants didn't think. Rather, individual ants did not think—although Dr. Porter knew that an entire ant colony, considered as a whole, could be said to represent a viable consciousness, carrying on its necessary function to support the ongoing life of the whole. An ant without a colony would simply cease to be—like a single cell fallen out of a body. For ants, survival was a social event.

Because she was a social person—more at ease among people than without them—Dr. Porter believed that for human beings, too, survival was dependent on social bondings and the ensuing practical divisions of labor.

Never could survival depend, in her view, on individual resource or will. She had said it often to Tristam Saunderson during their years together: Religious worship led to idealization of individual glory, individual suffering, individual perfection both inner and outer—the equivalent of individual salvation. Better to divest a society of that nonsense and get on with the business at hand, which was a group—not an individual—effort: physical survival. With full stomachs, clear eyes, healthy limbs—only then could a people deal with spiritual requirements.

Yes, he had smiled, had shaken his head in that dreamy way, yes. But it is not that simple. And he'd fallen strangely silent. It always came to this concerning the matter of religion: her quiet but firm proclamations, his lack of argument, and the silent daydream look that would follow.

Yes. Yes. But it is not that simple.

Crouched over the blood-soaked white body, Dr. Porter thought she was beginning to see his point. She looked up to the faces of warriors, all covered with a thick green paint so features were washed away as effectively as any mime's. Their bodies, too, were covered with green, and only breasts distinguished the females from males. Some held spears, sharp chipped points of stone. A few had guns—old-issue army rifles from some long-ago European war. The eyes stared tiredly down at her, light brown in green faces. Then the bodies parted to make way for another. This one was slightly taller, larger-boned but trim—it was a body on which the muscles were corded and stretched, living on the tightrope between sufficient nourishment and deprivation—yet still maintaining its strength, as well as the impression it gave of grace, of power. The face, arms, torso, legs—the body in its entirety—had been painted with meticulous green-and-white diagonal stripes, dizzying to look at for long. You'd have to look away, rest your eyes or shade them with a hand.

Dr. Porter squinted in the firelight. She stared up.

"He's dead."

The striped face nodded.

The other green bodies were half bowed now, one hand shadowing each pair of eyes while the other clutched a spear or old-issue rifle. When the striped one turned to them and began to speak in the short, guttural sounds of their language—a language Dr. Porter had only begun to decipher— they bowed lower still, and some pairs of eyes closed completely with an expression almost of pain, as if suddenly exposed to too much light.

There were murmurings in response to what was said; not unhappy sounds. In the firelight, Dr. Porter glanced around at the dark convex mounds of surrounding huts, and beyond them, above, all-encompassing, the jungle through which no starlight drifted or cool air seeped. Somewhere a child cried in sleep—the cry stifled itself in the same soft suddenness with which it had begun.

There was silence. Turning to her, the striped body stepped closer.

Dr. Porter looked up. "What is it you usually do? Bury them?"

The striped lips laughed, eyes flashed dark out of the masklike face with a sudden bright humor, the head shook.

"Well, he ought to be buried. Or cremated." Dr. Porter was all professional now; her concern must be for the still-living. "I am considering sanitary factors. Disease spreads."

Ant colonies, she thought. Then for some reason she wanted to laugh, too, but kept silent. She wanted to stand but sensed somehow that to do so would be a grave error. Despite the status so recently conferred on her— all due to another harm-filled ritual in which she could not believe—despite all her status as heaven-sent healer, she understood instinctively that certain limitations accrued. In the presence of this striped body, she must not stand while others bowed. Never. So she remained crouched over the bloody white fire-lit corpse, and inside she sighed. Nothing logical about rituals, she knew. She sensed that, with most rituals which could not be explained as having a socially productive end, the discomfort involved in participating was a major essential ingredient. Things for which one did not suffer were— in the eyes of the worshipper—suspect in value.

But the real truth of her life, she had to admit, was connected to motives far removed from political or religious philosophies. In one of the dome-shaped huts where children slept, her son slept also. She had a child and was therefore bound by claims other than dogma, strapped firmly into life by coils of love and terror. For the tiny life that was her son she would do anything, she knew, travel anywhere, betray everyone, serve any god.

In the strange, guttural language which Dr. Porter didn't yet understand, her own hut was called the House of the Healer. Warriors were now stationed at its entranceway, where torches blazed at the tops of poles that sprouted from the ground. Their spears were planted point-down in earth, faces expressionless beneath the masks of dull green. Inside, rituals occurred which they were not permitted to witness; things concerning only Healer and Goddess. Their job was to wait.

On the small flat table woven of branches, candles were set in glass trays; both candles and trays were rare commodities, but in her position as Healer the doctor was granted special privilege. By candlelight she knelt to one side of the striped body which sat cross-legged on a pallet, immobile under its burden of unexpressed pain. Dr. Porter held bandage shears and reached carefully between the breasts, found cloth that had been painted to match the skin. Her fingers located its outline and she snipped away.

"How do you feel?"

The zebra mask smiled. "Sometimes uncomfortable. Sometimes—oh, not too bad. The swelling's gone."

"Let's see. Yes. Yes, good." Carefully the doctor peeled away strips of bandage to expose the underlying gauze. She began to slowly separate gauze from the skin beneath. "Good. No more infection." Her fingers pressed; if the body winced sometimes, there was no expression on the masklike face. Green and white streaked in diagonal lines down from the head, stopped just above both breasts, continued their interrupted journey below the line of breasts and went down and down to the cloth-covered area where thighs joined hips, down both legs. Even the toes were striped. "I'll put more ointment on. After next week I believe the bandages may come off, but I tell you, you're playing a dangerous game."

The mask chuckled. "There are no games, Dr. Porter. No games, no coincidences—have you forgotten?"

Manella reached for the open metal kit beside her, picked out a tube of salve and more gauze padding. For a second, both pairs of dark eyes met, held, evaluated. The doctor sighed. "That may be. Nevertheless—"

"*Nevertheless?*" The voice teased.

"Nevertheless I am a doctor first and foremost. So I tell you, you ought to create different rules for this goddess of yours! Different rules, ones less brutal. I'm considering your physical health—your body has limits."

"Now, now, Doctor. Limits? A goddess should be without limits." The mask moved, smiled. There was a hint of weariness in the smile. "Do you think they'd believe in Her if She never risked pain? Or if She flinched? No! The key to divinity is its limitlessness—come now, you know that. Do you think they'd swallow your politics or risk their lives for an abstract concept? Do you think they'd follow socialist dogma with the same passion they would their Goddess? For Her they'll kill, or even die, because She weds them to the earth and earth marries the sky—a rhyme!—and without Her your ideals are nothing, Doc. Saunderson knew. All your ideals, nothing, because they don't even know they're doing anything except following the will of the Goddess. You need *Her* more than you need dogma. Her. Me. Oh—" The body shuddered, green shimmering dizzily into the stripes of white for just a second as the doctor's hand smoothed ointment gently over cruel red gashes criss-crossing both breasts.

"I'm sorry if this hurts."

"Not as sorry as I am."

Dr. Porter grinned. Then her face grew sad, examining the savagely slashed breasts. It had been a long process of healing, with still longer to go. No wonder. Always, while carefully tending the damage done, she was reminded of that horror mingled with fascination she'd felt upon witnessing the ceremony. Blood of the Goddess. Taken annually from divine breasts in lieu of milk. The green-painted faces had clustered around, fire lit the backdrop and children were shooed away to sleep; this was the time of the Moon. She had come out from trees surrounded by warriors. Stepped simply, easily into the center of the circle, spread both green-striped, white-striped arms and two warriors bowed before each outstretched arm, their own breasts brushing damp earth, before standing, laying down their spears, uncovering their eyes. They had stepped behind her to seize an arm each. The doctor watched with a curiosity that was beginning to be touched by fear: another green warrior body stepped out into the center of the circle, woven strings of leaves dangling around the neck and wrists and arms, head obscured by a wooden mask with a flat, round white surface on the front, small holes cut into it for eyes and mouth—the Moon, Manella knew, the Moon. In her hand, the Moon held a knife with wooden handle and long, sharp-chiseled stone blade. Firelight brushed everything shadowy gold, flickered, and jumped. Someone had begun a whining, monotonous chant; soon all were chanting, the same strange words rising and sliding back down in seemingly endless repetition. The doctor felt herself swaying slightly in rhythm. She would not forget it—not the sound, the dim swaying, rocking sensation, the sudden silence in which golden light danced up, sank lower, dark eyes watched intently from faces plastered green. There was the swift, intentional lift of the knife. Quick jab downward to slide along the green-and-white flesh of divine breasts and up again, down, again, and again, again. Something moaned. She heard the moan rise from the ground and felt herself inside it; she realized it was more than one voice moaning, a chorus of voices moaning in unison with each slash of the stone-edged knife, each swelling of blood that mingled with the green and white of each slashed breast. She saw the striped neck arch, striped eyelids close in agony, but from the lips no sound escaped. It was a chorus of watching voices that moaned instead. And the doctor felt herself moan, too, her eyes shut, then open to let out tears.

"What I appreciate about you, Doctor"—the voice teased again, brought her back to this hut, this time, this antibiotic ointment she was spreading over healing breasts—"is your sense of humor. Most radicals have none."

Manella Porter smiled. "There's not too much to laugh about!"

"Oh, I disagree. Here we are, on the same side of things—I think that's funny. Not funny hah-hah, but *funny*, in the sense of being absurd. Come on, Doc, give us a smile. There! Would you have imagined it, any of this? You wanted to abolish hierarchy. You wanted to abolish religion because you thought it was the same thing. You wanted revolution for the sake of *the people*—not just an individual person, no! That would be too small, too divergent from your idea of the group as all-important. Except that no collectivity thrives without a soul! Without many souls—*ah*—"

"I'm sorry."

"Go ahead. No, go ahead Doctor, it's all right. There. So what did you find to give your revolution a soul? Religion! You put it in the framework of religion. Intelligent of you. Of *Saunderson*. You set up your god, and you went out and found yourselves the Goddess. Lucky thing I happened to be there, wasn't it? If you believe in luck—I don't. No coincidence, Doctor. No games—"

"Hold the gauze on, like this."

"No games. Saunderson knew. He saved me for a purpose. And I saved you for another, you see: you serve my purpose while I serve yours." The voice laughed painfully; despite the pain, there was a husky, musical quality to it, and it still hadn't lost its teasing edge. "Heal the Goddess, Dr. Porter. Keep Her alive, otherwise your purpose goes unfulfilled. They only follow gods. Not mortals. It's good. It's good! This way they can't possibly know what they're up against. Knowing what you're up against—that makes things much more difficult."

Dr. Porter cut the last strip of tape, wound it in place on perspiring skin. She looked up and their eyes met again; was it her imagination, or did the large, mad dark eyes staring fixedly back at her have in them a spark of something approaching sorrow? She couldn't make it out. "You are right," she said softly.

The head nodded, shoulders stooped now with pain.

"And mortal," said the doctor.

The laugh came again, quietly goading. "Around here, Doc, truth is in the eye of the beholder, as they say. Mortal? You're the only one who holds that view." The zebra lips smiled. "A minority opinion."

Outside, spears dug deeper into ground, warriors shifted feet as they stood watching, waiting for their goddess. In the hut candle wax dripped to cluster in dull white globs on glass trays. Both women sat, and were silent.

INTERNATIONAL PLAYTHINGS, INCORPORATED

The District Manager faced what was ahead in an outwardly calm manner. He'd requested this meeting after careful consideration. Other men—lesser men—might have considered it a last resort. But he—and this was why, he reminded himself, he'd become Manager at a relatively young age—looked upon it as the logical extension of circumstance, something which could not be avoided. In addition, a part of him anticipated it with curiosity. He'd never met Zachary before.

The New York headquarters of Zachary Chemical Corporation was in the area of Manhattan affectionately referred to by the in-boys at Corporate as International Row; this because if you knew certain things you could look up and down streets and avenues in this area and count off the sky-scrapers belonging to companies owned by International. Royal Hotel Corporation sat almost directly across the street from Fujiyama Video, which in turn nestled against the administrative headquarters for Northern Lights Pork & Beef. Just down the street was a building shared by several smaller but highly profitable International-owned concerns: Mont Rouge Mineral Water, Complex Carbohydrates, Inc., *Tour de France* and *Ultramarathoner* Magazines, LS Athletic Concepts and Scott-Simmonds Adventurewear, Inc.. Several blocks uptown were two publishing concerns, a motion picture company, and Zachary Chemical Corporation.

Walking through the halls of Zachary Chemical, the District Manager had been struck with the difference in design and color scheme between these headquarters and Royal Hotel's. He approved. It was good policy to allow differences to flourish like that—keep the umbrella open and everyone clustered happily underneath, but encourage a certain amount of differentiation. His ability to approve gave him confidence now; he was, after all, going to meet someone much his superior by any standard of the Corporate echelon. But the District Manager wasn't one to shirk challenge.

He'd been led by two silent secretaries through several green-carpeted rooms in the executive suite. They arrived at a room where a Louis XV desk with matching chairs beckoned; following an inner voice, though, the District Manager settled himself on the plush-backed sofa instead. There was no sign of Zachary. He accepted coffee offered by one of Zachary's girls, watched it poured into white, initialed china cups as the steam rose in faint clouds, watched tray, cups, saucers, and spoons set carefully on a cherrywood coffee table in front of the sofa. He continued to follow his inner voice and let it sit untouched. He wasn't thirsty anyway.

He glanced at white blinds drawn over the long window to his left. There was a dimmer installed somewhere, so the office had sufficient light; but this light was adjustable, pleasant, felt faintly warm to him despite the artificially modulated temperature, gave the room's thick carpet and thick-paneled walls a womblike, inviting glow.

The District Manager shut his eyes.

I wish to report, sir, on our progress.

The phone connection had been poor. He'd attempted to listen to Santigo's words at first but couldn't make them out. Then he'd thrown one of his rare tantrums, had his girl put the call through again on a special Corporate line. And this time, when he'd understood that he was getting a progress report—which would either corroborate or conflict with his own sources of information—he could feel himself begin to perspire. But he'd replied calmly:

Yes, Mr. Santigo. Please go ahead.

Santigo's voice crackled along thousands of miles of wires again. Despite the continued interference it was a voice the District Manager could recognize—rapid but nevertheless assured; he recognized it as one he'd heard before, and the familiarity was that it reminded him in some way of his own. Despite the differences in accent and texture, despite the differences of culture, the separation of miles.

I wish to report that Mr. Connery has arrived, sir.

Yes. You've been in touch.

Sir, we have.

Good, said the District Manager, *then everything's on schedule, I take it.*

I am in contact with certain elements of the military—

The voice got lost in static. The District Manager didn't bother listening for lost words, though; this subtle evasion of his question—were things on schedule?—indicated something far more important to him: the possibility that things were not on schedule. Or that there'd been some hitch in plans. If so, he'd have to root it out.

I'm aware of your contacts, Mr. Santigo. You're doing a fine job there. I want you to know it hasn't gone unnoticed.

There was silence at the other end, silence which the District Manager could sense was a mixture of pleasure and unease—even from thousands of miles away, he could sense it. He continued:

You have a great deal of support here. We want you and your people to succeed, Mr. Santigo. So if there's any problem—

There is one slight problem, sir. One minor problem has arisen.

The District Manager had been drumming his fingertips briefly along the desk surface. Now he leaned back, waiting.

Santigo's voice seemed faint until it leaped strongly across the wires— erratic connection.

The problem of Miss Zachary, sir. It was our understanding that her movements—interference crackled, obscured, then the final word shot out— *monitored.*

The District Manager nodded. He remained silent, waiting.

This was our understanding. But it seems she has—slipped away. It seems—more static—*nevertheless.*

The District Manager waited. He was careful not to wait too long. That might appear to be indecision on his part, and that he'd never permit. Not to a superior; still less to an underling. *I see,* he said. *Yes, I see. Well, Mr. Santigo, that's something we'll have to deal with in the near future. I will see what I can do about that. In the meantime*—he leaned forward against his desk, felt himself smile because, despite everything, he was proud of good work when it showed itself and, despite everything, this work was good work all in all—*in the meantime, stay the course.*

Very well, sir. Will I be contacted?

You'll be contacted.

Sitting on the plush-backed sofa in the executive suite of Zachary Chemical Corporation, the District Manager opened his eyes. Someone had sat, silently, beside him.

"Do you take cream?"

The face that turned to him was stocky and handsome.

"What?" The District Manager blinked.

"In your coffee. Sometimes the girls forget to ask."

The District Manager swallowed his surprise. He felt his palms slowly dry, shock dissipate from his face, and when he was sure not a touch of nervousness remained he offered a hand and introduced himself. Odd, sitting here so close on the sofa. He'd imagined meeting the man standing face to face, but now he had to turn uncomfortably to his side, and the face meeting his at a slight angle seemed, in the dully glowing light, to be of indeterminate age. Zachary shook his hand. He said he was pleased to meet him.

"What about that cream?"

"I'll pass on it today, Mr. Zachary." The District Manager patted his vest-covered belly half mockingly. "Hurts the squash game, if you don't watch out."

Both men laughed.

"Good that you play." Zachary grinned. "Compete?"

"Level B," said the District Manager.

"Manhattan Racquet?"

"No. Squash and Swim Club."

Zachary nodded approval. "A man's got to keep in shape, with all this sedentary living, eh?"

"I agree."

"Tennis?"

"Some." The District Manager spoke carefully. "A little college varsity." He examined his own hands, spread casually on his knees. Then he decided to take a calculated risk. "That must be your game, Mr. Zachary."

"Clay court!" Zachary beamed, obviously pleased. "Don't like grass or indoors. *Didn't*, I mean." He gave the District Manager a wry laugh. "These old bones aren't up to par lately. It's been a long time! Not much of a game for an old codger, I guess. Although I still say"—he leaned forward, slapped the District Manager's knee in a friendly way—"I still say an old codger like me could whip one of you young hotshots around the block. One on one—"

The District Manager laughed modestly.

"—winner takes all. Experience wins! Experience!"

"Mr. Zachary," the District Manager smiled, "you're right about that."

Zachary stood, moved a little restlessly across the carpet. The District Manager took him in: a tall man; despite the thick gray hair he looked younger than his age; broad torso, a well-contained paunch. Something bordering on delicacy underlying the handsome thick rigor of his face— were the eyelashes long for a man? the nose almost dainty? It couldn't be pinpointed, but was nevertheless there—an intimation of childhood delicacy and beauty. Zachary turned his back and the image vanished.

He sat behind his desk. The District Manager stood.

Zachary pulled at a drawer. In the room's quiet glow the District Manager could hear the faint slide of the drawer on its runners. "Here," said Zachary, "you'll get a kick out of this."

Crossing to sit opposite him at the desk, the District Manager was aware of an odd lack of sensation: he couldn't for the life of him feel his feet. They'd numbed; it was as if they'd vanished. He knew that couldn't be. They were carrying him silently, gracefully, assuredly, across the carpet. Facing Zachary, he sat.

Something had been set between them on the desk. Examining it closely, the District Manager saw it was a sort of model, several complex components mounted on a single platform. In miniature scale he saw the thin-surfaced table mounted, the miniature net strung across the table at the halfway point dividing it in two, the two miniature figures, miniature paddles in hand, at each end of the table. The District Manager noticed that two levers protruded on his side of the platform. Above the levers he noticed a company insignia: International Playthings, Inc., and above that the initials of International Communications Enterprises.

"Table tennis," Zachary said. "Ever play?"

Slowly, the District Manager shook his head.

Zachary grinned. "Well, you know what they say. There's always a first time."

He reached to flick a switch on the model platform. Something whirred softly; the miniature players on the platform lit up suddenly with a reddish glow, twirled in a complete circle and stopped, facing each other across the little green table.

"Your serve," said Zachary.

"Sir?"

"Your serve!" Zachary winked. "I know they say age before beauty. But today—well—you want the right lever, my boy. It's the right lever you want first."

Hesitating slightly, the District Manager touched the right lever. Immediately the miniature green table was lit like a television screen, and across it, from one player to another, wafted the image of a ball. Fascinated, the District Manager watched it float in a straight line toward the miniature player on Zachary's side of the platform. When it had drifted almost completely off the table's edge, Zachary calmly touched a lever and the tiny white image of a Ping-Pong ball began floating eerily back in the opposite direction.

"Right lever serves," Zachary chuckled. "Left one returns. Remember that. I've been in touch with my man Connery. I've been in touch and I know the whole story."

The District Manager felt his mouth go suddenly dry. He pressed the left lever too late; the ball had drifted completely out of sight. A small red dot appeared at Zachary's end of the table—one for the old codger, he guessed. The District Manager tried not to pause too long. He touched the right lever again.

"Mr. Zachary. I've spoken with Santigo—"

"Who? The hell with your Santigos. Ah-hah!" Just in time, Zachary returned the serve. "You really think they're important? Your Santigos, I mean. No. No, my boy, they are not."

The District Manager glanced up briefly, but for too long a time to return the serve. Baffled, he stared down again at the glowing green table swept clean of its circular white image. He pressed the right lever and served up a ball. At Zachary's end of the table glowed two red dots.

"I run my own ship, and I don't need any hotel flunkies from Corporate"—he returned the District Manager's serve in the nick of time—"coming around here, trying to tell me how to keep it clean. You understand that?"

At the last possible moment the District Manager pressed the left lever, returned the serve. For the first time in many minutes, he felt a surge of hope and confidence. "I've been asked to point out, Mr. Zachary"—his voice remained carefully polite—"that nearly a third of that ship is presently owned by Scott-Simmonds Adventurewear. You've seen the latest printouts yourself, I assume. All recent transfers of stock—"

The District Manager paused. He suppressed a rising gasp of triumph. The ball had disappeared off the edge on Zachary's side. He was proud of himself for the calm lack of expression he maintained when he looked up to meet the man's eyes.

"The recent transfers, as you know, are causing a lot of questions to be raised. Not just with your other big shareholders. I'm talking about some of the boys at Corporate."

Zachary kept his gaze. He pressed a lever, served. "Connery," he whispered, "is on top of things."

"I've been asked to point out some of the problems concerning Lee Simmonds, too. It seems"—he flicked the left lever, glanced happily at the table to see the tiny speck of white drifting away from him—"no one is certain of how much he knows."

"He thinks Connery's on the up and up."

"Are you sure?"

"Absolutely, my boy. He thinks he's hired himself a nice clean professional. And don't you worry." Zachary glanced down, smiled. He returned the serve. "Connery's on top of that one, too."

The District Manager looked at the glowing green table, one dot glowing red on his side of the scoring mechanism, two at Zachary's side, miniature ball of white floating toward him.

"And Miss Zachary, sir?"

It had come out quietly.

He waited until the last possible moment before pressing the left lever with firm deliberation. Perfect timing. The ball returned; disaster averted in the space of a wink.

Zachary eyed the table with mounting concern. "It would seem," he breathed, "that my daughter's been kidnapped."

"Kidnapped?"

"Kidnapped."

Both men watched the miniature table intently. Their features were blank, riveted. Their inhalations were intentionally suppressed; tension was in the atmosphere, hanging over the International Playthings table tennis set.

"I've been asked to inquire," said the District Manager, "as to what you propose concerning Miss Scott."

Zachary glanced up. "Who?"

"Miss Scott," the District Manager insisted. "Raina Scott."

"Oh." Zachary glanced down again, in time to see the white speck drift off his side of the table, another red dot glow into being at the opposite end. Two all. Zachary didn't serve again. He leaned back in his chair, smiled slightly. It was a curious, almost gentle smile; the District Manager couldn't read it. "Do you really think proposals are necessary? Personally, I think she's dead." The smile remained; the eyes meeting the District Manager's were a deep, pure blue. "Even if she were alive, at this stage of the game I guess you'd have to employ some pretty extreme measures to find out, eh? Send in the National Guard, or the bloodhounds. Or maybe just smoke her out. But let's assume—just for the sake of argument—that they found her after all. I think they'd find her dead." He leaned forward and the smile faded. "I'm sure of it."

After a while the District Manager nodded. "I see."

"Good." Zachary smiled again. It lit his face, gave a ruddy tinge to the cheeks and forehead. When he stood, the District Manager stood too. They shook hands. "Give my best to the boys at Corporate."

"I will," said the District Manager, "I'll do that."

"Keep up your squash. I'll be watching the rankings."

"I'll do that, Mr. Zachary."

When he'd gone, Zachary sat quietly, flicked a switch and the table tennis game stopped its subtle whir, lights went out. In the suite was absolute silence broken only by his own sighs. He'd loosened the knot of his tie, and once in a while found himself sighing for breath—not out of any physical trauma—he didn't quite know why.

He remembered something from many years ago: the long, sloping expanse of a white hill in winter, dropping down and away from him; the hard sensation of steel and varnished wood beneath his hands—his sled. You steered it by working the front rudder. He'd loved that sled, spent breathless hours going downhill speedily, rudder in hand. Wind screamed past his muffed ears with a thick, whipping sound. His boot toes dragged behind.

THE GREAT WHITE CIRCUS

The Zachary family had many residences. European apartments. Estates in California, Florida, Minnesota—the list went on longer, and the grounds of these estates were always described as "rolling hills," whether there were hills there or not, and regardless of whether these hills rolled.

Growing up an only child—for once he was a child, too—John Karlen Zachary remembered spending more time at the Minnesota residence than anywhere else, at least until he was six years old. Sometimes, they'd stay the winter. His father, John Arthur, liked the isolation of the flat, frozen territory and would spend hours gazing out at rapidly forming thick white crust along the window ledge. At these times, the weight of material wealth coupled with a certain emotional austerity seemed to drop from him and he became merely a man, shoulders slightly bowed, a lone figure lost in contemplation. Perhaps it was the illusory expansiveness of memory—was it? John Karlen would often ask himself—which made the boy, later the man, recall that these contemplative sessions in front of windows appeared to last an increasing length of time with each passing day. Peering around half-closed doors, John Karlen marked the silence, the winter-darkened silhouette of his father, back turned toward him in half-shadow. At six, he was a boy accustomed to marking silences. The thick, unruffled silence between his parents which sometimes continued for so many days that when it was eventually broken by a commonplace phrase it was as if every icicle dangling from the eaves and ledges of Zachary House had fallen at once, chorus of crashes echoing along the frozen road leading somewhere else. Once he peered around another door and saw an embrace. He watched, eyes wide with curiosity and glimmerings of half-knowledge: it was a long, extravagant kiss, his mother's head tilted slightly back, exposing her slender neck in pale shadow. The thought came to him that his mother was beautiful. From the walls, clocks brushed minutes by. He saw his father's hand nestle against a well-clothed breast, fingers stroking. Outside it snowed.

That Christmas he'd been given a large, intricate model. When assembled, it was a delicately engineered circus ring. Elephant in frills, caged lions suspended through burning hoops, brightly dressed animal trainer, girls balancing by nose tips on horseback, juggling clown, and several acrobats on swings and trapeze—all were there. He spent the long hours of that winter manipulating the figures, speaking to them, naming them and creating adventures for them to enact. Within the world of the ring heroism prevailed and disaster was always a step behind. It lurked, imminent, like an unseen shadow. The barest flick of a finger, the slightest alteration of an acrobat's concentration, and disaster would flood in to alter forever the brightness of the ring. There was something about this situation which appealed to the boy, touched him deeply in a small, secret corner of his heart.

His mother, Elizabeth Karlen, came from money that had originally been German. Arms manufacturers who moved into metal works as the times demanded, and made sure that their daughter married well. She'd grown up surrounded by showcase models of various guns from the old Karlen Weaponry. When she married a Zachary she brought some of her favorite models along. The Minnesota house seemed the perfect place— walls could be lined with glass-encased guns—it was the most rustic of all the Zachary residences, the most masculine, the most solitary. These long winters made her think of pioneers. She fancied herself a pioneer wife, calico-clad, in the subtle beginning throes of cabin fever. She wondered what those lonely, awkward first farmsteads looked like to the native Plainspeople who'd trod this ground centuries before—like the tiny nub of something unknown? Some bleak beckoning thing? Holding her son's hand, she promenaded along the hallways on late winter afternoons and would stop sometimes, open a velvet-lined glass case with a silent turn of the latch, inspect and gently caress what was inside. Once in a while she held John Karlen up to see. The odor came to him of old oil. He reached out once to touch but was gently prohibited: *No, no, you mustn't play right now.*

He was occupied with the circus that afternoon. Outside the snow had stopped. Winds had eased to nothing so that beyond the picture window was still, white air and a fall of several feet to the frozen cushion of white. He felt a chill against his back, something change in the room's air. Or perhaps there was no chill; perhaps he'd simply had a touch of flu that winter. He was a frail, tiny child, susceptible to everything. But he remembered, later, sudden cold and then a mild wave of warmth that followed, wrapped him in its cozy glow. He turned from the circus ring, where daring artists of the physical painted imaginary arcs in air, and noticed that his mother had come into the room, letting the large burnished door fall shut softly behind. She'd come to play—this thought arrived from nowhere, without reason—his mother had come to play, and he was glad. She carried something wrapped in ermine. Her eyes were warmly blue; not crystalline but a dark color. They were friendly eyes with a hint of something childlike in them. The beauty of her face was a ripe kind, a fullness that asked for color instead of the flat winter pallor forced upon it.

Her hands lost themselves in the ermine-draped object. John Karlen watched with fascination as she raised it toward the walnut mantel and the portraits of his father, his father's father, a line of oils of all the fathers who had in one way or another sired this moment.

"Bang," she said. Then giggled.

In the room's cool, high-ceilinged hush her laughter echoed. He began to laugh too, abruptly, contagiously. The navy-blue eyes focused mildly on him, arms swiveled toward him with pointing force, hands vanished in ermine. His mother smiled. She made a clicking sound with her teeth.

"Bang."

Nervously, the two exploded in laughter again. He felt giggling swells expand his stomach, pound out against ribs to the point of aching. He felt himself gasping for breath. He felt his face begin to redden, strain, and the waves subside, hysteria lessen. His mother sat on the edge of a velvet-upholstered high-backed chair facing him. Her own giggles had settled to quiet and, though her cheeks were still flushed with a peculiarly triumphant glow, she breathed calmly. She wore a dress that billowed loosely around her knees. The material had a sheen to it, a sheen accented by the room's lamps, and when she spread her legs in a sudden, sweeping motion he heard the rustling silky white of her slip beneath. The ermine-covered hands lowered, hovered between the knees. He watched the ermine begin its slow slide. Up toward her, brushing both thighs, the thing between her thighs a sort of eyeless, brainless animal that was a combination of fur and her two hands and some foreign, unidentified other thing.

As the dress folds parted, underclothes brushing white between white thighs, he was desperately conscious that he was not supposed to see this. There was something wrong in viewing it; he had the quick sense that it was analogous to sticking a finger in cake frosting when no one was looking— more serious, even, than that—not what his mother was doing, but his own act of witnessing. Fascinated, he stared. Small, high-pitched chuckles froze in his throat. The ermine crept up, part of it beginning to disappear beneath the shimmering flimsiness of the dress. John Karlen stared at his mother's face. She smiled back calmly with a slight, secret smile that had to it an almost reassuring calm. Behind him something creaked softly. It was the tiny form of an acrobat, swinging by legs from a miniature trapeze, arms flung open to catch the miniature woman who any moment might hurtle towards him.

John Karlen saw the ermine explode and the gun revealed, his mother's smile freeze, then change, and he was moving backwards more quickly than he had ever moved in all the six years of his life, noticing red streaming down the young, white flesh of her legs, the slip, the sheen of dress folds bursting sudden blood-red. He noticed the model circus he'd played with all winter standing, oddly intact, noticed the slight back-and-forth swing of the acrobat, legs hooked over the tiny trapeze and arms wide, waiting. John Karlen took it all in with the odd sense that there was plenty of time—for what, he could not have said—took it all in in much the same way that his own daughter, years later, would face the rapid approach of a Ping-Pong ball from across the table with a calm, dreamy feeling inside of herself, as if the other end of the court were many miles away, the blurred speeding white of the ball a large and easily-dealt-with object, the fleeting seconds between the arc of the ball and her reaction to its approach stretching limitlessly before her, all the time in the world, all the time in the world. Sometimes she'd almost yawn, stretch. And wait. John Karlen fell back leisurely. Somehow the hard surface he fell against cracked. He heard a sharp antiphony, shattering glass. First behind. Then all around. The explosion echoed, blood burst, acrobat swung in still chandelier-lit air. Then all that fell away from him as he fell away from it through the glass panes of the picture window, fell out and through and backwards and the shattering glass all around him vanished in the sudden omnipresent white sheet of cold.

From his elbows, the back of his neck, the backs of his tiny legs, cuts streamed red and froze on contact with the air. His shirt and trousers clotted red in tiny frozen spots. John Karlen didn't notice. He was running in the snow.

Meeting sky, the snow seemed pure white; the air above slightly gray, and darker with late afternoon. It was all quite still. There were the sounds of small feet crunching once and a while through surface. In certain areas, the surface had a rainbow tint caused by a few stray smatterings of lighter-than-gray daylight. John Karlen saw the horizon: silver line against the mirror of white. He headed toward it, fell. His face cracked once on the frozen surface but he didn't feel a thing. He stood and ran again, heading for that far-off horizon of silver he knew was attainable, somewhere away from the explosion of guns leaping out of ermine wrapping, the gush of blood down a pale exposed thigh, swing of miniature acrobats from a wood-and-glue trapeze. But his small limbs seemed to shrink, feelingless. He lost the gray contrast of sky, face cracked again on a hard, ungiving mirror of endless white.

John Karlen dreamed.

Against snow, he smiled in his sleep. He dreamed of the great white circus, and of cherubs flying through air. Under hot ring lights their bodies gleamed, carved of gold. Wings wrapped one over the other like birds sheltering birds in a nest. The cherubs intertwined, flew blended together. One male, one female—but he could not tell which was which because the figures were so solidly intertwined. The ringmaster pointed up to where golden cherubs hovered, stopped in flight and blended one body into the other. The ringmaster nodded calmly, smiled.

Behold. Thy love before God is like the love of man and woman.

The elephant snorted agreement. And the crowd went wild.

The crowd was a moving, shouting mass of bodies stripping in harsh ring lights, clothes flung everywhere, arms reaching, flesh white, flesh brown, bodies moving together to blend one into the other in frenetic imitation of the suspended golden cherubs. Approving, the ringmaster smiled. Amidst the pandemonium he was untouched, calm. In the great white circus there was everything, he told John Karlen, everything, and all things were quite all right.

All things are holy before the Lord thy God, blessed be He, Creator of the Universe, Master of all Splendor.

Impaled, intertwined, the glistening bodies of the ringside crowd seemed to blend until the whole mass was one chaotic body of a million wriggling legs and swaying hips, breasts crushed to breasts, and down thousands of pairs of thighs ran streams of red. Feet washed with red and he was about to panic until he realized his mistake: this was not blood, not a substance coming from bodies themselves. The ground had turned to violet; they were rolling in grapes. Bunches of grapes streaming purple, trampled to crushed pulp under feet, staining the rolling frantic bodies wine-red. The lion hoop caught fire and shot up into air above, a circular torch, a demented halo.

Blessed be He, the ringmaster sang in a flowing, rich baritone, *the Lord our God, King of the Universe*.

Some bodies wilted, paled against the background of wine, stiffened; faces brightened in some sort of—what was it?—some sort of ultimate sensation, of bliss, of death. Some died. But the cherubs were still, suspended, and the ringmaster nodded again. Everything was all right, he said, in the great white circus. All life. All death.

Though I walk through the valley of the shadow of death.

John Karlen opened his eyes and white blinded him. Then, slowly, against the blinking white he saw faces of men he did not know. Beyond them, the face of his father.

Of the shadow of death. I will fear no.

He closed his eyes again, returned to the circus where acrobats flew now, flipped from trapezes with brilliant ease and caught one another in the nick of time, well-oiled limbs, hands rosined for firm grips, dressed in flashing, spangled white. In red-stained bleachers the audience was naked, stained red like the wood, and wrapped in each other's arms they all seemed to sleep with utter calm. His mother smiled invitingly to him from the center of the ring. She opened her arms. Then one hand flew to her chest; she supported a naked breast and pressed it out toward him. Her other hand held a snaking, winding stick. Her smile was entirely peaceful, as though produced by some soporific drug: calming, reassuring. And in the background John Karlen heard the strange musical chanting of many voices, a foreign lament.

"Hypothermia," said a doctor.

The acrobats froze, white angels suddenly stilled in air, outstretched arms turning swiftly into white-feathered wings. The wing tips touched—just barely. Another particle of an inch and they would have grasped one another, been assured of safety; but here they were, frozen instead in the air in perpetual promise of a safety they would now never attain. Two alabaster figures, ivory carvings facing each another, wings outstretched and touching. The acrobats smiled. Both were female.

"—Mr. Zachary, sir."

His mother raised the twisted, curling thing that was her wand. John Karlen huddled before her. Something poured on him from the breast she squeezed. He felt warmed then, entirely comforted. Above, the ivory angels hovered, wings touching, and in the bleachers all slept naked with a sound-less sleep like death. The many-voiced chanting increased. It was a language he'd never heard before, yet it seemed he could understand it completely.

We shall burn incense to the Queen of Heaven and shall pour her libations as we used to do.

An image came to him of his mother's pale thigh streaming red. He shook his head on the pillow, banished the image forever.

We, our fathers, our kings and our princes in the cities of Judah and in the streets of Jerusalem.

The warmth increased, became a steady, pleasant heat. The boy's head rolled against white sheets, face blasted a sudden hot feverish pink.

For then we had plenty of food, and we all were well and saw no evil.

John Karlen made small sounds. Voices talked above him. Half in, half out of the great white circus, he was confused and began to cry.

But since we ceased burning incense to the Queen of Heaven, chanted the voices, *and pouring her libation, we have wanted everything and have been consumed by sword and famine.*

White drops spattered from his mother's breast. They fell on him, cooling now in the bright heat of misery where he rolled, burning, tiny body stretched out in the sheets of a hospital bed. John Karlen opened his eyes, looked up suddenly. What he remembered later was a skylight—and he would wonder, idly, how that could be. No such thing as skylights in hospital rooms, not to his knowledge. It must, then, have been a hallucination. Still, he remembered a skylight, and the dark starlessness of the night it framed, and falling softly through darkness onto the panes of skylight glass were thick, soft drops of white. He reached feebly as if to touch the drops. Reached up for the snow.

Rolling his chair back from the cleared desk and swiveling around to face the window, John Karlen Zachary had left the spindly image of the child behind and was a full, muscular, aging man verging on plump. He had a roundness to his eyes and cheeks, that flushed thick German look.

He was in New York for a week. Then out to Chicago. Then back for a while. Then L.A.

Outside, the city was hot, cotton shirts melting into sweating skin on street-level backs. His offices in every part of the world were the same, though, all protected from extremities of weather and circumstance.

Turning back to his desk, he reached to press a button.

Venetian blinds turned their edges farther down over the window. The office was dark save for a small, oddly intense circle of light emanating from the bright fluorescent desk lamp.

He pressed another button and the desk top began to glow. It glowed in the shape of a large rectangle, blanching the dark surface. When he reached to flick off the lamp there was still a broad rectangle of light shimmering before him.

He loosened his tie. This slight movement was somehow out of place in the room, incongruent with the man himself. The man himself was stolid-looking. He didn't seem to be the kind from whom quick, nervous motions would come; still, the rapid jerking at the neckline betrayed something about him. Fingers—usually thick and at rest—quivered for a second against the loosened silk knot, then dropped to the glowing desk top. Fingers tapped in some sort of rhythm known only to him, and as they did so they made enlarged, distorted shadows against the background of white light.

John Karlen pressed a third button and the light began to change.

Every person has about them a public truth and a private truth. The public truth is a daily enacted drama of mannerisms, of words spoken and ideas brought vividly, momentarily to life with a single gesture, a way of dressing, a way of walking or of hesitating before picking up the phone. This public truth is related to a person's idealized vision of himself; it is a continual attempt to appear to be what one might hope to be, or what one might hope others expect one to be. The private truth is different, composed of half-remembered dreams, lingering fears, nervous involuntary motions and spontaneous reachings for joy, or for the cessation of solitude. It is a sort of shadow world in which time defies its own rules, works sometimes in reverse, mingles the daughter with the grown woman, the boy with the man, so that in private moments the truth of one's life can work even physical distortions upon a person: sometimes a noticeable shriveling takes place, or a strutting way of walking when one thinks nobody can see. Sometimes the person talks to himself, acts out over and over again that grasping for the elusive, dimly recalled visions of childhood. Neither truth—public or private—is more fundamentally true, or real, than the other. Both public and private create the person; the person creates both, and the outside world—as macrocosm of individual needs, desires, reachings—runs on the combined steam of both truths. John Karlen Zachary, sitting in his office, was in a limbo universe now of combined steam. He was halfway between the public and the private truth of his own life.

The desk glowed softly to a cartographer's crayon-like green, and as the image came into focus the color brightened until it became harsh, tainted the ruddiness of his face a sickly shade, shadowed his gray hair the color of limes.

John Karlen leaned farther over to see. He followed lines curling into and around the map which had glowed to being on his desk top, circuitous routes into the interior of Bellagua. Each squiggling line stopped abruptly at some point; the squiggles angled in from various starting points along the island's eastern coast, and if you gazed long enough it could be seen that the abrupt end of each line, when viewed from above, delineated some kind of invisible boundary; that all the lines' end points, taken together, seemed to delineate the border of a certain territory in the central part of the interior. It was as if every zone had been penetrated save one, and this zone was at the core of things, circular, waiting, unyielding.

He pushed another button and subtle changes occurred in the map glowing before him. The lines vanished, and on various areas of the bright green background appeared small splotches of white. John Karlen gazed at this a while. In the green light surrounded by cool darkness, his lips opened as if to speak but nothing came out. He looked a long time.

He touched the button again and this time the change was more radical. That entire central territory—invisible boundaries delineated by the crawling, tortuous lines now vanished—faded slowly to be replaced by a large patch of white. It was many times larger than the surrounding, random ivory splotches, a solid white thing like spilled paint, or a torn remnant of canvas.

John Karlen's fingers tapped again in sudden speed on the map's green rim, creating long, stabbing shadows across the white-splotched surface.

He closed his eyes.

Time was sometimes nothing—this knowledge he could feel swell inside as he slipped from public consciousness to private—time was often lost when memory took over, and the experience of the past could sometimes be relived so vividly that one's heart would match the exact same elevated pulse it had beat once upon a time, that time you were remembering. So he did a slow pan of furniture, of closets lining walls, closets packed with trousers, closets wrapped in furs, rooms filled with shoes. He'd clambered over and through a vast assortment of things, textures, colors, to reach this point in his life where he sat quietly, eyes shut, in air-conditioned darkness.

Miss Scott. I wish to protest your revolting relationship with my daughter.

Sitting across the desk, she'd looked at him in slight surprise. She seemed barely perturbed. There was silence in which, after a while, she shrugged.

Gazing out from the cool white fury inside, he was aware of some dim, half-remembered thing; something which knocked at his primitive memory and told him it had always been this way.

It is immoral, and obscene.

She leaned toward him, her arms stretched on the desk. The aggression of the gesture surprised him and he sat back with a brief, nearly hidden stab of nervousness.

Really, Mr. Zachary. Are you suggesting there's something obscene about the nature of our relationship? She paused. She smiled briefly, mirthlessly. *Is that what you're suggesting? I hope not. Oh, I hope you're not. Your choice of words, Mr. Zachary—it's all wrong.*

He stared. She was framed against the half-opened Venetian blinds that let sun through the window in geometrical patterns. The sun streaked diagonally across her shoulders. It bleached the left side of her face when she leaned back into it, so for a moment the face coolly returning his stare was part shadow and part white. He noticed her eyes, boldly examining; she seemed, now, to be slightly curious, and the dark eyes had in them a teasing spark. John Karlen kept looking. It had always been like this, he knew. His people versus hers.

Sitting across the desk staring back at Raina Scott, he could almost remember.

Are you threatening me, Miss Scott?

She sighed. *If those are your terms. Maybe I ought to explain something to you, Mr. Zachary. It pleases me to protect what I love. And if you try to hurt her in any way, I will come after you and hunt you down and I will kill you.*

She stifled a yawn. One hand swept lazily, gracefully, to her lips. How strange, he thought, strange that she'd just said what she had and seemed so at ease. He felt a reluctant twinge of admiration.

John Karlen opened his eyes. White-splotched green glowed before him. He noticed that he'd spread both hands on the desk. They stretched across the mottled surface, five-pointed shadows. He ran fingers caressingly over pools of white, then pressed a button and the map before him changed back to what it had once been: crayon-green broken only by small, wiggling dark lines that invaded it and abruptly ended.

In his mind, he superimposed a face over everything before him. It was the face of his daughter Karlen. He watched it change, age slightly, until it had completed the metamorphosis from infant to woman, the woman still young, still beautiful. She had that pouting look. It was the one she always gave him; it came after her wounded look, and was followed by the sight of her back as she walked away. He couldn't even count the times she'd turned with sure grace and simply walked away—her most successful mode of getting what she wanted. Still, much as she'd ruled him with these subtle tantrums, in giving in to them he ruled her as well, became her source, her sustenance, the spring from which all her desires would be met. She'd stick her sneaker-clad feet on the polished edge of some dining room table, racket pat-patting insolently against one hip while she crossed arms over her chest, waited. It seemed she was always waiting for something from him—some demand, some praise, a bauble or high-priced trinket he invariably brought back from one of his trips. He outfitted entire rooms for her pleasure: Ping-Pong tables measured to professional specification, racket-lined walls, indoor basketball courts, volleyball nets waiting to be unraveled, hoops vibrating on walls with each lay-up shot. He reveled in what she was becoming: a graceful, slender, swift creature, androgynous in the precision of each goal-driven motion, wiltingly beautiful when she stopped and tossed her long, thick brown hair back and her eyes sparkled particles of green. He reveled in it, and at the same time was disappointed because it failed that other, more traditional standard—the one which would demand softness of her, a girlishly clumsy demeanor and hands which were uncalloused, heart that pattered timidly instead of slowly and strongly, a body used to slipping into the folds of silk and satin designers' dresses, eyelashes fluttering, subtly tinted cheeks blushing, feet arching painfully down to curve into stiletto heels. He'd made her, somehow, unafraid. At times he found himself mourning her lack of fear. It was dangerous. Lack of fear—that could get her in trouble some day. He knew it. Could get her in trouble with people, with men, men like himself. But he had made her unafraid. So much so that she'd had the nerve to stray far from his houses, his credit cards, his modes; she'd strayed far from his love, been so unafraid as to jump into the great beckoning void of love for another. And he'd lost her.

It seemed to him this wasn't the first time he'd ever lost her but only a slightly different repetition of some older time, some other time, when he had lost her to violence or love. Sitting there, he could almost see the face grin mildly at him, a child's once again. He could almost see her blink, mouth broaden in that smile she had bordering on sly; he could almost see her wink. The way she'd done, maybe, ages ago, all the other times he'd lost her. This time, he would find her.

John Karlen shook his head and the image faded. He gazed at jungle that was the interior of Bellagua. Somewhere in there was his daughter. Somewhere in there was his daughter, and Raina Scott. He'd accepted the inevitability of it painfully, over a long period of time—the inevitability of knowing that if one was found, so would the other be. Because they were attracted like magnets; the truth rolled inside him with a foul taste. They repelled and attracted and somehow blended together, and he knew that in order to get her back he'd have to perform an irremediable sort of surgery.

So be it.

He pressed the button again and the desk-top glow faded to darkness.

John Karlen stood carefully. He was momentarily stooped with a heavy kind of weariness. He crossed to the window, lifted an edge of Venetian blind so sunlight shot through, stabbed a streak of bleached white across the back of his hand. For a moment he thought of acrobats clad in sparkling white. For a moment, he harbored his vision of the great white circus, bright ring lights, a little boy stumbling in snow and spatters of blood flying from his elbows, spotting dark against all that glittering pallor. He closed his eyes. Behind closed lids the acrobat tumbled, swung, twisted and grinned, hurtled toward him through the air with the twinkling white certainty of a shooting star, of death.

This time, he'd find her.

I'm going to find her, Daddy. She'd stuck her feet on his desk again. It reminded him of old times. He noticed she no longer wore Keds, but LS Specials—that new line of athletic footwear he'd seen promoted everywhere, another company owned by International. Then he knew which company it was and who owned it, and something in him died again, shut off to the beckoning warmth of nostalgia. He glared across the desk at her. She seemed not to care. Still, there were tears in her eyes. He felt glad for a moment, savagely glad, to see tears in her eyes. *I'm going to find her. No matter what you did I'll find her, Daddy. Don't you try to stop me.*

John Karlen Zachary opened his eyes to the dark of his office, sunlight shafting through. He stood there at the window and his shoulders relaxed. Then he was no mogul, no madman, no monster—merely a man. He was the latest in a long, long line of men burdened by possessions, by their own sense of loss. Lonely men, standing at windows, staring out at the great, blank expanse of what they owned.

THEY'LL DIE IN OVERTIME

When he got out of the hospital, Pablo took to walking a lot.

His ribs hurt at first; the legs had remained sound, though, and with his right arm held a little crooked and twitching at unpredictable times and the fingers of his right hand curled inward—crushed nerves, they'd told him—and some small muscle on the right side of his face gone permanently lax so that side never smiled, he had a strange, mean look to him. He took to walking all over the city, at all hours. No one ever bothered him.

He'd gotten back on the last flight out of Bellagua. Somehow, when he'd been still unconscious, basic first aid had been administered, things arranged in that way they had of being arranged. Pablo figured there were a couple of worlds operating in the universe simultaneously. The world where things could be arranged, deals made with the flash of a smile, the rattling of phony ID papers down unknown corridors—this was the world invisible to him, yet existing side by side with the one in which he had moved, dreamed, and tapped the lens cap of old Alfredo comfortingly. So he'd awakened in a hospital bed in New York City with a sense that something irreparable had finally happened to him—and that, somehow, he'd been waiting for it all his life.

His phone calls to Zachary went unanswered. So did the calls to Nash at Royal Hotel—*Urgent!* he pleaded with cool receptionist voices, *Please say it's urgent!* But for him the real kicker was that even Joe Goldberg wouldn't return his calls. Pablo could never get through. The man at the other end was always busy, always on another line, out sick, out to lunch, at a meeting. Several days of this and Pablo'd gotten the message: he no longer existed. He'd been scrubbed from the blackboard of their professional lives; why bother returning the phone calls of a man who didn't exist? Still semi-dazed from aftereffects of painkillers and anaesthesia, the thought spun through his head that maybe this was the way it would be from now on. *Those bastards*, he'd thought before; now, he had some idea of who *they* were. The only problem was that they were so many. This new-found knowledge didn't frighten him, just depressed him more. He was surprised to get his first check from Royal Hotel in the mail, on schedule.

He still hadn't opened most of his mail. It was piled high on the kitchen table, some he'd just thrown away without a second glance. He had some insurance money, had some money saved, plus the rest of the newly arrived Royal Hotel advance. There was all the time in the world, he told himself— though for what, he could not have said. Three days out of the hospital he got a letter from Gabriel's wife, which he opened. She had heard, she wrote in bad English, about his accident, and felt much pain. When he was better, she wanted him to come to Jerusalem for a long visit. Gabi also would love that. She wanted much to meet him. She signed it Love, Yael, and he felt warmed for an entire afternoon before throwing it in the garbage with some other mail. Pablo went for a walk. He walked all the way down-town, decided to take a subway local back. He'd been gone several hours when he felt it: a ripple up the spine. Then he knew someone was following.

He didn't turn around.

The sensation lasted. He rode subways for hours—up, down, crosstown. Someone followed.

It was a muggy, desolate 3:00 A.M. that night when he found himself face to face with wall graffiti on the station platform at 96th and Broadway. It was small handwriting, oddly neat, almost unnoticeable among the pro-liferation of other words scrawled everywhere around, and it was etched deliberately, darkly:

RAINA

That was all.

Something stung his eyes. He felt tears, for a moment wondered why, and for a moment forgot what the word could mean. The tears vanished before spilling; then he had it, knew it, and touched the fingers of his left hand gently to the wall, traced the outlines of letters etched there.

His fingertips traveled down, found the + symbol somewhere beneath a multitude of coarse words swirling illegibly. His eyes followed. Somewhere along the opposite platform a drunk sang, stopped to hiccup. Pablo searched. He pretended the things scrawled over what he searched for did not exist— they were words painted or carved or crayoned along the rough, grimy surface, would vanish if he willed it and leave only words he wanted to see: RAINA + —followed by the name he willed into being.

K, his thumb caressed. A. Written in the same small, intense, deliberate block letters, etched with the same edge of some sharp object. K. A. He bent closer to the wall, could smell alcoholic piss. He looked for a final letter under the maze of garbage. His second finger zig-zagged, touched. He had it. Z.

Pablo stepped back. Behind him, the tracks were lit with approaching train lights and animals scurried off to holes out of reach. The drunken singing was obscured by the sound of a train clattering nearer. He looked at what he'd found. A simple, oddly unoriginal thing to carve into walls or trunks of trees; the only item missing was a heart's outline to encompass both names. Although maybe, he smiled to himself, maybe it was there too, just more indecipherable than the other letters, more hidden beneath a barrage of fresher banalities.

RAINA

+

KAZ

That was all.

Someone watched. Pablo could sense it.

Behind him everything screeched, train doors grumbled half open and nobody got out. The drunk was into blues now. *I don't care where they bury me, Lord!*

The train went on. Its racket clattered away, vanished. From the ceiling, occasional drops spattered to the platform's cement edge.

Pablo bent farther down until his ribs hurt. He pressed his right cheek to the dirt-greased wall and it stayed there, lax, unsmiling, forever numb. He knew what letters the cheek was pressed against, though, could feel it somewhere inside beyond irreparably ruined muscle and the skin covering it, and for a minute he forgot about being followed and felt he'd finally reached home. He wondered when she'd etched it in. Some late night maybe, some long, wandering, aimless night of after-party nausea and emptiness, with your lover gone off to Java or somewhere to nab a few thresher sharks and there you were, lovesick, forlorn, no volleyball practice until next week and the only comforting sound in all the world that familiar pat-pat of a wooden paddle—no, *racket*—against your hip, sheathed in its beaten hand-stitched leather case; on such a night, after a few too many Millers or Heinekens, on such a night you would wish for decent champagne, maybe; maybe you would burst at whatever seams you had, and since the lovesickness bursting in you stemmed from the sort of love that is generally not shouted from rooftops, not seen walking hand in hand along midtown streets, not sanctified by the marriage ceremony, you might strive, on such a night, against this stomping of societal boot heels on a feeling so intimate, so profound. You might strive to create something, anyway—even though in the act of proclamation something else got defaced, you might justify this by the thought that even brilliantly applied oils deface the purity of canvas. You would snatch out the pocket knife no one knew you carried, draw a heart's outline, maybe, with a thin childlike arrow through, and deeply, deliberately, etch in the right names.

He heard the faraway screech of another train. The drunk hadn't shut up yet, he was singing the same line over and over. *I don't care where they bury me, Lord!* Pablo breathed deeply with a sense of sudden clarity. He pressed his numb cheek harder against the wall, the letters etched there, and for a second could have sworn there was some vanishing twinkle of sensation. The clack of the train wailed closer. Pablo could feel her. He wept.

As he groped toward the nearby bench, his left hand casually brushed its top, touched one item of graffiti among all the others carved there. His fingers seemed to stick. Something like chill shot up to the elbow. He had to stare a long time to make it out, but there it was—the same sharp-edged instrument used in the same terse, deliberate script:

KAZ WAS HERE

His fingers searched frantically in the maze of letters, trying to ascertain the date that followed, but it was blotted out by other things.

José 95. Beni sucks cock. Pray and be happy God loves you. Beware the fascists posing as gods for they will bleed your soul. Renaldo Numero Uno. Suck my dick mama. Pray to the Lord our God. Only He can Save you.

And next to *Pray to the Lord our God. Only He can Save you,* more tiny block letters leaped out at him, caused his hand to pause, and tremble:

WHO DO YOU THINK YOU ARE, JOE?

The electric hum spread inside him. He blinked at the mutilated bench surface. Something was here—he knew it. Behind him, someone watched; he sensed their approval. What was it she'd said? Extrasensory perception? And asked did he believe in it, and he'd said oh, he hadn't thought about it much and so she'd said she was glad, glad he didn't think about the things he didn't think about—sure, he remembered. But something here was flooding him with a sensation that couldn't be defined as physical but was just as certainly not hallucinated, and as far as he could tell was unrelated to any emotion except maybe what you'd feel bursting through layers of tough substance to find something—some*thing*—he didn't know—akin to truth. It had come to him of its own accord and now he opened his arms to the thing he'd never thought much about and let it take over, let it whisper in his ear stuff he hadn't heard before. It told him he would come close to something soon, if only he believed. It told him to be patient, persevering. Told him that was why he'd been driven underground. Everything had its purpose, it told him; everything had its price. And if only he believed, then he would draw nearer to the thing—the thing he'd dimly sensed in her, the thing she'd imparted to him in half-truths and lies, the thing he had tried all his life to capture in photographs, the thing he had been damaged for. It would lead him there.

A train was coming.

The telling, tingling sensation was no longer so elusive as hours went by and he continued his search through the station. Sometimes he'd feel like she was walking beside him. Smiling coolly, staying just out of reach.

Mentally, he listed the growing legacy of graffiti she'd left behind there.

RAINA
+
KAZ

AND

KAZ WAS HERE

AND

WHO DO YOU THINK YOU ARE, JOE?
FOOL,

she'd written in response to someone's proclamation that the Knicks would defeat the Celtics in an upcoming game,

THEY'LL DIE IN OVERTIME.

When the train shrieked to a stop he wheeled around, thought he caught a glimpse of color, a shirt, a body scurrying into the first car, carrying something—spray cans?

After the train screeched out of the station he saw it. He wondered why he hadn't noticed it before—it was on the wall right across the tracks. Someone had spent some time on this one, had carried along a few cans of different paints and taken the trouble to apply it carefully. And even if the art was crude, it had a certain power to it, sprayed with attempted care over a tattered advertisement.

It was a landscape of green. In the forefront sat a blurred white snowman, withered brown stick arms, brown button eyes and mouth curved in a grin. To one side, the landscape was signed in brown, wiggling script: *Carlos.* Beneath the landscape's green were more brown words, letters erratic and sprawling. But they could be deciphered: *¿Cuándo hay Figuras de Nieve en las climas tropicales?* When are there Snowmen in tropical climates?

White arrows pointed the way.

A few panels down was another landscape on another faded ad poster—this time a green half-mound with a crudely drawn palm tree sticking up out of it—recognizable as a stilted representation of an island. Next to the palm, another snowman on a slightly smaller scale, same withered arms, same hollow eyes and distorted grin. *Ask Frosty,* said the words scripted below in English. Same handwriting. Also signed *Carlos.* And beneath all that, in the same brown scrawling paint, an address in the West Forties, third floor. Pablo sat again suddenly, shaking. He was alone in the station. The battering sound of an approaching train on tracks came louder. He memorized the address.

It was one of those old, shitty, black-stained buildings filled with floors that had once been factory outlets, floors where two-bit vending companies kept their offices, unrented floors where ancient prizefight posters still peeled from the walls. There was a guy in uniform keeping one eye on the elevators, one on the door. Pablo had to sign in. Late afternoon. He hadn't slept, but he'd remembered to go home, shave, change clothes. So he looked tired and the usual weird, but other than that presentable.

The elevator chugged up a couple floors. It stalled midway between the second and third, lights flashed on the door panel a little crazily, red, yellow, red. Then they went dark, there was a groan from somewhere below and the elevator picked up again, chugged its way to the third floor and stopped uneasily, doors hesitating before easing open.

Pablo sidled out. Behind him the elevator squeaked, clanked shut, and he heard pulleys complain. He was in a large old gymnasium. The floor had that polished piney sheen; he noticed basketball hoops folded up, backboard mechanisms extended out above a few rows of empty bleachers. A couple of exercise mats had been stacked against one wall. He took it all in—the old sweat smells, varnish, the open high-ceilinged emptiness—before noticing the insistent, rhythmic sound coming from the other end of the gym. Pablo turned, felt his right arm twitch and grabbed it savagely with his other hand. The volleyball was served against a wall, plunked there with a brutal, ringing thud, and bounced back to the server with sure speed. Slowly, he walked toward the other end of the gym. In between thuds and bounces, he could hear his tennis shoes squeak on varnished wood.

She was dressed in shorts and a raggedy old tie-dyed man's undershirt from long ago. The shirt's rainbow colors were highlighted against the dark wood-brown of her skin—a background so smooth, warm, and burnished that the rainbow seemed insignificant in comparison and the thought of white skin ridiculous. She was long and slim and tough, broad-shouldered. The legs, sprouting sockless out of ancient racing flats up into thighs that disappeared too soon, were wonderful; they were like the legs of an animal designed for speedy and graceful movement, arching flexibly with each serve, relaxed, ready, waiting. She focused intently on the ball in her hand. She hadn't noticed him. The ball spun up, fist hit forward and up in a perfect bullet-like arc and arm followed, reaching long and solid, dark and rippling, after the flying ball.

Each movement was precise, yet smooth and unselfconscious. Jet hair pulled back tightly from her face in a severe ponytail, tied with a scarlet ribbon. Her cheekbones were high. Something about the long, straight bridge of the nose reminded him of hieroglyphic illustrations on Egyptian tombs. A faint scrim of sweat veiled the face. Pablo watched her profile. He was a little in love.

"Who you want?"

She never took her eyes from the ball but served perfectly, watched it thud with powerful deliberation against the wall, opened a hand to receive it on the second bounce back. She served again with no break in motion. She hadn't looked at him once.

Frosty, he whispered, then realized he'd spoken too softly to be heard. He cleared his throat and it still came out hoarse.

"Frosty."

One hand stopped the ball. This time, though, she paused. She gazed ahead at the wall, then dribbled a little, still not looking at him, spun the volleyball on one finger and clasped it to her chest. The tie-dyed rainbow clung where she'd sweated through; he saw her bold, perfect outline. She wheeled around to face him.

"Shit. Look what the tide washed up."

Despite himself, he laughed.

She laughed too then, and they both stood there while the sounds of laughter echoed to the high ceiling and got lost, ghostlike. She was spinning the ball again on a finger. Then she stopped laughing. He noticed she was about an inch or so taller than he.

"All right. Who you want, turkey? Who sent you?"

He shrugged. It was the only way to keep from freezing up inside; he felt the right arm begin to quiver and reached for it quickly, held it half crossed over his chest and belly. He tried a grin—a partial smile—all there would ever be. The name came out by instinct:

"Carlos."

Her expression soured to one of annoyance. "Damn. That nigger. What's he want *now*, huh?" The dark, enormous eyes fixed on him. "Huh?"

Pablo could barely feel himself breathe. By instinct, he told himself, instinct. Inside there was the faint inkling of something, some tiny sputterings of the telltale electricity he'd come to know. He let words carry him along. "He just said"—it came out a sigh—"to ask Frosty"—he stopped, throat clogged. She frowned impatiently.

"Ask what?"

He breathed. "About the Snowmen."

He thought he saw a nervous quiver near her eye for a moment. She muttered under her breath.

Pablo got a firmer grip on his right elbow. It was jumping uncontrollably, arm moving against his belly in spasmodic jerks. He forced himself to speak into her eyes. "So if you see Frosty"—he tried another half-grin—"tell him Pablo's looking for him."

The ball dropped sullenly. It bounced a little, rolled toward the wall; she stuck both hands on her hips and stood there glaring. Despite the threat of her gaze, he sensed she was a little frightened. But she managed a quiet chuckle.

"That mother. All right, what's your story?"

"I'm looking for—"

"*I'm* Frosty, you turkey." The noble head moved from side to side. Then she'd stopped smiling altogether, was examining him with an almost professional sort of skepticism that he couldn't place. She sighed. "I guess you got to take what you can get, huh? Shit. You don't look like much to me, boy. What's your story? AWOL? You jump parole? They looking to float you with bricks?"

The electricity shot high. Near, near, he could almost smell it. He blurted words out desperately—words, any words—maybe they would purchase more time.

"We can talk about it. Let me buy you a drink."

She sneered. "Who you think you are, Joe?"

"My name's Pablo."

Then he stopped, mouth open. And wanted to shout. He wanted to bow down to her, or plant grateful, tearful kisses all along the sleek burnished brown of her body. He risked everything.

"I'm a friend of a friend, maybe. Karlen? You know her?"

Against the wall, the volleyball scuffed sadly. It was the only sound in the empty gym. Through slits of windows up near the ceiling, afternoon had turned into evening.

"Shit," she said. The large eyes were suddenly damp, about to cry.

They sat on the lowest bleacher. Pablo felt a distinct, gnawing lack of privacy. Or maybe it was just that he'd waited so long, felt so raw and exposed in the face of meeting someone who'd known her.

He told her everything, figured somehow that was what he had to do. She dribbled the ball between her knees whenever he paused. She gave an occasional sad smile. At those moments her profile became quite dramatic: rose-tinged black, sharp definite lines of the face stunning in a way that reminded you of time's beginning. Nefertite had looked something like this. Cleopatra. Jezebel. And around them, small white men had bowed down, spilled out their hearts. Pablo could sense all this. To confess in her presence was quite correct. It made him feel he was returning to the rightful flow of things; or rather, joining the flow for the first time in his life. Sometimes she'd shake her head—*crazy bitch!* she'd mutter—and the sad smile would stay a little longer.

After a while he was silent.

She began to talk herself, then, voice muted, faintly sad. They'd played for the same team. Volleyball. Karlen was tough, strong serve, went right to the net—no messing around. You never would have known she was a little white rich kid, not from the way she played. And she didn't give out much at first; no telling what was on her mind until you'd hung around a while, hung around the showers, the locker room, maybe traded hairbrushes, borrowed shampoos back and forth, assisted in some last-minute volleys and gone out later for a couple beers. Then you'd hear her bitching, maybe. Bitching about some other shitty one-night-stand with some stupid wombat. The old joke—she smiled at Pablo, unabashed, and her full dark lips were taunting but in an almost friendly way—the one that was good for a few laughs over beer with the girls afterwards: *What you got there? If that was a little bigger it'd look like a cock.* Some more old jokes too. Pablo winced but kept listening. The night someone said to her, Hey, you always shittin' about what lousy fucks all these men are. Whyn't you try a goddamn girl, honey? And the beer glasses stopped midair, voices stopped, bitching stopped, a nervous giggle sounded somewhere, and Frosty caught herself halfway through swallowing, realizing those words had come from her very own mouth. But Karlen was a crazy bitch. Shit. She had those little things of green in her eyes. Pretty, you had to admit it. But it was more, too— she just had a way about her. She'd looked straight at her, smiled a little, said, At this point, *anyone* will do. And they all cracked up then so the nervousness died. But Frosty was suddenly hopping mad. She pressed the point with wicked grins—*Come on girl, maybe you queer and you don't know it yet!*—and Karlen slid her glass across the beer-slicked tabletop until it clinked to a stop right next to Frosty's. She shrugged a little like it was no big deal. *Then show me.* She invited calmly. *Show me someone who will hold my attention.* Frosty turned to Pablo and rolled the ball in her lap. Her face had softened somehow, looked sort of sad.

"Crazy bitch."

"Did you love her?" Pablo gave himself a wry smile. It seemed this was becoming kind of a habit, sitting around asking some beautiful woman if she loved some other woman. But in a way the idea was a turn-on; it left him out of the action but also out of the way of danger—gave him the entrée of a voyeur without any of the attendant stigma. Frosty gave a non-committal smile. It occurred to him then that her nickname was a perfect one; she was cool without being too forbidding. And despite the toughness, there was something delicate about her. Black ice, he thought.

"Love? Nah." She frowned. "*Love.* Shit. That's a funny word, boy. I don't know, maybe a little. We messed around some." She laughed. The sound soared and dissipated, echoing like antiphonal voices in a theater whose acoustics had gone wild. "Some. But whatever we were doing just started us laughing. It's funny sometimes, you know." Keeping his gaze, she winked. It was a sudden, deliberate movement in the dark, still face, like a bright marble rolling suddenly across blank surfaces. "It is. One day she's acting like the ball could blow up right in front of her face and it wouldn't make her yawn, you know? Next I hear she's in love with some bitch. In *love.* I mean, she had it bad. Then this bitch she's with disappears.

And she's cruising everywhere—I mean, she's paying off some rough people, you know—swearing all over town how she'll find her. Then *she* disappears. And I'm the one's left with the dirty work, and I'm in it ass-deep. But you think it stopped me? No. So it's something bigger, isn't it? Huh? You think? I mean, something bigger says when you gonna find someone who all the sudden *holds* your *attention*." She shook her head. "Crazy bitch. She was always blabbering about this white whale shit. Get a few beers in her and no shutting her up. Chasing whales, my ass. Like she didn't have enough problems. You know what I mean?"

Pablo nodded. He thought maybe he did.

The ball dribbled, thuds echoed. Frosty clamped it between her legs. She turned to him. "Yeah. Well, you better see Carlos, I guess. Tell him I say okay. Tell him—" the smile reappeared, froze her lips for a second in that enigmatic expression which was unyielding and also strangely tender. She shrugged. "Nah. Just tell him I said okay, okay? And you better go now, turkey." She squinted up toward the windows, noticed darkness for the first time. "You gotta be there by ten sharp and I *do* mean *sharp*. You got a pen?"

He shook his head. Then he wanted to ask what all this was about, but something warned No and he kept his mouth shut, everything inside stretched tight and quivering. Pablo was silent. He searched through himself for sounds; there was neither a lack of fear nor fear's presence; nothing but an all-encompassing waiting silence that he'd never felt before. No, he shook his head dumbly. No pen.

She met his eyes. "Good. I'm gonna tell you once and that's it." She leaned forward. He felt the dark lips brush his ear slightly, address whispered, and he repeated it to himself with silent insistence, number and street and apartment singsonging in his head until there was nothing else there.

The ball rolled out from between her feet. She laid a brief, deliberate kiss on his ear that made him shiver suddenly, made him memorize— along with the address—the rainbow streaks of her tie-dyed undershirt and her musky, female smell. The kiss ended as definitely as it had begun. She pushed him savagely to his feet. There were tears in her eyes.

"Get lost, turkey. You better go."

Pablo glanced again at the window slits. Why, he wanted to know, why— of all the things that had happened so far—was it the sight of those little windows up there that made him uneasy? As if they were blank eyes, watching everything. Here, closed in a sweaty old gymnasium, here he felt somehow vulnerable, and quite exposed. Then he looked back to her and realized, without knowing why, that his concern was more for her. Did she know, too? Know how easily people could disappear?

"Will I see you again?"

No, she told him, she didn't think so. But then you couldn't ever tell. She smiled, then stood and began twirling the ball on one finger, hand on hip, giving him that look which taunted without offending. No, you couldn't ever tell. Not in this crazy world.

When the elevator doors closed on him, she was practicing serves again. Between winking red lights and the heavy door that groaned shut, he saw the volleyball spin, dark fist slam it just so, then arc through hot wooden air.

He had to go down to Fourteenth and change to the LL. Riding, he gripped an overhead handle so tightly his forearm ached. He was getting there, getting there. He had no idea where *there* was—only knew that it was where he had to go. Pablo felt his shirt cling.

He got off before Brooklyn. Going upstairs to the street a gust of sudden cold hit him, uncharacteristic for summer. When he'd reached the street the chill stayed a while. He went east to Avenue A, then south, then east again. He thought better of it all and backtracked, walked uptown a few blocks. Then he retraced his steps. Some dark slits of eyes from above could be watching—you never knew. Not in this crazy world.

Pablo passed crumbling stairs leading up to pitch-dark hallways from which glowed the tips of cigarettes. Voices murmured sadly from the crap-filled, fenced-in yards left by demolition crews: one voice explaining, cajoling; another demanding; deals were sealed, money changed pockets, hungry cats walked on the rusting tops of fire escape banisters. Sometimes words came to him in Spanish. Laughter echoed out of a second-floor window and looking up he'd see makeshift curtains flutter, dim light shine through from the background. Babies squalled. It reminded him that for some reason the sound of a baby wailing in an atmosphere of Spanish had a sharper, more staccato, immediate tone than it would in any other language—and the sound made him homesick in ways he couldn't have expressed. He was aware that nothing he did here would go unnoticed. The seemingly lazy eyes regarding him from doorsteps took everything in, and if they seemed not to see him, seemed instead to be steeped in their stepside card games, swigging tall cans of Budweiser and sharing a continuous running panoply of inside jokes the way they did every night with all the other guys, this was merely deception. Pablo guessed he wouldn't necessarily be considered an easy mark—he looked like a creep. Now, though, he was just being figured out. He guessed, too, that he was being regarded with just a hint of uneasiness—no one tried to sell him anything. No one was even obvious about glancing his way.

Pablo wound through all the blocks like this until he came to one where the buildings were silent. Windows had been boarded up and some of the boards torn off so only black spaces stared out.

He turned to look but no one was following. He gave another glance up at the remains of fire escapes. No more eyes. There was just the night above, sky fogged slightly with heat so no stars peeked through. He heard a gurgling sound and stared at the curb. Someone had taken the cap off a fire hydrant up the street; water gushed toward sewers in a dirty bubbling stream.

It was into a hollow-eyed building that he turned, barely catching the half-erased number above the doorway. His shoes sifted through damp garbage. He thought he heard something scurry away to his right. In the dark, Pablo stopped. He stood absolutely still, left hand clasped around the right elbow, and standing like that he began to feel very small. When he heard breathing he realized it was not his own. It came, instead, from some space directly ahead.

The Bic lighter flared two feet from his nose. It revealed the zip gun aimed calmly at his forehead, the pimpled young Hispanic face like a crazy mask in flickering yellow light.

"One step closer, *hombre*, you gonna suck on this."

Empty inside, Pablo accepted the sensation of fear almost with joy—it had been a long time—and his hands rose to shoulder height immediately, right one quivering like an injured hawk's claw. He could feel the sweat pouring. Good old sweat, he thought vaguely. Then he wanted to faint. His mouth opened with the dim notion of speaking; he saw the flashing black of small, close-set eyes glittering back at him and his mouth snapped shut. No. He didn't want to suck on anything.

"What you want?" asked the voice behind the gun. It was a young voice, slightly nasal. The pimpled lips smiled nervously. "You gonna be in trouble, man. What you want?"

Carlos. Pablo heard himself from far away. Then he sighed, called up one last reserve of energy and felt his voice return with a stab of pain. "Carlos. Frosty sent me."

The Bic sputtered uneasily. Blue glowed from the flame's center, dribbled a faint, ghastly glow on the ruined walls behind and around. The Bic moved up, then down; the lips with their pinpoint acne spots sneered after a while, and through a dissipating layer of terror Pablo recognized it as a sneer of acceptance. He was being examined.

"*Claro*," sneered the lips. The tone was of resignation. "Okay, *hombre*, I don't kill you yet. You got a name?"

"Pablo."

"Pablo what?"

His hands trembled. Maybe he'd die now. Maybe. Something in him wanted suddenly to force the issue, make this kid murder him in cold blood; he yearned with a cold, tiny kernel of desperation to perform some heroic act and let it lead him to an inevitable death—surely, he thought, certain deeds would all but dictate a fatal ending—then he thought of Raina. She flashed through his mind, shirt blood-soaked, grinning, grinning. And he went blank again. No. No. No, Pablo. This was not the time to die. He wouldn't even have known what cause he was dying for. There—there was the pain of it all: once you knew what cause you were dying for, fully understood and treasured it, you'd prefer to *live* for it instead. Perhaps perseverance was a truer form of heroism. Pablo shrugged. On his forehead, sweat dripped. "Just Pablo."

The dark eyebrows arched. "*¿Tú hablas?*"

Pablo's hands dropped to his sides tiredly. He leaned against some slimy wall and inside there was no more fear, only relief mingled with a bitter exhaustion that couldn't be cured by sleep. "*Sí*," he said simply. The zip gun still pointed his way but wavered a little; it had lost its intention, he knew.

He was led farther back along the black hallway, feet shuffling rubbish with each step. The kid walked cautiously behind muttering unintelligible words. The bizarre thought came to Pablo that it had always been like this. He had always walked at gunpoint down unlighted dead ends. Someone behind him had always clutched some weapon or other, mumbling a litany of foreign sounds. Eventually they'd find out that he was—in some way even he did not understand—an imposter. A clever pretender, who had come this far on luck and instinct alone. What would they call him then? When they found out? Jew? Kike? Traitor?

Queer?

Did it matter?

A cellar door got kicked open with metallic groans and the zip gun pressed his back to indicate the way. Pablo turned and stared down steps that were crumbling dark stone. Beyond the faint light of the Bic he could see, way down at bottom, more faint light.

Pablo took the first step. Inside him, something laughed.

No, the something laughed, no, it doesn't matter. They gonna get you, *chico*. Maybe sooner. Maybe later. Gonna get you, gonna get us all. Who? *Them*. The ones painting this world the color of pigeon shit, that's who. Jew. And if they can't get you for one thing, they gonna get you for another. Kike. Traitor. Jewboy.

Queer.

Pablo laughed silently. He took another step and the zip gun nudged his spine. He was going down toward the light.

Shit, he asked the something inside, you think so? The something laughed with him, nodded sagely. Yeah, *chico*. Sure thing. You think they differentiate? All those labels, all those names—it all means the same goddamn thing to *them*. And *they* gonna get you sooner or later. Guaran*teed*. If they don't call you one thing, they call you another.

Then why not be everything? Everything that you are?

Yeah, laughed the something, *why not?*

He took the steps one at a time, steadily, felt himself suddenly floating in a strange kind of bliss.

"Why not?"

The zip gun moved along his back. "What you say?"

"Nothing." He kept moving. *Why not?* he said to himself. Why the fuck not? And he stifled the laughter. He had a brief urge to turn around and tell the kid something like: I love you, I love your zits. Say something like: What you got for me, *hombre?* I wanna suck on something.

Maybe that was what he wanted.

But Pablo kept walking. What he didn't want was to die.

He hit the bottom step, turned a corner into the sudden flood of dim light. There was a room. There were fold-out metal chairs and men sitting on them. The chairs faced a blackboard, chalk scribbles, and a tiny, quick-stepping man whose leather-gloved hands held chalk while he talked. His head was hooded in a black and green ski mask—the green bright like a Christmas tree.

FREEDOM FIGHTERS

Carlos strutted. His gloved hands waved flamboyantly while he talked, and there was barely a hint of accent in his words. Once in a while he'd motion toward the blackboard with a thin stick of chalk; these motions were vague, seemed to have nothing to do with the various lines scribbled there, white-headed arrows pointing the way to a circle smack in the center of the board which was blank, unidentified. He noticed Granito slide in from upstairs, some creep in tow. He didn't let on that he'd noticed, just kept talking—it would be more impressive that way. He'd had careful instruction in the art of leadership. It worked like magic; he knew that the men sitting there watching him and listening had also noticed another presence in the room. Taking their cue from him, though, they did not turn to look—all eyes remained fixed on the gloved hands, the magnificent ski mask.

Watching, Pablo knew it was Carlos. The gun pressed haphazardly against his back again and, taking the hint, he sat slowly on a metal chair. The pimple-faced kid was behind him. Pablo began to listen. Nothing, he knew, would come as a surprise. There would be no more surprises—not ever, not for him. Sweating, smelly, looking like shit, Pablo nevertheless felt himself drift in a cool, pleasant space of calm and comfort.

"—to the interior," Carlos continued. "This is their plan. Since they can't surround an army that doesn't stay in one place, but disappears instead all the time, and spreads out"—the ski mask almost grinned—"through the jungle. Their solution? To defoliate. Defoliate, strike, then move inward. In a circle, like this"—the chalk drew faintly on the blackboard's center— "always inward in circles that grow smaller and smaller each time. Until there's no place left to hide. Then, the final air strike. This is their plan. We know this from intelligence sources. Now." He strutted to the left, the right. The gloved hand rose, chalk flipped through air and was caught delicately, precisely, between two fingers. "Unlike the real Army of the People of Bellagua, the National Army there is bullshit, comrades, I'm telling you right now. A bunch of trigger-happy incompetents and mental defectives. The Civil Guard, even worse. Just forget them, they don't count. What you've got to concern yourselves with—" Breath issued from the ski mask's mouth in the form of a sigh. Carlos paused, turned so he was in masked profile against the chalk-scribbled blackboard, and the chalk did its neat flip through air again like a headless acrobat. "The elements of real concern, comrades, are the Snowmen. They're imported. Free agents, fascists with a lot of special forces background, guerrilla warfare experts, you name it. A few *Americanos*, a lot of Europeans. Scum of the imperialist war-mongering system. Racists. Capitalists, all of them. There's plenty of western imperialist money involved here, and these scum will do anything for the right price. Got it? So you watch for Snowmen. In basic training you've been taught to recognize them. Impersonate them. And eliminate them."

A leather-clad hand smudged the blackboard; a finger drew one long, clean line across smeared chalk. Then another line, cutting through the first: a giant X marked the spot.

Carlos turned to his audience. The ski mask didn't crack a smile. He leaned forward, his next words hissed with special emphasis. His voice was commanding, earnest—as if the faces staring back at him were somehow noble instead of what they really were: the dazed, slightly crazed faces of men who'd taken the long ride so far down that they would do anything— and not even for the right price, or any price, for that matter, save the cost of a bare necessity. Still, they could all talk and walk. At least the absolute bottom layer had been weeded out. "You are freedom fighters!" the voice spun from its black and green hood. "You are proudly dedicated to the defense of the world's proletariat! You are committed to defending *the people* against all the Fascist, Capitalist, Imperialist, Zionist swine who continually oppress and murder them. Got it? *Good.*" Carlos raised both hands.

On ruined walls, slime dripped. You couldn't hear or see it, but in some way you could feel it: the weight of the streets above, all the crumbling buildings and rusted sheets of metal swinging loose off broken nails, slow paws of tired, homeless dogs meandering through garbage; it all seemed to weigh down through the sidewalks and cracked pavement to the basements below. So for a second, the ceiling in this place—with its sole light bulb rattling above—seemed to Pablo to sag, and sigh, slump ever so slightly downward toward the reaching human hands. Maybe this was all there ever was, after all: raised fingers clutching air, not knowing that they were straining toward an inevitably sagging earth; if the earth caved in suddenly those fingers would writhe and claw as did the fingers of deportees in Auschwitz gas chambers, scarring even the chambers' stone-hard cement walls, and the freedom they fought for would be that most basic one of all—the one for which all newborns fight with every shriek and gasp—the freedom merely to breathe, and so live.

Neither asleep nor awake, Pablo tried to concentrate. The meeting over, they'd separated him from the other volunteers and taken him farther underground, to a room that was the kind you saw in old war films—swinging hot white light bulb, a sweating table, a chair. He sat in the chair automatically and looked up to the green and black mask that was Carlos with an expression of expectation. They asked him questions, most of which he wouldn't remember later. Some he did, though. From South America? What country? What kind of name is that? A Jew? A Jew? German, he told them.

He told them about the pictures. He told them he'd had the film on him but Zionists had stolen it. And that Frosty had sent him. He told them what he knew about snow.

A roach scuttled up the wall. Beyond the light's glare they were discussing him. It was too late, someone said in Spanish, we leave in two weeks. There's no problem, someone replied, run a check and if he clears, take him. The revolution needs a photographer.

He was blindfolded and his trembling hands were tied, the right one balling to a fist inside the left. He was led somewhere else. They weren't careful and he kept banging into walls. He was led up steps, stumbled once too often until somebody tripped him, then hitched rough hands under an armpit and dragged him along. When the air lost its close urine smell he knew he was outside; he turned his face up, standing unsteadily, and felt rain splatter down. His left shoe stuck in shit and the stink drifted up. They were shoving him along. They were making him bend low, giving him a push from the rear until he sprawled headlong against a vinyl seat cover, banged his forehead on the cracked surface of an armrest. In the car, he sat upright. There were others with him: men, he could tell by the smell.

"The photographs, man. Where are they?"

Pablo breathed. "In the hands of Zionists."

"Hey," someone said, annoyed, "let him off the hook. He's all right."

"Are you telling the truth?"

"Sure," Pablo whispered, "I'm telling the truth."

After a while they seemed satisfied. The engine was started up. He felt the dull bump of shattered pavement beneath, heard the whine of smooth-worn tires. The car stopped several times. Each time someone got out the sound of rain drifted in with fresher air and there was the scent of streets; the door slammed, the motor idled. Each time someone would get back in, the engine sputter back into gear. Once in a while someone muttered and there'd be an answering murmur. Mostly, though, they were silent. Pablo could hear each breath—theirs, his own. He waited for the breath that would signal his end. He waited in a blank country of terror so strong he felt removed from it, as if all this were happening to someone else and he was there by chance, looking in on things in a detached way.

The car slowed, he heard the door swing open and a rush of city air, the sudden gushing sound of rain. Pablo was shoved out into puddles. He bruised a cheek on the curb, felt his face in a tepid stream of water and his tied hands wedged under him, eyes blindfolded, and he lay there a minute, patiently, in the rain.

Someone yanked him to a standing position. In two rough movements his hands were ripped free, blindfold pulled off, and he was blinking directly into the delicate dark brown face of a man he'd never seen before. The man pulled him along—roughly, but not cruelly.

"*Bienvenida*, comrade. *Venga*. You come with me. I'm your Commanding Officer, Carlos."

His real name wasn't Carlos. It was Naphtali Lev, Israeli Military Intelligence.

His original assignment had been to infiltrate the ranks of an American terrorist group with bitterly anti-Zionist tenets. He'd then been assigned to infiltrate a splinter group of the original organization, which had become in recent months the Foreign Brigade to Aid the Army of the People of Bellagua. Naphtali Lev, alias Carlos, had infiltrated well enough to be given a position of trust. He'd infiltrated so well, he'd become their leader.

Now Carlos walked through the rain-drenched streets of a shitty New York neighborhood, hauling along Pablo Klemer, photographer—the brother of Gabriel. Naphtali Lev was supposed to keep an eye on him. And the easiest way to do that, he knew, was to keep Pablo right by his side.

GABRIEL

Something about Mediterranean heat made it different from heat in other parts of the world. It had a quality—almost a smell—that set it apart. Maybe an intimation of age. All the centuries of baking heat that had come before; the races of people that had breathed this air, black, brown, and white bodies falling gently earthward with each passing year until the bleached bones crumbled, grew bleak and pasty, became grainy dust like the desert that refused them shelter. Yes, Gabriel knew, it was the air's antiquity. The Middle East, they called the area—the westerners who saw things only from their own geographical and political point of view—because to them it was the middle of what seemed to be east. To Gabriel, though, it was the center of the world. This bleak land that on maps made a barely discernible speck was the core of his universe. And if others did not know it, that was their problem. His profession came in handy when those others tried to make it his problem. Then would follow meetings with a select few—Gabriel was always among the few—in secret places. Certain plans would be made, men assigned to carry them out. Invariably, these plans led to death. It was as simple as that. Death to save life; when anyone felt the need to justify it, this was what they said. Usually, though, there was little time to waste on justification. The game they played could be fatal. They were constantly measuring the cost of each countermove. How many lives in exchange for how many deaths? They'd been forced into this

game of death-dealing blows. Gabriel was one of the tools of death at times—
at other times an expert gatherer of information. He could focus on relevant
details and collect one pertinent fact after another with the ease of a practiced
pickpocket. He could aim any of a variety of weapons with perfect accuracy,
pull the trigger without an instant of remorse. If there was remorse it took
place long before the deed itself. Gabriel lived through all doubts in advance.
By the time he pulled a trigger there was nothing to stand in his way; not
even himself.

"Peace, Gavi!"

"Peace." Gabriel sat, glanced across the desk and noticed Arik had lost
some weight, looked healthy, firm, more unhappy than ever. Not much
new. *There is nothing new under the ass of the sun.* An old Middle Eastern
saying. To himself, Gabriel grinned; the face he showed the world remained
impassive, hard and intelligent in an odd, rough-cut way, very tanned.

"What's new, Gavi?"

"Not much. Everything was all right, finally—"

"I heard."

"You heard."

"Sure. Congratulations."

Gabriel shrugged.

Outside, barracks stretched flat and brown, seemed to stretch forever
while you gazed until, blinking, you'd realize that in the heat your vision
had doubled; actually, there were only a few barracks wilting bleakly against
the gray-white desert. The window seemed to melt while you gazed, too,
steam rising to join the pale sky. Gabriel looked out awhile. At predictable
intervals men walked by, rifles lax along their shoulders. They were all
young men. Sweat soaked in large dark spots on the olive-green uniforms,
under their arms, along chests and backs. In the distance were mountains.

Arik had been standing and now sat abruptly. He clasped his hands on
the desk. "There's no question about it, Gavi, it's the right material. And
the photographs—a perfect match."

"Sure," said Gabriel quietly. "You can thank my brother for the photographs."

"I heard. Your brother's all right?"

"He's alive. He walks and can speak the same as always. I heard—"

"You heard—?"

"Naphtali's keeping an eye on him. There was some physical damage
that will be permanent. But I think, above all, there was psychological
harm—" Gabriel stopped, seemed to catch himself and then was suddenly

silent. He flashed a strange smile Arik hadn't seen before. "Or spiritual. A wounding of the spirit."

In the silence, both men could hear the rapid hum of the room's two fans—air conditioning broken again, Arik had apologized—swirling hot air in useless currents that gave the brief illusory impression of cool. Arik's fingers tapped the desk a little nervously. He was a few years older than Gabriel. The pale, thick hair matted against both temples was beginning to gray.

"Time, Gavi. Everything rests with time." Looking up, he saw with surprise that the pale eyes staring back, usually so hard, had a slightly injured look. Arik felt he'd momentarily trodden forbidden territory and glanced down, ashamed. "Naphtali's a good man. A good man for the job. He'll watch very carefully—"

Gabriel nodded.

They talked briefly about other things. Gabriel almost didn't listen to himself responding—yes, his wife Yael was fine and city life seemed to agree with him, yes it did, if only he would have the chance to live it. They smiled in unspoken agreement. He politely inquired after Arik's wife and children, did not listen to the answer. He looked out at the desert's heat, colorless sky, and the few man-made buildings small beneath it, withering with each passing hour. Olive-green uniforms stalked by. Gabriel himself was in civilian clothes. He fingered the open neck of his shirt.

After a while they were silent again.

"Arik." Gabriel held his gaze. "You have something for me?"

"You heard?"

"I guessed."

Arik grinned—his sudden, unhappy grin, as of old. "Good. I'm glad you don't hear everything."

"Only what I want to hear."

They laughed. Then both men settled more easily into their chairs, the room's tense edge of expectation muted by a kind of resignation, the resignation itself somehow familiar, not pleasant but in its familiarity oddly comforting.

"Listen, Gavi. If I could have a choice of men for this assignment—"

"There is no choice." Gabriel shrugged. "Let's not waste time."

Good, Arik told him. He reached into a drawer, pulled out an envelope about ten inches long, eight inches wide. It was firmly sealed, thick with material, and unaddressed. He set it on the desk between himself and Gabriel, patted it gently as if it were the back of an old friend, and folded his hands again next to it.

"A few passports, and other things you'll need."

Gabriel nodded. "Where am I going?"

"Back to Bellagua." Arik glanced quickly across the desk; there was no discernible change of expression on the dark, hard face gazing back. "The National Army there is seeded with a lot of white mercenaries from everywhere. Please find out who's paying. If any of this comes to a United Nations vote it will be nice to know which side to swing with—but that's the least worry. There are other things."

Gabriel gave one abrupt nod; of course, the nod said, no need to explain.

"Besides which"—Arik leaned forward, elbows hunching nervously on the desk edge—"it will also be nice to know who's paying for the Army of the People. Now there's some faction in America to think of, too—apparently they're sending supplies—"

"I heard."

"Good, then. You know the situation there better than any of us. But don't worry about this American group—it's under surveillance. Just find out who's paying for what over there."

Gabriel waited. Easy enough. There had to be more.

"And"—Arik settled back in his chair now, gave an almost satisfied half-smile—"a little clean-up detail, too. In here"—he tapped the envelope lightly—"you'll find photographs. The three clipped together, you will see, are of a man we've been wanting a long time. American. Once a Marine. He turns up all over—Africa, South America, Asia—we think he was involved up in the Golan in seventy-three, too. You'll see. A different name every time. It's all listed." His fingers tapped the envelope again. "You'll see, Gavi. Remember: he takes money from anyone, so everyone thinks he's doubling up or is a free agent. But he seems, really, to work only for Zachary. You understand, when dealing with him you must be on your own. Unofficial. So you'll need to be careful—there can't be any questions, nothing too messy or obvious. Aside from that"—Arik shrugged calmly—"please resolve this problem with all finality. The method is at your discretion."

Gabriel gave him a questioning look.

Arik smiled. "Sure. We cleared it with our American friends. Whoever he is, he's not official. And supposed he disappeared? They don't want to know about it."

Gabriel reached for the envelope. He laid a hand on it. "What's my time limit?"

"You'll be notified there."

Gabriel pulled the envelope closer until it sat at the desk's edge. A lot of material to become familiar with.

"Gavi. This matter of Raina Scott. There are different organizations involved—it becomes very tricky. Several of them are in contact, and apparently own more stock than Zachary—but it's messy, you must not appear to be aligned." Arik looked up again. The unmoved eyes of Gabriel met his. "Unless, of course, there's no choice. You must evaluate the situation as it develops—"

"Of course."

"—and changes. So." Arik slapped the desk edge firmly, gave another tense grin signaling that he was nearly finished. "Everything's been arranged. You leave tonight on a cargo plane."

"Cargo plane?"

Arik nodded apologetically. "Some supplies we're delivering—a favor to our South African friends. We owed them a favor."

"Supplies?"

"Supplies." Arik leaned forward, something in his eyes now that turned the blue of them darker with vague threat. "Listen, Gavi. Listen to me. You give a little, you get a little. True?" He sat back again, the cloud still hovering. "You want to call Yael from here?"

The package slid into his hands; Gabriel stood, stared at Arik calmly. "No. I'll just go up to Tel Aviv, it's better this way. You call her tonight."

"Whatever you wish. There's a car waiting."

"And *chauffeurs?*"

"Of course."

"Be careful, Arik. You'll spoil me."

Both men laughed.

The room was quiet then, except for fans whirling both ways and the sudden, nervous tapping of Arik's fingers against the dull-surfaced desk.

"Arik."

He glanced up.

Gabriel cocked his head slightly—in some sort of perplexity, Arik thought—then shrugged and gave his customary mirthless grin. "No. Nothing. I'll go now."

"Peace, Gavi."

"Sure," said Gabriel, "I'll see you."

Arik watched the white cotton of Gabriel's shirt as he moved to the door; sweat had plastered it against the back. It was a broad back, broad shoulders, waist trim and legs, arms, hands, all very strong—everything kept in a condition optimal for quick movement and rapid, spontaneous bursts of strength precisely directed. The right man, Arik knew. The right man for this job. At the door, Gabriel turned.

"You'll speak with Naphtali?"

After a short hesitation, Arik nodded.

"Tell him—tell him from me." Gabriel stared coldly. There was nothing in his voice, though, to mark it, nothing at all across his face. "Tell him to be careful, Arik. Tell him to be careful with the life of my brother."

The face turned, white back turned, Gabriel went out the door. He left soundlessly, seemed to glide out sideways without actually moving.

Sitting in a small hotel room in Tel Aviv, Gabriel gazed at the face of Ricardo Albrecht—his own face—staring back from inside the front leaf of an Argentinian passport. He looked at a few of the other passports, all at his disposal, and decided to let circumstance dictate which ones he'd use. Secretly, though, he hoped it would be appropriate to remain South American, and while he examined other material he began intentionally to think in Spanish, to speak Spanish silently with that rapid slur and vague lisp of Buenos Aires middle-class society, to speak English silently to himself with the emphatic drone of an Argentinian accent.

He rummaged through the other things: stockholder reports from International Communications Enterprises, Inc., Zachary Chemical Corporation, Royal Hotel; from canning companies, a television and motion picture corporation, a publishing house and its subsidiary presses. An ad agency. Computer software firms, a limousine service, a swimming pool manufacturer, several thousand heads of cattle and a few major midwestern farming corporations, along with their granaries. A toy company. A strip-mining firm. The list went on. International was everywhere. And Zachary Chemical was a big business—but not the only one belonging to the parent corporation in which Zachary held plenty of shares. There were other big ones, too. Zachary's holdings were of considerable importance; his companies had good profit margins quarterly, it seemed, and a superb annual rate of growth. But International was too large for any one stockholder to dominate. Gabriel guessed the internal setup had taken that into account; dissipation of individual power in favor of corporate expansion was entirely intentional on the part of Corporate. He ran through the great bulk of information again, this time more carefully. And this time, his eye caught what it hadn't before: the initials following "Zachary" in the stock listings weren't always J.K. In fact, "Zachary, J.K." showed up, he approximated, sixty or sixty-five percent of the time. The other thirty-five to forty percent was in the name of another Zachary: "Zachary, K.A." And most of the stock belonging to Zachary, K.A. was in Zachary Chemical Corporation. The rest was divided among Royal Hotel Corporation and a few other firms that had solid, steady, but undramatic growth rates. He went through the information a third time, more carefully than before. This time he caught the name of a company with a fabulous profit margin and a dramatic pattern of expansion: a running shoe and wilderness apparel firm. Simmonds, L., and Simmonds, R. Scott, were the major stockholders. They held an equal number of shares. And while Simmonds, L. owned stock in a few other companies under the aegis of International, Simmonds, R. Scott turned up all over the list, in many more places. Gabriel ran through the material again, combed it line by line. He noticed that the name Simmonds, R. Scott often appeared on corporate lists where the name Zachary, K.A. appeared. He noticed what stocks had been transferred where, or sold. Zachary, K.A. had done some transferring lately and a lot of selling. Scott-Simmonds Adventurewear, Inc., had absorbed nearly all the transferred stocks.

Gabriel memorized figures, names. He scanned the reports on Bellagua's National Army—nothing he didn't already know—and surveillance reports on the Army of the People of Bellagua, much of it speculative. He knew what to take with a grain of salt. He looked over the intelligence file on Raina Scott. Nothing much could surprise Gabriel, but once in a while his face, intently reading, would take on a look of disbelief. He wondered how much of the file had been borrowed from their American friends or, worse yet, their European friends; he wondered how much to accept as fact. Glancing back and forth from stockholders' lists to the intelligence file, he decided to remember everything but accept nothing. Knowledge was important and—coupled with verifying circumstances—would dictate the appropriate action. Gabriel plucked out a sheath of black-and-white photos that had been clipped together. In each photo—some old, some out of focus, some quite recent and clear—he saw the face of a particular man circled in black marker pen. He studied the face: a dark, strong, ruggedly handsome face he'd never seen before. Gabriel memorized the face and the pertinent information. This was the problem he must resolve with all finality. After a while he stood, stretched in the small Tel Aviv hotel room where window shades stayed drawn against outside light and bored young soldiers yawned, leaning against the door and walls, watching him. He asked one of them for a box of matches; he separated passports and other necessary ID material from the rest of the information; he put the rest back in the envelope. An apologetic young soldier trailed him to the bathroom where

Gabriel shredded the envelope and everything in it, dumped every shred into the sink basin and set fire to it with wooden matches. He dampened the ashes with water, then gathered them up, flushed them down the toilet. He cleaned out the sink, raised the toilet lid to make sure no black speck still floated. Glancing at the soldier's face, he gave a casual grin and shrugged. The boy blinked, somewhat astonished. Then raised his hand in a vague salute.

SNOW

Memoranda would be written concerning it, and their authors later claim to have no recollection of writing them. Arguments would be set forward in staff meetings; the recorded words would later be denied. One after another, men in various stations of power in many powerful governments would sit behind desks, clasp their hands formally on desk surfaces and speak earnestly to inquiring newspeople: No, no, they certainly did not remember having done so or having said so—to act thus had not been within their realm of responsibility. Although certainly someone might have done so, or said so. Someone. Yes, it was definitely a possibility. Yet when it came down to details, they could not say, not at this point in time. Documents? No, they did not remember.

In Spanish it is *nieve*, in French *neige*. Israelis call it *sheleg*. The English-speaking know it as snow. White flakes that fall from the sky. It is associated with winter, and with cold. Father Winter—the lean, somber flip side of a perpetually cheery and corpulent Santa Claus—is shown in fairy tales and fables to linger with night's frost, sweeping in on the tails of freezing winds. He is linked to the planet Saturn, celestial representation of the Greek god Thanatos, god of death; later muted by Christian mythology to a cranky old image called Father Time. As Raina Scott once wrote: *No wonder Time was a father! The Christian concept of time is linear, stemming from the Hebrew monotheism of the post-pagan era. As such, it is inextricably bound to the concept of hierarchy, itself an offshoot of patriarchy, each action a step up the ladder, each step following a straight line from the last one, the line leading, as time always does, inevitably toward some end. In ancient Hebrew writings, this is the End of Days. For Christian fundamentalists, the apocalypse. To the ordinary person living anywhere, in any age, it is death.*

Gabriel's military duties had led him many places, forced him into strange avenues of research. He believed in the utmost preparation before beginning any endeavor. He believed that thorough knowledge of a situation was the key to controlling it.

Back on Bellagua, he decided to further research this question of snow.

It was the kind of research that couldn't be conducted in library shelves. It required, instead, brief meetings near street corners in obscure parts of Sagrabél, vague acknowledgments murmured in many languages. It required ducking in and out of dingy cafés and bars through sweltering tropical streets to make contact. And the bad copies of classified documents would be burned later, he promised. Despite any promises, if an occasional document appeared to have some bearing on matters relating to his own country, he'd photograph it in miniature and immediately divest himself of the film in another café, through another brief contact. He knew he had to keep always on the move. Gabriel was a photographer too.

He learned more, too, about the Snowmen—an internationally linked organization of great concern to his own superiors. The Snowmen had a long history, spanning several wars and countless deaths.

They were all men, the majority of them white. Change had been slow within the organization, but like many time-honored and exclusive societies they were forced to keep up with current trends in order to retain both membership and financial viability. So, with the progressive establishment of chapters worldwide, certain men of color might be sponsored for membership, admitted in due course, and they too could eventually become Snowmen. At one point, it was suggested that the rules be changed again in order to admit women. This was one step too far, though; this movement never went anywhere within the organization, the proposal never even came to a vote and was soon forgotten. As a chapter president said at the time, *Certain traditions must not fall, for they constitute morality itself!*—a phrase which was much quoted among Snowmen everywhere.

It was a secret brotherhood—secret in the style of the Final Solution, the Klan, and the Bomb—one of those secrets everyone knows about but no one cares to admit. The Snowmen were secret but far from clandestine. It was a gentleman's club in a way. Like many other clubs it distinguished itself first among the British gentlemen's-club circuit of nineteenth-century London, but even then it claimed a long history stretching back further than the typical gentleman's eye would care to see. Back to the dawn of recorded time, some claimed in whispers over after-dinner cigars, when Christ had not yet shown His face and human beings were doing all sorts of nasties to and with each other; gentlemen, however, did not discuss such things, and at any rate there were wars to consider. The Boers. Indescribable pagan filth going on in India, the colonies of the Caribbean. Order and common sense had to be spread quickly, before it was too late; things were getting out of hand with each turn of history's page. Order, yes, and with it of course enlightenment: the enlightenment of trade, of industry. The colonies were like naughty, energetic children, filled with bad ideas and throwing tantrums atop mounds of natural resources. Get them to reap all that raw material they were sitting on, offer it up to a paternal governing body for export and processing; then ship it back to them, charge high prices and put them in debt to the company store, tame them—all that sort of thing. Old chap.

The Snowmen were dedicated to enlightenment via the spreading of trade and the gospel of industry throughout the globe, not to mention at home. Things went on right under their very noses, things so vile they ought not to be written of. Prostitution. Onanism. Uranianism. Inversion. And while a certain gentleman of enterprise had tried to put a halt to the first of these unmentionables, his endeavors were nowhere near sufficient; the lower classes swarmed with moral vermin. Even at the time, his methods were considered a bit extreme. Indeed, it was debated whether this gentleman, who fancifully called himself J—— the R——, ought not to be cast out entirely from the organization. Luckily, calmer heads prevailed. The police were notified, payments made; the matter was allowed to blow over as, with time, all matters are likely to do.

After the turn of the century, Gabriel learned, Snowmen began wearing identifying gold cravat pins inlaid with a miniature ivory dot. This was their signifying mark, like the old school tie. They acknowledged one another on the street by a nod, a brief tip of the hat.

Snowmen were nothing if not respectable. Among them were men of lineage and enterprise. Colonial viceroys and secretaries to viceroys. High-echelon military men. Their ranks even included a few artists and writers until the time of the Wilde scandals; then it was determined that in the future, as a matter of policy, artistic types would not be admitted. Trials were always bad publicity, unless you were Queensberry or some such chap, or unless you were the prosecuting chap or the judge; so artistic involvement

of the membership would thenceforth be confined to wives of members—
and their activities in turn further confined to patronage rather than participation. If the wife of an admiral or viceroy was occasionally rumored
to harbor peculiar tastes for effeminate young musicians, well, that was all,
as they say, in a day's work. So long as there was no social embarrassment,
the women might do as they pleased. *Give a filly some rein*, they'd joke,
and she'll handle smoother in the hunt. Then they'd share a laugh, order
excellent whiskeys and tamp good Dutch tobacco down in their pipes.

Tradition—it was everywhere. It was everything. Tradition created families of bishops, families of naval officers, shipping magnates, physicians,
morticians; the sword of tradition was handed down from father to son to
grandson. So, too, was the Snowmen tradition—no better sponsor than
one's own dad. Like any society, the Snowmen had an internal hierarchy:
nobility at the top, hired help at bottom. Even among the bottom echelon,
tradition reigned supreme. There was, of course, the mercenary tradition.
Sometimes unpleasant things needed to be done in obscure parts of the
Empire to ensure the establishment of trade, enlightenment, industry, and
order; sometimes Her Majesty's troops were a bit too bound by the dictates
of bureaucracy to operate in a manner most suited to the completion of
unpleasant—but necessary—tasks, and then what was needed was an easily
mobilized special task force. Funding from the private sector simply assured
greatest efficiency. In the eyes of the Snowmen, they trespassed nowhere;
the task of both public and private sectors, when it came to colonial diffi-
culties, was one and the same. They were merely patriotic.

As for the substance itself, Gabriel's research had led him first to his own
back yard.

The experiments of Dr. Ernst Kalbsbratten at Maidanek, 1941–43, were
actually the first time "snow" was used—in an early, crude form which was
gray and very grainy; it hadn't yet been distilled to the fine, sheer white that
would later characterize it. These experiments were carefully documented.
In fact, they were in the library annals at the Yad Vashem Memorial in
Jerusalem, to which Gabi had easy access. He'd been unexpectedly delighted
to find them, used as he was to looking long and hard for things.

You could tell, glancing over the documented evidence, that Dr. Kalbsbratten was no slouch. He was also no drunk—many of the entries in the
laboratory journal were in his own steady, concise hand—and from this
evidence of sobriety it could probably be deduced that he wasn't an S.S.
man. Furthermore, he was probably no great fan of sadism. Full-fledged
sadism requires that the victim have some awareness of his or her anguish.
No angel of mercy, he; still, his methods showed a very businesslike ap-

proach. Suffering was not prolonged. When an experiment neared completion, the participants were taken out and shot. And the doctor would use only *musselmen*—the Camp's walking zombies, whose minds had long since ceased to function—as subjects or controls; inmates with demonstrable consciousness would be rejected, sent back to work.

In the Kalbsbratten annals at Yad Vashem were photographs: bone-gaunt bodies, the eyes already dead, a ravaged arm raised so the camera could get a better view, a deformed leg held out for inspection. From the experimentally treated limbs, skin hung in strips. What replaced the skin were patches of bubbly white.

From the doctor's records and verifying records found in the supply department at Maidanek, it could be seen that limited quantities of the substance were shipped from Munich in sealed metal containers marked as fertilizer. It was developed in the newly established chemical laboratory division of the Reichstag Munitions Works, formerly the old Karlen Weaponry. The district manager at Reichstag, a Herr Bleischlift, was arrested by the Gestapo in '44 for selling industrial information to the British, executed for treason in October of that year. Before then, though, he and Dr. Kalbsbratten had evolved a friendly business correspondence.

29/4/43
My Dear Herr Bleischlift:

In response to your request for further data concerning experimental usage and racial distinction: Our tests thus far have shown no differences among the biochemical reactions of Gypsies, Slavs, Jews, Communists, or Homosexuals. Enclosed please find statistical and photographic documentation. Please note that we have been able to detect no correlation between race, age, sex, and rapidity of the development of experimentally induced pathology. They all simply die.

My regards to your lovely wife.

Sincerely,
Ernst Kalbsbratten.

In November of 1944, Dr. Kalbsbratten was arrested by the Gestapo. The charge: selling industrial information to the Soviets. He was executed for treason in December of that year.

It was a group of mercenaries hired by a modern chapter of the Snowmen that originally spread the substance known as "snow" for defoliant purposes—it was a professional soldier who coined the word.

In crude form, the substance had shown up in an obscure part of Africa after the Second World War. While used at that time in a purely experimental way, it was linked to a sharp rise in the infant mortality rate of a particular tribe in the region. Combined with the concurrent rise in regional deaths of herbivorous wildlife and the pathetic crop yield three seasons in a row, its usage was later acknowledged as a major factor in the rapid extinction of the entire tribe. And while the national government then in power gave a great deal of lip service to this matter of poor crop yield, and voiced considerable concern vis-à-vis the region's devastating infant mortality rate, they did little in the way of aid. This particular tribe had been known to be a hotbed of dissidence.

Several years later, it appeared in the Orient. Still, its use was limited to the experimental; other defoliants were more popular at the time. So the substance which had been dubbed "snow" was used in small quantity over relatively small areas of natural foliage or crops. It was spread at night by unmarked helicopters in whose cockpits sat mercenaries of various nationalities, dressed in civilian clothes. One of these men, an American ex-marine, called his helicopter Rudolf, and—while in flight—thought of himself as Santa Claus. Ho ho ho, he said, pressing control panel switches as Rudolf hovered, let loose a measured gust of the substance and moved slowly on for a short distance, spewing snow. Ho ho ho. Merry Christmas, boys and girls! And Gabriel merely nodded, sipped his own coffee and smiled back in a friendly way. The longer he lived, it seemed, the more often he came across these amazing coincidences—Santa Claus was the man he'd been looking for, the man whose face he had memorized from photographs in Tel Aviv. Whenever something like this happened, he would experience an uneasy sensation; it always gave him the feeling that there was something going on in the world which even he did not know about.

Connery laughed suddenly. "I don't believe we've introduced ourselves, have we? I'm a free agent these days, nothing to hide." Offering a hand, he winked at Gabriel. "Craig Johnson," said Connery, and then was pleased with himself. It had come to him by whim: an honest, solid name.

Gabriel shook hands warmly.

"Ricardo Albrecht," said Gabriel, "I'm pleased to meet you."

"Albrecht? Let me guess—Chile."

Gabriel beamed. "Argentina."

I'll drink to to that, said Connery, and both men laughed. Gabriel ordered amother small pot of coffee.

It was by no means the worst espresso Connery had ever tasted. Years ago, in the pathetically makeshift capital of a tiny Asian nation that had risen to sovereignty suddenly, briefly, and was then in the throes of a predictable, equally pathetic collapse, he'd sat at the outdoor café of the only hotel in town and sipped an espresso that was mud gone sour. Somehow, this morning brought back the memory, although—he smiled to himself with a resignation bordering on sorrow—all these places reminded you of all the others. There was a terrible similarity in everything that went on; it was history's endless repetition droning in the background like machine-gun rounds. He smiled across the table at Gabriel, remembering: that morning, sitting outside the hotel he'd checked into as Art McDowell, businessman, he'd sipped bad espresso without tasting it and someone had sat across that table, too—one of the nation's newsmen, a reporter whose radical editorials had tossed him into a favorable limelight with the first overthrow and now, with the second, guaranteed his demise. He'd been a frail, copper-skinned little Oriental like the rest of his countrymen. And Art McDowell was telling him not to worry. Things could be arranged. The little guy—by now, Connery had drawn a blank on his name, wondered if he'd ever really listened for it in the first place—nearly cried with hope and thanks. He'd reached across the table unreservedly, something Orientals rarely did. He'd gripped the big white hand with both his own, said in badly accented English, Thanks Art! you don't know how much this is important to me! So Art McDowell sipped the last of the rotten espresso, smiled back and nodded a casual goodbye as the little guy walked away, knowing just how doomed he was. He'd looked up when another rapid series of explosions sounded from across the street; the frail body was spinning along the wooden rim of a vegetable stall in the deserted market, spraying blood. Art McDowell watched calmly. Soldiers grouped around the body after it had stopped moving—one of many in the streets that day—rolled it over with the barrel end of a rifle. He'd gone upstairs to his room later, waited a while, even fit on one of his combat vests just to get back the feel. But eventually a message came: his services would not be required after all—things had gone more successfully than originally thought possible. For his time, he was paid in full.

Now he sat with this fellow Albrecht beneath the awning's shadow, feeling early morning cool desert the air, watching Civil Guard stroll by and, occasionally, an army truck filled with soldiers, automatics pointed skyward. Sometimes a soldier would fire aimlessly at a cloud and the explosion scatter whatever scrawny chickens happened to be roaming through the streets, cause carefully balanced baskets of vegetables to fall from shoulders as their owners made for the nearest alcove or alleyway. Still, things had settled down a lot closer to normal in the past couple of weeks—both men knew that from experience. And while you might once in a while come across some bloodied corpses left here and there throughout the streets of Sagrabél, some shop windows—glass was still a rarity—shattered and hollow, the fruit markets sparsely populated and far-off gunfire sounding well into the night, all of this was simply to be expected. Give it a few more weeks. Then, business as usual.

Gabriel smiled across the café table. Craig Johnson this time, was it? In a couple of other places it had been Art McDowell. And other names in other places—lots of other names. Sure. Well, he was Ricardo Albrecht. Had the face smiling back at him been up north in '73? The Golan? Had he smiled the way he was smiling now from the cockpit of a fighter plane, from the cockpit of a tank, spewing snow? Mr. Connery, Gabriel thought, Mr. Connery, I am very glad to meet you. To finally meet you, Mr. Santa Claus. Ho ho ho.

They talked business. Ricardo Albrecht was in the meat industry—top echelon, executive management; beef was a big product in Argentina. There was the matter of grain imports for the feeding of cattle. There was the matter of grain storage; the shipping industry was involved, which meant you had to be, at some level, international. In his country, Ricardo Albrecht explained as they exchanged knowing grins, international involvement meant involvement with the national government, the military—oh, it went on indefinitely, these involvements, before you knew it you had to have a firm hand in certain affairs of international politics. Didn't Craig agree? Craig Johnson laughed, nodded. He certainly did.

And that, Ricardo Albrecht continued, led sometimes to the obtaining of certain substances developed in nations other than his own. Sometimes a government might bargain with elements of another nation—elements which, in Mr. Johnson's country, for example, were called the private sector. Because it was all essentially business, was it not? Every government was in many ways a corporation concerned with profits, with losses, with productivity and efficiency and internal cohesions and divisions—why shouldn't one business bargain with another? For necessary items. Such as fertilizer. He had inquired as to the effectiveness of this particular fertilizer. Number 88 in the Zachary Chemical Corporation catalogue, wasn't it? Still being evaluated; not yet available for mass marketing. But there were influential groups in his own country—where, Mr. Johnson understood of course, the public sector and private were often one—influential groups that had requested he attempt to obtain a modest quantity of this fertilizer from Zachary Chemical Corporation. For a price, of course. They were, after all, businessmen.

Ricardo Albrecht ordered more espresso. Craig Johnson smiled pleasantly at him, seemed to consider a moment. When the fresh espresso came he took a sip, kept smiling and raised his cup in a toast.

"Ricardo. I'll see what I can do."

They drank, and talked a little about vacation spots in Europe. After a while they stood; Ricardo Albrecht paid the bill, and when they shook hands passed a small letter-sized envelope to Craig Johnson filled with German marks: a down payment. Craig Johnson slipped it casually in a pocket and neither man remarked on the exchange. Craig Johnson told Ricardo Albrecht where he could be reached in a few days' time.

You're a dead man, thought Connery. He grinned in open friendship at the face of a dead man.

This time's the last for you, thought Gabriel. He grinned back at Connery. In the meat business, Santa Claus, you are what Americans call dead meat. He wanted to tell Connery that somehow he'd known him always: through the years, the centuries, through the wars. Knew that he'd been everywhere, assumed every identity, played every fatal game, led people of every race, every belief, along the broad white road to oblivion. Sometimes they'd stood on the same side of the fence. But often not. This time, for instance. And it would be the last.

Gabriel waited a short while, watched Connery walk casually away along Sagrabél's main street. Then he stood, and followed.

INTERNATIONAL AIRLINES
FLIGHT #848

International Airlines flight #848 left New York on schedule, 12:15 P.M., as Pablo had known it would. Rigid and sweating in his aisle seat, he kept a grin plastered across his face and fondled Espía Pequeña in his lap over the obediently fastened seat belt. Carlos had bought him the camera—a nice little Leica. He was dressed in the regulation three-piece suit, shaved, cologned, hair neatly trimmed. He'd slipped a briefcase under the seat in front of him. Sometimes the left hand strayed, plucked at a small gold-plated pin on his lapel, at its tiny circular ivory inset.

Soon, something beat in his head. *Soon*. He glanced at his watch. That rippling anguished sound of takeoff was over; the seat-belt sign remained lit overhead and the picture beneath it of a crossed-out cigarette was extinguished. He glanced at his watch one more time, hung waiting, breathless. His right hand, balled to a fist next to Espía Pequeña, tingled slightly.

"Ting" went something. Pablo blinked. There was the click of seat belts unbuckling all around. A pleasant American female voice announced that the captain had turned off the seat-belt sign. She said other things—Pablo didn't listen much. He just drank in the sound of the voice, that delicious "ting" that meant time had passed just as planned, and he could feel his shoulders relax back against the airplane seat, because now was only waiting.

He glanced across the aisle. Another businessman there, his three-piece immaculate, the white shirt beneath the vest a little rumpled with sweat.

But the hair was neat, the face smooth-shaven, manicured dark-skinned hands folded with deceptive ease around a rolled-up section of the New York *Times*. In his lapel, an ivory-dotted, gold-plated pin. He glanced back at Pablo and their eyes met once, held for a fraction of a second. Pablo looked ahead. Some fundamentalist Christian sect from Idaho up there— clustered together in groups of seats—beaming middle-aged faces under straw hats or white sun visors. All of them wore plastic name tags on their shirt fronts. One stepped past Pablo now, smiling openly on his way to the toilet. The shirt was sky blue. The name tag flashed yellow, plastic glistening.

HI, MY NAME'S HARRY
CHURCH OF CHRIST
THE INDESTRUCTIBLE COMPASSION

Pablo wanted to stop the man, reach out a hand. *Harry*, he'd say, *Harry*. Then be speechless. He would take Harry's hand in his. He would lean his head tiredly against Harry's shirt front, nestle his nose against the sky-blue belly. He'd ask Harry to be his father. Promise to convert, anything. As Harry's son, would he walk peacefully to gatherings on the Sabbath? In churches? Become a willing member of the congregation of the Church of Christ the Indestructible Compassion? Yes. A thousand times yes. Pablo knew it suddenly—knew he'd convert to anything. For a moment more of life.

But the moment passed. Harry was gone down the aisle, slipped into the toilet. OCCUPIED flashed across the closed door in three languages. And Pablo grinned, relieved. He felt the temptation of thought drift from him again; again he was pure, a waiting machine, and he glanced at his wrist-watch.

Sitting next to him was a young couple. Honeymooners, spanking new wedding bands gleaming from their fingers. Mom and Dad paid for a sojourn in the tropics as part of the agreement—who said dowries were out these days?—and the guy was a nice kid, said he was in the air conditioning business, held his new wife's hand the entire time he spoke.

One of the guys he'd seen before was heading down the aisle: middle-aged, straw-hatted, sky-blue shirt and the plastic yellow tag.

HI, MY NAME'S CHAS
CHURCH OF CHRIST
THE INDESTRUCTIBLE COMPASSION

Another bathroom call. Pablo stuck a foot casually out into the narrow aisle and tripped Chas. He felt a rush of joy when his foot felt the impact, instep bruised in sudden pain. Silently, he apologized to Chas and to the Church of Christ the Indestructible Compassion—cruddy action on his part. And Chas was staggered but not fallen.

"Sorry!" Pablo half stood.

"No problem!"

"You okay?" Pablo spoke too loudly and blushed. But he couldn't hide this sense of joy he had, this confirmation that he wasn't mad yet. Getting there, maybe. But he knew, he felt, that he could hold on awhile longer. At least through another roll of film.

Chas smiled, eyes tiny and blue behind thick steel-rimmed spectacles. "I'm fine, friend."

"Good," said Pablo. There were tears in his eyes. "That's good."

Pablo sat back down. He glanced across the aisle and blank, dark eyes met his again, same dark hands gripping the *Times*, same gold-plated ivory pin in the lapel. No, he was not mad. Not yet.

He shut his eyes.

Gabi, take me home.

That was from long ago—his childhood. For a second he went back in his daydreams to being a skinny little brat. He'd lost his way and it was after dark—all the suburban streets loomed menacingly altered before him, with a strange eeriness which in daylight they could never possess. He'd broken into soft humiliated sobs, looked up, and there was Gabriel standing quietly in the dark. *Here, Pablo. What are you doing?* The voice humorless, but more welcome then than a Mars Bar. Tears dried swiftly on his cheeks. *Gabi, take me home.*

He opened his eyes.

Pablo, he told himself, Pablo, what is happening now is that you are going slowly out of your mind with fear. And you must not let it happen. Not until you have the pictures.

Who was speaking?

He looked down to where the voice had come from, ringing in his head without sound: the camera, Little Spy. Gratefully, he patted the lens cap with his left hand. Pablo touched the ivory-inlaid pin in his lapel. Then he dozed again.

Duerme, said the camera, *sleep, little brother. I can watch. I can watch from my hill while you sleep. I have all the eyes. And it will be okay.*

Sleep.

* * *

An accordionlike funnel attached to the plane's mouth at one end, airport entrance gate at the other. Through it, Pablo felt himself floating. The floor was carpeted green, worn and soft from the soles of many shoes, air conditioning blowing toward him from ahead and behind. He had a feeling of déjà vu. But no lurking sense of doom this time; instead, he felt almost weightless, somehow glad, as if he'd take off any second now and fly on his own imaginary wings. Here at last. Back on Bellagua. He'd been afraid maybe he wouldn't make it. But here he was, after all, closing in on things, getting closer somehow to the core of whatever life was for him, some truth. *Destiny*, some called it. He tried it out, liked the feel of the words: *My destiny*.

To his left, his right, behind, men dressed as he was. Three-piece suits, neatly groomed. They all carried leather briefcases. All sported ivory-inlaid gold-plated lapel pins. Pablo's camera swung around the neck, rubbed the buttons of his matching vest. Straggling ahead was an assortment of honeymooners, vacationers, and the straw-hatted, blue-shirted members of the congregation of the Church of Christ the Indestructible Compassion.

He glanced at Carlos, who nodded back with a half smile.

Pablo felt himself go calm and cold inside. He measured each soundless footstep along the corridor. He was walking through this tunnel toward Bellagua, toward her, the vision of her face, the thing that drove him mad, his rolls of new pictures, new souls, his destiny. He whistled with a sharp, bright, ecstatic sound.

SOULS OF ATLANTIS

Leaves seemed to sprout from the sky as well as the mud. There were hardly any more patches of sunlight leaking through. Things dipped and clung in a perpetual state of night.

For Kaz, it wasn't all delirium. There were times when she could walk on her own; sometimes there were hours of lucidity. In these hours, things swarmed around her with a slow, painful clarity, and she saw her life— each action, each motion—in bright relief, saw herself small against the stars, twisting like a ridiculous puppet foolish enough to believe it had a mind of its own. She couldn't tell how much time passed, or if it passed at all; she seemed to wake sometimes, sometimes to sleep; she could feel herself being carried, the sweating insistence of men's hands clutching her ribs to support her.

"Do you wish to continue?"

She looked up to the tired, green-toothed smile of Captain Something-or-other. She fought to answer, could only nod. She heard his words through some kind of haze:

"Dangerous to continue. Perhaps."

She grabbed for his hands. *Raina*, she thought. Then wondered if she'd spoken the name aloud and, if so, whether or not it would have any meaning for him. He gently tried to disengage his hands but she clung almost forcibly.

Tell me, Raina. Tell me. What's happening to me.

"We must stop now," he said.

She shook her head. She could feel each eye fill tearfully.

"Why?" she blurted.

"To continue is dangerous."

Continue, she sobbed.

"Dangerous. It will cause more pain still."

Kaz grinned. It had come to her suddenly, a sort of flashback. She felt his dark hands pressing her forehead now, felt herself sweat coldly, and with a wave of nausea the delirium seemed to lessen. She knew it would return— it always did—but she was thankful for the periods of clarity.

Kazzy, the Jews apparently have a saying made just for me!

Oh yeah?

Yeah. "What does not kill me, makes me stronger"—what do you think of that one? Whoever said it first must have had me in mind. Raina laughed. Kaz remembered the laugh: husky music filling the room in Number Twelve, touching her with a sense of loss—as if it was the last time she'd hear Raina laugh like that, as if each time Raina laughed it was the last time—but she'd laughed herself, bathed in its warmth.

A good saying.

I'll say.

Kaz blinked at the dark male face.

What was it she'd said?

Pain's a signal to stop and stay inside the rule book Kazzy, isn't it? But how do you find out what's there if you don't step outside the rule book? Physical pain? Oh, it's really a signal that you have to continue and get beyond it. There are different layers of it. Like there are different layers of knowledge. You've got to strip away—just strip away! and keep going. It makes me—she'd smiled, laughter stopped, a cool, calm tone to her voice; when her voice was like this it made Kaz sit up and take notice—*It makes me proud, so proud, to persevere. To persevere—that's the point! And then*— her hands spread before Kaz, palms up in a concluding gesture—*then it's all over. Because everything starts and ends and it's just a matter of time, anyway, isn't it, before it's all over—the pain, I mean. And once it's over, you know what you didn't know before.*

Green teeth smiled down at her. Kaz grabbed for his hands again and sat upright.

"I'm okay. Really."

"Do you wish to continue?"

She nodded, sick to death. "I do."

* * *

She fell in and out of fever. She reached through the pockets in her leather vest for antibiotics. Lucky little rich kid, she told herself in moments of clarity, lucky little Karlen, to have access to all those chemicals. And she'd pat the other secret pockets sealed tightly on the inside of the vest; these compartments strained at the thread binding them shut, stiff rolls of money stuffed inside. So much money. Lucky little Zachary. She was a walking bankroll, a delirious casino.

In her hours of lucidity, she rested while one or more of the soliders dozed. Captain Something-or-other seemed never to sleep. She sometimes spoke with him. He was an earnest, educated man, she realized. Genuine earnestness in men had bothered her once upon a time, but now she appreciated it. He talked a lot about this man Saunderson. The Captain was educated in the ways of white people—he'd been to school in Britain, and there are no whiter people on earth than the British, except maybe the Germans. Saunderson was a sort of prophet, he explained, a sort of moralizer, calling his people—the Bellaguans—back to some of the old ways. The old religions. According to the ancient beliefs there were a finite number of souls and an infinite number of lives to be lived, the Captain explained to Kaz. So a soul could be kept very busy—his green teeth showed in a smile—very busy, yes. Reincarnation? Kaz asked. He told her yes, perhaps. Souls that stemmed from time's beginning. Or rather, from the end of time and the beginning of *history*. Or rather, the end of one world and the beginning of another.

Kaz listened to the story of a world lost in floods. It had been inhabited by an advanced civilization, that world—and the Captain smiled again with his crumbling teeth, saying of course it was all highly dependent on what one meant by *advanced* and what one meant by *civilization;* but for now it would be sufficient to say that this ancient society had been fairly complex even by the standards of today, had utilized the sciences of agriculture, irrigation, architectural engineering, to its advantage. It had been a society with an intricately structured pantheon and many attendant rituals, a society skilled in defense and destruction. One of their gods was the Bull God of land, the Black God who rose from earth and gave the earth sun. More powerful still was the Goddess of the sea, White Goddesss of moonlight, bestower of victory in war, and guardian of fertility—which came directly from her breasts, like milk from the breast of a nursing mother. The two were chastely wed, being brother and sister. Sun and land, Moon and sea— coexisting, but separate. When floods came the Sun hid; the Bull God vanished in the sea to resurface later, much altered, with few survivors— so few because most of the world's land sank out of sight to become swirling mud beneath the rising floods, and this mud carried with it the matured hopes, beliefs, dreams and nightmares of billions from the most *advanced civilization* ever sheltered by earth. Discarnate, these souls went spinning through the universe. And waited. They waited the centuries of evolution through, began to incarnate themselves as soon as human form had evolved enough to contain a soul in search of its fulfillment.

Kaz smiled. It was night, and she huddled in shabby blankets for warmth. They spoke in whispers. They'd made a tiny fire—nothing that could be observed from any distance—and by its fading glow she saw the outlines of the Captain's face. "No." She shook her head. She looked steadily at the Captain and for a second her smile faded; she was afraid. "I believe death is final."

In the dull light, he smiled kindly. "Perhaps. But Saunderson says even something dead continues to change. He says that all things transform with time. That is the function of time—to transform. Saunderson says"—the grin broadened—"that in these days it is called progress."

According to the old beliefs, he told her, the soul left a body that had physically died. Once dead and buried, the body decomposed—the process of decomposition itself merely one other form of transformation, from one variety of substance to another. Eventually, meaning simply *in time*, it became part of something else: the earth. But, as Saunderson said, did particles of earth remain the same throughout time? Why should they, when all other things in the universe were transformed continually? Nothing ever remained the same. So death itself—even death—did not for a second stop the process of transformation to which things existing *in time*—organic, inorganic, all things—were subject. The soul itself, traveling away from the dead physical body, was on a long journey. Perhaps a journey that never ended. Perhaps, too, it was the soul's way of transforming, of growing to become something different like all other things in the universe—and like all other things the soul traveled in time too, took different forms.

Kaz was silent a while. She stopped staring at the glowing green teeth and stared instead at the faint orange of their fire—all this, wasn't it ephemeral? Didn't it have a finite existence, a definite moment of birth and a cut-off point just as definite? What if you did not believe that destruction was absolute? Then you could do anything, couldn't you—kill, maim, destroy at will—the only absolute was transformation, so morality became an unnecessary superstructure that obscured what was really going on in the universe. Eternal existence. That's what every religion always promised. Crucify in the name of eternal life. Gas in the name of the eternal empire. Kaz shook her head once, gently. She smiled back at the Captain.

"No go, Joe. It's a one-shot deal."

"What is?"

"Life."

"Let me guess," he grinned quietly. "There is a certain consolation, perhaps, in your way of thinking, because if you live only once you must also only die once."

"Sounds good to me."

"Saunderson says that history's repetitions are endless." His black eyes met hers calmly, and in the last remaining glow of flame they glittered like stars. "Perhaps your soul thought the same in a former life."

"In Atlantis?" she teased.

"The world of old," he nodded. "Perhaps."

What about before? she teased gently. What about the Great World that was there before the Great World that was there before all the Great Disasters? And what about before *that*? Then Kaz broke into chilled sweat and felt suddenly sad, sad for a world so filled with endless repetition, and with the endless repetition of its own destruction. Or—the word crept insidiously through her train of thought—*transformation*. The air had sounds, if you listened carefully: things being torn down, being built, erecting, sagging, whimpering; there was the erosive fall of rain on glass—a memory: Raina tossing thick dark hair back in one aggressive motion, and laughing, laughing; the sound of rain, the silent fall of snow. What if this Saunderson guy was right, and there was no end to it all? What if things went on this way indefinitely, repetitiously, without limit—you faced the meaninglessness of your own minor spark of light in the world, then, tiny insignificant body slipping and sliding across the vast expanse of a journey without end— wouldn't you, nuts or not, sometimes harbor the thought of putting an end to *everything* for good? Expression of ultimate power. End it all—the limitlessness, the repetition, the indefinite process of transformation—rip out the molecules of change from the earth and plaster the ocean frozen white for all eternity and tear the air from the sky. Make life significant. Make death utterly final—and the only absolute.

Kaz broke through the chill to smile again. She looked into the Captain's eyes and thought for a moment she'd seen someone else there—a hot, arrogant face grinning back—but then it was gone. "Okay," she said softly, "forget all that one-shot deal stuff." Then she felt a sort of fear creep through her. Because there were, she realized, at least two essentially different ways of looking at things—oh, she'd always realized that, she guessed, but never before had they clarified themselves so to her. And if you did not look at things one way, if all your potency and all your striving went toward rendering your own small life significant, then somehow, somewhere along the way, you would have to do some damage. Because you had ripped things out of the context of time, taken them into your own incapable, unaccustomed hands; you had beliefs to uphold. You might now have to kill. Out there, in that other world she'd left behind, she'd merely been disowned from further inheritance for breaking one of those unspoken rules— but what now might happen to her in the jungle at night?

Looking at the Captain, Kaz was afraid. For a moment she cursed her soul. Stupid vehicle it had chosen for this part of the journey, wasn't it: a small body, already deteriorating, and—like all living bodies existing *in time*—exquisitely sensitive to pain.

Pain is the fire of transformation, Kazzy! Anger is one fuel, desire the other!

Kaz was dizzy. Huddled there in dirty blankets, she let her head sink to her hands; she felt delirium about to press down again. She opened her eyes and squinted at the dying fire's tiny glow. It reminded her of something. Some thought at the tip of her mind, some idea at the edge of the universe. And then she knew it: viewed from many light-years away, what had happened in the past would still be perceived as happening. It was in the power of light to defy time like that. To preserve all things. To render each action ongoing. Each flame perpetual. The heat seemed to reach out and touch her fingertips.

Peekaboo. Raina let the white quilt slip gently away until she sat there naked. *Come and find me.*

Kaz blinked away tears. She'd understood it: somewhere in time the quilt was still falling away, Raina still half hiding, asking to be revealed, lover still searching—and she understood that, somehow, it would be all right.

She could feel the twin fuels swell up inside now: her own helpless desire, and a healthy dose of rage.

Okay, you cunt. I'll find you. I'll find you no matter how tough you make it. You can't hide from me—you understand? Miss Hotshot. Miss Goddess. The tears dried hotly along each cheek. *You know, Raina, you're such a bitch.*

She stood unsteadily and wondered: was this her destiny? To play hide-and-seek with some crazy bitch? Slipping and sliding in a tiny, insignificant way across the background canvas of a million laughing stars and pockets of darkness?

The sleeping soldiers had awakened, and began to gather their gear and stand too, but Captain something-or-other shook his head at her, spoke coaxingly. It would be better, he said, to rest now. They would proceed in good time. In good time, but she was too ill to continue at present. Kaz grinned nastily, knowing that she was the one who really gave the orders around here after all, sensing it in his deference, in the half-frightened way their dark eyes settled on her before looking away. Knowing this, she laughed. It was the spoiled brat in her that spoke.

"Captain, don't you say that. We're going in there. Don't you try"—she smiled at him and he smiled back, a deep, gentle sadness in his eyes— "don't you try to keep me from what I want."

SLOW TWITCH FIBER

Lee Simmonds' suite in the west wing of Royal Hotel-Bellagua was a mess. Uncharacteristic. Lee had always been a meticulous man; shorts and sweatshirt laid out just so on the bed each morning, shoes carefully selected and set next to the sweatband he'd run in. He was the kind of man whose worship of discipline had bred in him not a militaristic attitude, but rather an appreciation of all that was the end product of creativity: good music, fine furniture, innovative business proposals. He saw in excellent products a symbol of dogmatic pursuit fueled by passion, tempered by an unremitting discipline that was born of love. So all things he loved recalled to him his own sense of physical discipline; likewise, this discipline reminded him of everything he loved, and for that reason a good 5,000-meter race had once, in his prime, made him feel that he'd taken his place among the artists of the world. Early on, he'd even said that amateur athletes were like artists, in that both pursued their endeavors out of need, or love, against many obstacles, and more often than not without financial gain. Lee came from money. Not millions, but enough of a blue-blood American gentry background to ensure comfort and a deeply bred sense of Protestant values— so he could say such a thing without the slightest hint of complaint.

Later on, of course, money came. It came under the table, under chairs, passed along in envelopes, from quickly established bank accounts, through college counseling offices, via the pocketed hands of track coaches. *These boys are willing to pay for a good 10,000.* Lee realized quickly there would be only one way to keep his respect for those surrounding him—he'd have to become one of them. Even though he appalled them at first, made them nervous when he seemed on the verge of refusing gifts, he would just have to understand for the first time in his life that no one cared about all this. The world was composed of perpetually turning backs, and watchdogs who were always looking the other way. The world created by men of good breeding was one in which only scoundrels could really thrive. So in order to thrive in the world of their making, men of good breeding had to develop the scoundrel within themselves; if they were to gain and attain the pinnacles which they and all their ancestors had defined as success, they'd have to lie and wink and smile and lie again. This was, after all, the *real* world underneath the superficial one of rules and laws. He saw that the way to future success lay in not looking down gift horses' throats; he must pretend to go along with things. In pretending, he'd act as if he was really accepting money, living expenses, gifts. The only way to act as if he really was accepting it, though, was to really accept it. So Lee really did.

He rose to wear the velvet wings of hero for a few years, top man in both the 5-K and 10-K, record breaker, record holder. Wasn't he deserving of it, if, indeed, anyone was ever deserving of anything? Lee got used to making money.

But there was always a part of him that stood back from everything and observed. This part kept itself unsullied somehow, somehow refined. The good breeding was there still, the open, friendly manner, excellent taste in music and furniture, the sharp mind for law. Or business. Business, eventually, won out. He'd learned that in order to accomplish anything ideal in life one had to split a significant part of oneself away from the shining soul of light and goodness; this split-away part had to do a lot of dirty work.

In Lee's suite, things were thrown everywhere: half-filled glasses of water here and there, shirts hung haphazardly over chair arms, a few opened boxes of running shoes. They were experimenting with a new heel stabilizer on one of his long-distance training models, and no matter what he was involved with at the moment Lee liked to be up on things. Pads, pencils, official letters were stacked on coffee tables and ledges. There was a tape recorder, a casette player; there were casettes marked as various works of Beethoven, Mozart, Tschaikovsky. In reality, these were recordings of telephone conversations between Lee and the Cultural Attaché at the American Embassy in Sagrabél. Connery had suggested it. Something about Connery was compelling. His suggestions were tantamount to commands—you'd invariably adopt his vision of necessity as your own.

Lee examined the photographs.

He'd looked at them more than a million times before. There were no revelations there any more, just a tugging sense of perpetual recognition that pleased and pained him in ways he couldn't define. He was hunched over in a chair, photos set one next to the other on the coffee table before him.

The three pictures were black-and-whites, poorly focused. If you stared closely, the background could be seen: the kind of thick leafiness that would blur in distance—dense, omnipresent, and in black-and-white merely dark instead of green, gray shades blending to charcoal. From the darkness blurred several faces in varying shades of gray. One face was a lighter shade. Staring at the photo, you could call it white.

Hand twined in a paper cocktail napkin, Lee examined every inch of the photo with close attention. It was difficult to make out, in the photographic blur, what exactly these bodies were doing. They sprouted indistinctly from dense foliage. Two appeared to be carrying some long, dark object in their hands. These objects had the length and general form of rifles. Lee knew nothing of guns, but could recognize the shape well enough.

In this particular photo, the white face had been circled with red marker pen. Lee bent closer. He stared at the face of Raina. Because it *was* Raina—of this he was sure, too—there were the eyes, same shape, firm line of the nose, familiar chin. This face looked back at him and didn't even seem taken by surprise, seemed instead to be calmly accepting a sudden request for a publicity shot, almost smiling. Was the face cruel, or merely clear-cut for a woman? Were the features firm and hard, or simply *there?*—somehow immutable, as if they'd gazed fuzzily out at many men from the painted cave walls and illustrated pages of history. He'd never known for sure. Even close up.

He couldn't remember the sensation of holding her in his arms, although certainly he'd done it many times. In some essential way, Lee had never held her. Perhaps she'd been unseizable. She'd never slipped from his grasp, either, never exactly denied him; she'd just been there, gazing back with that hard, almost-smile and the unanswering darkness of eyes; even when touched she remained out of reach. Her skin, her hair—he couldn't remember the texture of her, or her smell. What he remembered was something not quite tangible; he called it her presence. Once she was in a room, even without speaking her presence dominated. Eyes would look to her, shift away with unease, then look to her again. And it wasn't even the amazing things she'd done, or her amazing discourses on them—it was simply her being. She attracted people the way lanterns attract flying things at night, the way the sea attracts lemmings in certain springs; it wasn't an erotic attraction so much as a compelling quality that seemed, in some way, inevitable. Years ago, Lee had made up his mind that he'd travel far to be with her. He'd cross many brutal terrains, if necessary. Perhaps he'd known back then he would have his chance to do that; she seemed hell-bent on putting all sorts of brutal terrain between herself and everyone else. In a barely touched recess of his heart—the same part that had first been touched by the strange reality she stirred in him—he wondered why she'd willfully drive herself so far. The fact that she would go so far, so purposefully out of reach, constituted a part of the attraction she had for him—and, he thought, for everyone else. Ebullient, social, riveting, she was also unattainable. For this reason, people scrambled madly after her. They couldn't go where she went; couldn't know where she'd been and what it was like, not really; they could only listen to each tale with a careful attention, promote and market her and sell her image to their public version of glory. But comprehend what she experienced? What she was all about? No. No one could touch her.

Until she fell in love. And it was not—he reminded himself—it was not he with whom she'd fallen in love.

Had she really fallen, though? Secretly, Lee didn't believe so. Rather, she'd finally chosen to become a lover. She'd stalked the object of her choosing with all the care given to any major hunt. No, he couldn't imagine Raina *falling*. Merely pausing mid-flight to examine something from the air; then maybe she'd swoop down. And if he didn't know her the way he thought he did—if he was all wrong, and she really had fallen—then he was sure it was because she'd chosen to fall. He believed almost superstitiously that Raina wasn't subject to twists of fate because in some way she had a hand in twisting it herself. He'd always felt himself sliding tortuously along the twists and turns she managed to carve out—now no longer with her but alone, left to his own resources. Sometimes he felt he was heading slowly, foolishly toward disaster at the end of this crazed trail because he was following Raina, and in following her had forgotten the thing he did best: he'd forgotten how to back in and take his mark, and run.

Yes. This face staring from the jungle was Raina's.

The rest of her was obscured by out-of-focus darkness, so he couldn't tell whether or not she held something in her hands, too, or whether her hands were bound. Was she captive? Held against her will?

Lee laughed out loud. Because he was certain of a couple of things: one, that Raina's hands would not be bound. Nobody'd dare bind her. Two, if she held something freely in her hands, it would not be a gun. She'd never set hands seriously on a weapon from which, along with death, true art would not flow—it wasn't her way. He knew that no matter how far she'd gone and how barren the terrain, she'd insist on certain things. All the more so because she had a lover, although it wasn't he. So now when she dealt creativity or death, pain or love, she must do so with a tool as finely wrought as her intention; she must be as tuned to its nature and its use as she would be to the body, the desires, the inner voice of the one she loved.

Connery sat on the other side of the coffee table. He glanced at the photos upside down, then back to Lee's face, which he scrutinized. "Is it anything I ought to know about?" he asked quietly. He'd practically memorized the pictures himself. Though his own copies were ashes now in a drainage pipe, he remembered particularly the one Lee's gaze was fixed on now, white face gleaming fuzzily out of uncertain shadows.

Lee shook his head. "Nothing new. I just can't believe—" He looked up, lips open—a look of futility, Connery knew, futility touched by pain and impatience, the beginning edge of rage.

"What?"

"I can't believe it. Yet I do. I think it's what she'd do! Yes! Given half a chance she'd do it if there weren't any other options, and yet I somehow just can't believe"—the jaw stilled, lips trembled, he blurted it out with a voice dulled by fatigue—"that she'd go so *far*. I mean, in the emotional sense." He grinned tiredly. "As well as the physical."

Connery's voice was steady, soothing. "My guess is that, for her, the two were the same. Every new event was some method of exploration—"

"You keep speaking of her in the past tense," Lee interrupted irritably. "I wish you wouldn't."

Connery's big hands rose, palms opened out in a gesture of humility. "I'm sorry, Lee. I wasn't clear enough. I'm speaking of the psychological truth here, if you will."

"What do you mean by that?"

"Just that, in a very significant way, she appears to have buried her previous life and undergone a kind of change. The woman you knew two years ago might be gone now, or changed for good."

Lee laughed. Sure, he said, sitting back in his chair for the first time all night and relaxing, it sounded reasonable if you didn't know Raina. But he'd seen her go through every kind of conceivable hell, absorb punishment that would kick most ordinary mortals right over the bucket, and come out the other end walking on her own steam, even managing a smile. Each time she'd learned something new but remained essentially unchanged. Nothing could render her unrecognizable. Not Raina.

He laughed again. Through hell, he told Connery, through every kind of hell and back.

Connery nodded, his dark face shifting until it was gentled around the eyes, voice kind. Lee bet he was all he was cracked up to be, one of the best, worth every cent you paid him—insightful and competent, something calming about him. He listened while Connery talked. The large hands slapped a table edge, tapped there monotonously. Connery told him yes, of course he believed that, without question. She'd gone through all those extraordinary circumstances she'd put herself into, and come out psychologically intact. "The difference being, these were hells she chose for herself, Lee. She planned everything to the last detail—you've said so yourself—she was pretty meticulous—"

Lee nodded vigorously.

"So she had some kind of a mental framework to receive and process all those painful stimuli, a set of expectations—she'd gone through everything before it even happened. I'll bet you've done it before a race. It's like, say, envisioning yourself in action before an event. Maybe you'd run through a mental picture of each quarter on the track. Or even each stride. You'd see yourself performing successfully every step of the way—"

"Yes!"

"I thought so. Well, you understand what I mean. But what if—suppose something different turned out to be the case."

Connery leaned forward over the coffee table. After a while Lee did too, a puzzled expression settling gently on his face.

"What if you were used to going through everything in your mind before it happened—any event, any race—and having things turn out pretty much the way you'd envisioned them. Within certain limitations, of course. You might not always win or make great time, but you'd finish, you'd still be there on the track running, good form, doing your hundred percent. Nothing bizarre was expected beforehand. For instance, it never crossed your mind that the race would suddenly turn out to be twice as long as it was supposed to be. Or that the track would turn to mud for no reason, or turn to ice. Or turn upside down, for that matter. What if one or all of these things happened anyway? Your stability would be challenged, wouldn't it? Not to mention your physical resources. You see what I'm getting at?"

Lee fingered the edge of one of the photographs listlessly. He said that he thought he understood.

And the unsullied part of Lee held itself back from everything Connery was saying. It made sense in the abstract. Perfectly reasonable and believable; had he read it in a psychology journal it would have seemed acceptable.

But it didn't describe Raina. No matter how accurate it was in all other cases, it did not, could not describe Raina and what she was about. It was too much linked to rational patterns of ordinary life, ordinary people. Raina wasn't ordinary. She'd envisioned the track turning upside down—mud, ice, and all.

Weeks after the coup was pronounced a success, Lee and Connery went into Sagrabél for a drink. Over the radios a new government was announcing itself: a government dedicated to the abolition of terrorism, and to the pursuit of free enterprise.

The roads were open again.

Connery loosened up. He was at that point in the process of drinking when reflexes seem as good as ever, speech is not yet slurred, but one's perception begins to be tinged by a mellow, golden blanket of benevolence. And he liked Lee. Only goddamned man on the island with a brain left, he thought. Not that Lee Simmonds was entertaining by any means, no— in fact, Connery thought, Lee lacked creativity. He was a man dedicated to discipline, to business, and now to the single-minded pursuit of Raina Scott. After a while even the most passionate dedication could become boring to any outsider. Connery, though centrally involved, liked to keep his emotions locked away with the laundry. Only way to succeed in his profession; stay hard and cool.

So drinking was a welcome diversion. A little drunk, Lee became kind of like a bright mascot: his observations always got a laugh, and he was physically so opposite from Connery—slender, fair—they made an odd, intense-looking pair.

Lee figured what the hell. This coup—nerve-wracking in its sudden totality—threw bureaucracies into chaos. And his plans would again be put on hold, he knew it. He felt a sudden swell of desperation. Of wanting, desperately—her? Or something. Something else. What, he didn't know.

Connery had chosen a bar along one of Sagrabél's side streets—a dim, musty little place sparsely populated with foreigners. Not tourists, these, though they were white. They looked as though they lived here. Worked here. Some of them obviously were here to fight a war.

They'd sat at a ramshackle table near the back. Away from the bar, the door, the light, faint whirrings of the ceiling fan made shallow background noise. Connery chose this table, Lee guessed, because of its proximity to the dart board. Much used, hanging half off the wall, it beckoned. Connery had grabbed a handful of old darts from the bar on their way back there. Now he aimed haphazardly over suds from warm, foaming beer. Lee watched, a little fascinated. He had that feeling of vague unease which comes from the knowledge that you do not like a particular person as well as they like you. Oh, he was becoming somewhat fond of Connery, appreciative of that appealing combination of intellect and obvious physical prowess. But there was something else about Connery he didn't like at all, and this he couldn't pinpoint. He guessed he just didn't trust the man. Which was all right; no law on the books that said you had to trust everyone. Or anyone. He held himself in reserve now, though, because of that, let himself seep slowly into misery-free inebriation, but he was a little on guard.

"Play?" Connery offered him a couple of darts.

Lee shook his head.

Connery took another sip of warm beer. He wished himself anywhere but here and threw. Way off the mark. He jammed the remaining dart into the table with a gesture of mild disgust.

Lee turned to see a couple of white men in combat vests wander through the door talking, gesturing. The sounds of a Germanic tongue. Maybe Flemish. Something about it made him shudder—he shut it out, turned his back. This bar was the kind of place that reminded you of disease. You'd want to wipe off the seats before you sat. Think twice before putting your elbows on the edge of anything.

Connery settled back in his chair, seemed to relax. Actually, he was observing—observing Lee and the subtle changes of expression on the fair, Protestant face, observing the entire bar and who came in and who left. Even drunk, his power of observation remained in full force; it was, by now, an instinct. He'd arranged the darts before him in a moonlike arc, plucked one from the lineup and tossed it. Not a single bullseye.

Connery laughed, a reflective sound tinged with bitterness. He glanced suddenly at Lee. He was pretty drunk. "You know something, Lee my boy? All human relationships are a piss in the bucket. Water under the bridge." He looked up to meet Lee's eyes, and in his own Connery could feel a slight twinkle of desperation shining through. "I mean in comparison to something really big. History. Something affecting large numbers of people. You take either of the World Wars. Take any war. Any earthquake. A tidal wave happens—bam!—no more village. Or the extermination camps." He snapped his fingers. "Voilà! make a few million people disappear. And the world changes in the space of a couple of years—it's just that easy. So I think"—he raised his glass in a sort of toast, downed half of it in one gulp— "it's sort of a pity to waste all kinds of time trying to figure out why one insignificant individual is making it with Jack or making it with Jill. You agree, don't you?" He paused, examined Lee carefully. "I'll bet you do.

Everybody alive is going to die—that's for sure. And when the tidal wave comes you're in it and so's your friend. History will lump you together regardless of individual tastes or practices."

Lee drank some of his beer. He managed a numb grin at Connery, but he was shaken. There was something at odds here, in the man in front of him. Some essential contradiction which he found intangibly treacherous.

He tried to shrug off the feeling. He was a little drunk himself, and spooked by things in general. "That's a pretty strange way for a man of your profession to look at things."

Connery laughed then, and Lee could see him relax. The shoulders settled, face smoothed. He asked in a joking tone for forgiveness. He'd gotten a little carried away again; it happened sometimes, he'd start spouting his philosophy of life and death and forget where he was. And if there seemed a split between his philosophy and his chosen profession, well, he guessed he could be a mass of contradictions at times, like everyone else. He winked good-naturedly. Something, he said, that he was working on. Contradictions.

Now he'd gathered the darts in one fist, caressed their feather tips with his palm.

Lee kept his hands spread firmly there on the beer-soaked wood, and didn't even have time to speak before Connery calmly dropped the darts, one by one, in the spaces between his spread fingers. They stuck there in the table, points firmly stabbing wood. Lee froze. They could have stabbed his flesh instead. He glared at Connery's hard, handsome face. Barely audible Flemish sounds drifted to him above the click of the fan.

Connery smiled.

Lee grabbed a dart and threw it. It missed the battered board and plunged into the wall instead, stuck hard, jammed to the hilt.

Sometimes Lee woke up in the night afraid.

He'd think of Connery, and this would for some reason intensify his fear.

Connery had suggested that they give the diplomatic circuit a little more time to come through. If things didn't work out that way—he smiled knowingly, a little regretfully—and chances were they might not, well, there were other channels as yet untapped. Still, they ought to try things through American channels first. And if the truth about Vince St.-Peters and what he knew had to come out, it ought to come out only after things on the straight and narrow had been exhausted.

Lee stepped out on the balcony some nights and glanced down at the Royal Hotel courtyard. The pool was open twenty-four hours a day; drinks were served to the all-night people sprawled on cushioned lounge chairs, and in the brilliant light of courtyard lamps the bright blue pool surface had a flat, false glint. Sometimes laughter drifted up. Lee thought he heard gunfire from far away, amidst the occasional laughter and gentle clinking of cocktail glasses at 3:00 A.M.; once he thought he saw fire bursting momentarily across the sky, something scream like flames through his head, and he heard the shatter of an explosion rock far-away earth, plant-damp earth, jungle earth. But each morning he told himself he'd imagined these things. Aside from the few weeks' cessation of activity, things on Bellagua had just about returned to normal: the airport reopened, shops in Sagrabél reopened, the all-important bars reopened. And though the season had just begun, the island was flooded with tourists in a way to make promo people on St. Maartens or St. Croix jealous; Bellagua was catching on as a good place to go to, a place to be seen. The coup had been a flash in the pan. It received minimal coverage abroad. When newspapers and magazines were allowed through again and newsstands in the hotel lobby stocked once more, up-to-date—although, Lee noticed, the stock had considerably lessened in variety, someone somewhere was being extremely selective—he pored through everything and came up with only a few back-page mentions of it. The fact that war still continued went unmentioned; it was as if the soldiers, the Civil Guard, the shocking-white faces peering out of army trucks bound for West Reef, did not exist—as if they, too, were figments of his imagination.

Grasshoppers, rum and cokes, piña coladas, sloshed in frosted glasses down on the pool patio. Leaning over the balcony, Lee imagined his sweat dripping down to mingle with someone's carefully mixed refreshment. Rain from the sky. Or maybe he'd just whip it out and give them the Golden Boy's piss. Let them drink something of him up their fucking straws. Yet he was one of them, catheterized by them somehow as he stood there shivering despite the climate. He remembered what had waked him almost screaming: something he'd seen in Sagrabél just after the coup. A single torn leather shoe, tossed against the side of a shop whose windows had been boarded up for the duration, laces stained, resting in a puddle of still-wet blood that splattered the boarded windows, glistened on the curb and dripped down to join rotting fruit rinds in the street. All that blood, and one broken shoe, and although he'd been sipping beer in a café across the street for hours he hadn't heard a single scream. Just once in a while gunshots whining from streets far away. Or the panting sounds of someone running by, then the clatter of boots and bayonette clink soon after, while hot sun beamed down. But no scream.

He'd been horrified by a sudden knowledge: he would not be able to run fast enough. His muscles were mostly slow twitch fiber, more capable of being trained to endure then to sprint. In a pinch, he would not go the hundred yards fast enough to escape from whatever it was that tore him with fear. That shoe lying in blood had been the shoe of a slow twitch man.

Laughter drifted up. Someone dived into the pool.

Lee ran a hand across his forehead. He looked up and saw the moon. It was a bright, cold off-white with discernible vague dark streaks dotting it here and there, almost a half moon.

Raina, help me. I'm afraid.

A winged insect fluttered to the balcony railing, buzzed there briefly before taking off for the courtyard and beckoning lights.

Raina, help me. I'm a strong man, but what if it's not the right kind of strength?

He glanced down at his hands. They were long, clutching the railing for dear life. Lee liked to know what he was up against. Here, he didn't know. He only knew that somewhere things were happening. Terrifying things. They were happening as he drew his next breath, and the next, and the next—happening in secret places far away and in cellars close by—blood was spattering walls, the blood of men who'd run the wrong way, or who had not run fast enough.

Silently, Lee talked to Raina. He asked her to forgive him. He told her he was afraid.

What was the fear? he asked himself.

Was it fear that made you run? Or was it running that made you afraid?

When he turned back to look indoors Lee noticed that the bedside lamp had gone off. He stepped through from balcony to carpet. Something about the smooth brush of carpet beneath his feet calmed him, and standing there in the dark he felt suddenly cool inside, clean of all fear. It was a feeling he'd sometimes had years ago, waiting for the starting gun: that moment of breathless calm before a fair strike, that complete physical security flowing in and of oneself. So glancing toward the armchair near the foot of his bed, Lee was oddly unsurprised and unafraid to see a man in shadows sitting there.

"Mr. Simmonds."

Lee nodded. Quite calm. He'd expected this somehow, he told himself, expected this all along. Even though he did not know what *this* was, he had—somehow—expected it.

"I'm pleased to finally meet you."

There was a matching armchair by the side of the bed. Lee sat in it, faced the unfamiliar shadow outlines and waited. He'd caught something strange in the voice—an American voice, he thought, but there was a slightly guttural tone to it, an alien rhythm—the voice of an American who had, perhaps, lived a long time in foreign lands.

"Please accept my apologies for intruding. I don't mean to alarm you." The shadow leaned forward. "May I introduce myself? I am Captain David Ben-Lavi, Division Three, Special Forces, Israeli Army Intelligence. In real life, of course"—the voice was a gentle baritone, friendly and relaxed— "I'm Gershom Kol, owner of a construction firm in Be'er-Sheva. And before that—before that, I was Bruce Edelman of Baltimore, Maryland. A lot of things change when one immigrates." The shadows shifted. Watching, Lee could almost have sworn that the face in darkness grinned. "But all that's beside the point. I just wanted to assure you, Mr. Simmonds—we're on the same side. I've been instructed to tell you only the truth."

Lee felt himself smile—an odd sensation, as if his face had become rubber and the lips rubber bands. Maybe he was dreaming. It was certainly possible. Maybe that was why he felt such lack of fear; he'd entered calmly into the world of his dream, and now when he heard himself speak the words sounded back with odd detachment. "The truth?"

"The truth."

'That's good." Lee's voice was quiet, amused in a tired sort of way. "I used to know a certain truth, Mr. Kol. Or is it Lavi? I think I even used to run for it and win for it. I also tried to love for it. But you know what? That truth? I forgot what it was. And now, it seems to me"—he stopped, felt his head shake slowly; it was definitely a dream, he knew it, felt it— "it does seem to me, now, that there are lots of truths floating around, and everyone has a different one. That's not counting all the different versions there are of the *same* ones. So—" Lee chuckled. "—I'd be pleased to hear your side of things."

After a while, the shadowed face nodded. "My side of things is also your side, Mr. Simmonds. Allow me to explain."

Gabriel leaned back in the chair and spoke easily, calmly.

Lee listened.

Once in a while he caught himself on the verge of dozing. Then he'd straighten, grip the arms of his own chair. What he heard was astonishing— or rather, he thought to someone less jaded by circumstance it might have seemed that way—but Lee found it simply interesting. None of it surprised him. His experience with business contracts had prepared him for this, this country of conflicting truths in which explosions were ignored, and no one heard you scream.

Gabriel spoke of snow. He spoke with authority; he'd spent plenty of time on research. Before Lee's drowsy eyes were painted vistas of grainy, barren white, dotted by the pale shriveled stumps of trees. Ponds where fish bloated, stank, turned over in death on the surface; fields where cattle ate odd-shaped, white-tinged weeds and vomited blood before dying, or lived and produced deformed calves; trees, grass, the land all turned to white. He spoke of tiny communal settlements on Middle Eastern mountain ranges, tracts of African plain where crops would no longer grow; and the newborn children of years following—children born with no fingers, with no toes or feet or hands, children born without eyes. They were called monsters instead of babies, and, in his country, locked away for life in secret government institutions along with the horribly maimed of many wars—national morale was of prime consideration. Early experimental sprayings in the Orient. Although there, of course, other methods had initially been preferred. At that time, the substance was not sufficiently developed, not in its present state of maximum potency. Because in its present state, he believed—as a man familiar with military strategies—that, given certain pre-existing conditions, no other method could be preferred. Certain conditions: dense foliage covering strategically crucial terrain, where the cost could not be accurately estimated because the nature of the terrain itself was to hide, to obscure. In some of the earlier testing phases it had not been dropped from the skies but, rather, *planted.* Thus its false identity as an experimental fertilizer. What was its number in the Zachary Chemical catalogue? Number 8. Or 48, or 88—he'd forgotten exactly—it was there in boldface type and block letters in the catalogue of substances being developed, a legally sanctioned process. Fertilizer. Development of said substance funded by a special intercorporate grant established by International Communications Enterprises, Inc. to encourage innovation as well as unusual endeavor in the private sector. The same series of grants that Lee Simmonds had special access to. The same money that had funded the production of their most popular line of long-distance training shoes—an innovative last that was able to correct runner's pronation. The same money that had funded Raina Scott's expedition into the interior of Bellagua. Members of that expedition simply had to return a few favors, had to carry several small samples of a fertilizer in with them, number 8, or 88, or 48, fertilizer provided by another International-owned corporation. International liked to think of itself as one big family. Best benefits in the world. It wasn't too much of a favor to ask.

Gabriel paused. Lee saw the shadow of Gershom Kol, alias Captain David Ben-Lavi, lean forward again.

"Your wife, Mr. Simmonds. Sexually—I am trying to be somewhat delicate—she was inclined a certain way—"

Lee heard his own whisper. "That hardly seems to matter, Mr. Kol, does it? In the face of all you've been saying, I mean. How could it possibly matter?"

The voice that answered was smooth, but somewhat embarrassed. Lee recognized the embarrassment and wanted to laugh it away. Poles up the ass—all of them. Himself too. Surprising how any knowledge at all made its way through the world; men of good breeding everywhere seemed dedicated to sparing each other's feelings by ignoring anything that was not socially condoned. Still, how could it possibly matter a damn? His own embarrassment at listening was—he laughed silently to himself—just as predictable.

"It doesn't matter at all to me, Mr. Simmonds, I assure you."

Lee didn't believe him. It came down to this again, in the midst of everything he'd just heard: he was being held in low esteem because of his wife's sexual proclivities. His manhood was, in the eyes of another man, somehow diminished.

Gershom Kol, alias Captain David Ben-Lavi, paused before he spoke. In the silence Gabriel believed, for just an instant, that he actually was Gershom Kol, formerly Bruce Edelman of Baltimore. That his truth was unassailable, and absolute.

"I assure you," he repeated softly. "Miss Scott's habits don't matter to me at all." He caught himself; he'd unthinkingly used her maiden name. "But they might matter to others. If my name was John Zachary, if I had a child—all this is speculation, you understand! I myself have no children— if, perhaps, I had a peculiar love for this child of mine. You must understand, Mr. Simmonds, my job is not to judge the tastes of others—"

Lee nodded.

"—so I say again that all this is speculation. But also I am instructed to tell you only the truth. I use my discretion in these matters."

"I understand." Lee could barely hear himself.

But part of him didn't understand. It was this part now that spoke to the shadow figure across the room, words slipping out dreamily without his conscious control. How could it be? he asked the man sitting in shadows. How? Was it really conceivable, in this day and age, that a man would meddle with the fate of nations merely to satisfy a private need? Commit genocide on whim? Ah, the shadow figure answered slowly, contemplatively, why—*especially* in this day and age—was such a thing *in*conceivable? Was there not always an element of the intensely private in every public catastrophe, some small, personal motive from some key figure somewhere which, unknown to many others involved, was actually the thing that acted as catalyst? Who could know the inner truth of a man's life? Or a woman's? Or know that, in an age when millions could be obliterated by the push of a button, there existed any greater sense than that: that private, small, inner need which—given the right external circumstances—could create empires, or destroy a people.

"The American Consulate is a dead end, Mr. Simmonds. I'm telling you this now because"—the voice cracked tiredly—"because I hate to see a man of my own side waste time. At twenty-three hundred hours tomorrow, excuse me, that's eleven o'clock p.m., a brown Mercedes Benz with diplomatic plates will be parked across the street from the West German Embassy in Sagrabél. If you also are there, no further time need be wasted. I have clearance to remain in contact with—with certain elements still active in the present government here. Your wife represents an important profit margin to various interest groups in your own country, Mr. Simmonds. Also, she is Caucasian." The voice laughed with a dry, weary sound. "This would make any—shall I say *accidental*—fatality involving her much more visible. Such a thing would constitute acute political embarrassment to certain parties, you understand—as well as considerable loss of potential profit. I'm sure you know that quite well yourself. In this world, Aryan blood is still precious. Money, more so. Good night, Mr. Simmonds. You may use my name at your discretion."

He stood—outlines of a man, the features hidden, angular body looming larger than reality—for a moment, in darkness. Lee was locked into his dream; he stayed in the armchair almost sleeping, watched the tall shadow through dreamy eyes.

"Ah, stupid of me. One last thing, Mr. Simmonds. Terrence Connery—he works for everyone at once. Do you know what that means? Our intelligence file on him goes back a long way. The matters I spoke of earlier—Africa, the southeastern part of Asia—he also was there. For your own sake I would suggest you stay away from him."

Lee laughed. His dream voice drifted out into the room. "Connery's straight and clean. I had Corporate run a check—"

David Ben-Lavi shrugged. "He comes in many forms, Mr. Simmonds—don't blame yourself. How would you be expected to know? Good night, now. Good night."

* * *

Lee slept past the morning, into afternoon. He woke sometimes, felt himself relapse into the odd grip of an exhaustion that seemed out of proportion.

The sliding glass doors to the balcony remained open. Sometimes, on waking, he heard the clink of glasses from the pool area below, saw sunlight streak through to blanch the room's dark carpeting, heard the crash of water splitting apart when someone out there dived in. The sounds he heard seemed not to change from hour to hour. On this part of Bellagua life went on regardless of anything else, and it was always the same kind of life: the kind that took no heed, rolled over and back into money, alcohol, tanning lotion and carelessness. By evening he found himself awake once more, leaning toward the night table in a haze of exhaustion and dialing Connery's room number. Outside, sun had faded. Things were dimmed; patio lamps went on with a dull glow, and when he gazed out the sky was tinged with that light purple of just before nightfall.

Yes? the voice responded.

Lee spoke easily. "We ought to talk. Out on the beach, say, in half an hour?"

"Of course," Connery said. "Anything happen?"

"Half an hour. By the way, I know. I know about you."

The voice on the other end paused. Then, "What," it said coolly, "what do you know?"

"Oh," said Lee, "everything. Everything. Half an hour." He smiled into the receiver—it was a tired smile, more for himself than anyone else, and he couldn't have told where the urge to smile came from. "By the way, pal, don't bother coming by before then. I'd find some way to kill you. She taught me—Raina taught me how."

Lee was betrayed.

He felt it for the first time in his life: *betrayal*. Curious. He'd never felt betrayed by Raina. Anything she'd done had been open and aboveboard— often agonizing, but never had she lied. Lee was beginning to understand himself. Perhaps he was incapable of feeling betrayed by a woman. Perhaps only a man could betray him, truly; had he known this all his life? And only now allowed the realization to take conscious form? Maybe. Yes. Yes of course. Plain as the Protestant nose on his face. And why—in the midst of public catastrophe—he should find himself focusing such energy on a small, personal, intimate sense of betrayal, he didn't know. He only knew that he was beginning to understand some things for the first time, and beginning to really understand what the voice in darkness had told him last night: the public act could always be catalyzed by the private self. It often was. So that waves of history, rippling one on one over each other, might originate from a private, personal source of seemingly small proportions. And he didn't know, anymore, if he really wanted to find her. If he'd have anything to say to her; if he had any minor twinges of desire left for her; if he'd want to do anything in particular except stick her in the middle of another advertisement for wilderness apparel and watch the money coming in; no, he didn't know that he really cared that much now. He didn't know if she could count on him for certain things at all anymore, didn't know if he could count on himself.

Connery's handsome, dark face loomed suddenly near him, smelling of beer. Connery sat on the sand. Warm air wafted from the bay, settled over both of them like a gentle blanket. After a while, Lee sat too. Connery fished through a paper bag. Lee glanced sideways. Connery didn't look armed—just a little drunk. Along with betrayal Lee felt a sliding, sickening sense of unease. Maybe he'd accused Connery falsely. Sitting there, he couldn't remember for a moment what was true, and real, and good, realized all those things were up for grabs anyway. Nothing was true, or real, or good any more. There were too many sides to each issue. And everyone involved had his own private reason. He wondered what Connery's was.

"Tell me, Lee." Connery's voice slurred. "What do you know?"

Lee was silent awhile. He was remembering the first glimpse he'd had of Karlen from across a crowded room—way back then, in the other life he seemed to have left behind for good—Raina tapping his shoulder, pointing proudly. There, there she is. What do you think? Pretty, he'd said, and blushed. Is that all? She'd scowled a little. He shook his head. No, beautiful. Just beautiful.

Beauty was a combination of factors. Someone could have all the features that might accrue to beauty and still not be considered beautiful; in beauty there was also an essence, an emanating glow that spoke of other, intangible things. Karlen had it. She seemed without particular lineage, although he knew of her father's power and wealth; she might have stepped from a Renaissance painting and seemed the same; she might have spilled from the depths of an Irish pub to reel drunkenly in sunlight and still have been beautiful; there was something strange about beauty in a woman. It was always there. External trappings couldn't change the essence; they might alter the accent—but the glow would remain.

Glancing back at Connery, Lee knew suddenly who he worked for, understood intuitively that he'd been sent here to kill—as he'd been sent so many other places, in so many other circumstances and so many other times, for the same purpose.

"Who pays you? Zachary?"

Connery laughed. Beer sloshed in his mouth. He nodded, the same Connery Lee'd seen tossing careless darts in Sagrabél, a little mean, a little out of control. "Everybody pays me, Lee. You too!" He laughed again. Breeze rippled against his face, cooling him. "I have orders, you know, a man's got to make his living somehow. I have orders"—the face leaned toward him, handsome and reeking—"to bring one back dead, and the other alive, or both dead if necessary. Okay? And so what if they're white, smartass. They'll blend right in."

"What makes you so honest just now?"

Connery shrugged, spat in the sand. "Why not? You don't matter. A faggot who runs fast, so what—know whatever you want, *faggot*." He sipped some beer. "Remember that little guy who was poking around for a while? That photographer, a little Jew, well, they took care of *him* all right—don't think it wouldn't happen to you, Lee my boy. But you'd be an ass to poke around too much. Believe it or not, you and I are on the same side, Lee. I'm just protecting your parent corporation's business interests. They've got grand designs on Bellagua. Forget running shoes, my boy. Let's talk precious minerals. Let's talk oil—"

"Was there oil in Vietnam, too?"

Lee was almost surprised at how collected he seemed, even to himself. He had the sense he'd had last night that he was moving in a dream, that all fear was stripped away leaving him clean and clear inside, not courageous but simply moving freely in the strange absence of fear.

The mention of that country, though, had unsettled Connery. He could see the man shift uncomfortably in sand, gulp extra long from his bottle of imported beer and toss it far, far down toward the shoreline before opening another. Connery grunted. He seemed to struggle. Watching, Lee felt oddly gratified.

"Look, don't run that crap past me again. If you want to believe it, Lee, if that's the way you tie the world up into some neat fucking little package and put it away on your shelf, go to it. Only don't come lecturing me with it, okay? Keep it to yourself." He stood, threw a pearl-hued shell toward the water and settled back down to the sand. He retrieved his beer, which had been stuck bottle-neck up in crumbled sandcastle ruins, and took another sip. "What I don't get"—and his voice was different now, genuinely curious—"is the whole frame of mind behind that. I mean the frame of mind that on the one hand allows you to see a bunch of natives in some backwater country sitting around a fire eating ceremonial weed and puking their guts out, and on the other a bunch of Americans in a football stadium eating hotdogs, and say that the first is beautiful and the second ugly. Who gives you the right to judge that? What makes anybody think that what's native or natural or wild is somehow always beautiful? Or even the way it *should* be. Tell me." He turned to Lee, eyes bright with beer, questioning, challenging. "If you think it's a great idea to take a crap anywhere you feel like it, and grow worms in your stomach, and have your skin rot off because tradition says you don't wash with water, and your teeth fall out because you never heard of toothpaste—or maybe if you think it's a beautiful thing to burn off your daughter's clit when she hits puberty because that's tradition and that's the way it's done—if you think all these native things are great then go to it, Lee." But Lee was silent, staring at darkness ahead over the water, and Connery took another few sips of beer. He emptied the bottle, began to fill it with sand. His tone became quieter. "You know, I've thought a lot about this. I feel it most when people start talking about Vietnam— you know the old liberal line, I'm sure you believe it yourself—about the big bad Americans and the good little orientals. Well those boys were in a jungle—a *jungle*, and I'd like to get a show of hands from all the critics right now and see how many of them have been run through survival tactics in a jungle and come out standing. And a lot of those boys got put in bamboo cages and got their eyes poked out by a lot of good little orientals who fed them to rats. Now, I'm not saying they were any better than what they were fighting, you know, I'm just saying that there weren't any heroes there, nothing beautiful or natural was going on there on either so-called side and there's not a single goddamned person who can come out of something like that righteously. Because in a jungle you see a lot of shadows. So maybe you're going to shoot at your own, or maybe you'll hit some white boy or maybe some boy with slanted eyes—what does it matter? You're in a jungle, that's what matters. The enemy is the jungle, right? It's the jungle and it's everything in the jungle, forget about arbitrary divisions like politics and sides in a war, after a while you start to hate that goddamned jungle and everything in it and all the people who come from it and the whole goddamned country the jungle grew out of. And after all that, you can start to hate yourself for just being there. Because you're part of it too." The bottle got heavy with sand. Connery grabbed another handful, let it filter down into the open neck in one smooth stream. He chuckled quietly. But in his voice there was a kind of regret. "Listen, Lee, maybe you'll tell me to stuff it. Go ahead. That's been done before. Only I want you to think about this: think about what it means to keep yourself alive in there. Really think." Then he tossed the bottle, sand-packed, as far as he could and sat with an abrupt motion. "You want to go in there? You want to look for your queer fucking wife in there? You'd better chuck the track shoes, boy, and pack a nice high-powered rifle and a good knife and a couple of handguns, that's my advice. You go in there alone, you'd better leave a legal will."

Lee stood. There was sand in each shoe, sand wallowing in his shirt around the elbows. He wanted to do something, he didn't know what. Maybe slug Connery a good one right in the teeth. But his fist stiffened at his side, immobile like the rest of him, he couldn't move for the bitterness.

"You don't have to agree with me, Lee. Plenty of good people don't. But Raina would." Then Connery was laughing. Lee listened to the sound as it became more and more not laughter at all but something violently unhappy, uncontrolled. When it stopped Connery avoided looking his way. He stared at sand instead, fingers etched mindlessly in it. They could hear sounds from the hotel strip, women's voices raised cheerily, low murmurings, clinkings of glass, some faint music. "Maybe it's better to go in a novice," said Connery softly. "That way you don't know. Maybe there's less fear involved. Maybe. Me, I know all about it. And I'll tell you right now, this is something I'd just rather not do. I'll take a clean toilet any day. I don't care what happens to this goddamned island, Lee, and I almost don't care what happens to those two goddamned women either—but let me tell you whoever gets to them first had better do it fast. So if you want to be the first then more power to you, boy. You'd better find them fast, though. You'd better! Leave tomorrow, or tonight if you can swing it, and make it pronto before they defoliate the whole godforsaken place from here to kingdom come."

Connery's face was a white outline in the dark. In front of them placid bay water, behind them hotel lights and sounds, stretching to either side the sand, the night, and somewhere a thick tangle of jungle trees and shadows. He took a few steps toward Connery. He crouched so they were almost face to face. Lee didn't know what to say. Maybe that he knew Connery was a survivor—and an epic sort of survivor, too—but that surviving didn't mean you were good and it did not necessarily make you noble, or right. He wanted to tell Connery all the ways he was wrong. But it was difficult to thread out the wrong things he'd said from the things that made perfect sense. So Lee was left with a maze of half-truths, and the feeling that he understood much less than he had before coming here.

"Terry."

The face turned to him suddenly, drunk and almost startled.

"Listen," Lee said calmly, "I don't know about all this. If you pointed some weapon at me right now I don't know if I'd defend myself or just let myself be killed. I guess you know what you'd do. Well, maybe you're lucky to know that about yourself." He swallowed. His throat was dry with the hot saltiness of the air and the feeling he had of pervasive exhaustion. "So don't bother telling your friends about me. I'm probably no threat, I don't know how to shoot, anyway. But Raina does. And she would." He paused. "For certain reasons."

He watched Connery's face. It was broad, handsome. It was one of those hard, fearless faces, and perhaps the hardness of it was what made him so surprised to see a soundless tear work its way down the cheek.

Lee heard himself with a sort of curiosity. It was the steady, cool sound of the words that made him wonder—did the words really belong to him? They seemed to. "Maybe she's crazy. She probably is. Only I don't think she's out of her mind. You understand the difference, don't you? I think— don't ask me why but I believe this, I just do—I believe she's mad but not in the head. I think she still knows what she loves. And you wouldn't want to harm anything she loves, Connery. Or any*one*. You wouldn't."

The tear had dried, the face still stared back, expression like a solid dark wall now, impenetrable. Lee turned and started walking. There were things to take care of. He guessed he had to pack.

"Simmonds!" It cracked his back like a whip. "If you've got a brain in your head you'll leave for stateside tonight. I can hold them off awhile but sooner or later they're going to find out, and if you think they were joking around with that little Jew you've got another thought coming. You stay the hell out of it."

Lee stopped. Ahead, steel drums wove a delicious hum under bright guitar chords. He heard laughter. He could see the light now, twinkling across the black expanse of beach. He turned one last time. His hands and arms were twitching, shivering, but he raised his right one—high, so Connery would see. There wasn't any moon but still you could make out shapes in the dark. He lifted his middle finger deliberately and held it a good long time. It was straight, an obscene arrow. For Connery's benefit. Pointed at the sky. Because he didn't have a gun. And, like he'd told the man, he wouldn't have known how to use one.

III

THE
WALKING
DREAMS

NO BONES IN IT

sweet thing, like candy. I miss you. I can't wait until I'm back. Oh, I
suppose to be honest of course I can wait, but... I'll kiss you all over... I'll
kiss...

Why were Raina's love letters boring? And insipid?
Raina herself wasn't boring. According to Kaz, Raina was never boring.
And if you'd taken a survey of everyone who had some contact with her
before her disappearance, not a single one would have used the words *boring*
or *insipid* to describe Raina Scott. Still—

I feel humbled by your beauty. Or maybe your youth, which can be
the same thing. You have a freshness that's almost innocence, as if you
were my child. I want to be everything to you...

Humbled? When was Raina Scott ever humbled by anything?
John Karlen Zachary found himself smiling. Number Twelve had been
oddly preserved—rent paid in advance for months. But the phone was
disconnected. And she'd slipped up a little in her role of happy homemaker:
the gas and electric bill had gone unpaid, so there weren't any lights. John
Karlen knew his daughter better than she'd thought he did. Anything could
be arranged, he knew, with time and money; he'd had appropriate keys
made up, then simply walked through the streets like any ordinary man,
stepped past the raisin-faced doorman who'd been compensated for looking

the other way, taken the elevator up. Research into the address had unearthed another interesting fact that made him give his shy, almost-smile: the building where they kept their apartment was owned by a real estate company that was itself a subsidiary of International Communications Enterprises. And John Karlen sensed she'd forget to pay Con Edison. So he brought along a flashlight. Now, sitting in the great armchair in Number Twelve with one of Raina's file cabinets broken open before him, he passed the beam over dark African death masks, figurines of grinning goddesses and leering twisted demons, the stark glimmer of teeth protruding from an open jawline, light reflecting in the shark's glass eyes. On one shelf he found semi-melted candles in varying lengths and colors. He lit a few.

John Karlen felt himself sinking into the chair. When he finished one letter he folded it and put it back the way he'd found it. He was trying to ferret something out, but he hadn't yet found it—no revelations, nothing that might condemn, alarm, or incriminate, nothing that would interest Corporate or anyone else for that matter—and this lack left him vaguely dissatisfied. Here was nothing but personal material, neatly filed, obviously left for posterity; the gall of it irked him. Like many letters, diaries, and notes of the famous, Raina's were dull. Only once in a while did he get a real peek at anything poignant that rang true. And even then it was tied to the commonplace.

> Kaz, did we pay the phone bill this month? I forgot to check before leaving. Then I thought maybe the phone was tapped. But why? At Kona I remembered it suddenly. They know me there, it's a better hotel than the one in Honolulu.

Maybe the phone was tapped. But why? Why, indeed?

> Oh, forget all this—you know my paranoia. I saw a puppy today that I wanted you to have. A griffon, the dam is a champion with—get this!—documented lineage, et cetera. Just for you, Lady Zachary. The little guy has a name already, too: Fitzwilliam Harrington or something like that, something ridiculous. Oh, I know you and defenseless little animals. I'm checking out the possibility of bringing it back on the plane. The only hitch would be quarantine. I can't see leaving it alone all that time.

Phone bills. Laundry. There were things to be rented, payments made, stamps to be put on envelopes and R.S.V.P.'s sent. Reading over these letters, it was easy to see who did all this. Not Raina. She was too busy bringing home the shark meat. Maybe she knew it; maybe she'd stopped long enough, somewhere along the way, to let it embarrass her a little.

> Don't let me oppress you. I know how easy it is for me to be that way. I'd say pull out now, before the going gets worse—it will, you know, because of who I am, get lots worse—but every time I try I find I can't. Instead I just keep saying Please don't go. Sometimes I wake up in the middle of the night saying it. Please don't, Kaz. You're the only one I trust.

The carpet was full of dust. John Karlen rubbed the soles of his shoes across it, heard the gentle scuff, the faint hiss of a candle wick smothering in wax. Something depressed him about these letters. The ones to Kaz were subtly different, he realized, than most of the other love letters before him. His daughter become an entity called *Kaz*—the thought made him wince. But there was something pleasing about the sound, too, and this confused him more than anything else—the pleasant, cocky sound of the new name that wrenched her away from him for good. She'd finally found a lover. But in an odd way it wasn't Karlen who'd left him, because in leaving him she'd assumed a new identity, hadn't she? When *Karlen* became *Kaz*, she'd transformed herself. Was the daughter in his memory really gone for good? Or was she locked all the more securely away inside of him now? The woman had become Kaz, the daughter Karlen shed like molting skin. Still— in her unintentional way—she'd left him her original identity, left him with something. Maybe it wasn't Karlen, after all, who'd found a lover; maybe it was the intermediate persona caught in a web of private transformation—that persona somewhere between the Karlen about to be left behind and the Kaz about to *be*—who'd gone out without a single weapon to her name, been hunted by a consummate huntress and carried off like a trophy of war.

Raina and Kaz—they were lovers, certainly. They'd lived together. There was no doubt in John Karlen's mind that, for the woman his daughter had become, it was the most intimate of all her relationships. Yet these letters from her lover were oddly devoid of outright expressions of love. The love was more often than not alluded to, shrouded with practical detail, buried in seemingly casual affection. This offhandedness on the part of Raina should have made him gloat. Oddly enough, it did not. Unfolding, folding, replacing them in well-hung file envelopes, John Karlen couldn't help but conclude that those other love letters that gushed and cooed and contained passion expressed in the most banal of ways, were not to Kaz at all. Wise in the ways of posthumous legalities, Raina had kept copies of everything but left all addresses off. She'd write a letter to Kaz one day; later on that day, an insipid love note. To Kaz? John Karlen doubted it. To some*one* else? Maybe. Or to *many* others? Probably. Raina was a woman not easily satisfied. He recognized the omissions born of subterfuge and, perhaps, a little consideration—what if it had been *Kaz* who broke into a file cabinet? Raina would have had quite a lot of explaining to do, wouldn't she, especially if the names and addresses were left on.

A candle sputtered. John Karlen reached into a pocket for matches.

Certainly Raina had a reason for addressing only Kaz by name. Those others were referred to by different endearments. There was Sweet Thing. There was Darling. And—the one that for some reason made him cringe most—My Child. *My Child.* Shuddering with the consistent rush of near-shame he experienced when coming across letters to this particular one, John Karlen realized it was the frequent use of the word *child* that sent pricklings up his backbone. Something about it was vaguely disgusting. *My Child.* The woman thus addressed couldn't have been all that much younger; the correspondence indicated she was at least several years beyond legal adulthood, and one shrewd cookie to boot. Raina was rich in her own right, cared nothing about money, and she was always throwing it around or giving it away. If you struck her fancy, life could get easy awfully fast. Not that anyone ever really took her for a ride. Raina was too tough for that, too fully conscious.

My Child. John Karlen looked away. There was something obscene about that. He lit another candle and melted its opposite end to the glass holder. Obscene?

Or was it, somehow—oddly, unexpectedly—intimate? Expressive of certain yearnings? Revealing in ways that Raina Scott, had she been aware of it, would not have chosen to be revealed? Therein lay the sense of shame; for the first time John Karlen felt himself trespassing.

> My child...you're beautiful. To me. I said once it was your youth.
> It must be, because I know women more beautiful, but I think...of
> how smooth your skin is because it's young...My feeling is of maxi-
> mum power. I want to protect you from everything. I could, you know,
> I'd hold you in my hand like a bird and feed you from my fingers...

It was hard to make sense of all this crap, but he kept reading. Once in a while, John Karlen stood and shook dust from his elbows. He paced, feet slipping on carpet dust. Once in a while he'd go to the window and edge the curtains aside, poke fingers through a fully drawn blind. It was dark outside.

Shadows made dark contrast to spasming light on walls, shelves, artifacts. He would not get her back. A thick hand went to his collar, but his tie was already unknotted, hanging loose around the white shirt neck. She was gone and he wouldn't find her. His face dark in the shadow, John Karlen knew somehow that there might well be no reason for any of it. He understood this dimly yet concretely; it was knowledge rather than an explicit thought. He would not get her back. Had she known of her lover's disloyalty? If so, had she cried at night? Threatened? Pleaded? Left a hundred times and returned? He would not, could not, know. The truth of their relationship was forever obscured from him no matter how many facts he obtained, no matter how many file cabinets could be broken into, how many love letters exposed. The bond they shared, tormented, betrayed, and reveled in would never be understood by him; he was forever shut outside of it. He'd never find her. Who could pinpoint the truth of a single life?

When he returned to the armchair his shoulders curled and sagged. Candles flickered as he slid past.

John Karlen sat. There were other drawers to rummage through.

Time passed. Candles melted to nothing. He shone the flashlight over shelves and found others to light until he was surrounded by glass trays holding long, tapering candles, tiny flames flicking monstrous illusions on the dust-caked walls and furniture.

Once, for a second, he thought he'd found something.

> could tell you lots of aboriginal myths about the offspring of unions "such as ours." Ignore me, I'm just trying to cheer you up. Myself, too. I want to tell you what I felt like after Wednesday night, Kaz, I was miserable with all the things I wanted.

John Karlen paused. The hand strayed again along his chest, found the unknotted tie. His fingers curled with a sudden nervous motion around one silk strand. It was a long letter filled with lame flippancy—obvious that Raina had felt uncomfortable, or in some sort of pain that she was clumsily trying to overcome. And this in itself was odd. Raina doing anything clumsily didn't seem right. Again, it came to him that he ought to feel a kind of gloating triumph but again he didn't. His fingers twined in silk, thumb rubbed the tie's end into a crude knot. He scanned a couple of paragraphs again before stopping to really see.

concerning your lack of motherly instincts. You know I don't believe it. When I let myself, I see you bouncing some brat on your knee, or breast-feeding it. When you say things like what you said Wednesday, what I want is to give you a baby, the way you say you want—you say you want my child. If I could I'd manufacture the right stuff and put it deep down inside you to grow. It would be ours. I don't let myself see this very often. You know I can't, and don't.

John Karlen blinked at his wristwatch with surprise. Three forty A.M. How had time passed so quickly, without warning? It seemed only seconds ago that he'd walked across the thick, dust-filled carpet, blinked out between the blinds to see city darkness dotted by streetlamp lights, moving car lights that illuminated curbs in shifting bright splotches. Without knowing why, he felt a strange burning in his throat and nose, a full blurring of the eyes. Tears? But he couldn't remember ever crying. And now, when they seemed to lurk without conscious reason, it was too late to begin—he no longer knew how. Raina's thick, cream-colored stationery crackled dryly on his knee. A pricking, almost frightening feeling inched along his neck. Outside a taxi horn honked, the echo fading on its way downtown.

Kaz, why did you say it? When you said it I wanted to cry, I wanted to kill you.

John Karlen read on. Raina wanting to cry, to kill—what she wrote was all strangely uncontrolled, as if a valve had been turned on full blast, a plug unplugged. Ever since Wednesday night, she wrote, she hadn't been able to shake it—no. She could have brought or bought Kaz anything else, could have given any other thing but the thing asked for in some half-conscious moment that Wednesday night—a baby. Natural urge, perhaps, one felt deeply when there is much love; a desire that followed the logic of the gut. Kaz wanted a baby. Not a baby in the abstract, but *Raina's* baby. Maybe she'd blurted it out during some high aftermath, tears dribbling suddenly as urgent arousal peaked, eased, and the world returned. Maybe in that instant Raina envisioned a child bouncing on Kaz's knees. It looked like her but had her lover's eyes: dark cat eyes, specks of green.

Listen, do you know who I am? I am Raina Scott, do you understand what that means—it means I never feel pity or terror, do you understand? Not for you. Not for myself.

She would not, she wrote to Kaz, suffer this. For Kaz, she'd wanted to be everything. But now there was this image in the way—of her child, bratty dark little thing with emerald dots sparking the eyes; and Raina Scott, who could stand pain that would send most mortals six feet under, couldn't tolerate the pain it evoked. Because, she said, it made her feel she might fail sometimes. Become mortal. Be insufficient. And she didn't want the image of this baby. So she was taking it far away where Kaz couldn't see it. No, she would not give her a child. Not ever.

> You ought to know, Kazzy, sooner or later that's what life with me means: no brats, no endless lineage, no promise of life eternal. The buck stops here.

This was finality—loving her—it was no promise of beginnings, but only the end of things.

> and I'll tell you a story, old North American myth. Two tribeswomen courted, wed in secret, then they ran away into the woods. They mated the way—oh, you know how they mated. One of them became pregnant. But when she gave birth it was to an amorphous kind of fleshy blob. See, this was the only offspring to be expected from such a union— some kind of deformity. So they had to kill it because there were no bones in it. I have reservations to Athens from Cairo for both Friday and Sunday, just in case, so unless something comes up I'll be home either Saturday or Monday. Do you want to take a week and get tanned? I thought Turks and Caicos. It would be relaxing. Or maybe Bellagua. Think about it. Whatever Lady Z wishes—does that surprise you? Believe it or not you are the love of my life. Probably of all my lives. You said once you didn't want to live without me, and if you feel that way when the time comes I'd take you with me. Cheer up, Kazzy. That's not so bad now, is it?

Touching the cream-colored paper, John Karlen's fingertips felt hollow. They traveled up his own thigh, tingled suddenly with surprise. He had an erection, for the first time in years.

One thing was obvious: Karlen Addams Zachary—the Heiress, the Beautiful, the Faithless—had become unswervingly loyal once fallen off the edge of respectability into Raina's arms. And *Kaz*—the lover—was blind in ways that Karlen could never have been. Once committed, she saw things through a rose-tinged monocle. But did she see falsely? Hard to tell. It seemed, at times, that Kaz could zero in on something important, ignore a lot of peripheral nonsense and, in so doing, was able to guts it out along a difficult trail, shape some kind of partnership with a partner who defied shaping. She'd put on blinders and so saw straight ahead. What she saw was quite simple: her lover. And quite monumental: the only *other* she'd ever experienced intimacy with, the only other for whom she felt unquestioning desire. What was Raina's power, then, to make her feel all this? Who knows. Kaz was not unique in that she loved. She would therefore choose to be unique in *who* she loved.

John Karlen touched himself lightly. His fingers shivered.

He listened to the dreary sounds of cabs racing downtown along empty streets. Three fifty-five A.M. There were echoes of heroism running through everything Raina did—grudgingly, hatefully, even he would grant her that. Not heroism maybe, but grandeur. Even the crummy things she did. Mortal or no, Raina as Raina, in a particular time, was in many ways a woman of her time and made no attempt to be otherwise. She might stick to bows and arrows for weapons, but when it came to traveling she did it in jets first class, when it came to material things she was a woman of vanity. And her string of lovers was merely an acquiescence to modern creed: self-indulgence, lack of fidelity.

Then again—could you really call it lack of fidelity? Maybe not. Maybe she was loyal, and exclusively faithful to Kaz in her own way. Raina was pompous as hell with all those anonymous recipients of bad letters, and consciously stylized. For all these elaborate gushings, no one else was ever invited to move in or pay the phone bill; no one but Kaz was offered pet griffons; to no one but Kaz was her paranoia revealed, her pettiness, her pity or terror or genuine wealth of affection. In the pantheon of Raina's love life, Kaz was not to be displaced. So when it finally came to her— that bleak, taunting hope to plant life, a child—it came to her with Kaz. No one else.

> *Believe it or not you're the love of my life.*

Not much invention there. Still, it rang true somehow.

> *You said once you didn't want to live without me, and if you feel that way when the time comes I'd take you with me.*

Maybe she did. Isolated, deep in the jungle—could she survive herself another time? Raina knew greatness. She knew her limitations. Maybe she knew that she could not make it through all alone this time; maybe she sensed that this time the end would loom probable, very near indeed. And mortal or no, she was definitely telepathic. So she summoned all her powers from the borderline of madness and goddess-ness, pulled a little telepathy out of the hat and called for her lover. Mortal or no. And despite all that goddess stuff. What was it, anyway, but religion? Being telepathic, sensing oblivion, she'd also sense that the thing she flirted with now could send any goddess plummeting to another death. And in the face of it, all she had left was to love. So she called her lover, got serious about religion. John Karlen had been tricked, thinking he had the means to destroy her simply by sending her far away or sabotaging her means of survival; he'd forgotten how epic a survivor she really was. He'd underestimated her drawing power. His own daughter was the precious metal thus magnetized. In attempting to save *Karlen* he'd ensured her permanent removal from the face of the earth. She'd taken him up on his challenge. One on one. She was looking for her lover. She'd disappeared into the folds of a great white blanket falling to cover the world. Because if she could not have life eternal she would take the next thing on the menu of eternity: oblivion. She'd take Raina. One on one. And he'd lost them both for good.

> Kazzy, once I thought I could talk about anything. Now I don't know. There's a recurring dream I have, I've wanted to tell you about it for a long time but somehow I can't—what do you make of all that? Come on, you're the brain around here. Everything I touch I'm so used to, everything habitual, but sometimes everything seems strange. Mysterious. As if I keep heading toward something completely unknown and keep wanting it, without understanding what it will turn out to be. If I ever have a grave, what would they put on the stone? I'm in one of my paranoid moods, I guess. Hunting tomorrow. I should be asleep, or resting, or concentrating. Something. And yet—

And yet—then nothing. What was there to say, when faced with the mysteriousness of things? Raina sought her own end. She was no different from any other human in so doing; it was merely her method of seeking that set her apart, made her a household name, made her a commodity, made her a star.

Had Kaz understood all this? Touched it? Touched Raina?

John Karlen drifted around the large, cluttered apartment, blowing dust from objects here and there. Books stuck together in the shelves when he tried to pull them out. Several were inscribed. They'd bought books for each other constantly—each birthday, each month or year marked off a different anniversary of sorts, their revision of traditional custom.

To appease Kaz after some argument, Raina had presented her with a precious leather-bound edition of works by an Italian poet. In it she'd inscribed a series of apologies, and recapped the poet's life. A brave solider, fighter pilot during the First World War. He'd lost an eye in combat for the port of Fiume, emerged decorated with medals, adored by all, popularly christened Il Comandante, enamored of a series of beautiful women, endowed with a continual appetite for living well, endowed with a fortune, with awards for poetry and scholarship, newly endowed with a slowly murderous venereal disease. The great love of his life an exquisite dark-haired dancer who left him for another woman. With balding head and wrinkled black patch over the dead eye's socket, he'd stalked the marble halls of his villa in increasing bitterness, paranoia, and gloom, suffering more and more frequent spells of the madness that ate away at his brain. Raina had written it all hastily, returned to fretful apology at the end of the inscription:

> Forgive me, Kazzy. You know how I can be. After you forgive me come and find me again. However you want. But please don't leave me.

John Karlen slid the volume under one arm, wandered past candles that hissed after him. He teetered uncertainly on the threshold of the bedroom. The feverish glow of background light urged him on until he bumped against the corner of something and bent down to feel its surface: a bed. The cover a kind of fur, he thought, thick, dusty, somehow warm, a pale shadow in the dark. John Karlen inched forward until he was stretched over the width of the fur-covered bed, rubbed his face in it. He rolled onto his back, felt his neck embellished by soft, dusty fur, and one hand clutched the book to his chest while the other searched down along his belly and thighs, touched his groin. But the erection had vanished. He felt a sensation overwhelm him then, sorrow mingled with a deep, hushed sense of peace. He eased the leather-bound book down to his thighs. He could feel it through his trousers: the heavy, dull pulse of his blood beating against it. He spread both hands on top of the leather cover and laced fingers together.

John Karlen slept. He dreamed of snow.

He woke and blinked in surprise—the darkness was complete. Then he realized the candles in the front room had all burned out. If someone had looked down on his face, it would have been hard to tell what was there. Tears? You couldn't have seen. His eyes were hidden in dark.

He would leave the way he'd come—silently, officially unnoticed. The file cabinet would be put back in its proper place and doors shut beneath broken locks. He'd carry the leather-bound book under one arm, almost as an afterthought.

OPERATION SNOW

When drops fell, they looked almost silver in the night. No sporadic dusting this, but a systematic, circular sweep that painted a thin white ring along the outermost edge of Bellagua's interior. Preliminary tests were over. Time for the real thing.

The real thing had been planned a long time. Strategic Command in Sagrabél did it with some help from foreign friends—*advisers*, they were called—who, dressed in civilian clothes, devised charts displaying statistical estimates of probable losses on both sides. They presented maps of the interior, concentric white circles overlaid on green until each one looked like an archery target.

On West Reef, rotting fish lined the shore. In one village, two children died without known cause; it was said wicked spirits possessed their souls because they collapsed suddenly, convulsed, eyes rolled white up into their heads.

In another village, a child was born with no limbs at all but the head was perfectly formed. The child died within hours. Some said the mother had murdered it—this, however, was just rumor.

Three young men of this village walked for days to reach Sagrabél. They traveled by night, avoiding National Army installations along the way, carried baskets of fruit as a gift to be presented to medical doctors they hoped to contact there. *The soldiers will not listen,* they were instructed to say, *they pretend not to see what has happened, there is a curse on things. The trees crumble and leaves turn to white. Everything becomes like ash after a fire. The fish die, also our children.* But in Sagrabél these men were detained by hospital authorities. It was obvious, reports stated, that they were delusional. They were admitted for involuntary treatment but not heard from again; somehow, the records were lost.

This was the first circle of defoliation.

Operation Snow progressed as planned. By night, helicopters dusted in a wide, sweeping circle around the rim of the interior, laying down another strip of white.

On West Reef, human bodies floated to shore along with the corpses of fish. These bodies were barely recognizable. At first, it was thought they'd been painted. Then it was realized that what streaked across each naked back and chest, arm, leg, face, neck, was not paint but something ingrained into the skin itself, like a burn or rash. Where flesh had peeled away, the underlying tissue was soft and bubbly on the surface; it was whiter than a white man's skin, pure white.

This was the second circle of defoliation.

By the second month of war, refugees were trickling daily along Bellagua's only highway. They passed army convoys, the army convoys passed them. No acknowledgement was made on either side. The terribly thin, dark-skinned refugees walked along as if invisible. There were children clustered in stumbling groups behind mothers, children clutching the hands of smaller children, adults holding half-filled baskets by straw handles. At first glance, you couldn't tell men from women. Everyone looked the same—all had hungry, wrinkled faces and blank eyes staring straight. The difference was between the tall and the small. Some children carried baskets on their heads.

They were heading away from the interior. The National Army trucks traveled in the opposite direction. As they passed each other—the dark, uniformed men in trucks, the half-naked dark people walking barefoot along the road—there was a mutual understanding of sorts: no one would recognize the other; there would be no connection made here, on this road in the light of day, between what each side had left behind and what each side hurried toward. They were ghosts, one to the other.

"Rather a shame," said the pilot. He turned to Lee and the helicopter hovered, a giant bumblebee hanging in air, sides unmarked for intelligence purposes. The pilot was a white man, South African, and had immediately recognized the name of Captain Ben-Lavi. Lee had been taken under certain people's wings, ushered into dull rooms in the smoky, beer-smelling section of Sagrabél, duplicates of his photographs shown to him again and again. This matter of Raina Scott was bigger than even he had realized.

He'd been out once before with this particular pilot, but never during daylight. "They've lost whatever they had, you know." The pilot shrugged. His pale young face wasn't without sympathy, though. "There wasn't too bloody much to speak of in the first place, of course. Still it's rather a shame. Little shacks, fishing rods, whatever all else—as they say, *kaput*. Rotten business."

Lee looked down.

All the bodies moving along the road made a long, wavering line in the day's bright heat; dark-skinned people, gazing straight ahead. He couldn't make out a single figure that looked white. No Caucasian woman glancing casually up at the sky with mad, bold eyes, sunburned, strong-boned, androgynous in appearance and maybe gaunt from years of tough living, deprivation—

Raina!

No wife. Lee searched. No wife, no Raina, not yet.

Hey! Raina!

What did he want her for? Some last gasp of completion?

Where are you?

God forgive me, thought Lee. Then he brushed a hand across his forehead in surprise. He'd never been a religious man. And what the hell did he need to be forgiven for, anyway.

Up here, Raina. Up here.

"Heard about this new crop duster they're using?" The South African spoke cheerily, trying to make him feel better; he hated seeing a man down. "Quite something! Smokes them all out—that's what they say, at any rate."

Up here, Raina. In the sky.

THE MOON

The cell was small, and secret, located among a row of similar cells. Still, the space in which a person dies need not be large, or public, or particularly unique. The cell was dark because outside was night; a tiny barred slat up near the ceiling let in light during the day. One night he had watched hours pass through this slat. He watched the shadows go from red to purple to black, to gray and to sunlit yellow again. Once, he saw a star.

He was on his back on damp concrete. There was nothing to be heard, nothing to be seen in the dark. He blended right in. He was just a sighing breath there, coming from the night.

One eye was swollen shut. There were other bruises, because he'd been beaten around the head for many days, but surprisingly almost no blood. Sometimes a trickle from the nostril. Even he couldn't tell. It might have been water. Saliva. It might have been any wet thing on skin. And the skin itself throbbed beyond pain now. It could have been anyone's skin, detached, floating like sighs in the dark.

Daylight is a cornucopia of stimuli. Darkness has a texture all its own. This texture is an absence of things, rather than a composite—absence of color, of sound. You put your fist in, and through it. Your eye. Then you refuse it, and the refusal is a denial, a deceptive game of sorts. You embroider it with visions instead—visions that come with the memory of daylight. So the hollowness is filled again with what seems familiar—an illusion of things idealized, remembered, imagined—because no one understands darkness, no one is equipped to face it fully and without the aid of illusion, or the anticipation of approaching light. His eye watched. He played games. He remembered. He imagined.

The slat was a doorway and he poked an eye through it. Colors flashed back. First there was a bird, taunting, fluttering with its many colors and the limpid flash of its eyes. He saw naked women; his eye traveled along the length of their bodies. He saw one woman out of all the others. She was dark, her hips broad, long slender arms and hands. She had soft lips that laughed easily. Her eyes were large. He saw that her left breast was bigger than the right. She'd always joked about it and said well, she was nevertheless still standing upright. His eye moved along her thighs until he sank into her, dark eye blended into the near-black of her skin. When she passed by with the multicolored bird he was looking up at another face, also a woman's, but this face a white one. White was not quite the word for it—it had been darkened with sun, sand-whipped. But it was Caucasian. Then things reversed and he was looking down, examining the feverish lines of this white face with amazement and concern. Even insane with fever, the face was more arrogant than pained, more defiant than anything else. There was on it the toll of physical misery, but no trace of fear. That was what marked it—the lack of fear. He'd noticed it then, looking down through thick leaves at the half-mad eyes gazing straight up into his. He saw himself bend over carefully, pull away more foliage. He saw himself gingerly lay the flat of his palm against her forehead. It burned him. He saw himself reach to hold her wrist gently, measure a heartbeat that had shot giddily high, flying close to the sun, close to death. And the eyes, unblinking, fearlessly meeting his.

Nearly gone, said a voice. Whether his or another's, he couldn't tell.

Something poked through the slat. His eye blinked. It seemed the beginning of some sort of light—but he knew morning was far away. For a moment he tensed, back pressing down against damp concrete. He could hear things in minute detail—the click of beetle legs on the cell wall, the passing away of seconds an almost visceral thing. Time bled on and he felt it inside himself. Then he let go. There was only him now, his eye which saw things no one else could have seen, and he floated free of time in the cell's dark womb. There wasn't any pain. Strange, he told himself, he'd have expected a considerable amount. But he laughed silently. Expect what you would, it didn't matter once faced with the reality of a place you'd never been before. And he should have known that. He should have known that better than others.

With his eye, he reached for his son's hand. The fingers that clutched at his were childish, soft. There was a tenderness to the flesh. He picked his son up with his eye, fondled him there a moment. He made him stay for a careful embrace. And he was trying to impart something to the boy— a certain wilting away of all his reserves at the feel of the dark soft skin, the thick-curled fresh hair against his cheek. He made his eye stay on the boy and hold him there a moment longer. Patience, he murmured to the eye as it grew tired. Just a little longer. Patience. He was trying to do things right. And there was time, he told himself, enough time, surely, for this.

Then the boy was gone. And he was left with more time. Suddenly, the thought of still more time flooded him with despair. He'd said all his goodbyes. And dying was the nowhere place—an intangible process between one mode and the next, the incessancy of it an agony beyond any mere physical pain.

Cerebral hemorrhage, someone said.

Then he was relaxed, nearly peaceful. Not long. And he knew how it would be. He was a doctor himself.

Like a thin, dry bone, an image came to him of England. It was dull, countryside green where it was not flat industrial shades; white women grinning bad-toothed grins at him through train windows and nasty accents grating against his ears. They had suggested he take a permanent leave of absence from his studies. All the gray men in suits, their gold-clipped ties bearing insignias of private clubs in London. He'd been careful not to search out their eyes, afraid of what he might see. He sat cautiously still on the hard polished walnut of the chair. *Inquisition.* That word came to mind, left quickly, he gave himself a secret smile. Outside graduate students walked by, their shoes crushing sweetly against grass. It was raining. He remembered that—the crushing sound of shoes on grass, and a light drizzling patter of rain. He'd thought at first to engage in intelligent debate. For a gentleman, surely, surely, he told himself, all things were possible or at least imaginable. And then he allowed himself to meet the eyes of one—one of these gray men in carefully pressed silk—and what the eyes told him was that he was not one of them and never would be. There were several species of human being, those eyes said, and he was one of the lesser ones. He'd nodded. Smiled, nearly laughing, so his face attained the look of a prankster there in the walnut room exuding tradition. Exuding power. Theirs was a fait accompli. He smiled in defeat. The sound of rain.

Not much longer.

He explored the slat. Something else would flow by and through, inevitably. The eye wanted to droop but he kept it open.

What came through were faces—a crowd of faces. Some he recognized, others were new to him. He reached out his tongue for them. The texture of people, he could feel it on his tongue like food and it went to the core of him. He'd eaten them before. All the times he'd been denied food, these faces had come to him and he'd hungrily lapped them up. And all the times food was his for the taking, sitting in a carefully guarded tray across the small space of a room, his for the taking after days of hunger—if only he would issue certain statements, if only certain retractions were made and documents signed in pen with his name, by his hand. For the taking. But he'd eaten his people instead, their faces pouring in like shafts of light, while pudding cooled across the room and fresh-cooked meat steamed silently.

People. His food. He felt them on his tongue, with his eye, in his hand, the way he'd felt their presences so often before in the days that turned to dark and left him wasted. His. And the insect-eyed guards who smiled at pain. His too—them, too. Sometimes the thought made him vomit out what little was left inside. Still, it was true.

Bird feathers flapped. Colors tantalized from the faraway slat, wings spread, inviting. He wanted to fly off with the colors, become one of the leg-clicking insects scuttling down cell walls, scuttle up instead toward the narrow opening and out into the strange beginnings of glimmering light.

The faces insisted. They smiled darkly down. White, some of them, some of them brown, some reddish gold, some nearly pure black so only the flashing of cornea distinguished the eyes. All his. The same person. Every man has many colors inside himself. Many colors and many ways of being. Every man the same somewhere inside, the same potential cells lingering in wait, every one a potential hero, every one a potential villain. Every Jew a Nazi. Every Nazi—somewhere, in the most frightened recesses of the heart—a Jew. Every face the boot that kicked it and every boot the face bleeding in pain. The same person, the male the female. The female male. You fat men of power, you eat so much and take so much because inside yourselves you are malnourished women and children, you are powerless and starving somewhere inside. So you eat so much and take so much to compensate. Only natural. Like the animal licking its torn skin to heal it, and only making it rawer thereby, natural. So he had said. So he told them when they asked. And he'd asked them: what is it in these things to frighten you? What is it in these words that can possibly harm you? They stared back, fear shining brightly somewhere in the background of their own eyes. And he'd tried to understand, despite his own fear of physical pain—he knew they would hurt him. But still the questions continued under hot white lights in shadow-filled, airless rooms—what had he said here? And there? So he told them. *Every Jew a Nazi. Every Nazi a Jew. Every white man a black woman with child. Every woman a man with a whip. All sadists seek unity with a masochist. All terrorists are victims. All people of violence strive to crush the deep-rooted lust for peace and tenderness inside themselves, for they fear it is insufficient. All who are strong hide a private weakness, and the weak likewise hide their strength. Cancer is life unlimited. Life unlimited is death.*

What was there to retract, he wanted to know? What was there to retract, in verbally acknowledging that order and chaos exist in equal measure throughout the universe, and make love nightly? So that, where the one element seems to be in abundance, the other lurks always underfoot?

Are you saying—they leaned down close to his sweating face—that the rich will become poor? Isn't that what all this leads to?

He laughed. He told them no, no, that was not what he'd meant. Although perhaps that, too, would happen. What he meant was that in the pursuit of love, hate was not the enemy; in the pursuit of physical strength, the enemy was not physical weakness. What he meant was that the true antithesis of brilliance was not stupidity, but mediocrity. Mediocrity—the flabby need to conserve a passionless status quo—was far more destructive of passionate good than, say, an equally passionate force of evil. So he told them.

Through the slat, light grew stronger. He wondered, vaguely, what it was.

Everything else was a peaceful, seductive darkness into which he felt himself sink easily. He was drifting toward the last part of this limbo, he knew, and the dim sensation of weightlessness was graceful and without pain. Still there was that light. He kept his eye opened.

And it came to him, suddenly, a bright globe obliterating every face before him. It glowed pale white through the slat, far from earth now—he could see the firm white curve of it dividing the slat into light and darkness. The moon. His eye reached out for it. Something in him grew to desire. He wanted to touch that cool light, be calmed by its silver coldness and glow.

Sister, he said. The whisper echoed meaninglessly. He didn't know why he'd said it.

Now it was changing color—the smooth curve distorting, beginning to bubble along its horizon line, drift from white to golden yellow and then to a burnished, bloody red. Then it burst. It flared up larger, obliterating the slat's dimensions, pinwheeling in through the larger hole toward his eye. Its flames made scarlet spokes that whirled around as if in a strong wind. *Sister*, he said again. He couldn't have shut his eye now had he wanted to. It was opened almost by force, and with it he watched the moon on fire twirling toward him.

Then the rattling in his head broke apart. He felt it spurt open and his back arched, hands twisted soundlessly clutching out at the dark, his legs spasmed and then were still. Things flowed out of him—from the nose, the eyes, both ears and from his mouth—fluid things, red and yellow and clear damp wet on the darkness of his skin, and he was still reaching. He went out through his hands. Something tapped out to join the rest of the dark, the silence, crowded with faces and whispers. He slid out quickly so both eyes in the broken body left behind rolled suddenly open, blank. Still the hands reached, hands twitched. Stars sprayed from his fingertips. Until, spent and cold, his arms fell to the concrete with a tired thud, and the body of Dr. Tristam Saunderson cooled rapidly in its dark place in the small and secret cell where he had been beaten to death. The narrow slat near the ceiling regained its former size. Not a single charred mark would be left behind, not a sizzle of smoke, to show what had burned its way inside and conducted this theft in hot secrecy.

Outside, star-spattered darkness twinkled calmly. And the moon, grown paler and smaller, had not a trace of flame on its cold white surface.

THE INDESTRUCTIBLE
COMPASSION

Finally, there were prisoners of war. Rebels emerged from white-dusted frond huts, eyes dulled in shock as they gazed to the disintegrating plant life around them and the ashen, shriveled tree trunks sticking up out of ground covered by a grainy substance. They emerged with skin peeling from backs, chests and limbs in loose, bubbly white strips, hands weaponless, arms raised and outstretched like muted brown Christs.

Near dumping grounds outside of Sagrabél, the body of Dr. Tristam Saunderson decomposed in its unmarked grave.

As prisoners of war, the rebels were first herded into small wooden cages in which the only possible position was to crouch. In these cages, they were sometimes kept for days; they were kept there in the sun of midday, along the road to Sagrabél. So now, during the third circle of defoliation, Bellagua's highway had a sight in addition to men in army trucks heading one way, half-naked refugees the other: small wooden cages lining the roadside, with here and there a white-blistered hand sticking out between slats in silent, frozen supplication.

"What the hell is that?" The helicopter hovered, pilot chuckled a little sadly and flew down at an angle to hover lower in the sky. Do you know? Lee asked him tiredly. Do you know what those are, those brown boxes?

"Prisoners of war. A bit savage, don't you think? Keeping them in boxes to rot, I suppose. That's what they say. Soften them all up a bit. Soften them up for interrogation, you see."

"Oh," said Lee, "I see." In the cramped space his knees ached, Achilles' tendon ached to remind him of years ago, spiked track shoes in the rain and a two month layoff for injury. He laughed. Little brown boxes. "Jesus," he said. "Jesus Christ." Then he laughed again, and the pilot—who didn't like to see any man down—cheered up a bit himself.

After they'd softened up a bit the prisoners of war were dragged out and forced to stand. Most couldn't; their knees had locked, quadriceps severely weakened from the long hours of stationary strain. In being forced to stand, many sustained their first internal injuries—muscle tears, ripped tendons.

Interrogation followed standard procedural guidelines not mentioned at Geneva. Bellagua was a struggling nation, and could afford no expensive equipment. However, the Civil Guard—having matters relating to inter-rogation of P.O.W.'s under its direct jurisdiction—had long been able, where such matters were concerned, to make do with the stuff at hand. The simplest of implements can cause extreme pain: a belt, a boot. Indi-vidual tolerance for pain varies, but every man and every woman has a breaking point after which there is no morality, no personality, no truth or lie, only a land of lightlessness and physical suffering. Great soldiers risk falling into such territory time and again—it is a surer test than the risk of death. Great athletes are trained to endure in this land of pain longer than others—it eventually becomes, not performance itself, but the tolerance for extended physical suffering which separates the great from the good, the hero from the mere idealist. These soldiers from the Army of the People of Bellagua weren't soft men—their life of tremendous hardship had made them tougher than the average civilized human being—but within the context of their life they were ordinary men, not trained specifically to endure high levels of pain for long periods of time. And after the breaking point, a human being will do anything. Say anything. Sign anything. Of all human truths, this one is absolute; and the Civil Guard interrogators knew it well. They were carefully selected for their job. The key to productive interrogation is a certain curiosity, after all: what is each man's breaking-point? Interesting to note various levels of tolerance. The more scientifically minded among them compiled results, made graphs delineating differences in age, shade of skin color, time spent in the interrogation cell.

During interrogation, each prisoner of war was asked two questions re-peatedly. The first:

Who are your gods?

Later, they'd be shown a photograph taken a long time ago in the interior. In this photograph, dim and badly blurred, were several figures. One appeared to have white skin, and its face was encircled with red marker pen. The prisoners of war were asked:

Do you know of this person?

What the prisoners of war weren't told was that their answers did not matter in the least. In the interrogation cell was only pain.

Repeat this now, they were told, *Tristam Saunderson is a liar, a liar. Not a god but a liar, a dirty, shitty liar. Tristam Saunderson is shit. His followers are shit. My mother is shit. My father is shit. Saunderson is shit, shit, shit, shit, and a liar.*

Then the picture would be shown them again.

Repeat this now, they were told, *I do not know who this is. I do not know who this is. I have never seen this person. I do not know this person. I have never seen this person. I have never seen this person. I do not know who this is.*

Later, a pen would be put in the hand of each. They would make a mark at the bottom of a piece of paper on the dark-stained table before them, a mark which stood as each man's signature. All signed. There were no exceptions, save several who expired before they had a chance to sign—of pneumonia, the official report stated—but aside from these few everyone signed. It was only a matter of time. Interrogators are trained in patience. patience.

After signing, the prisoners of war were taken to other cells. In these cells they would lie on the floor and wait. Some waited a long time. Some seemed to have been forgotten. But after the period of waiting, each prisoner of war was dragged from his cell and forced, again, to stand. He was hosed down with disinfectant and then cold water, and given a sack-like pair of gray trousers and formless gray shirt to wear, and after being dressed in these clothes he was marched down many corridors, pushed down long stone stairways in the dark; he was blindfolded, and shoved into the back of an unmarked truck, driven far away, then marched from the back of the truck, led down another series of hallways and up flights of stairs. When the blindfold came off, each prisoner of war was in a courtroom of sorts: there was a long table, on one side of which sat several military men from the National Army, a representative of the Civil Guard, and a white man—a foreigner—who made no notes on the proceedings and remained silent, once in a while nodding.

Each prisoner of war was charged with treason. In evidence a piece of paper was presented, at the bottom of which was his symbol of signature.

I, the undersigned, hereby confess to treasonous activities perpetuated against the lawful and internationally recognized government of Bellagua. I hereby denounce all such activities. I denounce the Army of the People of Bellagua as a group of traitors and criminals. I denounce Tristam Saunderson as a charlatan and a liar. I now believe in one God, the Lord Jesus Christ, and in the sovereignty of the government of Bellagua. It is my wish to stand trial for the crimes against the state of which I am accused, and to abide by the verdict of this court.

Signed_____Date_____

Afterwards they were taken out into a yard, and shot.

With the fourth circle of defoliation, the Army of the People of Bellagua was forced to retreat deeper toward the core of the interior. Now there were wounded among them. There were fewer trees to hide in along the jungle's devastated rim. So the area they occupied was becoming smaller and smaller. Their base of operations was being peeled from them like onion skin.

At the same time, this forced conglomeration rendered each advance by the National Army more costly still. The areas into which they advanced were darker than before, even thicker, more unknown. They were guaranteed to be peppered with rebels, and each advance saw more desertion from the National Army ranks, a higher rate of mortality resulting from ambush. Sometimes now, strange illnesses swept the ranks, making entire units useless for days: inexplicable vomiting, dizziness, fevers, the occasional sudden collapse. *Psychosomatic*, said the white doctors who were there as medical advisers. They'd shrug. These illnesses were all temporary, it seemed, even though some of the symptoms tended to recur. The Bellaguan doctors whispered among themselves. They looked around to see that there were no white faces nearby before conferring. Their own faces would show worry, strain born of more than physical fatigue. But what they talked about, no one knew.

Word was getting out.

Foreign newsmen, hungry for copy, would sometimes lurk in the airport asking questions. Why the continued news blackout? Was there still a substantial amount of civil unrest? Why was the government having such difficulty quelling this unrest when it had previously claimed that the period of martial law would be brief?

How did the government account for the disappearance of hundreds of Bellaguan citizens during the past months? Was this a political matter?

Why was there no new official information concerning the welfare of Dr. Tristam Saunderson?

Was there any truth to the rumor, rampant among radical groups in other countries who maintained connections to similar groups in Sagrabél, that Dr. Tristam Saunderson was, in fact, no longer being held in protective custody? If so, where had he been taken?

Was there any truth to the rumor, rampant among radical groups in other countries who maintained connections to similar groups in Sagrabél, that his common-law wife, Dr. Manella Porter, had in fact not fled the island at all, but was living under the protection of armed rebel forces based in the interior?

If there were, in fact, armed rebel forces based in the interior, did this not imply that they were well organized? And if that was the case, who was their leader?

The more vocal of these newsmen were deported—sometimes with the aid of their own nations' embassies, headquartered in Sagrabél. The quieter ones were closely watched. They were hounded by overcharged hotel bills, flat tires, lost credit cards, harried by taxi drivers who couldn't follow directions; they were mugged by hooded assailants in dark streets when coming out of Sagrabél bars, assailants whom the Civil Guard seemed helpless in tracking down. They were helped by no one, admitted nowhere.

Still, word was leaking out.

On the same morning that Cycle Four of Operation Snow was completed, Dr. Manella Porter—rapidly attaining stature and fame among underground radical groups worldwide—played games with her young son Yosh somewhere in the interior. The thick, chirping darkness was unruffled by sunlight, night fires gone from the firepit and all, all continuing as usual—children's voices sounding quietly between domed frond huts that looked like leafy igloos, the sound of hand-shaped stone pounding vegetables to a thick paste, not the hint of a warrior, or Goddess. Grinning, Dr. Porter tossed her son gently into the air. He was tiny, dark and soft, dreamy-eyed, curly-headed. She tossed him again, caught him, pressed the boy quietly between her breasts. She tossed him again and caught him. Again. He giggled with delight.

In its unmarked grave, Tristam Saunderson's body decayed steadily—*transformed*, he himself would have said. Covered by earth and garbage, the skin had long since rotted away to reveal rotting tissue. Tissue in turn nourished enough bugs and worms until much of it had disappeared and revealed bone. The essential man, perhaps. A body sinking busily into dirt, one and the same with progress.

Gabriel hadn't slept in a couple of days; too busy. His life was composed of detail. He'd learned that the price of not concentrating on detail could be loss of life. So he'd elect sometimes to sacrifice sleep. He was busy with more research, busy with plans. The arrival of flight 848 had complicated matters somewhat. Nevertheless he saw it as an opportunity of sorts, albeit a dangerous one, and he was waiting for further contacts which so far had not materialized.

It was nearing the end of twilight when he rounded a corner in Sagrabél, heading away from the bar district toward the more elite side of town and, as always, taking a few twists and turns along the way. Maybe it was his tiredness—warped perception? he wondered—that made him imagine his shadow stretching long, long before him on the crumbling sidewalk, ill-defined in dusk. The shadow seemed to grow with each footstep, each footstep to echo louder than the preceding one. For a second, he thought everything stopped: all movement, all sound; there was a flash of time in which no cargo ships signaled their basso wails from the harbor, no noise from surrounding city streets reached his ears. Gabriel was alone. The completeness of it encased him, then stretched out empty before him—an infinity. He stopped. A brush of air behind his left shoulder.

Gabriel ducked. He twisted in a half circle and came up under the lunging body, hand chopped up between legs to a muffled growl of pain. He stepped back and stood taller. The body lunged again, coming toward him. Odd how slow this seemed. Something ran down his neck and shoulder. Gabriel side-stepped, a little off balance. He reached and pushed in—moment of entry and that hushed gasp, a shudder. He felt the slide in, pushed again. He kept one hand free while the other held on, thrusting, gripped, twisted from side to side and then around, around. The handle went slippery but his grip was strong. Gabriel saw it all in slow motion, calm and clear, huge body bent over on the blade of his knife. He pulled the blade out only when he was sure. Then in slow motion the body fell, thudded, rolled over, and in the gray end of twilight something dark spilled from the mouth and nose, bubbled down along the neck, joined the great bubbling splash of dark across the sky-blue shirt front. Gabriel reached down to wipe the blade on a sky-blue sleeve. He repocketed his knife. He could feel himself breathe. In. Out. And every thump of his heart. Then he thought for a moment he was crying. But no. He crouched to examine the body of the man he'd just killed.

Something attached to a front pocket glimmered faintly and Gabriel leaned over to see. He glanced quickly around but this was not a residential area and he was alone, no one had seen, he was sure of it. He reached into his pants and brought out a pocket flashlight, snapped it on to shine over the plastic name tag swimming there in blood:

HI, MY NAME'S CAL
CHURCH OF CHRIST
THE INDESTRUCTIBLE COMPASSION

Gabriel reached into his trousers again and brought out a folded pair of thin rubber gloves. He fit each one on, reached gingerly for the name tag and beamed the tiny light over it again. He lifted it. Attached there by clips. But something else shone from the back of the tag. Squinting, Gabriel could see that the back wasn't yellow plastic at all, but appeared to be dark velvet. In the center of the velvetlike backing he saw a small thing embedded and, touching it with gloved fingers, jiggled until it came out: a tiny pin, like an old-fashioned tie clip. It seemed to be gold—he couldn't tell—and at its center was a small white dot. Ivory.

Gabriel reached into his trousers, took out a small plastic bag. Carefully, he dropped the pin into the bag, sealed it, set it back in one of the internal zippered compartments in his trousers and put the rubber gloves in another compartment, the flashlight in another. He stood, felt his left ear sting, then ran a hand along his neck and left shoulder, felt the wet stickiness there—blood, his own. He did not think it serious. Still, he set a slightly quicker pace and stayed in shadowy sidestreets, fingers straying once in a while to the razor-slashed ear.

STRANGE MALADIES PECULIAR
TO WAR

Gabriel walked up the steps to a Swiss chalet-type place in the elite section of Sagrabél, hand pressed to his left ear. In the dully glowing doorside lamp it could be seen that his left shoulder was soaked with blood.

Gabriel let himself in. Within minutes several rooms were lit. Shadows of men bobbed up in windows to hastily pull shades, draw thick curtains.

In the blue-tiled bathroom, he pulled off his shirt and bundled it into a bloody ball, threw it with a splat into the bathtub. He filled the sink with cold water and stuck in a washcloth. He was busy cleaning off blood from his neck, cheek and shoulder when a man appeared in the doorway, medical kit held high. With the other hand he saluted.

"Relax," Gabriel muttered. He squeezed the washcloth over his ear, glanced sideways in the mirror. Just as he'd thought: not bad at all really, the earlobe not even severed. And it had almost stopped bleeding. "Relax. It'll be okay."

"Better let me stitch." The doctor smiled. He spoke Hebrew with an accent—from what country originally? Gabriel wondered—then he had it: Iraq. "Let's see."

"There's no time."

"This won't take long."

Gabriel pulled down the toilet lid and sat.

While his ear was being stitched others wandered in through the bathroom doorway, saluted, spoke with him briefly before wandering out again. Gabriel dispatched two men to his hotel room, had them memorize the address and agree on telephone signals in case of difficulty. The sink's fluorescent light made everything paler—blue tiles, the hands of men gesturing—and Gabriel's lips, pressed together sometimes in thought, looked thin and hard tonight.

"Two minutes more." The doctor whistled some melody. Final stitch made, he left.

Gabriel looked up to see someone else in the doorway, a tall, slender man with graying hair and an oddly gentle face. The brown eyes twinkled sadly. Gabriel straightened a little and saluted.

The man told him to relax.

"I wanted to avoid coming here. There was no option."

"Don't worry. We're almost finished." He smiled tiredly, examined Gabriel's face. "Our old friends the Snowmen, eh?"

"Two hours and they'll be spilling down the chimney."

The man shrugged. "So. We only need an hour and a half." He slid down against the door he'd locked behind, until he was sitting on the floor and his whole long, tall shape seemed nearly folded in two. "We planned to get in touch with you later tonight. But"—he shrugged again—"so life had other plans. You're okay?"

"I'm fine."

"Fine. I'll give you the message directly then. Two weeks, my friend. You understand?"

"I want my brother."

"You'll get your brother."

"I want my brother alive."

"So. You'll get your brother alive."

Staring at the man, Gabriel's eyes narrowed. "No legal complications? Nothing political?"

"What complications, Gavi? I don't know what you're talking about." He stood, one gaunt hand reaching to pat Gabriel's shoulder. "Let Naphtali take care of all that business. And don't worry about your brother. Finish up this assignment and everyone's happy. True? Good. So get the things you need, my friend, then let your people know whatever they have to know. And stop by to see the cartographer. Third room on your right, down the hall. He'll have something for you."

Clean-shaven, with a fresh shirt, hair brushed and a flesh-toned Band-Aid set neatly over the stitch marks on his ear, Gabriel did what he had to do, got the information he needed, dialed a phone number. He let it ring three times, then put down the receiver. He dialed another number, let it ring four times. Then he left the Swiss chalet-type house, walked several well-lit streets and turned, changed direction, walked for many minutes until he was nearing the embassy district. He hailed a cab.

The cab slowed considerably as they came close to the heart of the city— the dock area, where everything was very old, close together, hot and dirty. There were always people crowding the narrow, twisting streets here, always the smell of beer and cheap alcohol on lips or wafting from dirty opened doors, skinny dogs and roosters scuttling noisily along the gutters, and on every corner a Civil Guard in uniform accompanied by a soldier from the National Army. Curfew had been lifted recently in this one area of Sagrabél, called the entertainment district—for economic reasons, Gabriel guessed. One of Bellagua's prime drawing cards was its black market. That and cheap drugs, a thriving prostitution racket for interested tourists, off-the-record businesses that ran twenty-four hours a day. For a native of Sagrabél to make any kind of living he'd have to work in some branch of the tourist industry, and the most profitable branch by far was the illegal one. Gabriel had the cab let him out on a wrong corner. When it had driven off he turned back and wound through more hot, crowded streets, looped around again and passed through the open door of a bar. The sweetish-smelling, sickly hot darkness struck like a wall he'd come flat up against. Gabriel smelled sawdust, sweat. He looked briefly at the men crowding the bar— a few white, most not—and headed for the back.

Someone bumped into him and Gabriel stopped to brush himself off. Then he looked up—another white man, dressed in loose-fitting flowery shirt and light beige summer jacket—and his face brightened with recognition. "Hey Jack!" Gabriel spoke in English. "What the hell are you doing here?"

Jack's face also lit with surprise. "Speak of the devil. Bruce, it's good to see you. You here on vacation?"

"Nah. Had a little business to look after. But I'm cutting this trip short."

Jack slugged his shoulder good-naturedly. "You're kidding."

"Nope. Had to change some plans on short notice." Bruce winked. "Business. So I'm getting a little fun in tonight."

"Well, I hope you can get everything taken care of."

"Oh, sure. You know me. Look Jack, how about a drink?"

"Sounds good. Just one though!" Jack smiled, hooked an arm around Bruce's shoulder on their way to the bar. "Tom-catting tonight, you know how it is."

They wiggled through to the bar. Bruce ordered two bourbons and beer chasers. "You here with the family?"

"Just the wife."

They raised their shot glasses to one another. "How are the kids, Jack?"

Jack downed the shot, followed it with a gulp of beer. The empty glass settled on the wet counter next to Bruce's still-full one, next to dark elbows and filled shell ashtrays. He smiled at Bruce. "The kids are fine. My boy's at Yale this year."

"That's great!"

"Yep. I think he's going to stick with pre-med. Kids." Jack shook his head but, like all his gestures, this one was also good-natured. "Hey, you know who was asking about you a while ago?"

"Who?" Bruce sniffed at his bourbon, set it down again without drinking. "Arnie."

"That bastard!" Both men laughed. "How is he, anyway?"

"Oh, he's fine. Doing great. He asked if I knew how you were doing, and I told him I hadn't heard from you in a while. Anyway, he sends his regards."

"Thanks. If you see him, give him my best."

"Will do."

"Tell him I'm fine, business is good as planned. Tell him I'll be back in Cleveland in a couple of weeks, and I'll give him a call."

"Will do. We ought to have lunch sometime anyway, Bruce, you and me."

"Sounds good."

"Want me to give you a ring?"

"Do that." Bruce grinned. "You do that."

Jack finished about a quarter of his beer and slapped Bruce on the back again, told him to take care and they'd get together soon.

When he'd left, Gabriel waited ten minutes. Then he threw some Bellaguan currency on the bar counter—large, brightly colored bills that on the world market were worth less and less each day—and made his way outside.

The next bar he went into was just down the street. But Gabriel took another long route, cutting and dodging along crowded sidewalks, looping more buildings to come around from the other direction. Once inside the bar he went straight toward the back. More dim light, more sweat, more sawdust smells, men lining the bar three deep. There were a few more white faces here—businessmen from other countries—and sounds of many languages mingled confusingly in the dark. Gabriel spotted a table where one white man sat, tan summer jacket and open-necked white shirt, dark-framed glasses sliding down the short bridge of his nose. He made his way over and pulled out a chair.

"Hiya, Morty."

"Bruce!"

"Been waiting long?"

"No. No problem. I just got here a few minutes ago."

"Good." Bruce signaled the waiter. "What are you drinking?"

"I'll have a beer."

Bruce ordered two beers. He turned to Morty, grinned calmly. "Well, how are we doing?"

"Okay. I'll tell you though, Bruce, coffee futures are looking bad. They'd better straighten things out in Brazil."

"Personally, I think they're stockpiling for a rainy day."

Morty shrugged. "Who knows. It's a good thing we pulled out when the getting was good."

"You bet. Did you talk to the boys here?"

"Sure. It looks like we'll get the go-ahead. Everyone seems to think a clearance office is a good idea. Right down near the port—it'd catch the foreign trade."

Their beers arrived, and Bruce paid. He raised his mug, winked at Morty. "I've got news for you, Morty. We already got the go-ahead."

"No kidding!"

"Would I kid you? Now come on, drink up."

"You're kidding. When did you hear?"

"Just this evening." Bruce blew beer suds from the mug's foaming top. "Let me tell you, I was almost as surprised as you."

"Well, well! Any idea when you'll be able to firm up the deal?"

"Oh, in about two weeks."

"That soon?"

"Yep. The green light's on, Morty. So I'll just wrap up all the details—"

"Great."

"—and I still miss out on my cousin's kid's bar mitzvah down in Florida."

"Miami?"

"Nah. Over near St. Petersburg."

Morty downed some beer. He twirled his mug on the brown wooden tabletop. "Which cousin is that, Bruce? I know him? That the one you were talking about—with the old man who's filthy rich—"

"Probably. My Uncle Zecky."

"Yeah! That's the one. So. So this bar mitzvah's a big deal?"

Bruce shrugged. He blew more foam from his beer and it splattered on the table. "Big family affair. You know how it is. They hired everything but the kitchen sink—you know, one of those deals. But the big secret is"— Bruce leaned across the table and spoke in a wry tone of voice, stage whisper—"it's not my cousin who's paying. And it's not Uncle Zecky, either. Guess who's paying for the whole mess?" He sat back triumphantly. "Zecky's daughter, for Christ's sake. You believe it? Some family feud no one's supposed to know about. Anyway, she's got a thing for my cousin's kid, or something like that. So she went ahead and sold off some stocks or something to finance it—Christ, you wouldn't believe that side of the family. The richest bunch of fucks you've ever seen."

Morty chuckled. "I believe it. But they don't hold a candle to mine, Bruce. I got a brother—know what he did for his kid's bar mitzvah? He flew the whole damned guest list to Tel Aviv. No kidding!"

"Private plane?" Bruce joked.

"Just about. Everyone got the invitation and it was like some kind of military command, you know? You will be at the airport next Sunday at eighteen-hundred hours sharp, et cetera. I mean, we were just about expecting to get herded onto this plane by a bunch of paratroopers. Anyway, that's exactly what the invitation said. It was something, boy. That ceremony was something."

Bruce laughed, loud and long. "I hope you had a photographer on board."

"Sure did."

"Good," Bruce chuckled, "I'm glad."

They talked awhile longer—weddings, bar mitzvahs. Then they talked business. Clearance office in Sagrabél. Investments down in South America. The Pittsburgh office, the Cleveland office. Bruce told Morty he'd be wrapping things up just as quickly as possible. In less than a couple of weeks, if at all possible, but—he winked again—the Bellaguans operated on a different time schedule than the rest of the world. Which was why this place was great for a vacation, difficult for business.

Both men left the bar together and, outside on the street, Gabriel went one way and his contact another.

The defoliated land was now clear of trees and leaves; the National Army soldiers could march through it without fear. Ambush squads had no place to hide for miles.

From the ground it looked like a winter wonderland. No trees—just stumps—no leaves, for miles. Just white. Just snow. Then after some distance a sudden dark wall of jungle trees, rich green foliage. Winter sat smack next to summer. From the air, it looked like a big green platter fringed by concentric circles of white.

After touching a whitened tree stump, their fingers would tingle, burn. The sensation of burning would become increasingly uncomfortable over a period of hours, then gradually diminish until it was almost gone. But sometimes it returned in the night. It would creep through the palm, wrap itself around a wrist, continue up to the elbow. Some men got the feeling of flame rolling over in their intestines, and vomited. A few collapsed. Fatigue, the doctors said. Nerves. These men were removed quietly from the front lines. A rumor circulated that, in a unit farther along the West Reef area, three enlisted men had turned up dead in defoliated territory with mouths swollen open, tongues stiff and pure white between their lips. But this was only rumor.

As hostilities continued, there was a growing increase in the number of troops seeking medical attention for a variety of complaints the doctors seemed unable to explain: sporadic sensations of internal and external burning, vomiting, sudden fainting spells; a general sense of physical malaise that would make men sit suddenly in the middle of a forced speed march, their hands drooping to the ground and gun sinking tiredly. Sometimes despite the yells of commanding officers they would not respond or obey.

MY FRIENDS, I SAY THIS:
THEY WILL TURN US ALL WHITE INSIDE AND OUT.

This message, badly mimeographed, showed up on hundreds of thin slips of paper mysteriously distributed throughout all units. The next day came another.

KILL OR BE KILLED?
JOIN HANDS WITH OUR BROTHERS FROM THE ARMY OF THE PEOPLE OF BELLAGUA.
LET US FIGHT TOGETHER AGAINST THE WHITE MENACE THAT WOULD DESTROY US ALL.

After this one, tents were searched and ransacked by military police. Certain enlisted men were brought in for questioning, but nothing conclusive determined. And even while suspects were in custody, another brief message appeared on hundreds of slips of paper scattered through each camp:

MY FRIENDS, I SAY THIS:
ONE GOD ALONE WILL NOT SAVE YOU.
WHITE MEN WITH GUNS CANNOT LEAD YOU.

Rumors trotted at top speed through every unit. It was a group of mischief makers, some said, nothing more. No, argued others, it was a subversive group in the National Army itself. Still others argued that a group from the People's Army had infiltrated National Army ranks, and were issuing these notes as a terrorist tactic to break morale. And many men remained silent when the topic was raised. Silently, they folded their thin slips of badly mimeographed paper deep into a shirt or trouser pocket. Sometimes at night, a man would reach quietly into a pocket, draw out a faintly crackling thin slip of paper and caress it between his fingers.

G.I. JOE SAYS:
MURDER YOUR SISTER.

WHITE MEN WITH GUNS WILL ONLY DESTROY YOU.

Tristam Saunderson, some whispered late at night. The Doctor has returned.

THE WHITE GOD OF FOREIGNERS WILL LEAD YOU TO DEATH.

Dr. Saunderson, they whispered among themselves, in corners of tents, by the dull light of outdoor generators. He has returned to join the Army of the People.

MY FRIENDS, I SAY THIS:
THE GODS OF YOUR MOTHERS WEEP FOR YOU.

These messages are from the gods, some said. They fingered the crosses around their necks absent-mindedly. Nervous, they wiped sweat from their faces, crouched smaller still in the corners of tents. They swatted bugs from their bare hands and necks, spoke to one another while their eyes shifted fearfully from side to side. *From the gods. As it was told. The Black God will die with the Sun. And the White Goddess light the night for hunting.*

THIS IS A WAR OF FOREIGNERS, NOT BELLAGUANS.
THIS IS A WAR BEGUN BY EUROPEANS.
THIS IS A WAR SUPPORTED BY AMERICANS,

AND BY ZIONISTS.
THIS IS A WAR OF THE RACIST, CAPITALIST,
WAR-MONGERING SYSTEM.
LET US JOIN HANDS AGAINST FOREIGN FASCISTS.

Can you read these words? some asked, offering the slips of paper with
shivering hands. What does it say? What is a capitalist?
    An American. A European. These white men are capitalists.
    Ah. What is a Zionist?
    A Jew.
    Jew? What is a Jew?

G.I. JOE SAYS: FORGET YOUR OLD GODS,
JUST KILL LIKE I TELL YOU TO.

WHO DO YOU THINK YOU ARE, JOE?

Pressing the lever on the mimeograph machine in a sweaty basement in
central Sagrabél, Pablo hoped she'd forgive him for that one. But he was
running out of slogans, and anyway his talent had always been sort of
derivative. Like he didn't have any soul of his own, he kidded himself, so
he had to go out stealing them all the time. Just to feel sane. Just to feel
human. Until there was suddenly nothing before him one day but a warped,
dark-skinned little body, no legs, no arms, no eyes—where was the soul in
that? And for stealing the image of this nothingness he'd been punished,
punished badly. Oh, he had a stake in all this just as much as the Bellaguans,
he guessed: stop all this destruction of souls; otherwise there'd be no pictures
for him to take. Sometimes he wondered what Gabriel had done with the
pictures. Sometimes he'd be willing to bet that when the prints were developed they were blank—no soul, no nothing; nothing there at all.
    Carlos liked the one about the Zionists. He told Pablo to keep at it, some
sort of interorganizational promotion might be in the offing. And Pablo,
who hadn't entirely missed out on Basic Training, saluted.

    In a National Army unit, a soldier vomited white liquid one day and
died. The cause of death appeared in the medical report in words that were
used for the first time but would be repeated countless times again—words
that would become well known and joked about in nervous whispers by
National Army troops. *Cause of death: strange maladies peculiar to war.*

One morning came the sound of light artillery shelling, the buzzing of planes overhead that weren't helicopters.

Later that day helicopters appeared, swooping over green jungle territory, spattering liquid onto the trees. This marked the beginning of the fifth circle of defoliation.

Cold, careful, removed from everything he touched or said or did, Pablo considered himself a mere observer now. If there was a secret corner of passion buried inside, some inner world where his dreams tossed and turned, moaned at night into the image of an exotic female face, this world was sealed off from conscious expression. He was a revolutionary now. Sometimes the word brought a slightly twisted smile to his lips—*revolutionary*—it was so formal. Always, there was the part of him that stood back from it all and said: *Me, a goddamned revolutionary? You're kidding.* These guys he'd volunteered with were a bunch of assholes, rejects, society's refuse. Throw in a couple of rich kids with severe mental problems and there you had it: The Foreign Brigade to Aid the Army of the People of Bellagua— another excuse for not making an honest living.

At least, that's what the detached part of him said. The rest of him was in the thick of it. The rest of him was grinding out ersatz slogans on cheap mimeograph paper in a damp, roach-infested Sagrabél basement, calling everyone around him *comrade* and saluting Carlos, their superior officer. The rest of him was taking pictures, mug shots of every member of the Foreign Brigade; Carlos had even gotten hold of a semi-decent spotlight and set it up in the basement; he ordered each member to pose for front and profile shots, made sure Pablo had some chemicals and darkroom space to develop the film. History of the revolution, Carlos told him, smiling from behind mirrored sunglasses.

Their dependence on Carlos was complete. He set up work rosters, made sure there was food at least twice a day, sent some to bed while others stood guard at the basement stairs. He filed away all of Pablo's photographs in his own secret file to which no one else had access. Carlos gave the orders. He had a plan. And there was a kind of blind faith they all had in him— he knew what he was doing, the organization had known what it was doing when it appointed him operational leader.

On Bellagua, they waited.

They waited a long time, obediently, patiently; they were trained to follow orders. The destination reached, some of them, had their minds possessed real clarity, would have been disappointed. They'd come expecting hand-to-hand jungle combat and found instead an unaired basement with mimeograph machine. The dangerous drudgery of it all made them very tired. Still, sleep was difficult. They were too busy grinding out thousands of mimeographed pages of slogans each day, too busy scattering the pages in National Army encampments each night—long, silent drives in unmarked trucks down the highway, off the road to evade blockades, truck lights permanently darkened. Some of them risked their lives every night. And despite the heart-stopping, sweating fear of it, it was still drudgery.

Carlos kept the photographer to himself a lot. The photographer never went out on night missions. The revolution needed to document itself, Carlos said, and good photographers with the right credentials were hard to find.

"Pablo, my friend." Carlos took a break sometimes when just the two of them were there in the basement, machine leaking mimeo fluid and sweat soaking through every inch of their clothing. He'd light a cheap cigarette, smoke as if enjoying some rare delight with each long puff. "Pablo, Pablo. The world's a funny place, my friend. The world's a funny place. If you want to do just a small piece of good"—he'd squeeze his thumb and fore-finger nearly together to show how small—"you need to commit a lot of evil deeds. It's funny." He'd laugh, blow out foul clouds. "It's a funny thing!"

Sometimes Pablo felt a surge of sincere affection for Carlos. He wondered if it was part of his general deterioration; he felt himself sinking into some-thing, he didn't know exactly what—some sort of large, gaping pit—more and more with each passing hour. He felt himself sinking into the dissolution of that thin line between public and private truth. He could almost see the wire dissolving inside of him, the tightrope no longer safe for walking.

Hours passed in the basement in Sagrabél. Pablo sweated them away; he worked efficiently. Why was it that everything he did seemed tinged with sadness now? He only knew that the memory of her face, of the specks of green in her eyes, was getting farther and farther away from him somehow, and somehow he was unable to fight this sinking down and away. The camera swung around his neck; he'd used up many rolls with mug shots. Something was profoundly wrong; he knew it, felt it—was it madness?— because he knew that was where he was heading, toward madness. Still there was the sense that something was left undone. He had some mission here, his life had led him to this point, this place and time; that much he knew. Strange how life did that: led everyone to a particular place and time of their own, often absurdly, often haphazardly, but always the final result was that you wound up *somewhere*, became part of the continuum of what they called history. Maybe that's what Carlos meant by saying the world was a funny place. It was nothing, the world, but a place where multitudes of lives were lived out; and some of these lives would intersect in space, in time, would touch each other. That was the absurdity of it, and the ultimate mystery—that he had taken the picture of Raina Scott, and later met her lover, and now he was here on Bellagua again for another reason, with another camera. Was there some meaning to all this? Pablo didn't know. He had little sense these days of what was physical reality and what was imaginary, hallucinatory, dreamlike. He wondered if all that really mattered, anyway—distinctions. What kept him functional was this unshakable feeling he had of being on some path or other—a path inevitably led somewhere, didn't it?—that whatever he was doing, sanely, madly, meaninglessly or significantly, it was a fulfillment of something called his destiny. And destiny, like history, was odd but unswerving; like history, it played itself out within the context of time. It was his lot never to comprehend what an hour might hold. Even if the destiny made no sense in terms of justice or morality or any other man-made configuration, it was nevertheless always there, patiently waiting in time, motiveless like the ineffable pace of time itself, or history, or love.

Some nights, bugs scuttling across the tattered folds of his sleeping bag and the cellar floor smelling of mimeo leakage, Pablo woke with the hint of tears in his eyes, a throaty ache consuming him. He'd want to speak the words he thought aloud.

I love you.

Who did he love? A face? Maybe he'd had a dream that reminded him of love; maybe it was the darkness itself he'd grown to love, after all, and his continual sensation of teariness and pain. Sometimes the face of Karlen would come into his mind; sometimes the face of Gabriel, or even Carlos.

I love you.

Karlen—had he loved her? Or only wanted her? Or maybe loved what he sensed about her, even then, before beatings and the madness of the world—that she was inextricably bound up with his destiny which, senseless or heroic, was still his own. Maybe it was Raina he'd loved somehow, or what she'd represented: a life uncluttered by considerations of fear or circumstance, so firmly was it committed to the realization of its fulfillment, its destiny, its end—Raina poised in the bow of a small boat, ancient weapon held with the ease of perfection, death swirling around her in circles, circles ever smaller—this was the essential Raina, the Raina history books would remember. And of all this he'd been a part, albeit a small one. So at the approach of his own fulfillment, his own hour, perhaps what he felt was a twinkling of that same awe—a wonder akin to love. Maybe it was this waiting hour he awoke thinking of—the hour that was his alone somewhere along the path—maybe it was this hour he loved.

I love you.

Who or what was the *you* that he loved?

He'd wonder.

And wonder who he himself was now, really—who was the *I* that loved the *you?*

No, it was all too difficult when you began to analyze. There was no subject and no object really, only the feeling; it was seeing every face he'd ever known. It was seeing Raina, poised forever there in time, weapon frozen in position and body perfect, strong, like the goddess she claimed she was—Raina daring everything to burn brightly ahead into her inevitable hour—that daring to blaze brightly, maybe that was a sort of love? The defiance of it what Karlen had loved, its brightness evoking in her for the first time the feel of it, of love—a daring to desire despite history, despite time, despite inevitable doom, burn the bright flame of *the wanting* high. Raina was both weapon and wound; she was moth and lamplight. Chasing down white things until—as somehow she had known they would—they turned to find her. Seizing beauty from the hands of faceless gods, luring it away across time, space, across continents. *I*—she had said—*I am always in love.*

Some nights, Pablo slept.

In the pre-dawn morning Carlos woke them all, whispered new instructions to everyone—up and muster, regulation dress, they were going somewhere, another phase had begun—Pablo wasn't surprised. He was sad instead, yet filled with expectation. He cleaned, dressed. He hung Espía Pequeña around his neck, walked out into the hot, cramped little streets of Sagrabél next to Carlos, the two of them followed by the Foreign Brigade to Aid the Army of the People of Bellagua. He breathed deeply. This early, the air was permeated with sea scent, clear and invigorating. He wasn't surprised to see limousines waiting for them, their dark windows opaque. Carlos waved him into the car he'd ride in himself. Behind mirrored sunglasses he was grinning again with assurance. And Pablo caught himself on one deep breath, for a minute just froze—he'd forgotten his wristwatch. He wouldn't know the hour when it happened.

But he eased into the back of the car, left hand guarding his camera. He supposed this was the way it always was, had to be—your hour would come, and you'd go ahead to meet it. Often you would not even know it.

* * *

Bellagua's National Airport appeared suddenly across the expanse of long, flat distance, its buildings dark, roadsigns pointing the way in several languages. It was Sunday, the road pretty much deserted. Not many flights left on Sundays. Most of the duty-free shops in the airport were shut down, and everywhere in Sagrabél the bars were closed. Bellagua was officially a nation of Catholics. And if crude wooden icons of a strange female figure, staff in one hand, other hand clasped invitingly beneath breasts and large wooden eyes blankly slanting, often appeared on shabby slum shelves next to plastic dashboard versions of Jesus, this was never discussed in church. Sundays found everyone except tourists in church.

Pablo settled into the smoothness of the dark seat. In front was the driver—faceless, because he'd never turned around. In one of the back seats Pablo sat hemmed in by three-piece suits and sweat; another back seat was occupied by more comrades and Carlos. Pablo turned once to look for Carlos' eyes. He saw his own face mirrored in the sunglasses. Carlos grinned.

Something like a ringing telephone started up inside Pablo. Was it warning him? He didn't know. He sensed, instead, some sort of elation, a bright anticipation. He cupped both hands around the Little Spy's lens, and his right hand quivered but he was feeling clear inside now. The ringing kept on like a mantra chant, almost comforting. He was getting there, he knew; didn't know where *there* was but realized that it didn't matter in the least because he was on the path, heading toward whatever he was supposed to be heading toward. And nothing could surprise or upset now—nothing; Pablo knew somewhere deep down under the ringing that the thing he was heading toward was his hour—his end—completion of his journey, unknown and somehow glorious in its finality. So he felt calm and hummed silently to himself. He was, he knew, the closest he'd ever come to happiness just now. Everything had slowed. The clicking of a small insect flying to its death against the windshield, glint of sunlight on the metal lens of the camera, the way he smelled, the vinyl, closed scent of the car—these sensations seemed to last forever. He knew he was closing in on things.

Pablo wasn't surprised when he opened his eyes to find the limousine stopped, motor off. The driver didn't move. In the car, no one moved. He looked ahead through a silent windshield. Here already: the airport; he could see the lines on concrete, could tell they were on a runway. Across the concrete blew a scrap of white paper that paused and rolled, then blew out of his field of vision.

In several parked limousines, windows tinted opaque, the Foreign Brigade to Aid the Army of the People of Bellagua sat and waited.

He wasn't surprised that hours passed, that he could tell they'd passed by the position of shadows along concrete. And there was that scrap of paper again, crunched to a misshapen white ball, blowing back and forth across the deserted airfield. Carlos told the driver to open the windows a crack. Silently, all at once, every window slid open about a quarter of an inch and hot fresh air seeped in. Pablo breathed gratefully.

He wasn't surprised when a click sounded, locks on each door were suddenly released. But every man sat still. Every man waited for the command. They'd been that carefully trained—to deny instinct—and they waited miserably, yet proudly. Because they could master instinct and become, in the end, utterly obedient—this was why they were proud.

Almost sundown. Pablo looked out at gentle blue shadows on concrete stretching longer than before. And behind the sudden sweat of anticipation what he felt was soft sadness, a sensation almost sweet, like a pillow to lie back on at night.

"Eighteen hundred hours, comrades. All out."

Carlos was last out the door.

They all stood there blinking for some seconds. Pablo looked around. The misfits, the creeps, the scum who'd jumped parole and psychos gone AWOL, stood tiredly around him in three-piece suits, each with its ivory-inlaid lapel pin. For a minute Pablo wanted to laugh. What must he look like himself? What must he look like to them, these volunteers for the Foreign Brigade to Aid the Army of the People of Bellagua? Did they know at all that he was using them for his own absurd purpose—a purpose as yet unknown to him—that he was riding along on their coattails? If so, did they care? Or were they all just riding along on the coattails of fortune, anyway—each would-be hero with his own private fear, his own misbegotten reason, hitching a ride with fortune. Or misfortune. It didn't seem to matter.

And he wasn't surprised, either, when Carlos touched his shoulder so he turned to face the two mirrors that smiled back instead of eyes. Pablo blinked. For a moment he thought it wasn't himself he saw in the double mirrors. For a moment he thought he'd seen Gabriel.

"This way, my friend."

Carlos' grip was gentle but insistent, tugging him around again, and numbly Pablo followed. Behind them came the obedient shuffling march of many feet. Espía Pequeña slapped lightly against his belly. Pablo realized that for the first time in weeks he had no desire to take a picture. No longer an observer now, in the thick of things, he couldn't step back and shutter-click. He was inside of something now, something *happening*. His guts surged. He moved along in a haze of bliss and terror.

They were heading toward one of the hangars. Vast sliding metal doors began to open as they marched toward it. He had a brief vision of her face. *Baby*, he said silently, and in his head lay naked on top of her, bringing his own face slowly down toward hers for a long, long kiss; he could taste her tongue, a vague hint of Moët—a good year. Pulling back he gazed down until she'd opened her eyes. Then the tiny electric green spots hissed up at him. He imagined himself afraid, and in love. *Karlen. Aw, Kaz. Aw, Baby. Baby.* Walking toward the hangar he could feel something move a little in his pants. Small beginnings of desire. Pablo, he said, how can you be such a jerk? Huh? How come you don't pay attention?

Dark-skinned faces grinned back at them from the edges of the hangar door. Each face had mirrored sunglasses. Pablo could feel Carlos' gentle grip on his shoulder. He could hear the steps pick up pace slightly behind them, expectantly, as each comrade saw the familiar mirrored sunglasses and sensed that the next Phase, long-awaited, had begun. The faces loomed nearer, darkness in the hangar beckoned. Keeping step with Carlos, he moved forward until his own face was almost parallel to the dark ones with mirrors grinning out obscurely. A few more steps. Just a few. The ringing inside began a long, sirenlike shriek. Pablo forgot to breathe. He was alive now, utterly, thoughtlessly—this was it, he whispered, this was it, his hour. One step more. They were parallel with the edges of the hangar door. Mirrors smiled back from everywhere—twin pools of mirrors leaping brightly from wood-brown faces. The hour screamed inside, white-hot ecstasy. The moment before death when everything is life.

Then Carlos' grip tightened around his upper arm and he was hurtling forward, dirt grinding up into his face when he hit the ground. Somebody pinned him and lay lengthwise on his back. The moment passed. Behind him the air exploded, gunfire whining rapidly, someone screaming in a strange, high-pitched blur of shock. The dirt curled under his lips. Pablo was crying. He was alive and crying; alive, and cheated. The Little Spy lay crushed, broken, against his chest. Something ran from his nose, and Pablo cried into dirt. They'd stolen it from him. They'd taken away his hour.

AFTER THE FLOOD

Pablo stared across the table. Staring back was Gabriel. He blinked, shut
his eyes for what seemed minutes, but the image wouldn't go away.
Gabriel looked tired. Some of that deep-grained tan had drained, the lines
on his forehead dug in farther than before. Pablo opened his eyes. He had
to conclude that this was no hallucination but the real thing. Then he
laughed. He reminded himself that everything was images anyway—Christ,
he was a photographer, he knew that stuff—all reflections and refractions
of light on matter that, without light, would be colorless; all of it, on some
level, illusory. Even Gabriel.

"Pablo, it's good to see you."

Pablo laughed again.

Gabriel nodded, dim hint of a smile on his lips. "I know," he said quietly,
"I know just how you feel."

Did he? Pablo shrugged. He noticed the bright light overhead, metal
cone shade sheltering it like an Oriental sun hat. In back of Gabriel stood
men in shadows. He sensed the shadows move in back of him, too. They'd
left the hangar behind somewhere, walked somewhere else—he hadn't
noticed where. And now there was nothing but this room: large, bare, dirt
floor and the bright metal-shaded light overhead, this metal fold-out table
and fold-out chairs on either side. Except for the ones in which he and his
brother sat, the chairs were empty. Lines from crummy old movies filtered
through his head.

We have ways of making you talk!

But no one seemed to want to make him say anything. So Pablo just sat there. He was frozen again in time. He felt protective of this numb sensation; who knew what the numbness was covering up? Better just to feel nothing. He glanced at the busted remains of Espía Pequeña on the tabletop. Too bad, he thought vaguely. He'd never developed a particularly close relationship with that camera, anyway—not like he'd had with Alfredo. He was sorry it had been ruined but not all that sorry.

Gabriel reached into the broken camera parts. He kept an eye on his brother, too. Even though there were experts lining the walls of this room, Gabriel never really trusted any man but himself. He extracted film from the camera reel. Then he fished through shattered lens remnants and came up with a tiny cartridge the length of one short finger joint and many times thinner. Unofficially recorded proceedings of the Foreign Brigade to Aid the Army of the People of Bellagua. A sorry organization, really. Too bad for those anti-Zionist tenets. Too bad they'd made contact with stronger, more lethal organizations. Under less malignant circumstances he doubted his superiors would have bothered with them—at least not bothered to infiltrate. Waste of precious manpower. And Naphtali Lev was top echelon. Gabriel juggled the tiny cartridge in the center of his palm. He pinched the film roll gently between fingertips, and from the shadows behind him men stepped forward, offered insulated plastic bags into which he dropped both cartridge and film. Gabi kept his eyes on Pablo. When these men had vanished once more into corners, he clasped his hands on the table surface and without turning muttered brief, succinct-sounding statements in languages Pablo couldn't begin to make out. A small leather briefcase was placed on the table close to Gabriel, a yellow lined pad, pens. Then men were filing slowly from the room. Pablo heard a door slide open, feet shuffle in dirt, then a tiny click—door closed now. He sensed no one behind him. Just he and his brother staring at each other across a long, blank table, broken remains of a tiny camera between them. Little Spy, he'd nicknamed it. Funny how things worked like that. There was nothing that happened purely by chance, not in this crazy world. Even the names you chose were matters of destiny.

"How are you, Pablo?"

He felt himself shrug again. He grinned foolishly. "What happened to your ear?"

"I can't answer that, *hermano*," Gabriel leaned forward earnestly, "except to say I cut myself shaving."

"Yeah. Close shave?"

Gabriel grinned.

Pablo didn't know he was sinking until the table surface loomed suddenly closer. Then he lost whatever numb control he'd had, knew the tears streaming down both cheeks were unstoppable.

"Gabi."

Gabriel reached across to grasp his arm.

"Gabi."

"What, Pablo." The voice soothed, inanely soft in the harsh, angular light burning down. "Dígame."

"Christ, Gabi. You look tired."

He cried fully then. He cried and cried.

The briefcase opened like an oyster shell. From it Gabriel extracted some official-looking documents. He laid these next to the pad and pens in front of him. He sketched on the pad for some minutes. Pablo watched silently.

After a while Gabriel slid the pad gently across the table toward Pablo. Pablo frowned. A sprouting tree of boxes connected by lines, each box initialed. The top box—the largest one, from which all the other boxes sprang—was initialed "S." Below it were several offspring; each offspring linked to several more of its own, tiniest boxes strung out in an increasingly long line at the bottom of the page. Pablo looked up in confusion.

Gabriel tapped the top box with a pen tip. "S." Funny English letter. It looked almost the same upside-down: a snake in miniature, minus the head. For a second he felt unbearably tired. He let it wash over him, the exhaustion bubbling always just below the surface, and in that second wanted nothing but to lay his head down. He remembered long ago, army basic training; men falling asleep at lectures, canteens being dumped over the heads of sleeping men. And he kept himself awake; the need for sleep passed. If his eyes gazing back at Pablo's were wearily bloodshot, they could still see what most eyes would miss. He'd never let himself forget that that was his ticket to survival.

"Listen, Pablo. I'll show you something." The pen tip drew invisible circles around the "S" box. "Each square here stands for an organization. These letters are all initials of organizations. It's all very simplified, like a family tree, you understand?"

Pablo nodded.

"This first organization here, the father organization"—his pen tapped the "S" dully—"is called the Snowmen. And all these other organizations are smaller, either offshoots of the Snowmen, or affiliated in some way. Now. This Snowmen organization is a very large one, Pablo. There are chapters all over, every country in Europe, many in the Middle East, they've infiltrated some nations in Africa, in South America, in the Far East, and they're all over the Eastern Bloc nations. This isn't taking into account the smaller affiliates—these small boxes here—you understand? What we are speaking of is a very large and efficient organization—"

"Like International?" Pablo grinned bleakly. He hadn't been able to avoid the crack. But Gabriel gave a little smile.

"Not quite. This organization is illegal. What do they say in the States these days? *Underground.*"

Pablo listened while Gabriel ran down the sprouting branches of boxes, name by name. Red October. The Black Berets. Arm of the Spider. The People's Liberation Front. The list went on longer. And somewhere toward the bottom, in one of the tiniest offshoot boxes, the Foreign Brigade to Aid the Army of the People of Bellagua. Interorganizational power struggles, Gabriel said. Sometimes, even the most efficient organizations became big enough for some subsidiary element to get out of hand. For some subsidiary element to disagree with overriding organizational policy, to attempt to break away or—if there was the proper manpower, proper funding from dependable sources—to pose a lethal challenge.

"This"—Gabriel patted the yellow lined page with his hand—"is a worldwide terrorist organization. Your Foreign Brigade is a splinter group, *hermano.* Originally of the Fifth World Liberation Army—you see here, this group—a very violent group, too. That bomb planted in the Gare du Nord—a few years ago, you remember? Among other things. Worse things. I could tell you a lot of stories but there isn't time. So you have the Snowmen here on Bellagua, guarding the warehouse—"

"What *warehouse?*"

"—and acting as mercenary advisors to the National Army. With more reinforcements on the way. In fact"—Gabriel grinned wryly—"these reinforcements have arrived already. Also—"

"What fucking warehouse?"

"—also you have the Foreign Brigade arriving here, a group sworn to the destruction of my country. Pablo." He leaned forward, groped across the flat yellow paper and almost touched Pablo's crumpled right hand, but did not. His voice was hoarse. "Listen, Pablo, things are funny sometimes. Imagine that you have before you a giant monster. You know that if you cut out some skin, more will grow back almost immediately. But if you chop off a finger, that finger will not grow back. So the monster has one less finger to hurt you with. Imagine that the Foreign Brigade was a finger—"

"You cocksucker."

"And imagine"—Gabriel's voice strained near breaking, regained its composure—"that at the same time, and in the same place, you have a chance to blow off an entire arm! Even though by doing this—" He stopped, hung his head miserably. Pablo leaned into the table with a kind of glee; he'd never seen Gabriel miserable before and there was something vaguely thrilling about it. His own voice was calm when it spoke.

"Even though what, Gabi?"

"Even though by doing this, you may ruin many other things. You may hurt or even kill innocent people. If anyone is innocent, that is—I don't know, Pablo. You may cause a lot of destruction, a lot of horrible things, by blowing off the arm of this monster. But if the arm is gone—"He shrugged. Pablo swallowed and something like stone seemed to roll down his throat.

"I don't know what the fuck you're talking about."

Tiredly, Gabriel nodded. Of course, the nod said half apologetically, I know you don't.

Pablo felt it snarl up and off his tongue now—were they his own words, after all? Or just propaganda that had become ingrained in him somewhere along the line? He couldn't remember. He did not feel like himself, but he'd forgotten what it might be like to feel that, anyway.

"You cocksucking Zionist swine."

Gabriel stared back at him unblinking. His eyes were red with strain but showed no surprise or rage. In fact, there was something almost kind about them. They looked bloodily out at Pablo, and it seemed to Pablo then that there was in them a glint of something close to tenderness. The fingers of his right hand spasmed, made the hand twist like a fish out of water there on the cold table surface. Pablo raised his left hand to shoulder level. He pointed an index finger at Gabriel, heard himself giggle. But his cheeks were all wet again, nose filled with tears, eyes watering and sore. Salty wet dribbled over a corner of his mouth.

Pablo turned his finger around, pointed it directly at the center of his own forehead.

"Bang," he said. "Bang."

They were silent for a long time. Until Gabriel reached gently and grabbed Pablo's hand, pushed it down onto the scribbled yellow pad beneath his own. "It's too late for that, Pablo. Don't you know? When you took an oath to kill your people you killed yourself as well. Who else but your people would save you?"

* * *

Gabriel had documents for him to sign written in Hebrew, French and English. He explained what each said. Pablo didn't listen much, just held an unused pen ready in his left hand. It seemed there were certain procedures here common for all new immigrants; certain others that were thoroughly irregular. But even the extraordinary irregularities pertaining to his particular case had, somewhere, somehow, been regulated, documented, and all in the most official manner. It seemed that the entity known as Pablo Klemer had ceased to exist as far as American authorities were concerned—all by agreement, of course. These matters must have required a touch of delicate diplomacy. Records erased, Social Security number expunged, bank accounts closed, credit cancelled and wiped off computer discs for good—a complex, painstaking procedure, to be sure. A lot of hard work had been done by a lot of people. Easy enough for a person to just disappear, but to wipe out all traces of him? Nothing easy about that. Still, as Gabriel pointed out with a tentativeness bordering on politesse, Pablo's traces were easier to wipe out than many. After all, he had no real close friends to speak of. No major investments. No debts. No lover. No children.

Baby.

He thought he'd spoken out loud, but no. Just that single, solitary thought caressing the air: her eyes. And the lovely, near-classical tilt of the face. But for a second he'd forgotten her name. She was merely an intangible image, an idea: *Baby.* Baby. Odd thing to call a lover, or would-be lover. Who was whose baby in matters of love? And if someone was baby, who was daddy? Who mommy? The idea of her had distilled to this, then, inside of him—this baby—yet he'd never consciously wanted a child. Had he? Wanted something left to grow on the earth he'd once trod, something that was far from inert, some*one*—a child? Seed of his body. All the pictures in the world, would they suffice if nothing was left to grow? Maybe he'd clung somehow to one last shred of his old identity by clinging to this idea of her. A Baby. But too late to want that, now.

Pablo had a new name: Guzman.

He had to sign this name on the documents Gabriel pushed in front of him one by one, as he patiently explained in a soft, monotonous voice Pablo did not listen to. He saw a tiny, wet splotch spread on the bottom of one paper sheet, then another; he traced his cheek with a fingertip. Odd to cry and feel nothing. To need documented proof of his crying. Perhaps he didn't really exist, then, didn't exist anymore at all.

Pablo Guzman signed everything.

Gabriel checked his watch. He slipped all the documents, the lined yellow pad and pens, into the briefcase, locked it shut. He told Pablo to come with him now. His face was more than tired; it was beginning to be old. Pablo touched his own face again.

He told Pablo he had a present for him. Something he wanted him to see. And then Pablo could sleep a long time—he'd like that, wouldn't he? Half smiling, Pablo nodded.

Pablo was strapped into a passenger chair, and in the chair next to him was Gabriel. In front, the pilot—a white man; another white man in uniform of some sort beside him. The helicopter buzzed through twilight, heading east.

"I'll show you something," said Gabriel, "that most people won't see. And then you need to forget you saw it, *hermano*." He leaned against the seat straps, spoke loudly to the pilot in another language.

"East Bay," he said after a while, motioning toward the side view. "You remember."

Pablo twisted sideways and looked down. Bright lights like stars speckled the darkening land below. He could see the dim outlines of hotel pools, carefully planted dark rows of palm trees, the strip of beaches, the oceanfront. The helicopter swerved slightly and was heading along the contours of the shoreline below. In a few minutes the helicopter's vibrations became slower, heavier. They'd stopped to hover. Gabriel caught his eye. There was a small, desolate smile on Gabriel's face. Tiredly, he winked.

"The Atlantis Project! You remember!"

His voice shouted hoarsely over the helicopter's buzz. Pablo looked down again.

Gabriel uncapped the face of his watch. It clicked away seconds.

Pablo looked back to him but Gabriel shook his head sternly, motioned to the side view. Pablo obeyed. He couldn't see much; twilight was just over. Still he could make out the water's rhythmic whitecaps breaking on sand, the massive dark contours of the Atlantis Project buildings, the crater-like darkness of the dig site itself.

"Watch!" Gabriel's voice was a cracked shout. He kept staring at his watch. Pablo opened his eyes.

Gabriel shot a glance at his brother. He remembered to breathe fully. The helicopter whined, buzzed and shook.

Two, said Gabriel. One.

Pablo stared down. He thought maybe time had stopped. Nothing was happening down there; he didn't know what the hell he was supposed to be looking for. Odd, though, how he'd ceased to feel the helicopter's vibrations, stopped hearing any noise at all. Then something down there changed. The darkness broke up; he wasn't sure how, only knew that it seemed to be shifting. The Atlantis Project seemed to heave in and out like an enormous creature breathing. Then it exploded, burst right up into open air. Things down there were suddenly sheer white, then smoky white specked by flashes of orange that flickered larger and larger until the entire area was covered with billowing white-gray smoke cut apart by the leaping jagged edges of flames. And what was it, spilling now into the waterfront nearby?— an enormous amount of liquid that covered an area of bay large enough to be seen from the air, white enough to be seen in the dark. Pablo's eyes were riveted. He had the same feeling he'd get at the movies: frozen in position, unable to tear away from the visions in front of him, yet apart from it all, viewing the silent screen.

A howl of victory cut through the whirring helicopter cabin. The pilot turned once to Gabriel, face flushed with a kind of joy. Then he turned back to the controls.

Gabriel's shoulders relaxed.

"There she blows."

He watched Pablo's back. All stiff, immobile.

"That's it, Pablo. That's the warehouse you asked about. We wired it like a hot plate. So the monster has one less arm." He smiled when Pablo swiveled around to face him. "No more snow," he grinned, "at least not for a while."

Pablo strained against the seat straps, reached sideways for Gabriel. He managed to stretch out far enough so the left hand grabbed a shirt sleeve, pulled with insistent, panicked strength. His brother was forced to lean out against his own seat straps, forced to clutch the grasping hand in both his own. Gabriel had to concentrate to understand above the roar of the moving helicopter what Pablo was trying to say.

"Find her!"

He shouted louder in the increasing roar of propellors.

"Find her, Gabi! You've got to! You've got to find her!"

Gabriel squeezed the frozen fingers between his. He felt something run down one cheek. Sweat, he thought numbly. A tear? But it couldn't possibly be. Gabriel didn't even remember the last time he'd cried—it had been that long ago.

Why, then, did his lips quiver? Tiredness, maybe. He could barely remember the last time he'd slept, either. So maybe it was a touch of exhaustion psychosis, after all—temporary trauma, he knew, which could be controlled if you were aware enough—that made him say what he did, scarcely knowing he'd meant to say it until he heard the words slip from him: All right, Pablo. All right, I'll try. I'll try to find her.

Evacuation of all tourists on East Bay began hours after midnight. Credit cards were of no use any more. Everyone must go, and now. Buses waited, trucks and limousines had been mobilized by command of martial law, and all hotel clients were roused from sleep by the pounding on their doors, down every hall in every hotel along the strip. Their bags had to be hastily packed. Angry husbands and boyfriends who protested could find themselves staring down the barrel end of army automatics. The soldiers threatening them would grin, and their dark-skinned faces be lit by sudden flashes of yellowed teeth. They enjoyed the tables being turned like this—even though the situation was an emergency, even though it came down through the grapevine that something horribly detrimental to the Operation had occurred. It was good, when from birth you were used to servility, to point a rifle at the face of the white pig who'd made you used to it. Even though times were bad, and half of some battalions hospitalized for strange maladies peculiar to war, even though you might not know when such a malady would befall you too, it was good, these days, to smile.

Rumpled, panicked, frantic at the thought of traveller's checks left behind in drawers, jewelry never checked out of the front desk safe-deposit box, tourists along the East Bay hotel strip began very quickly to look like refugees: hair all out of place, clothes strewn everywhere. Sometimes a National Army soldier would, for a joke, pierce through the breast of a designer's gown hanging in a hotel room closet with the tip of his bayonette. Then, despite any protest, he'd fling it over the balcony edge.

The parking lots filled. Lines of soldiers stood, white tourists in shuffling, dispirited lines before them, filing into the backs of trucks, being shoved along with the butt ends of rifles.

The highway was jammed bumper to bumper, horns blaring uselessly throughout the night and far into a morning that dawned dusty hot, unrelieved by sea breeze. Along the road walked dark-skinned people, some of them soldiers, some of them Civil Guard; and some of them vendors who were allowed by the soldiers to come close to the windows of buses stalled there on the highway leading to the airport, offer up warm cans of soda to white tourist hands clutching desperately out of windows. The price these vendors charged was exorbitant. They insisted on foreign cash.

IL VITTORIALE

News of the destruction of the Atlantis Project reached Zachary Chemical's B.O.D. quickly. From there, it was just a matter of time until Corporate got into the act.

The recreation room of the Zachary's Florida residence was cool, dark, deserted. John Karlen Zachary sat against a wall. His legs, stretched straight out on the floor, gave him a childlike look. There he was, gray and thickset, about to play with toys maybe. Slight sagging around his face's edges lent a pouting appearance.

The thought had crystallized today, out of nowhere—a small, lingering thought. It skipped lightly around inside him. At first he'd dismissed it as ridiculous, a morbid urge born of fantasy. But John Karlen was a man given to contemplation at times. These times would steal up to drop a thin, intangible web over him and tie the strands around, so he'd find himself wrapped up, contemplating almost unwillingly a tiny, dark kernel of thought, a desire, like the one which had announced itself today. It was a yearning to fall backwards into something. He didn't know what. Nor did he know what touched the image with such poignancy. Thinking of it, this sweet falling backwards, he wanted to weep.

A graying sheet stretched over the Ping-Pong table. Fine carbon-bladed rackets lined the wall opposite him. Dully, his eyes passed over them, returned to the sheet. Sometimes these days he found himself believing he was somebody else. He'd get flashes that seemed to come from different times, different ages of history. Always he was somebody else in these vague scenarios played out briefly inside him in living color: a man of wealth and power, but not himself.

Through the window came Florida sunlight, hot, yellow. It stained the floor, hinted a heavy marsh bouquet, flamingo feathers, tough browning grass, coarse palm trees and bright-colored gravel surrounding statuettes on front lawns. Sometimes he thought of olive trees—why? this wasn't the Mediterranean. Still, he thought of Mediterranean climates, salted fish, olive trees. These days it seemed to him that he couldn't get warm enough. So he'd come down here alone. Even though up north was the tail end of summer heat, here, he'd figured, heat would be omnipresent. And he'd finally feel warm.

John Karlen closed one eye.

A tre occhi. We will talk with our three eyes, you and me!

He saw himself bent and squat, patch strung over one useless eye. He saw himself limp down the corridors of a vast marble-floored place, outside the olive groves, scent of the Mediterranean. *A tre occhi.* He laughed to himself and the sound echoed against piebald marble, cane echoed against marble in broken syncopation with the shuffling echoes of each step. *A tre occhi! We will talk. Eyes to eye, painter to poet.* He limped toward a room at the marble hall's end, blinked his good eye.

In the Villa of Il Comandante, mellowed sunlight puddled like oil on balconies, down broad marble stairways, splashing the earth between twisted rows of olive trees in Il Comandante's favorite garden. The man himself retreated from light—from the sun, he said—these days. He sank further into solitude, calling his extremities of mood a *strange malady*, one which he'd had since the War. His attending doctors knew the origins of this degenerative madness; it stemmed, as had all the world's evils, from lust for a woman.

In the Villa, rooms once filled with guests were empty, gilded beds naked, floors filmed with dust. This was a symptom of the old man's malady: to admit no one. No one but servants, doctors, and the dancer Fraulein Ida—his favorite. And, of course, his longtime friend the painter, who signed each canvas with a single initial: R—the legs of the "R" weighted down by minutely drawn black chains. So the painter was known to everyone simply as R. It was, R said, easier that way; she laughed and blew out clouds of gray-blue cigarette smoke.

When John Karlen stood his feet felt strange to him, unused to stepping along floors. They did anyway, skirting the sheeted Ping-Pong table until he stood at the opposite wall. His eyes wandered along the line of rackets;

there was a dead feeling to them. You couldn't imagine a human hand holding one. His shoes scuffed high-polished linoleum. He wondered vaguely where the cleaning people kept themselves. Odd, to have the place clean like this yet deserted. Another tax write-off. He turned, rounded a doorless doorway. For a second he wanted to call out some kind of greeting. John Karlen paused at the base of the stairway and looked up. The stairs loomed unbearably long. He wanted to wave. There was no one to wave to. Tax write-off. To himself, he grinned. He shut an eye, peered straight up and ahead.

Il Comandante paused on his slow, shuffling journey down the corridor. He managed to scuttle sideways and lean against the wall—also marble; it was old stone, older than he was. Once in a spell of lucidity he'd banged a fist on the dinner table as of old, proclaimed loudly that he would not need a tomb for them to bury him when the Sozialistas came pouring over his garden walls with shotguns, no, he had a tomb already, one he lived in, he was a soldier and a free man and so—he'd sneered at the astonished faces of servants around him—would die in the tomb of his choosing: the one he had built around himself. Die in the arms of marble, the marble arms of God. And at that point all lucidity ceased; he began to ramble again, his fervor diminished and with it the old spark vanished. His servants muttered among themselves. Now, though, he paused, pressed an old hand against the wall and seemed to sink toward it, cane inclining with the stoop of his body, diseased flesh easing into stone. He was wondering about Fraulein Ida—long his favorite, now no longer returning his love. When was it that she had been taken away? He could not be sure, could not pinpoint the exact hour—perhaps there was no exact hour, after all, merely a gentle falling away from him, a drifting backwards into the arms of another. She was a dancer. Surely, he might have expected it to happen. He supposed it was the manner of its happening that had jolted him at first—the oddness and yet the familiarity of it. R had long preyed on his women—sometimes with success, sometimes without—but always they'd managed to maintain a strange understanding that overrode all else. They had a history made up of years, bottles consumed, paintings painted and poems read at the dim hours before dawn while fire burned warmly in one of the hearths at the Villa Vittoriale. He was the poet, the war hero; she the painter. And if he still burned with a fierce male light she was dark, muted moon to his sun, all her work tinged with icy melancholy—but no less a lover. This he learned through experience. He'd have to grin wryly, somewhat paternally, at yet another young beauty she had managed to steal from him and whisk away to the Rue Jacob, the St. Michel—she was of Parisian boulevards, gossip, sudden, stark laughter and an ironic bitterness that gave the edge to her humor. He befriended her because he was a man in love with women, with battles, poems, wine, and life; he gave her a laurel wreath in bronze— one of his old citations as poet *extraordinaire*—and allowed her to wear his military decorations from the battle for the port of Fiume. He gave her a stovepipe hat lined with black velvet. It will fit the interior canvases, my friend. Black velvet, like all your shadows. Once, she'd bent over him on a sofa while he half slept, drugged with too much Bolzano, firelight playing tricks over the dark patch on his eye. She leaned down to kiss him, kissed his eyelid and the patch over the other. She kissed his bald head and then the bridge of his nose. He'd opened his good eye to see her standing over him, smiling down, and her look was one of gentle sorrow. Almost regret.

When had the Fraulein Ida been whisked away, carried off on a bed of shadows—when? He couldn't remember. And if he ever did remember, the strange malady from which he suffered rendered all memory inconsequential.

He thought he heard dim laughter from somewhere: an open door ahead, rich dark wood rimmed by gargoyle heads. A sweet, faint smell seeped into the corridor's unstirred air—a smell of gardens, of women. Il Comandante slid his cane tip carefully along the floor. His feet followed slowly; he had the feeling that perhaps he might be discovered—although why he should feel that way he did not understand, this was his own property, all of it, all. He also felt a growing sense of rage. From one tired eye he watched the achingly slow progress of each shoe along the white-swirled floor, inched and inched until the cane poked around an edge of one double door opening in. R's studio. A room devoted to unfinished canvases, to palette's, easels, half-mixed dabs of oil here and there. R was given it to work in whenever she visited. Covered with damp sheet, a canvas sat on the easel. Aside from that, and other canvases stacked against a wall, some chairs, a small table, the studio was deserted. Laughter drifting through one of the enormous windows made the room seem more barren still. The windows opened out into the garden, hand-fashioned glass panes crisscrossed by thin strips of gold.

Standing in the doorway, Il Comandante listened. He waited for laughter or words. For a second, he sensed some momentous quality in this waiting— as if he'd been yearning for it all his life—but the second passed. He was still anxious, though. Expectant. He could not understand this, only accept it with the queer logic of a twilit mind. So he waited. He was a little breathless. He waited for the sound of laughter.

Sounds came—words. No laughter here but a soft sound, something sad, pattering lightly on breeze through the windows opening out; a woman's voice, gentle and desolate.

Please.

And another voice lower in tone, slightly husky, musical. But Il Comandante could not hear the words. Then the first voice again:

Please.

He heard the other's words this time:

But there's nothing left.

You think that—

I know it.

You think that now because you're sad. You're sick with sadness, so you think—

The breeze crept through aroma of olive trees and the bitter, sun-darkened smell of earth, the garden. Women. Faint, gentle sobs drifted through now, drowned in breeze, drifted in on him again.

—you think some end will come. But it's all inside like the dream you had. It will be all right. Please. Don't worry. Don't you worry.

I want to believe you.

Come here.

Il Comandante felt himself move almost without willing it. Flying had been like that. The soar, dip, hand frozen on a throttle rattling nearly out of control. He slid across to the stiff white floor cloth and leaned on his cane, breathing with effort. The easel and shrouded canvas a few feet in front of him and beyond that, windows. He strained to hear.

—like a chain my dear, a weight on both your legs—how could you dance?

Shhh.

At Lausanne I saw it. Exactly like the dream—avalanches—

Shhh.

—everything covered, all white. All dead. The voice rose in a brief bitter laugh. *There's purity for you.*

You think too much.

Ah.

And feel too much.

Il Comandante swayed on weak legs. The cane swayed, scraped raggedly over stiff floor cloth. He'd closed his eye and imagined the voices—that's what he thought when he opened it, head beginning to pound with the acrid smell of still-damp paint. These sounds had come from the core of his strange malady—in hallucination, he'd heard the voice of Fraulein Ida and then of R. He giggled softly. A thin line of spit trickled from a corner of his mouth, but Il Comandante didn't notice. It crept down the jaw, dribbled off and splatted with a dull, flat sound on cloth. And he froze; sounds came again; it had been no dream.

Fraulein Ida's voice drifted through the window. "Come here, come here. Don't you worry."

"I won't finish it, then. I shall store the canvas—"

"Shhh."

R laughed. "Store the nightmares!"

Il Comandante's cane crept closer and he sidled along after it. Then he stood immediately in front of the easel and the damp sheet spread over a sizeable canvas. One unsteady hand reached, fingertips tapped along the sheet to its edge. He blinked. He was slightly feverish, mind turning inside the recurring madness that seized him more and more often these days. Then he grabbed an edge of sheet, peeled gently until it fell off, and he focused with difficulty on the canvas before him.

It was white. A sheer, blinding white spread across the entire breadth of canvas, and against it raw-lined figures of gray. The elongated, naked body of Fraulein Ida, lengthy fingers sweeping against white, feet buried in the bright expanse of snow. Her hair was raven black and fell wildly across gray shoulders. Another gaunt, gray figure lurked naked beside her: R, black-feathered quiver of arrows slung around one shoulder, a black, warped bow held loosely by her side—she followed the gently pointing gray fingers of the dancer and both seemed to be staring ahead and down, examining symmetrical splotches of red that spattered a broken double line trailing off the canvas. Staring, Il Comandante's eye watered. His eye wandered to the other edge of the canvas. And he saw a figure he'd missed at first. It was much smaller than the other two, dwarfed, gray, bent double; the two main figures had not noticed it; their backs were turned to it. This was a male figure in miniature, limbs warped and horribly deformed. Il Comandante stepped closer. He peered at the warped gray figure crouching there, leering at the two unseeing backs. The figure had his face.

Above the customary "R" weighted down with two black chains in the lower right-hand corner of the canvas, a title was scrawled in black. If he squinted he could make it out, written in English: THE LAST HUNT.

John Karlen Zachary stopped at the top of the stairs. He wanted to turn and look back down; for a minute, he wanted to go back to the recreation room, to the shrouded Ping-Pong table, dusty rackets. But the minute went away, brought on the next minute, the next. Still he was frozen at the top of stairs. Then he moved slowly down the hall, across carpets; his hands brushed paneled walls, brushed past light switches, polished edges of bookshelves. He was standing at the bottom of another staircase looking up. One hand trailed to the wall, sought a switch. Flick, and there was a buzzing current in the air. Things became perceptibly cooler. John Karlen stood enjoying the air conditioning, swayed slightly on his feet. He shut his eyes.

My child.

Il Comandante's feet rasped across the floor cloth. The cane tip led—it was mahogany, black-tipped, the handle ivory. He laughed somewhere inside; he could not stop himself from doing this thing, even though it was a vast intrusion—it had been etched on canvas that he would do this and, in his heart, he shrank to canvas size. Half giggling, panting, he leaned against the window ledge and looked down.

The garden was a carefully tended chaos of flowers, vines, yellow petals brimming like sun over darker ones, and at the garden's edges began rows of olive trees, twisting guardians. On a wrought-iron bench they sat: one in baggy, ill-fitting men's trousers and a too-big white blouse spattered with paint, feet bare and absurdly delicate sticking out of overly large trouser legs, stovepipe hat set on the ground; the other in a loose gray blouse gathered at the waist with a red sash, black dancer's tights, black slippers. Her hair flowed black at crazy angles over her shoulders; her head bowed to cover both their faces, for R's face was hidden against her shoulder and, looking down, it seemed to him that the two bodies ran together into a single head of mad black hair. Hushed sobs came to him again. Breeze drifted up. A long, delicate dancer's hand stroked the hidden head, the back, then poised again in air, fingers sensing breeze. He knew what he'd see if Fraulein Ida glanced up: the pale skin become translucent, lips press together suddenly; her eyes would flash a defiant look up at him. And in the center of those eyes would gleam pinpoint emerald specks.

Il Comandante turned to scrape once more across the floor. The effort cost him greatly. At the door he was suddenly shivering, sighing for breath. For many minutes, he felt that everything had been stolen from him.

My child.

John Karlen stopped suddenly, looked around in surprise. He'd climbed another flight of stairs and now stared down to the darkened hallway. He'd gone up the stairs as if floating, his lips forming words that never sounded. He felt himself move forward again and wished briefly that time would slow for a while, seconds not rush by with such predictability. John Karlen checked his hands for tremors. There were none. Hands held stiffly out before him in the dark of another carpeted hallway—not a shiver. Still, he was afraid.

At the hallway's end he opened a door.

The room was small. He'd used it off and on as a temporary office over the years. The furniture, the phone, every object in the room was covered with dust-free sheets of plastic. John Karlen stepped across to the window. His hands on the curtains clenched strongly, surely; that surprised him. One motion now, one wide, flinging motion—there, curtains parted swiftly, and the room filled with sunlight.

He unlatched the window at top and bottom. He set both firm hands to the window and pulled up; it opened with a ripping sound and hot air washed in. He opened it as far as it would go. John Karlen leaned out: three floors down was the egg-shaped pool and the patio area. The pool had been drained this season. For a second, he wondered if he'd see eyes staring up at him: large, lovely, dark brown, oddly speckled with catlike green. Would he see that face? Perhaps he didn't want to anymore. Perhaps. He stepped back from the window, moved across to his desk. Gently, he lifted the plastic covering sheet away. He fished in a pocket and got out keys. Insert the smallest one, turn, hold, just so. The top drawer opened when he tugged.

Marble echoed with the rapping of the cane. In anger, the old man threw whatever his meager strength could lift: books sailed to smash against unlucky shelves or heads; sitting stools tipped over, crashed. The servants hid where they could. In the kitchens they conferred. It was decided to send for doctors.

Impossible! There will be no egalité! They are no better than the Sozialistas, all of them. He spat. *Women. They are damned. They are diseased. They come only to steal what is beautiful—they will die, all of them, die horribly.*

John Karlen reached into the drawer, picked out a flat leather case and set it on the desk top. He opened it.

Because all things die. Tell this to the painter. No! I must see no one! No one today!

In John Karlen's hand the metal object gleamed. It caught warm sunlight. It reflected light brighter into his eyes, so for a second he was blinded.

Down white-swirled corridors of marble echoed crashing books, a stabbing black-pointed cane, the feeble feet of the old man catching sudden, momentary strength—rage, insanity, a sort of mad anguish dancing speedily beyond pain. What had she said to him? *Je suis païenne.* Curling on the floor after a pas de deux, long and slim, swanlike, pale, dark eyes glimmering green. Dressed all in white. A pagan, she said. But God would make her pay. And while she'd danced for another, posed naked in studios he provided, dark eyes smiled at that male *manqué*, that travesty of a woman had dipped brushes onto the palette, stepped back to frown or beam, tilt the stovepipe hat on her head and stepped forward again toward the canvas. His favorite was seduced with oils and white canvas. When had R chosen to make the theft? When the old man's eye was focused elsewhere. A plot? Perhaps. Yes.

And desire. After all is lived, do you feel it still?

R's eyes glowed suddenly. She leaned forward too, eyes to eye. *Ah. I—* a hand tapped with austere pride at the breast of her man's jacket—*I am always in love.*

Metal gleamed in John Karlen's hand. He felt the full warmth of sun against his back; he'd turned his back to the window and half sat, leaning against the ledge. Something sounded from far away. A bird? He thought maybe he'd heard a single, lonely bird cry, flying south to marshes. Metal flashed, the instant froze. He sucked the metal and the instant up into his mouth. Finger pressed—but he was still frozen, silent inside, sucked up in a vacuum of soundlessness. Until he felt a momentary chill. Then he burst out backwards into the day, through the open window and backwards, backwards, head leaking red, falling backwards into soft arms of sunlight.

The warehouse demolition wreaked havoc with their plans. In Sagrabél, men in three-piece suits sat for long talks with men of the military. Heads would roll eventually, of course. No excuse for the lack of security measures. Their entire supply shot; well, almost. And with the internal chaos taking place back in the States at Zachary Chemical, no telling when a new supply could be shipped. Old man had picked a lousy time to pull a stunt like this. Heads would roll. But right now things were too suddenly unsettled; they had to get a grip on the situation first. Operation Snow must continue— because they were now committed. Evacuation of tourists in the East Bay area had already begun. The military made their presence known all along the highway and especially in the airport. No need to let anyone relax, or think that because of the temporary chaos they could sneak too much past customs without paying. But these tourists had to be gotten out as quickly as possible. There was the matter of biological half-life, the matter of birth defects; the last thing they needed was more attention. As if the foreign newsmen hadn't been trouble enough—now, at least, a complete news blackout would be called for. Under martial law there were reasons to shoot first, ask questions later—or never—and if foreign nations desired to ascertain the location of their missing persons, there was always the governmental bureaucracy to fall back on. Such searches could be made impossible. They could be rendered heartbreaking before they'd even begun.

Wilting, waiting, tourists crowded the airport for flights out of Bellagua. Under the eyes of men in mud-brown uniforms they huddled over suitcases. Vacation mirth had fled. In its place was a sweaty, silent kind of fear that deadened all laughter. No one spoke much. And the airport shops charged what they wanted to. Now was the time to stick it to them—all these white tourists, with their white money—a candy bar was worth whatever you had to pay for it, especially when you were hungry, your plane delayed indefinitely, no place to sleep but on a damp airport bench.

Another circle of defoliation began at night. It was decided that, due to the sudden depletion of supply, this spraying would have to be the last. At least for a while. It was a light spraying, a weak one. There were no more refugees to root out anyway—they'd advanced too deep into jungle territory for that. The only casualties would be rebel soldiers and villagers. Helicopters swooped, hovered, propellors whirred in the dark like methodical, mechanized bird wings, and white liquid sprayed down on trees in the night.

Afterwards there was a strange silence. In West Reef army bases, men noticed the silence; it was a thing of the air, a sort of blanket or heaviness, like a waiting storm. Against the beaches ocean lapped, foam slapped dead bodies of fish piled high by the tide.

EVERY PRINCE OF DARKNESS

Some men are afraid of the dark. Not Connery. He liked it, felt free moving in it, it was home to him. As a child he'd led make-believe search parties through dozens of back yards, over fences, garbage dumps, along strange fire escapes. Back then he'd gloried in it; these nighttime raids into enemy territory—even when the only enemy was an overaged guard dog chained at the entrance to some junkyard or other. He'd remember his father slapping his back in good-humored affection over all these imaginary conquests. *My boy, it's good training. Good training for life. A man's got to know how to fight, doesn't he? Got to know how to make a living, too. You go for a little respectability, my boy. Man's got to have a plan. A man's got to have one, Terrence.* Well, he'd gone for it. He proved himself in combat above and beyond the call of duty. And the seed for more of that was in him, too. So he'd gone free-lance for a while after his tour of duty. Why not? It was money in the bank—all that respectability had to be purchased somehow. No beggarman, he, and no thief. But natural intelligence—perception of motives, appreciation of some of the finer things in life—these qualities had long run in the family. To his father, Connery exemplified them; he was the vindication of a long line of top-notchers who'd never before attained the social status necessary for full appreciation of their skills. A soldier could also be a gentleman.

Connery had grace that seemed incongruous in a big man. He moved through thick foliage almost effortlessly, the suck and pull of earth didn't bother him. Like darkness, it was a thing he almost reveled in; it felt entirely natural to him. The pervasive lack of light, deadening wet heat, mud sucking to pull you down—they created a friction that to him was life itself. In here, he was in his element. And it didn't matter what he'd been yesterday or what he might be tomorrow. In the jungle interior he was the crystallization of an idea that had been formed over the ages: a well-armed man, stalking something along the face of the earth. Connery embodied centuries of conditioning—more than a tradition. In the proper environment, he became something essential and fine. That was why he moved with such perfection. In here, he was what he'd been born for. Carrying out a destiny as old as the stars, something mapped out before he'd existed. This urge in him was deeper than memory, more real than his age or name: to do the job. There was a job and you did it. And if it was a job you'd been trained for, bred for, destined for—all the better. A man had to make a living somehow. If he could make it and fulfill his destiny at the same time— that was a prince of a profession.

Moving silently, he paused sometimes; he'd bend cautiously to check a torn fragment of leaf, or some smudge beneath fresh moss that hadn't quite been overgrown. Tracking—he was damned good at it.

Snowmen were men of their times like anybody else, subject to the same waves of history. If they had a unique approach to the problems of life and of society, they were nevertheless *of* it all. Part of the problem. In their eyes and the eyes of a great many others, part of the solution. They had brothers, wives, children. They played rugby after work, or boxed, joined gentlemen's clubs and desired good music, good wine. When moving through city streets they dressed in the same clothes any other man of that particular time and place might wear. They swore, they drank, they prayed. They jerked off, and sang, or cried. Like any other man. They were out to make a living. Their function was to be of service. They had dreams, memories; and, like any other man's, some of these memories were sweet.

Connery was no different. Like the life of any other man, his was composed of the memory of sensation, complexities of reaction both physical and emotional, major peaks and valleys. But more important than peaks and valleys were the small, seemingly inconsequential details that filled the in-between times. Licking a peppermint stick at the age of six. A carnival ride, ferris wheel: the feel of wind rippling across his boy's crewcut like a subtle, cold hand with fingers briefly tapping. The taste of water. Feel of boots coming off hot, blistered feet—sudden shocking cessation of discomfort. Feel of a woman. A woman's smell. Connery had never much cared for women. For sex—yes, sure. He was a man. Still he'd never cultivated relationships—too much energy went into that, left none for fighting. But then, Connery had never cultivated relationships with men, either—not really. Sure, he had friends. But the part of him that was a soldier stepped back from all that. He'd never fully participated in anything he did. Perhaps that was the key to his survival in each endeavor; perhaps it was what made him dangerous. There was always the part that could look in and see himself moving. It was as if he had several pairs of eyes. In many ways, there was very little that had ever really touched him. Except for the small, nearly forgotten memories, he'd remained isolated from a certain flow of life, remained essentially alone. It seemed to him, thinking back on things, that the men of his family had always been this way. They'd functioned in the society of men as if in a kind of dream, drunk wine and talked with men, worked among men, taken women and married them and had sons—fulfillment of a duty, performed more or less as gracefully as possible—but their passion had remained apart from the common passions of common men. Their passion had arisen in solitary, elemental circumstances, when no one else could share it; stalking something, fulfilling a job they were paid to do, carrying on a long-standing tradition and doing so utterly alone. It was men like Connery who would cause things to happen—catalyze a roller coaster of events that eventually affected the lives of thousands of more common people, millions even. Yet he himself remained isolated from that flow of life affected by his actions; in the jungles he'd moved through, he was something apart. And when those thousands, or millions, felt the sting of a particular disaster, his presence as catalyst was invisible to them. They would not think beyond the ostensible workings of the world—the governments apparent to them, corporations selling stocks, store chains raising prices, crop failures; collective corporate blamelessness seemed to rule the day everywhere. Humans were essentially untrained to deal with the concept of individual responsibility. So men like Connery were never thought of. And the existence of the Snowmen would have been laughed about at most cocktail parties. Merely a chimera, some other hard-nosed radical's paranoid fantasy of conspiracy. This widespread propensity to disbelieve had enabled the Snowmen to operate, relatively unencumbered, for centuries.

Combat vest secure, Connery moved through the conglomeration of green blending readily into different shades of darkness. He'd expected a slight fever and dealt with it effectively—nothing new for him. Pity all the poor bastards who came in here unprepared. He popped pills at regular intervals and he drank plenty of water, was sure to eat every couple of hours. All survival mechanisms on go. There was a job you were paid to do so you went out and did it. But timing was of the essence. He'd traveled quickly since that night on an East Bay beach, caught up with unexpected ease. Two nights ago he'd been close enough to hear them breathing in the dark. He'd come within yards of where they were resting: the woman sacked out on rotting blankets, dark-skinned men dozing off and on, snapping awake to every real or imagined sound. But Connery was silent. Yards away, he'd watched and known it wasn't the right time. They were too close together, the woman still not weak enough. Though she'd been sick enough, he knew, to slow them drastically—their restricted pace operating to his benefit. He had no doubts about overpowering one or all of them, but had no intention of risking injury unnecessarily. This was tough enough terrain when you had it all going for you. So he'd just watched, waited. When you were on the offense, you had all the time you needed. When your existence was not even suspected, so much the better. The woman's breathing came quickly, dizzily. In the dark he saw the dark faces of men lean closer together, confer almost soundlessly, their brown eyes racing everywhere, always on guard when they weren't wearily half-closed. After a while they picked her up by the arms, and two of them carried her between them while the third man led the way.

That had been two nights ago. And the time not quite right. Connery plucked a leech from his wrist, reached for his canteen. Signs got fresher; he knew he was closing in. So he stopped, crouched, silently chewed dried foodsticks, swallowed silently while strands of moss settled on his shoulders.

International Communications Enterprises, Inc. had been glad to sponsor the Raina Scott expedition. International: private sector grants to encourage the creative and daring individual accomplishment—the TV ad that went something like: *Because we believe in the future. Your future. Our future. This program has been brought to you by a grant from Zachary Chemical Corporation, a division of International Communications Enterprises, Incorporated. Zachary Chemical Corporation—planning for the future—today.* They'd been generous in footing St.-Peters' medical bills and they'd footed the bill for the funeral, too. Sometimes, Connery wondered idly whether somebody somewhere had footed the bill for the gun St.-Peters used in the end—why not? Unlike much of the world, Connery saw things in terms of individual action, individual responsibility. Part of that came, no doubt, from his ancestry—from his long line of forebears—from his profession. You could have all the corporate red tape in the world, he knew, and still it came down to a single man signing a single name on a single sheet of paper—always, it came down to that. The buck could pass only so far before someone caught it. Corporate blamelessness was composed of many individuals who, all the way along the line, were responsible for their actions and all in some degree blameworthy. To go out on your own, do a job yourself—that was honesty. A return to the old values. Snowmen had always considered themselves members of an elite.

Connery finished swallowing his food.

He checked all his gear and took another pill for fever. Hand tightened again on the midsection of the bow. Nice grip there. He was strong.

It would be done silently, he decided, and in a way to induce panic. Get to the men first. Try to get them on the run, and with their sick burden they'd have an impossible task. He'd bet they were sworn to protect her on pain of death, otherwise they'd have dumped her long ago. He knew the workings of a jungle mind.

Connery scraped a couple of leeches from his hand on the bow. He drank more plastic-tasting water. Then he walked on in a crouch.

He stopped. What came to mind was a little boy's face, looking up at him in the dark, blood trickling from the nose. It had happened long ago. One of their postmidnight junkyard raids, streets silent under sporadic lamplight, winter damp in the air. They'd made off with rusted windshield wipers, a half-stripped wheel, dented hubcaps. And some kid bringing up the rear had fallen, bashed his nose, metal parts rolling shrilly around him on pavement. Connery had gone back for him, of course; he'd picked him up, jammed his own snotty handkerchief against the injured face and thrown a comforting arm over the boy's shoulders. He remembered it now. A winter night. He remembered looking straight up at the flat dark sky, feeling it first on his eyelids, his cheeks and forehead: the silent fall of snow. Inside him, something played like a wooden flute—quiet, delicate, faintly sad—something crumbled effortlessly and then rearranged itself, and, looking up, he felt himself changed. He felt himself older.

The toe of his boot touched something solid. He bent to peer at the object; cautiously, he picked it up. It was a stone carving: statuette of a woman in miniature, very old. Something like those wood carvings made by natives in Sagrabél—goddess amulets—they were sold to tourists, or worn around neck chains as lucky charms.

He shut his eyes tight. Brief visions danced across the blackness: men on hands and knees in a dusty pit, scraping away with teaspoons, with toothbrushes. One of them tenderly extracting a small object from the dry, exposed earth—a dirt-caked statuette. Clean it off and it was a woman in stone. Naked breasts full—with milk?—maybe one of the nipples had cracked off over hundreds of centuries. In one stone hand a wiggling stick— a wand of sorts, snakelike wand; over a shoulder what looked to be some crude sort of longbow. Hair drawn back from stone forehead. Hard, clear-cut, strong features neither male nor female. Only the eyes were emphatically female: large, slanting up at the stone corners, cold and blank yet with an odd delicacy—at once animal, human, and stone. While all around in the excavation pit other men paused, struck objects with their spoons, gently pulled Goddess figurines from the earth. Some minor variations. But all the same Goddess. Goddess Sitting Down. Goddess Standing Up. Goddess Squeezing Breast to Offer Milk. Goddess Stalking. Goddess Taking Aim. One layer deeper and they'd struck gold. Temple of the Goddess. There were alabaster fragments, statuettes which when assembled told a story never set down in the history books of men. Grapes inches deep in the Temple courtyard. Feet dancing on grapes until all legs were wildly purple to the knees; bodies rolling in grapes one on the other—women on men, women on women, men on men—rolling over and over, backs, thighs, breasts and chests stained violet. The High Priestess raised a wand. Chanting rose from grape-stained lips, seemed to rise out of the earth itself. High Priestess and her Brother Husband. High Priestess and her Lover—a warrior—a woman. Beads rattled in wind. Drums rattled, drums lightly tapped. Somewhere a flute piped and sighed.

Connery crouched fully, his back slid against a tree. He felt his legs lock slowly, then his mind lock, and he was frozen. It was all crap, all of it. Everything he'd thought for days.

You had to have a way of existing in the so-called civilized world. Well, he'd done that. And somewhere along the line maybe he'd believed a little too much in civility; maybe he'd actually allowed himself to fall—to become *civilized*. Was there a part of him that longed for the society of men? He half sat against a tree and could hear bugs crawl along his helmet's rim, and he wondered—was it that? Fear? The fear of a civilized man? Or was it just memory that got in the way again: the white of foaming beer; the smell of streets after a heavy snow, fresh wet and blank somehow, as if everything had been erased beneath it. Connery remembered playing in the snow, building snowmen on crumbling corners, pebbles for eyes, chain of pebbles in a moonlike arc for the mouth, a rock nose. They'd steal scraps of lumber wherever they could find it, give the snowman wooden arms. Rummaging around for a ratty old ski cap and setting it, just so, on the snowman's bald white head. Touch of the poet there. And Connery'd gone around all that white, frozen afternoon, manufacturing little snowmen on street corners. Everywhere you turned that day—a snowman—blank, round white bodies, rocky little eyes, pebble grins.

I am legion.

Sometimes—and he wouldn't know why—he'd be filled with words. Obscenities, mostly. Filth. He'd think these words silently; at times it was all he could do to keep himself from blurting them out. He'd get so full of it—the horror of these words; it was never arousing, merely frightening. Maybe the root of this strange urge was an incident that had happened in his childhood at around the age of four: his father coming home late one night, a little drunk, crashing around the house using abusive language—frightening, because he was a strong man and savage when out of control. And outside it was winter. Maybe the beginnings of snow. But Connery believed something he had never quite dared put into words—that somehow he'd inherited this propensity to silently speak foul words; that his feeling of being filled with obscenity and a kind of accompanying, unrelenting pain, horror, were linked to the practice of his profession—the traditional one of a soldier. Mystical explanation. Desire for the magical—infantile, infantile. Was the pain he experienced at these times also infantile? Also inherited? He'd never known. It seemed to well up from a source deeper than himself and much, much older. Once, he'd wanted to permanently lay to rest the public misconception that demons were cackling, gleeful creatures of evil. He'd wanted to prove somehow that this was not the case. *They are men*, he'd dreamed of saying, *men like you. Or me. Demons deserve compassion like any other man. Because they suffer. Evil is joyless. Evil never laughs. Evil is pure pain. Pity every demon. Every prince of darkness. For they suffer.*

But he'd never said it out loud.

He'd even wondered why he'd thought those words in the first place. The language felt stilted to him, not his language at all. It seemed to come from another time and place. Another man.

Painfully, Connery stood.

He proceeded slowly, careful to make no noise. Now it seemed that bugs had stopped crawling, moss stopped swaying. The leaves were silent cushions around him. The darkness that encased him was like an impenetrable coat of armor and, in it, what he willed would come to be.

With his pack, vest, automatic, quiver bristling broadheads from the large, cabled bow in hand, he was nearly twice his normal size. He moved in a hunched position, touched nothing, moved through the darkness without a sound. Connery himself couldn't even be seen—not a breath, not a flash of pale skin—it was almost as if he'd disappeared. And if you held a mirror up to his face, maybe you'd see nothing reflected. Or, if you did, it would be an amorphous dark mass moving forward, looming closer, in complete shadow.

The three soldiers from the Army of the People of Bellagua moved in silence, too, and without lights. They propped the sick woman between two of them, her weakening arms over their shoulders, and their officer led the way. It would have taken an expert to sense their presence, to determine any hint of noise that came from them. Only an expert of superior skill and experience could track them. But Connery was closing in. And he knew that he'd have them soon. The only thing that might buy them time would be animal instinct—if one stopped, sensed something, called an alert. It might buy them time now, but it wouldn't save them. He followed, listened with the ears of experience. How many times had he done this kind of thing? Often enough to forget how often. The times blended into one another. South America. Far East. Middle East. The times, the countries, the terrain. The centuries.

Several yards ahead a shadow paused, sniffed the air. Connery crouched low. He'd put on the silencer, fished out a spot flash in seconds, steadied the hand.

A tiny piercing light shone briefly. It illuminated the man he'd aimed for; the dark face turned back in surprise. Then the look of absolute shock. A tiny dark hole suddenly formed in the center of his forehead, dull, quick thudding sound rang. The light flashed again—like a single searchlight ray. This time the dark mouth turned in panic toward him had opened wide enough to reveal crumbling black teeth. The head arched up, neck spouted blood, and red trickled from the mouth's dark corners. The light blinked out quickly. There was the crush of leaves. Two dead men had recoiled, fallen, rolled, and the woman they supported between them had fallen too. Connery stopped. Cat and mouse now. Now, a game of the mind. He was trained for this.

Three bodies breathed quickly in the complete dark: Connery, stalking; a half-conscious white woman crushed between the bleeding bodies of two dead men; Captain Something-or-other from the Army of the People of Bellagua, now being stalked. And something else breathed above which they did not notice. They were too busy with the details of surviving; they were too busy breathing to recognize the sound of another breath that did not keep pace with theirs but was slower, calmer, deeper, more patient in waiting.

Connery slid forward until he nestled in leaves; until he'd soaked into the mud itself. On his knees, he reached around for a broadhead, drew it from the quiver slowly, taking his time—plenty of time now, he knew. This moment coming up would be limitless. It always was. And there was a vague sorrow in this for him: to inhabit, over and over again, this limitless sort of space in time, to proliferate like flakes of snow on winter days, to be legion, and everywhere, in all times, in all spaces, always—always to be stalking, to suffer the obscenities of centuries inside oneself and never have true access to the balms of society, to be always a foreigner intent on getting the job done for pay, essentially joyless, always feared, never loved. This moment just before a kill was eternity. And Connery was tired of eternity, dead tired. For a second, he wanted no more of this suffering. He'd have traded everything in that second for the limitations of a single life, a single name. In that second he aimed, and something rustled overhead, something else breathed. He sighted, released; his fingers flickered precisely and the arrow was gone, another shadow frozen in agonized shock among trees. Connery heard the rustling again as if in a dream, slid forward and turned around. Three dead men behind him; otherwise he'd never have turned his back. He moved sideways against a tree. He half crouched again, looked up. Rustling of leaves, gentle, rhythmic rustling, like musical notes turned flat. Breathing from somewhere—he couldn't tell where. But the breathing came slowly, calmly. He thought he had the direction it was coming from then and he smiled, plucked out another broadhead and turned to face the right way. He thought he saw something white flash. Something green. Breathing mere feet away—how could that be?—unless, in stalking, he'd been stalked the entire time. He thought he had it—a mask of sorts, quivering dizzily somewhere in front of him—thought he had a good sight on it, nocked the bow. Then he felt something splitting open on his helmet. The crack of leather, smell of oil, resin. Rubber wood. Leather split in half on metal. The handle of something plowed into his face. Unsteady aim there, but meant for the eyes. He felt blood gush from somewhere and he turned immediately with a fist thrusting out to kill, meeting only air. Then air rushed into him. It made a hole right through him—a long, primitive arrow of air, stone-tipped stick piercing right through his midsection and pinning him securely to the tree, nose bloodied, broken Ping-Pong paddle remnants rattling in the rim of his helmet, his face still fixed in a nervous, pained half-smile, eyes wide open and dead.

EXTRICATE, EXPEDITE, EXTRADITE

The helicopter's top-heavy nose descended at an angle. It shifted position until it was more parallel to earth. Lee looked down and saw the concentric circles of white, ashy substance that had once been jungle; the final faded circle interspersed with not-quite-destroyed trees—supplies had run out on short notice—and the sudden wall of thick jungle which stretched inland for many miles. Beyond this terrain, in the center of the island, were plains of tall brown grass. Then the rocky, uninhabited territory of near-mountainous hills, dry stone ledges, shale and dust. The rebels they'd captured referred to this territory as the Land of the Moon. No one knew why. Old superstitions, it was thought. But it was true that, from the sky, on a clear night, whatever moonlight there might be would paint this area a stark, dusty shade of pale silver. The silver would be cut by sharp rims of shadow—cliffs jutting out over dead valleys.

The South African pilot he'd grown accustomed to was gone one day with no warning, and a young Britisher settled in to take his place. Lee had been sleeping in borrowed rooms here and there; large houses in the wealthy section of Sagrabél, occasionally some dive in the crummy part of town where bugs crawled up walls and along the floor and came through ceiling cracks, and armed men whose nationalities he couldn't determine waited just outside his door. Always he was expected, his face recognized before he'd said a word of explanation. Always he was guarded, the address where he must stay on the following day whispered in his ear at the right moment, and the cars that shuttled him from one place to another carefully inspected before he got in. It was all so much larger than he'd ever imagined, this matter of Raina Scott. Sometimes he wondered what they wanted him for— they must have some use for him, this he knew—but with so much undercover efficiency on their side, what good could a husband possibly do? Even a well-connected husband. Sometimes he'd stay awake long into the night, listen to sounds from the street. Shoes running by. The clink of metal scraping brick. Crash of cheap beer bottles on crumbling pavement, the bark of a dog. Bird squawks. Sick roosters crowing before dawn, and the gentle, barely heard sound of someone humming, humming slightly, passing by—who? Woman with basket on head? Woman holding child's hand, walking out into the morning? Sometimes he'd get tears in his eyes and wouldn't understand why—unless it was due to this sense of overwhelming exhaustion he carried with him now like extra weight—it was a sadness that always seemed to be with him. It had the feel of permanence, and Lee didn't know how to save himself from it any longer.

The young pilot whistled, turned to him. The eyes were clear, blue, British eyes, cool and unblinking. Ruddy young cheeks and mild eyebrows. When he smiled the two front uppers were missing.

"Nice day, i'n'it?"

Lee nodded.

"What I say, they should've sent one of them Israelis in after her. Get a Jew for your dirty work, he'll do it every time. Know what I mean?"

Lee looked down again.

"What happens now?"

The cool British eyes blinked cheerily.

Ah dunno.

Lee had gotten used to that response, had come to dread it. What didn't this kid know? Matter of fact, what *did* he know?—that was more to the point. Lee guessed a little paranoia was natural under the circumstances.

"Dunno," said the kid, grinning. "Perhaps they'll wait, know what I mean? What with everything blown to smithereens on the Bay, don't suppose they got a full deployment on West Reef these days. I'd lay you ten to one"— he winked—"there's heads rolling in the old National Army. And you know these coons, mate, you been here long enough, when I say heads rolling I mean there's real heads rolling about, guts and all." He shrugged, still cheery. "But what I really mean is, things is going to take a bit longer now. They was going in there pretty quick with all them fancy crop-spraying devices. But now they got to get in more slow like, and fight. And one thing you know about them—they ain't fighters. Bloody chickens, that's what I say. They been saying how all this is *drawing* to some *conclusion* in a *matter of days*. Anyways, that's what they was saying six weeks ago. Then"—he flicked switches on the control panel and the helicopter nosed up again, began slowly to climb—"then it was a *matter of weeks*, right? And now— well, you know what they been saying. You think months? Personally myself, I say years. Well fuck me. Good money but a bloody waste of time. Personally myself, I like to go in somewhere, get the job done, come on back and have a couple beers. And I ain't the only one." The helicopter straightened out again parallel to earth, hovered idly. He'd been shouting over the propellors and still shouted, but the voice was calmer now, less strained. Lee listened with a kind of fascination. "Between you and me, mate, this goes on much longer they're going to be getting a lot of slackers in here. Lots of them jackasses gone over the hill, just out of jail, you name it, they'll wind up here—but not the real professionals." The young voice had deepened with pride. "Me, I'm cutting out after the next paycheck. And they can find some sucker who really needs it. But this sort of land here— this"—one hand swept toward the glass front of the helicopter cabin—"you don't want to go in without a good deal of backup, that's what I say. And these coons ain't it. Quite a sorry lot, actually. But they won't do the bloody job, neither."

Lee gave himself a tired smile. Find my wife and this will all be over, *mate*. Sooner than you think. She's what they want out of all this anyway— some nice commercial model for their Raina Scott dolls, someone to cosign for another big stock transfer. Find her and the whole game's off. And no more paycheck, *mate*.

He'd seen the men, white men, in cruddy back rooms, smoking endless cigarettes and pushing documents under his eyes for approval. Agreements to amend agreements. Lots of countries were involved because of all the corporate interests—lots of gold bars, lots of stock, lots of investors unhappy on lots of B.O.D.'s if one of International's major stockholders *and* major commercial properties had been lost for good—or, worse still, gone irrevocably out of her mind. Major commercial properties did not run off into jungles and lead revolutions. They didn't want to know about that; they didn't want anyone else to know it, either, particularly their public—not now, not posthumously or post-revolution. They had all the proof possible under the circumstances; evidence pointed in an unfortunate direction. And it would not do to have her turn up dead, dusted with white—would it? Better get her back. Extricate her pronto. Expedite. Extradite. You could smell phony headlines for miles:

RAINA SCOTT—ALIVE!

WORLD'S GREATEST ADVENTURER: HOW I SURVIVED YEARS OF CAPTURE

THE MIRACLE OF RAINA SCOTT—AFTER YEARS THOUGHT DEAD

THE RAINA SCOTT STORY, AS TOLD TO—

No. Lee didn't want to think about it.

And there was the matter of Zachary Chemical Corporation. B.O.D. in a mess. Zachary'd left all his holdings to his daughter. There was lots of money involved—foreign money—big-time investments, the sooner they came up with her dead or alive, the better.

You could see the thought shuddering in their minds:

HEIRESS TO CHEMICAL FORTUNE DISAPPEARS

You didn't want to mess with that one, either.

Sometimes Lee felt slightly nauseated. This nausea might last for hours, into the night. He'd wonder why they kept sending him up in helicopters. The best method of search, they said, and they even brought in so-called experts who spread maps and explained it all to him. But he hadn't seen Captain Ben-Lavi or whatever the fuck his name was since that night, and there were times when he suspected they were sending him up in these helicopters just to get rid of him each day. Even though the sky around them was speckled with helicopters, all swooping, sweeping down closer to the jungle, then ascending to move on farther inland, swoop once more and hover, search, search out some sign of a single white woman embedded in all that darkness. Even though this matter of a search was obviously dead serious, he couldn't help but think that somewhere it was all a sham. What if they did not find her?

What, then, would they do with him?

Raina, he said at night, *Raina, are you still alive?*

He received no reply—nothing tangible or intangible, yet he believed somewhere deep inside that she was alive. The sign would come, he felt, if she suddenly died—then he'd feel something definite. He'd know. They'd always felt each other somehow, when all was said and done. They were friends.

Raina. Tell me what to do.

But no answer came. Then suddenly a realization grasped him for the first time: despite all the seeming deference to his wishes, the care taken with his life, the documents politely submitted for his approval, he was under a kind of arrest. It was as if they'd taken him into custody in the most courteous manner possible and now held him politely but firmly. And one thing became so obvious to Lee that he wondered why it hadn't been clear before: unless Raina Scott was discovered, they would probably be happy to let the wrong three-piece suit through security, and this three-piece suit would be the one that would kill him.

The rationale for all this wasn't quite clear to him yet, but he sensed it by whatever instinct was left to him—just as he'd known it was Karlen he'd seen sitting on the Royal Hotel restaurant patio all those weeks ago, Karlen who had disappeared, her name gone from hotel registers at a moment's notice—so easy to make someone vanish.

Lee turned back to the pilot. Nearly twilight out here; they'd been hovering and swooping in the helicopter all day. Lee's voice was friendly.

"What do you say we pack it in?"

"Anything you say!" There was that semi-toothless engaging young smile again. And the helicopter nosed up, propellor roared, they turned to face east and the encroaching purple-blue of evening. They left the other searching helicopters behind, strung out over the jungle like enormous black insects, their flying lights blinking on as the darkness spilled west.

The helicopter descended onto its unofficial landing strip just outside the National Airport, and as its touchdown bump jolted him, Lee felt afraid and also sure of something for the first time since coming here. Greeting the customary dress-suited guards, white men all, who accompanied him from place to place and vehicle to vehicle, he stretched his legs, touched his toes upon climbing out of the helicopter, gave a friendly nod to the one who spoke with a strong German accent. More documents of extradition to sign? Stock guarantee to look over for Raina Scott—to be signed in proxy by him—yes, more documents. He was sure to give amicable grins, stepped easily across rubbled ground to the sedan they had waiting. Lee felt the evening leave him, felt the purple-blue lift, hover, soar and cry like a bird set at liberty. His mind was made up, and he was free. On the trip into Sagrabél he relaxed.

He was sitting across another table in another smoky room, papers about to be pushed across the table at him, pens ready and at least a dozen very official-looking white witnesses surrounding him. Matters had once again been explained in extraordinarily legal-sounding terms. Of course he understood it all quite well. Lee saw the paper sliding toward him. Near a row of black pens, his fingers quivered.

What was it she'd said?—some time once, after a race of his maybe; she'd come to watch. Both of them very young. Had he had some intimation then that they'd breach the borders of friendship for a time, actually become lovers, actually be wed and the marriage evolve to an agreement between friends written in stocks and bonds— had he thought about it then? And, if he'd sensed it, would he have had the guts to go ahead and do it all in the first place? But what was it she'd said? *Oh, it's hard but you do it, you just pretend there's something you love to be reached—don't you? You were wonderful, Lee. Your kick at the end there—that last quarter—ah! It was brave! I could feel it—in here—*and she'd pointed to her center.

Lee felt the sweat cool on his face. Calm now, and very full of presence— moment before the take-off, fair strike. He breathed calmly. Here goes, Raina. Here goes.

"I'm terribly sorry." He fingered a document, shoved it back across the table. "I can't sign any more of these."

Voices hesitated, rose to fill the sudden, dazed silence, but he waved a hand and overrode them. Lee saw his hand cut through smoke with a sudden, pale streak of clarity.

"Let me finish. It appears to me to be the case"—he paused—"that this would not be in the best interests of my wife. In other words, gentlemen"— he looked coolly around the room, the shocked white faces stared unbelievingly back at him—"I firmly believe she's doing, at this very moment, what she wants to do. As her husband, or just as someone who has loved her, I am"—he passed a hand over his forehead—cool, dry, with a faintly exciting, tingling sensation raising the top layer of skin—"I am quite incapable of making, in full conscience, any move against her. And I'd like to say now—well, I'd like to thank you all for your help. It's been most instructive. But I"—he shoved the pens with a finger; they rolled away, clattering into one another—"I choose not to betray her in any way. Not any more. So I've decided to give up this search for her, gentlemen. Starting now."

The room stayed silent awhile longer. Some cigarettes were lit.

Are we to assume, Mr. Simmonds, came a voice, *that this is your permanent policy?*

Lee smiled, a little triumphantly. He leaned back; he couldn't remember the last time he'd felt so relaxed or complete. He breathed in what felt like pure oxygen—liberating, invigorating. He'd take a run later, for the first time in a long time. He could feel the desire growing in him right now, adrenaline starting its giddy pump.

"Yes," he said. "That's a good assumption to make."

What did I tell you, Raina? It's done. Pretty good, huh?
It's done.

He was staying that night in some house on the fringes of Sagrabél's residential district—his room guarded as usual, dinner tasted as usual before he ate it, the long, palm-shadowed driveway guarded. But no one seemed ready to stop him when he stepped out of his room in old nylon running shorts, ripped mesh T-shirt and sweat-dried headband. On his feet were the new training flats they'd tested out several months before—the LS Trail Blazer—a nice, lightweight model in brown cut with white. No one stopped him on his way downstairs. He nodded pleasantly at every armed man he passed, gave everyone the same message: he was going out for a short run, no more than a few miles. Anyone who wanted to come was welcome along. They declined with easygoing grins. Keep his pace? Never. Yes, he smiled in response to each query, he'd keep an eye out for himself. Yes he knew the way back. Couldn't go far anyway—all the roads out of Sagrabél were blocked, and East Bay sealed off since the evacuations.

Lee stepped out into the night. He saw bugs whirling around doorpost lamps, closer and closer to their end; saw the dark shadows of men guarding the long drive out to the road. He stepped lightly down to the ground and began a slow warm-up jog. Step and step and step and step and. Get into a nice rhythm there. A little hard at first—sure, he'd let himself get out of shape these past few months—but basically more delightful than he'd have thought possible, like a return to an old friend. He jogged along the driveway, waved to each guard he passed, breathed out, in, breathed out the same message to each: going for a short run. Not too far. Not too far at all.

Lee picked up pace. Long driveway, this. Long, long. And as he settled in, step and step and step and step, breathe out, then in, he realized this running was different—felt lighter—than any running he'd done before, even what he'd done in college. This was freer somehow. Lee spotted a tall shadow at the end of the driveway. Last guard stationed. He picked up pace and felt he was going well. Not at the old winning pace, of course, but then this was a run for pleasure, and he couldn't remember enjoying the sensation of running so much before, not ever in his life. Freer. Breathe in, breathe out, step and step and step and step. Shoulders loose, arms supple, swinging slightly by his sides. The figure ahead was closer now. Soon, he told himself, soon. Then he realized what it was about this running he was doing, here, at night, on a half-ruined island in the Atlantic, that was different from any running he'd done before: he wasn't afraid anymore. So he was running without fear. Running fearlessly—and it felt wonderful, felt magnificent—his oxygen uptake limitless, legs flexible steel that would take him anywhere, farther than he'd ever been.

Sweat freely ran like the rest of him. Lee smiled. Breathing steadily, deeply, he almost laughed.

It's done!

The tall man's shadow was closer still, and he was running straight for it. He saw the shoulders set, legs spread in a stance. Saw dim metal flash, gun pointed, scope mount globed on the barrel, saw the shadow take aim. Would there be a flash? An almost silent thudding sound? Lee was suddenly curious. He ran faster. He ran to meet it.

GABRIEL

A single unmarked plane wailed over the interior in the colorless hours before dawn. The moon was new that night, sky lightless except for the stars. And the daily helicopter search had ended hours ago as it did every night; now only a solitary, point-nosed plane broke the bottom layers of cloud. Against the sky it was almost invisible, a flitting shadow passing across faded stars.

In the hull, equipment rattled. The entire frame shivered with a jolting, metallic sound. The metal floor was cold and, like the sides of the plane, rattling incessantly. Nevertheless, Gabriel slept curled against a side of the hull dressed in full paratroop gear, parachute strapped to his back.

He slept because after years of training and countless nights of sleeplessness, his body had learned to sleep anywhere his mind would allow it to; had learned that sleep, like food, was something to be stored against the future. Most often he was in such need of sleep that, when he did intentionally doze, his sleep was pure, unbroken and blank, a perfect rest born of necessity. There were things that must be done. A job not finished yet. Whole warehouses filled with poison had been demolished so he could finish this job, unsprayed, unmolested. For this job, he'd need as much sleep as possible. So he slept curled like a baby. On his darkened, hard-lined face, no trace of shame or worry. He slept earnestly, innocently.

On the rare occasions when he was home for extended leave, his wife had watched him sleep. She'd thought then that there was a kind of look peculiar to sleeping soliders: a man trained to defend and kill, resting in all his modern armor with a gentle, childlike pouting on the face that made him seem infinitely small, the weapons strapped to him infinitely large— an image tenderly absurd.

Gabriel dreamed of his wife Yael. It was a dream filled with soft colors. Not an erotic dream, just one of indistinct, gentle images. When awake, he'd wonder: was that the problem with gentleness? that it too often appeared indistinct beside outright brutality? But asleep, he thoroughly enjoyed this dream in all its soft vagueness.

When awake, he'd wonder many things if there happened to be time for wondering. He'd wonder whether or not it was really *love* he felt for his wife—this woman he'd met after too many years of service, courted briefly, finally married—after too many years of service he was old, much older than mere age, and she was very young, something fresh in his life when he stopped long enough to take count. Was it love, this melting sensation he experienced for her? Or was it just that he melted at the thought of a wife, a home, streets of a city in peacetime, no need for defense or war, no soldiers standing guard on rooftops or city walls. Maybe it wasn't her so much as all she represented—some of it attainable, most of it achingly out of reach except in brief, taunting moments. Or maybe he allowed himself to think it was merely what she represented that he yearned for in this melting way, so that he could avoid the reality of not knowing her as well as possible—because there wasn't time, because he was too busy with matters of killing, because he was, perhaps, afraid to attempt knowing her as more than just a wife in the abstract, a photograph to frame on the barracks desk. Every soldier needed a wife in the abstract, didn't he? To remember what it was, supposedly, that he fought for. At thirty-four, Gabriel felt as old as the hills he ran navigational exercises on to break in new recruits. And Yael, some ten years younger, was to him a girl. Perhaps that was why he felt oddly shy around her—the melting becoming a flood of embarrassment at different moments. He'd attribute it to constantly being around men in uniform or top-level officials in their crumpled white shirt sleeves. Too often he was simply exhausted; too often he wanted just to sleep next to her in bed. No song of songs. Home from maneuvers, he'd sleep curled around the fresh, musk smell of her body. In sleep, as in battle, Gabriel was alone. Exiled, Yael watched him at night. He looked very young. Absolutely still. Almost dead.

She'd watch and imagine him high on mountain tops. Or trekking across deserts in full combat gear, metal and canvas set with ridiculous weight on a body that had never been particularly large and, at first glance, seemed incapable of supporting it all. Or on rooftops, scrutinizing streets far below. In corners of the Old City at night, lurking, waiting. Always, she'd imagine him alone. On holiday nights he'd be waiting at a freezing mountain pass in the north. New moon, only bitter white stars for light, and on the peak above an ice-crusted capping of snow. Middle East. Outsiders thought it was all blistering desert or fetid valleys, but they were wrong: snow in the north, freezing rains during winter, wadis filled with sudden bursts of icy mountain water. She'd worry on cold holiday nights, imagine him standing guard in a snow-strewn pass between northern cliffs; see him stamping each booted foot in turn to keep the blood circulating, rifle ready on his shoulder, ears red and very cold. He'd rub his gloves one on the other to keep some warmth in each fingertip. Maybe the stubble on his face would freeze, dark eyelashes over the pale eyes glimmer dew and freeze—Yael worried about him, alone there in the pass at night. She knew he'd look down on the lights of valley settlements breaking the land's darkness like stars; he'd understand that those lights existed and the people behind them slept only because he shivered in a mountain pass above them at night, every night. She knew he'd feel a sort of happy pride then, forever touched by sadness. Shielding those valley lights, he was separate from them. As long as he remained separate they were shielded and their source of light assured, but as long as he shielded them he would be denied their warmth and company. He would never touch them. She'd watch him sleeping and not touch him, either. In this way, too, they were separate, husband and wife, she from him; in some sense they would never touch. She'd curl into him or flatten herself against his back, throw a protecting arm around, a protecting leg over his, settle her face against the back of his neck. She could feel him breathe, sometimes murmur in his sleep. And in this way she felt very close to Gabriel, closer than the times he was awake, his peacetime smile a sorrow-tinged barrier between them. In her imagination she knew him better than he suspected she did and, because she was not so inclined as he to question the source of whatever might be termed love, accepted what she knew. She taught schoolchildren during the day. When he was home she spoke to him in ancient Spanish spattered with Hebrew words, a soft, almost Arabic cadence in her voice.

Gabriel sat quickly in the rattling plane, stared up at the face of the man who'd shaken him to attention. Time now. Finish the job. He blinked.

He checked and double-checked all the equipment strapped to his body, his vest, ammo clips, canteens, first aid—all in order. The plane's roar obscured any possible communication. He nodded at the face staring down, stood, and headed for the right-hand exit. He turned to Naphtali Lev. The dark-lidded eyes smiled back at him. Briefly, they shook hands.

The door slid open.

Below was darkness—great, unbroken mass of it. Wind shrieked past; his knuckles felt instantly frozen. Gabriel stopped looking down, just looked straight ahead into the night. He kicked himself out, plunged, slipped toward the dark metal tail of the plane on a freezing stream of air, and then he was falling with arms crossed over chest and head lowered, knees curled up tight like an unborn child's, falling and counting silently in blasting wind currents.

Above his head, the black parachute opened perfectly. He eased his head up, legs straight, checked the cords for twists but everything was perfect.

In landing, you'd want to bend the legs slightly, plant feet together at the exact same instant and you'd lace fingers over the top of your helmet, anticipate the initial shock, the recovery roll. And keep track of time. Because you rarely felt yourself actually falling until you were close, quite close, to the ground.

Gabriel sliced through overhanging moss. A large, damp hunk of it dropped against his boots with a hushed sound. He wiped his forehead. The chills had started up again. Still, nothing serious. He'd seen worse before. He wiped the blade carefully across his vest and the wet stains were sharp, linear. He re-sheathed the knife.

There was another small trail here—he could detect crushed fronds beneath the new overgrowth—and this barely detectable path he followed. He stepped silently. Once in a while there was the rustling of his shoulders against leaves. At times a bird would call, lonely, shrill, far off—and he'd stop to listen. He judged the nature of the sound, the distance it traveled. Then he'd make a mental note to himself before proceeding. The eyes, which Pablo had sworn could see behind him, slid from one side to the other. Sweat dripped down his lids. Patiently, Gabriel wiped it away. He shivered. He was careful to drink from his canteen every few minutes. When the chills got bad enough to make his teeth click and chatter, he stuffed a tiny piece of handkerchief between the teeth on each side of his jaw. He wanted no sound to disturb the dark quiet, or interfere with the strange, lonely bird cries that came now at increasingly rare intervals.

Gabriel wiped his face. He thought of his wife for a minute but made himself stop. She had no place here. She was in Jerusalem. And he was glad—whatever he faced now, he'd have only himself to be concerned with and only himself to rely on. The strength, his. The terror, his alone. He'd done this before. He'd done it on military maneuvers, done it in deserts and strange foreign cities sweltering in sun. Every time was different, yes, and every time it was also the same somewhere because there was just you and the thing you were about to do—the stealing of some secret, the taking of some life. The thing itself stretched before you, limitless. So you played games with it, made it smaller—nothing but a series of minor steps which, effectively followed, led inevitably to one conclusion, one success, one theft, one death. You did not think about the thing itself except as one more minor step in a long road composed of minor steps. And you could then take careful aim. Fire.

The birdcall came again: crazed, alone, and shrill. He stopped, calculated. He looked down to see something alive coiled around one boot. He felt the shivering increase but told himself to go on ahead and he did. He watched as the pin-headed snake unraveled quickly, hissed into mud and moss and slithered away.

He stepped over hanging vines. Yellow leeches sucked their way along these strands, and he was careful to raise his boots high, avoid crushing things unnecessarily—he'd remembered the possibility of ants. His feet moved methodically. They were graceful, cautious. Sometimes they paused mid-step, listening. His teeth chattered on saliva-soaked pieces of cloth. Gabriel watched the ground, the trees to either side of him and all around. He kept walking. He sipped water continually. Quite a fever, but he felt all right. Very much in control.

He glanced to his left and there was someone walking beside him.

The brown-skinned man wore knee-length, patched-over trousers and a cotton shirt with many dark stains on it. His face was puffy with multiple bruises, and his glasses had been broken. They hung, cracked and lopsided, off the bridge of his nose. Still, he didn't seem in pain or at all disconcerted by his physical state. He seemed, instead, somewhat apologetic. He walked in silence next to Gabriel, bare feet soundless on the undergrowth.

Hello! he said cheerily.

Gabriel looked miserably away.

They both kept walking.

Don't feel so horrible, Saunderson said. You're forgiven, you know.

By whom? Gabriel felt his lips curl to a half-sneer. By you? You set yourself up to forgive, is that it?

There was silence. Gabriel glanced to meet the eyes once—they were warm, dreamy, looking squarely at him. Gabriel felt sweat blur his vision, felt his teeth rattling into nauseating damp cloth.

He kept walking. He could hear his own sighs in the heavy, wet closure of the dense green that surrounded. He glanced to his left again and Saunderson was still there. Gabriel felt rage build, tears sting his eyes to mingle with sweat. He spoke loud enough for the man walking beside him to hear.

You know, I hate people like you. You phony saints. You set yourself up with simple truths. You spout abstractions and people believe what you say. What you don't tell them—he laughed, nauseated—what you don't tell them is that your little truths don't work out so well in practice. So it's wrong to kill, you say. But you forget to state the circumstance! Does it occur to you that perhaps it's *right* to kill at certain times? No. You phonies. You priests, stupid rabbis, you Jesuses and jackasses. Get away from me.

Shhh, Saunderson said gently. Don't be so hard on yourself. I want—

*Christ*ians. Stinking Christians. Half of you are so busy butchering you can't see for the blood. Of course! And the other half are busily forgiving, forgiving, forgiving. So much forgiveness. Tell me, sir, do you ever mix a little sadism in with your love?

Saunderson's hand brushed his shoulder lightly. Gabriel shuddered. The heat was a wet cloak now across his shoulders. He told himself to measure the sound of each footfall. Take care of Saunderson first—he'd have to. Then for the rest.

My dear man, Saunderson whispered. You've missed the point.

Enlighten me.

I'm afraid—the man laughed gently—that I can't do that. It's not in my power. All I have is what you have—a tiny match in the darkness, Mr. Klemer.

You didn't behave that way before. All that talking in front of campfires, Mister Jesus. All your political meetings—

Oh! Saunderson protested sharply. They weren't political!

Gabriel smiled. Not political? Don't you know what happened to those people? For all your harmless talk? Do you care? You made a mistake, Mr. Saunderson. You loved people too much, you know. You did. Each and every one of them—they mattered to you. A mistake. For a leader, a mistake. You should have loved them in the abstract—in the abstract, like all your little truths. The way I love *my* people—

You don't *like* people very much, Mr. Klemer!

That's correct. I love my people in general. I despise most individuals in particular. I care about their basic needs being met. But beyond that I really don't want to know. I'll tell you why: there's no time for that, let them take care of their spiritual needs later. Let me take care of making sure they survive. That's more immediate—

Are you so sure?

"Yes," said Gabriel. It echoed against leaves. He swallowed saliva, nearly choked. *In the survival of a race as a whole, each individual member of that race must—on a certain level—be expendable.* The soul of each individual must take second place to the survival of the *people.*

The small, barely visible path grew wider up ahead. He could see that it was fresher, the broken fronds still bleeding, and he crouched suddenly and stayed where he was. From side to side, up and down, the eyes slid like a pair of roving lenses. But he could see no one. Gabriel watched, and listened.

Every Jew a Nazi.

Ridiculous, said Gabriel.

Every Nazi a Jew.

Quiet.

To save one group of people, you sacrifice another.

Sure, said Gabriel. He shivered, laughed silently. *And I will fuck with the devil himself to do it, if I have to. Do you understand?*

Saunderson's voice was soft, kind. I understand, Mr. Klemer. Certainly, I do. But white mingling with black as it always does—isn't the price you pay inordinately high? Doesn't it tarnish the value of what you achieve? If in doing some good, you also allow great harm to occur?

Gabriel had him by the throat. He was weak, Saunderson, the breath barely rattled in him. It wouldn't take much. And Gabriel was ready, felt himself surge with a sudden gush of desperation. Quiet. He had to have it, to remain undisturbed. His thumbs pressed down, found the windpipe, pressed harder. You moralists. You martyrs. All your ideas wiped out an entire village. You should have been more political. You should have.

Blood bubbled from Saunderson's throat, eyes behind the broken lenses wide, wounded with surprise.

What you said was right, Mr. Saunderson. I am the living proof. And I have something to tell you. Your philosphy leads to despair. That's all right. Don't feel too bad. All roads go there, in the end. They do.

It spilled out of Saunderson's mouth, dribbled down onto Gabriel's hands, foamed pinkish red on the waiting, upturned leaves. Then it was over and Gabriel wiped his fingers gratefully. He shuddered and nearly swallowed the cloth. Bad fever. But he was far from delirious, he told himself, yes.

He was in control. A wailing, desolate bird cry shattered the air around him. He flattened to a combat crawl. And he was moving forward, crushing the overgrown roots of an already beaten path, while behind him the broken body of Tristam Saunderson, twice murdered, disintegrated rapidly in thick jungle air.

The area Gabriel approached was flattened, leaves crushed to form a tiny clearing. He smelled the stench—dead flesh—he'd smelled it before along canals, in mountain places. But Connery stood against a tree openly waiting. Facing him. Eyes wide. Gabriel thought he almost smiled.

"Hey. Santa Claus."

The smaller gun was more convenient. He aimed with both hands, fired and the first near-silent bullet thudded in on target, right through the heart. But Gabriel was a little delirious; Connery made no motion. He stood there leaning against the tree, wide-eyed, half smiling. Gabi aimed again, again. He emptied the gun, and rose slowly to his knees. He noticed the lack of gushing blood, the smell of dead flesh. He noticed the feather-tipped wooden shaft sticking straight out of Connery's midsection, arms hanging stiff at his sides—he was pinioned to the tree. Mr. Connery was dead. He had been for a while.

Gabriel stood unsteadily and stepped forward to take a closer look. He stopped when he was face to face with the dead Connery. The features were already beginning a subtle disintegration. Gabriel wove back and forth on his feet. He spat out cloth. On his automatic, both hands shivered.

Gabriel froze. He thought something moved on the dead face before him. Thought he heard the throat clear, trying to speak. Then he thought he saw Connery wink.

He fainted.

The face loomed over him. Flesh peeled from it in thin strips. Lips rotted and hung low on the jaw, detached from the gaping mouth. But the eyes were alive, icily glittering as they watched him with a sort of amusement. Underneath the flesh now falling away were patches of a gleaming, bubbly white substance—as if all the tissue beneath layers of skin had been transformed, and what covered the skull was something other than human. The dead mouth smiled; a gust of wind came from it carrying an odor worse than he'd ever smelled before. Gabriel turned his head and vomited into the mud.

"Admire your pluck," said Connery, "but it's not much good anyway."

Chill had tightened around his neck. Gabriel tried to roll away but couldn't.

Connery chuckled. "Soldier boy. What's your dream? Illusions of peace? Too bad. The truth of the matter is nobody stops me. *Nobody.* Got to give you credit for trying, though. Nice little army you have there."

"Thank you," said Gabriel.

"I like to give credit where credit is due. What did you think was going to happen, anyway, once you got such a nice little army together? You thought everyone was going to kiss and make up? Sit around and play patty-cake?"

Gabriel shook his head. Foolishly, he felt himself smile.

"Teach a man to kill—if he's forced to kill once, from then on he's a killer." Connery laughed. The sound rolled out from a lipless mouth on stinking currents of wind. "You worry about that awhile, then—right?— all these nice kids, look what we did, went ahead and made them permanently killers. Then you get to rationalizing it all, I know how it is. You figure: well, these killers are doing it for a purpose, saving wives and babies, keeping the land safe for plowing and all that crud—right? Sure! And even though they're killers, they're still nice kids because most of them feel plain rotten about all this killing going on. Then—*then* you start feeling a little sainted, yourself. Because you figure: well, I'm doing all the really *bad* shit so everyone else can live innocent lives without having to even think of doing what I'm doing. Only somewhere"—Connery's voice spat, and something white dribbled down a corner of the lipless mouth—"somewhere deep inside, my friend, maybe you're a little bitter at all these so-called innocent people, living their lives like nothing's happening while you're there every night on the border getting your eyes ripped out. Come on, buddy, admit it! You feel a little used sometimes, huh? Sure you do."

Gabriel choked on something. When his throat cleared he was breathing heavily, staring straight up at the destroyed face. His own voice came out a whisper. "There are treaties."

"Yeah? You're right! There are lots of treaties, sonny. Lots of paper floating around the globe, huh? Plenty of people get born and raised to kill, too—plenty of people've got nothing to lose. That's where I come in. So let's can this crap about treaties. You know better than that."

The moldy skin across Connery's forehead slipped and fell off. Beneath it was sheer, glistening white.

Gabriel felt himself smile. He pointed in a sort of awe to the pure, shining forehead, felt a childish urge to touch.

"What is it?"

The mouth smiled.

"Snow," it said.

"Snow?"

"Sure. You know: snow, *nieve, sheleg*—come on, how many languages do you speak, anyway? It comes in the winter, cold weather and all that stuff, the right atmospheric pressure and bingo—snow." The rotting cartilage of Connery's nose hung from the face, then dropped away. Liquid oozed out to fill the gap, a pure, bubbly white. "It comes with the seasons. Kind of like patterns of history. You know all about history, don't you?"

Gabriel nodded. Sweat ran into his eyes and he pointed again, this time at the oozing white space that had been Connery's nose. "More snow?"

"You've got it. Peel a little more away anywhere—I mean *anywhere*—and there it is: snow. That's why it's no good, you running around trying to stop it. Look at yourself. You get into a worse mess than before. Plus you forget which fucking side you ever were on in the first place. It's no good, my friend, it's a royal waste of time and a royal pain in the ass—you're not going to stop it no matter what. Get rid of some, turn around tomorrow and there's more falling. Might as well try to stop a pig from rolling in mud—you know what I mean."

Gabriel used all his energy to prop himself into a sitting position. Mud soaked through his trousers. His back was slathered with wet moss and crawling things. He forced his eyes to stay open, stay steady, stare straight ahead into the icy bright eyes that looked back at him from a dead surface of glittering white.

"You're a liar," said Gabriel. "I've been keeping it away for years."

The mouth trickled white liquid. "Buying time, sonny. You're just buying time. Let me tell you something. You can *buy* time, but you can't *stop* it."

Gabriel fainted again. When he woke he was already standing, walking away from the dead body of Connery pinned to its tree by an arrow. He walked trying hard to focus his eyes, teeth chattering and every limb quivering with fever.

A bird shrieked close by.

He looked up suddenly to the pounding beat of wings he thought he'd heard, another bird cry sounding almost on top of him. Someone laughed. Gabriel forced himself to look up, and keep looking until he saw something just above him in the trees—a long, lithe form spread-eagled there, gazing down. Light bounced from the creature to him—green light, white light—in dizzying, swirling rays. Gabriel felt his own breathing cease. He had the feeling he was moving very, very slowly, and that everything had stopped. He felt his knees hit the mud. Then he was bending over carefully, moving completely by instinct—or some urge deeper than instinct—bowing to the ground.

You traveled a long way.
Gabriel nodded, walked slowly. "I had to."
A long way to do this job of yours. Tell me—in your estimation, now— does it do any good in the end?
I don't know, Gabriel told her.
They were silent.
Walking seemed easier now. Somehow, he was being supported. He felt himself floating—as if all the mud had vanished, foliage parted to let him through, the ground become a silky carpet leading easily to well-traveled roads.
Tell me. What do you make of it?
"Of what?"
This snow business. I used to think it was all just illusory—snow, I mean. But then I fell in love again and was convinced—oh, persuaded—that the substance was definitely not illusory, just something that transformed rather quickly. Like love itself—
Gabriel remained silent.
What do you think?
"I don't know," he breathed.
She pouted. The green and white mask moved beside him, dizzying; he saw her displeasure and for a moment was afraid.
You're no fun.
"I'm sorry."
Oh, that's all right. I expect too much from people. And anyway, you're a lucky man—you showed up a little too late for the hunting season. Consider yourself lucky—we had the same job in mind—
"I do."
I know. You must have something you love very much. Or someone. Are you in love with a woman?
"A woman?" Gabriel touched a chilled hand to his face, found himself crying. Something in him sank with despair. "I'm not sure. Perhaps. No. I'm not really sure." He sobbed the words without consideration: "But I plan to have children! Plenty of children!"
Yes.
The voice soothed quietly.
Of course you do.
Foliage swung before his face; she'd touch it and with a single movement

sweep it aside so they could pass. Everything was dark as before. Still, he felt them enveloped in a soft, glowing kind of light.

When we first came in here, it was all like this. They'd given us little vials. We were requested to break the seals and plant a few every certain number of kilometers—we did it as a favor, part of an ongoing agricultural experiment by one of the chemical companies, they said—they told us it was fertilizer. Everyone carried a supply of the vials, with the exception of Mr. St.-Peters and myself. He and I had the log books, you see. We didn't want any extra weight.

A striped hand edged vines aside, fingers flicked away the colorfully winged bug about to drop onto Gabriel's shoulder.

About half the vials were planted as directed. But some of the seals had broken in their packs over a period of weeks and soaked right through. That was when all the sickness started. Mr. St.-Peters and I—we watched it happen. There was nothing to be done. We tried everything. We used up most of the medical supplies. Force-feeding antibiotics, putting salve on these extraordinary sores that began developing all over their bodies. Oh, they weren't exactly sores—they looked more like burns, at least third degree. The tissue underneath was a pustulant sort of white. Amazing. I had never in my life seen anything—anything at all like it—and I've seen a great deal in my life. Of course nothing did any good. Every one of them died. Ten good men. Toward the end, Mr. St.-Peters and I took out the kit and did a crude chemical evaluation of the substance in one of the unleaked vials.

The green and white stripes shimmered. She turned to him and he had to look away, put a hand over his eyes.

Let me be honest with you. You're in this up to your neck, aren't you?—all this filthy business. I fail to see the logic in it. In order to accomplish one so-called good deed you commit a thousand acts of evil—no, I don't pretend to understand! Except in the sense that it's all so pathetically human. Oh, I even do it myself I suppose. I'd kill you now, too, if it weren't that we had the same good idea a while back. And I feel tired these days. It's enough hunting for now. For now. Somehow you bought us time—you did, didn't you, although maybe it wasn't your intention. How much time do you think? Several weeks? Tell me. A few months at most?

Between the fingers spread over his eyes ran tears. Gabriel couldn't stop them. "At most," he whispered.

He turned suddenly to face her and was momentarily blinded. But she smiled. It was a wonderful smile, white-toothed, split the mask in a dazzling way.

Thanks, then. For the few months at most. If the people in here knew,

*I'm sure they'd say the same. Thanks! On behalf of myself, and my lover—
I thank you.*

Gabriel shut his eyes. Green and white shimmered on the insides of his eyelids.

"Miss Scott," he said slowly, "I must ask you to come with me."

She smiled again. The eyes still glittered madly, but without anger this time. There was, in fact, a special indescribable sort of heat in them that reached out toward him and made him feel, irrationally and for just a moment, immune to all harm. But the striped lips opened haughtily, nostrils flared in a kind of stiff pride.

Oh, absolutely not. Don't you understand? I am Raina Scott. And Raina Scott has a standard to uphold. No, no. She would never go back.

He turned away then, dizzy again. When mad colors had stopped swirling in front of his eyes he found himself walking, breathing easily, his tears dried.

The walking became easier still. He moved in a dream. In his dream, the surrounding leaves became lighter green as they walked; the ground began to appear dryer, moss and hanging vines more sparse, and—once in a while—he could have sworn that faint strands of sunlight gleamed through.

Gabriel sniffed the air to make sure, and it came again; no illusion—a breeze. Again, and he opened his mouth, felt the cracked lips cooled by it, saw pools of sunlight shooting everywhere through the now scattered trees. Ahead were no trees but plains of grass, taller than a man's height and coarse, brown, thick, growing out of the flat dry ground.

You're in time, I believe. Yes, yes. And this is the place—I checked the coordinates on your map. Leave it to an expert.

Breeze blew past his teeth. It occurred to Gabriel that he was very thirsty. Both canteens rattled empty at his side. Turning to face her he found he could not. He found himself bowing slightly, eyes averted and hand shading his eyes. He could barely hear himself speak.

"What will you do?"

Now? Just love for a while. There's not much time for anything else. But there's time—some, anyway—for a little of that, isn't there? So I thank you.

Oh, Gabriel said, it's nothing.

He was feverish again, his teeth chattering. He cried.

Come on now, be brave. Be a man—hah!—go on, now. You've got a few minutes. Go on. Is your future bright? It is, isn't it. Go do the rest of it now—the future, I mean—really, you ought to. Go make those babies you said you wanted. Lots of children—remember? Better get started on *that. There's a good plan for you. Make some babies, have children—it's good! It's a good thing! Do it! Somebody has to. And I can give you three guesses—*she laughed and the laugh rang musically, bounced off the sun-filtered leaves and ended on a single, desolate note—*it's not going to be me.*

Grasshopperlike insects tickled his nose. Gabriel woke to stare at blinding sun that shone above the fluttering tips of grass.

He wrenched himself to his hands and knees with effort; every movement was extreme pain, every part of him chilled and burning, drenched with sweat. His uniform was caked with drying mud and crushed leaves. The sound came closer, changed from whine to buzz to roar, and he saw the helicopter's unmarked sides gleaming bright silver, circling, descending. He pulled every last bit of energy out and unlatched the safety on his automatic. No mistakes. Interception of coordinates always a possibility. Make sure of identity first—always—until then, wait.

The propellor made the grass around the area where it had landed twist wildly. It whipped up dust, too, so the surrounding air took on a whitish glow. Crouching, Gabriel thought he saw a man jump down from the open cabin door, machine gun held high in both hands. Machine gun lowered. Held high. Gabriel stood then and began to run. He ran toward the helicopter, toward the hand-held machine gun that appeared just over the top of the grass. He thought his lungs would collapse with the effort, running the several hundred yards toward the place where Naphtali Lev stood signaling.

"One hundred percent!" he shouted, and thought the shout would take his life away.

"One hundred percent burned!"

This was the positive code.

He collapsed, struggling to breathe. Someone dragged him by the armpits, hoisted him to a half-standing position, and now other hands grabbed him by wrists and arms, pulling him up from the grass into a bubble of glass and metal.

"On time, thank God." Naphtali Lev poured water on his face. "Lee Simmonds fell in with the wrong group, Gavi. Those bastards infiltrated." His dark-skinned fingers made a slicing motion across the neck. Gabriel shut his eyes. "You're not a minute too soon, friend. We clear out in an hour. Everyone. But it'll be okay. For all that, everything was finished according to plan."

Gabriel licked his lips and couldn't tell what it was he tasted—water, sweat, or tears. *Yael*, he thought, and smiled. *Yaeli, Yael mine.* Sounds wanted to tear him apart from the inside. His body shuddered with each loud sob. Each sob was drowned in the spinning whir of propellors, the rattling of control-panel throttles.

"Don't worry," said Naphtali, "a nice stay at the hospital for this one, Gavi. All that time in Jerusalem—and you get plenty of rest in the bargain— just think. It'll be okay! It'll be okay."

IN THE TEMPLE OF THE MOON

Dr. Manella Porter was rolling bandages.

The bandages were carefully stitched remnants of cloth. They'd been soaked and pounded clean, stretched overnight on wooden racks to dry. Now they had to be rolled.

Greatness, or sainthood, sometimes consists of merely doing what needs to be done. Those who tower above the rest in accomplishment and dedication—who attain the stature of heroism—are often those simply willing to see a thing through, to dirty their hands with the messiness of each necessary detail along the way. And while to members of the movement in Sagrabél or sympathizers in radical study groups around the world, Dr. Porter was growing in symbolic importance and considered a martyr to the cause, to Manella herself this was just another day. So she was rolling bandages. Someone had to do it.

Her hut was dome-shaped like all the other huts, ceiling of dried fronds intertwined with twisting branches. From the inside gazing up these appeared wormlike. Through an open passageway wet heat came bringing a dim light with it, sunlight that fought its way in dribbling lines through the thick foliage, wrote its name faintly on massive trunks of trees and gave to the jungle interior a soft, sporadic kind of glow that could be taken for daylight.

Dr. Porter hummed. Once in a while she glanced up from rolls of bandages, peered across at the sleeping female form wrapped in blankets on a pallet woven of leaves. The breathing came calmly now. Two days ago had been different: the body hot and shuddering with fever, lovely lips twisting incoherently around delirious words. They'd taken her from the arms of the Goddess herself—a gift! it had been whispered—and there were more hushed murmurings when the Goddess followed her into this hut, crouched beside the pallet and watched what was done, narrowed eyes examining each action with intense concern. Manella used two women of the village as assistants. Under the eyes of the Goddess they stripped the feverish body of clothes. *Gently,* She hissed once, angrily, and after that the hands of both assistants trembled so much that Manella sent them away. She washed the body herself and noted symptoms, decided she would probably live. Dr. Porter wondered why the fever wasn't a great deal higher. When she went through the stripped clothes she found out why: there were pouches sewn into shirt sleeves and trouser legs everywhere, inside compartments to the leather vest, each hidden cache containing plastic bottles of medicines, mostly antibiotics. Only one bottle had been opened, though. Penicillin. The doctor plucked each container from its pocket, began to stash them away in her metal kit and when she seized the penicillin found that a green-striped, white-striped hand had gripped her wrist. *No. She needs it.* The doctor looked up immediately, surprised; it was almost a plea. After a moment she placed her own dark hand over the striped one and tentatively touched.

"Of course. I'll see that she gets it."

The Goddess seemed to relent then, released Her grip and returned to crouch unmoving, the watchful tension as palpable as coiled spring. The doctor couldn't figure it all out. She'd been through some very strange things in her life but still couldn't guess what this one was up to now. So she fell back on her professional training, checked for wounds, injuries, moved each limb and finally eased some blankets around. The heartbeat was fast, birdlike and frantic. She forced the mouth open. She forced water down and doubled the dose of penicillin. After a while the woman slept, breasts heaving with each breath. Dr. Porter sat a few feet away. Night stretched long and still and outside the guarded fire pit was refueled at regular intervals. At the hut's entrance warriors of the Goddess stood, shoulders wilting tiredly as they leaned against spears stabbed in earth, the smooth green paint that covered their bodies glistening in firelight. They stood as hours crept by, patiently waited for the Goddess to reappear. They must stand there, hands on spears, for as long as it took. If need be they'd die standing.

Dr. Porter watched the feverish, sleeping woman, watched the Goddess, who was crouched at her side and seemed to have frozen in that position, staring down.

She shouldn't have come.

It was a thought spoken out loud, requiring no response. Dr. Porter simply watched. The one body pale, unconscious and rolling restlessly in its wrapping of blankets; the other silent and statuelike bent over her, only the pelvic area covered by a frail swathing of cloth and the rest naked, striped green and white, fierce eyes burning down. Once in a while, the doctor dozed. She woke at some point in the long night to see that the Goddess had moved closer to this woman, sat there crosslegged and was softly stroking her face, smoothing from it strands of thick brown hair. She fumbled with something around the woman's neck, her fingers lifting a delicate metallic line that flashed in firelight. She let the necklace resettle against flesh; odd tooth-shaped ornament which hung from it resting to point between the woman's breasts. Dr. Porter closed her eyes again and pretended sleep.

Shouldn't have. Oh, you shouldn't have come.

The voice was unusually soft, and sad.

Manella opened her eyes to see night settled for good. Fire glowed dimly through the entrance from outside. In its dull light she saw the Goddess stand and stretch slowly, her painted skin rippling zebra shadows with the sure, strong grace of each movement. There was an awesomeness in Her presence. Manella understood why they'd all been so impressed. Even though, she told herself, she didn't believe in any of their myths or rituals. Maybe it was her modern training, maybe her innate skepticism that allowed her to notice telltale signs of mortality: the face scarred by an exhaustion even paint could not hide; the paint itself beginning to slide with sweat and green bleeding random streaks across white.

You'll take care of her.

It was spoken in Her former language—a language only the doctor could understand. Manella looked up, quietly nodded.

Good. That's good. Now—She raised a hand, palm flashing sudden, shocking flesh-tone against the background of melting stripes—*this changes things. As soon as possible, I want her brought to me. Please see that it's done. You'll make sure of it, Dr. Porter, won't you? You will.* The hand gestured down. *She's mine. I want it understood. If she is hurt, everyone dies. Everyone.*

Manella watched. The Goddess smiled broadly. The smile made a curving pale slash across the face's diagonal stripes. Now Her hand had risen again, finger stabbed across Her own throat in a brutal, cutting motion.

Everyone. And the whole game is over.

She turned to brush through the entranceway. Dr. Porter heard the plucking sounds of spears uprooted from ground, the almost silent crush of warriors' feet against earth as they stood straighter, gathered weapons and followed. She heard the faint thud of knees on earth when men guarding the fire knelt, bowed their heads as the Goddess passed.

Today, Manella sat and rolled bandages. A few feet away Kaz woke up, forgot where she was, tried to remember and closed her eyes again. When she opened them she was gazing at a woman's dark brown face. She remained silent. She looked up wondering. She was waiting for something, it would come or it would not come, but in any event she was powerless right now to will it along; and she had no faith in her ability to speak. For a second, she'd lost all language and therefore all thought, was clean and blank inside, utterly innocent.

The face above her smiled. The lips were full and dark; the words came out in accented English: "How do you feel?"

She propped herself on an elbow. The fainting feeling came back. She shut her eyes until it passed. Kaz heard the first sound she made with surprise, she herself somehow removed from it—a faint laugh.

"How do you feel?"

She blinked dizzily. "Lousy. What's going on?"

The doctor leaned closer to hear the low series of whispers. Then she had to think awhile. If she answered that particular question, the answer, she realized, would take a long time. What's going on. She shook her head, gave a small, quiet laugh herself. Maybe she really didn't know what exactly was going on. Or maybe she did, and the knowledge—a wave of historical complexities whose crest she rode—loomed behind every daily thought like a waiting apocalypse. What's going on? *Some kind of craziness*, she wanted to say. *Some enormous craziness that's taken over all the world, that's feeding grain to pigs and cows instead of hungry babies, that's turning water into poison and the ground to ashes.* But she just smiled instead, and placed the back of her hand against this woman's forehead. Cool, damp, drained. No more fever. She gave her water.

"You lie down now."

Kaz did and her hands touched her own flesh—she understood that she'd been stripped naked and for the first time in many days wanted to cry. Dr. Porter saw the eyes glimmer tears, saw them half shut and then watched a pale hand reach out of blankets to search along the chest, the neck. The hand found what it was looking for, caressed the silver chain, and fingers wrapped tightly around the ivory moon-sliver of tooth. Then the tears receded. Across the lips spread a smile. It was the smile of a child sleeping secure in the knowledge of some sort of happiness, or protection, or anticipation. The doctor watched as the lips opened, formed a word, whisper sounded dimly in the hut's heavy air and the sound was a name.

Raina.

Dr. Porter barely deciphered the sound. She resumed sitting a few feet away on the hard, smooth-swept earth to roll bandages. From outside came the buzzing background chirp of insects, the occasional giggling of children and tiny feet racing bare on damp ground. From outside and far away came the long, harsh wail of a lone bird or animal. What is going on. Nothing, the doctor told herself. Nothing is going on. It was just another day of half-lit jungle trees—another day and she was rolling bandages. And at the same time everything was going on. It was going on and racing inward toward the center of this island, galloping ever closer with a slow, creeping thump like wingbeats at evening, sporadic blasts of thunder coming always nearer, like the inevitability of age itself, or death. It was happening everywhere, all the time. A chaos of money and machines that would soak these bandages with blood. She heard the same name whispered:

Raina.

Fingers clutching the shark tooth, Kaz slept. She slept with a sleep bordered by bright anticipation. She was quite close now. She could feel it. This nearness covered her while she slept. It told her she was approaching the source of desire now, closing in on the bright, white core of things. It assured her that soon she would touch what had beckoned so brightly for so long; that she was close now, very close, to attainment.

What it did not tell her was that attainment is also the end of a thing, the falling off because there is no higher place to go, the perpetually waiting little death. It was a death she'd known only through Raina—but a death Raina had known many times, in many ways. It had always been the doomed attempt to fend off this death that made Raina so daring; the end being inevitable, there was little to lose. It was what made her so adept at struggle. It was why she was so patient in waiting, and such a good lover.

Brown bodies blended into the sun-baked earth and dull rocks of the high places. They traveled by twilight. It was ordained by the Goddess; travel always at the time between times. Insects that fly above the clouds will not see you then. Eventually they came to where there were few trees and leaves grew thinner, the ground dry. Beyond that the plain of tall brown grass which had to be crossed. There were some women among them, some men. All were small, delicate-boned people of light brown skin, black hair and eyes; all moved lightly, swiftly, as if with each step they'd break into a run. Dr. Porter stood out among them. She was taller, broader. She was much darker. She walked slowly next to the pallet that had been lashed to long carrying sticks, every few minutes glanced over at the white woman stretched out on it, every once in a while would have them stop so she could hand her a squash-shaped canteen to drink from, hold a white wrist in both her hands and count the pulse. Sometimes the woman would half sit. She'd make sounds in her language—questioning sounds sometimes bordering on protest. Once she conferred with the doctor, then simply slid from the pallet and was on her feet. She steadied herself against the doctor's arms, breathing deeply and walking. She walked for many minutes. The pallet-bearers trotted along, burden eased.

She was striking in her looks, dark eyes flashed with another color in them—the color of the jungle—and once she laughed softly, weakly, so all turned at the sound. Their eyes were enormous, slightly slanted, gazing unblinkingly at her with a curiosity tinged by fear. When she crept back onto the pallet she slept despite the rolling, bouncing motion of their slow progress. Breeze blew with increasing frequency and strength through the trees.

Dr. Porter placed a steadying hand on the body that rolled slightly from side to side, aware only of the great burden of her responsibility. This was precious cargo. A tiny bruise, a cut, a relapse—none of that must occur. She must be delivered up whole. With her fate rested the fate of many; the doctor knew somehow that this woman was close to the center around which this entire game revolved—and while she did not completely understand the elements of the game and was not able to predict a given outcome from moment to moment, she had an instinctual grasp of the nature of the game itself, a wide-angled view of things. Sometimes, her own eyes rested on the woman's neck, and seeing the flash of silver, the small curved dagger of bone, she would come close to a clarifying vision. But the vision always eluded her.

Kaz drifted in and out of sleep.

Her clothes were crumpled, but had been washed clean. She'd refused to go naked. She'd seen it was the current style here, but current style had never much swayed her. Her sneakers had lost their laces somehow; the busted racket she wrapped with tenderness in her leather vest and used it as a sort of pillow. She told herself that the shattering of an outer form did not necessarily change an essence. Break an arm and it was still your arm. Torture a soul and someone could recognize it still—would know it if only they believed enough, if only they had opened up to and comprehended its true, essential nature—one that was nameless, unchanging, alone. Kaz slept and the crumpled shirt soaked against her back. The steadying hand of Dr. Porter made a damp imprint on cloth. Each muscle went limp in sleep. The burden of the pallet bearers was heavier then, and slower, as hours crawled toward night.

Kaz heard bird cries while she slept. The sound seemed to come from far away. Then the cries diminished, voices dropped from the chorus until only one remained. It was a long, lonely wail, something closer to an animal howl, or desecrated human voice. As she slept the sound took up more and more space inside her. It filled her head and seemed to become louder, closer. The closer it grew the less terrifying it became. Finally there was no terror to it at all; only a vast and overwhelming sorrow in the ringing hollowness of every note. She struggled to reach out and touch the source of this sound, eyelids fluttered faintly and—in her sleep—she cried.

She woke with a slight feeling of nausea, sliding from side to side. She woke to feel a subtle, hot breeze across her skin and the dark kindly face staring down. There were no more pools of sunlight, only shadows, and a gust of open air that said the terrain was changing. She woke with shock. Her lips formed a name.

The ground on their way uphill was scattered with objects that weren't sticks, though certainly that's what they appeared to be at first. They were bleached a dull brownish gray like the earth, knobby, angular things that here and there fell together in small dusty heaps or stuck solitarily from the ground like part of a broken spear.

In the twilight Kaz peered carefully. The farther they went uphill the more numerous these objects became. She could hear the pallet-bearers' breathing now, harder and harder as the incline steepened. After a while they stopped. She slid off the pallet, slid away from the doctor's gently pressuring hand and stood a little unsteadily, gazed at the flat, tablelike rock just ahead of them and a conglomeration of similarly shaped objects lined up on top.

The skulls seemed sad somehow, pathetically small. There were no mandibles left. The gaping holes for eyes looked like broken windows; the gashes once filled by nose cartilage looked a little ridiculous. Blank, expressionless. Approaching them on unsure feet, Kaz experienced a curious absence of fear. Looking down at the barely lit ground, she understood immediately what the worn soles of her LS Specials were crushing down against with each dry snap. She wasn't afraid but slightly revolted, resigned, and filled with a vague regret which she could not specify. Vertebral remnants, metatarsal bones, crunched beneath her feet. They mixed with the colorless earth.

"Here." Dr. Porter's hand rested on her shoulder. "Soon, now."

Kaz felt herself nodding in some sort of acquiescence: Yes, she wanted to say, yes of course. She turned silently toward the waiting group of small, tired people who had come so far today, carrying her a good part of the way. Soon now. Yes, she could feel it. But what did this black woman know? And how could she—or any of them—be trusted to lead her any-where? Or to understand the reasons for making this journey in the first place? Maybe they didn't know; perhaps they had no knowledge, not even an inkling, of their own expendability. Because surely, she told herself, surely, if they did, they'd have led her here only to be killed—symbolic sacrifice. Had they understood, they might have taken her as the spearhead of the vast white world that was closing in to destroy them. She brushed the doctor's hand from her gently. She turned and smiled, felt the smile's oddness. But her voice was just curious.

"Are you planning to do me in?"

Dr. Porter frowned. The ground twisted up, stalled here and there by flat, barren plateaus and clumpings of rocks. It went up to the high places, disappeared there in darkness.

"Well, are you?"

The doctor's attention fixed again on the pale white face before her, signs of illness and exhaustion mingled with beauty. She shook her head. "Are you so anxious for it?"

Kaz laughed.

The silence was strange. They resumed walking. Rest now, the doctor told her, but she refused and stayed on her feet. As twilight faded evening clamped down, air cooled and the bone-cluttered earth remained warm underneath. The air had a heavy, tangible quality; almost like a texture or sound. Kaz felt light and dizzy. Still she had no desire to stop. It was when they reached the next plateau that she stood and swayed, caught her balance against the arm the doctor offered. Stand, she told herself. She would stand, and remain standing; she'd go forward to meet what she strove for and be face to face with it, on her feet.

Something rattled in the dark.

The faces that loomed at them suddenly seemed to crop up from the dim shapes of rocks themselves. Eyes wide, black. Each face had been plastered with some sort of paint—each face and every body—a dark color which couldn't be made out in shadows. Each painted hand held up a stick. What rattled from each stick were bones tied by thongs; the bones rattled against each other with a dry, hollow sound.

Dr. Porter stepped forward to meet them, pulling her along. She was speaking rapidly to them now in a very foreign-sounding tongue. Once in a while she pointed to the white woman leaning wearily against her. The painted bodies fell into step on either side of their tiny group. They wore nothing but the smallest of cloths around the waist, tied between thighs; there seemed nothing but the presence or lack of breasts to distinguish one sex from the other. All were lean, black hair was swept away from each painted face and knotted, each movement catlike and strong, lightfooted. Dizziness was seeping into her now. Kaz could hear the ringing of her own breaths. On her feet. She'd stay on her feet this time.

The sound in her head got louder again. The chorus. Crying of some bird. She swayed on the flat, hard ground of another plateau, and looking ahead she thought this was the last plateau because there seemed nowhere else to go but across it and up a sheer stone peak leading only to sky.

The rattling increased. There was a slight chill—they were far up, she realized. And there were no lights here but, glancing above, she saw that a first star had glimmered out of nothing. Looking around she saw spears stabbed point-down in the earth among dull shapes of rocks. She saw the phantom fingers of dried bone swinging from these thin pillars, clicking against each other with each gust of breeze. A smell she didn't know permeated the air; it was so all-encompassing she hadn't sensed it at first, but now in the welcome wind ruffling sweat from her skin she was aware of it and wanted, for a moment, to run and hide. Something told her she wouldn't want to know it. And she'd always—yes, always—gone by instinct, made do with the stuff at hand when necessary. Still, she couldn't make herself smile.

Somewhere, someone laughed. She looked around but it didn't sound again.

She looked up, saw the source of the smell and for a second thought perhaps she'd seen something like it before. Some long-ago vision or memory from a long-ago dream. The male body hung, clothes in tatters, by its feet. The white arms hung down and were rotting in long lumps of detaching flesh. She couldn't see the face or dead eyes. It hung feet-up from a wooden frame several yards ahead, the frame sheltered by a wall of rock. Later, she wouldn't remember how she'd made it out in the dark. She'd think that perhaps it had been by the dull, glowing light of rattling bones that she'd seen this; then remember that she'd looked around again and this time could make out other shapes in addition to the dull outlines of large stones: crumpled, half-skeletal limbs haphazardly cluttering the spaces between rocks, dead hands clutching out, emitting rotted, shriveled odors from the partly revealed bone of each fingertip.

A match flared and was immediately sheltered in someone's hand.

Matches. She was surprised. For a second, she wanted to go back the way she'd come. Any way. The laughter came again; it was faraway, warm, cheery laughter—incongruous as the breeze that carried it. Another match hissed in the curve of Dr. Porter's large hands.

Kaz instinctively moved closer to the doctor. She felt her own fingers growing weak and heavy on the doctor's shoulder; then she pushed away to stand on her own.

There was movement around her. She couldn't make out what they were doing in the dark. Only Dr. Porter stood completely still, shielding an occasional lighted match between thumb and palm and glancing frequently up at the sky that had in it a single star.

Kaz could feel the day's pitiful vestige of recovering strength leave each muscle until what she stood on was nothing but a sort of willpower, a desire whose source she could no longer ascertain. Make do with the stuff at hand. But there was nothing at hand any more. Nothing but a sharp-pointed shark tooth dangling from her neck. She touched fingers to the tooth, touched them to her forehead. The ritualistic sensation of this motion calmed her. She felt one last surge of stability and kept on her feet.

Around her all movement seemed quieted. Several matches flared simultaneously, many green-plastered faces gazed hollowly at her with ghost-like expressionlessness as she stood there tired, sick, alone. Others had left the flickering ring of matches and gone to stand apart with their sticks of rattling bone, to perch on flat-topped rocks and gaze with a steady, careful scrutiny straight up at the silent sky.

Matches sputtered. Some went out and were relighted. The laughter came again.

It was a woman's laughter, nearer this time. It rang against rocks in the breeze-swept darkness. There was something tender about it, almost appealing. Then nothing. Matches had gone out and were replaced by a faint, icy glow; looking up, she saw that a pale sliver-thin moon had risen.

Here I am. Kaz opened her arms.

She felt things crumble away then. She felt it with a terrible sense of regret, apology; she'd wanted so much to stay on her feet. She waited for the crash of hard ground against her back and head, bones jabbing up against elbows, but it never came. Some arm had trapped her around waist and shoulders. Someone had caught her there, cushioned the fall, then lifted up and up with a certain, dizzying sweep. Opening her eyes, she saw the green-streaked, white-striped face gazing down at her like a hand-carved mask, features savagely obscured. She kept looking. Then recognized the eyes that met hers, stared wordlessly down. She fainted.

*   *   *

There were caves hidden in the high places. Some were winding, twisting labyrinths. All were very old. Hidden from the outside by boulders, camouflaged, the clean-swept hard earth floors of these caves were the only part of the mountain not littered by bone.

Torches lined the walls of the cave. There Dr. Manella Porter and her group of pallet-bearers were fed, guarded. There they curled up among themselves and slept. Beyond the guarded labyrinth entrance they weren't allowed to go; warriors of the Goddess stood there, stark and green, moved aside to allow Her to pass, burden dangling in arms. Then they closed back over the labyrinth mouth like flower petals clamping together. Bare footsteps sounded faintly down a corridor of stone.

The passageway wound through the mountain's innards, dipping, rising, narrowing. There were endless detours sprouting off it like twigs from a branch; other corridors leading nowhere and taking a long, dark time to get there. But the main passageway was indistinguishable from all these adjunct detours except for torches that flared at each rounded corner. The torches were hand-held. Green faces jumped above each torch. Each face lowered in a bow as She passed.

Time went by—a long time—but it seemed very brief. Or maybe it seemed endless to Her because She carried another body. Still, Her steps never faltered. This was Her realm, this sporadically broken darkness. She knew it all blindfolded.

The Goddess turned corners, went up and down rocky grades. Sometimes a spear would knock against stone from ahead or behind, and the echo ring for many minutes. It was on the diminishing crest of such an echo that She reached the passageway's end, where curtains of bird feathers hung over the entrance to another place in front of which stood two more green figures, silently guarding, who bowed as She went past.

It's frighteningly easy to become what you pretend to be. As in the famous quote of that anonymous German reflecting on the rise of Hitler: *One day we woke up, and we were Nazis.* Yes. But it's not that simple. The process of becoming anything can be nothing more than a series of simple, methodical steps. But these steps must be carried out with great attention to form, and the logical progression from one simple method to the next carried out with commitment and determination over a long period of time. So the decent German who said those words had, perhaps, pretended Nazism for a long time. In order to render the pretense believable, he had to pretend with vigor. He had to put some guts into it. In order to pretend with

conviction, he had to understand in detail the nature of what he was pretending to be, had to devote a good deal of time to boning up on things.
And like any athlete, artisan, orator—like anyone rehearsing a given set of
lines, rules, or movements—he had to practice. He had to practice hard.
Until the amount of time and emphasis that went into the pretense of being
a Nazi far outweighed the time and emphasis that went into being his own
self, the self that had stepped back and smirked a little and said: Okay now,
I'm really going to put one over on them. Until there was no time left
anymore to be the man who'd thought of pretending in the first place. And
that day came when, as he later said, he simply woke up and found that
he was, in fact, a Nazi. There was no room left inside to be anything else.
Like the boy Lee Simmonds had known back in high school who claimed
to be a good sprinter and then realized that eventually he'd be forced to
prove it. He practiced lonely, bitter cold months away on an obscure outdoor
track, limping back to the clumsily set starting blocks to rub his aching
thighs, aching calf muscles, while winter wind stabbed through his thin
gym clothes, and Lee, taking an easy cross-country jog after school at
sundown, would spot him sometimes from the snow-streaked crest of a hill
and grin down, unseen, at the awkwardness of an obvious beginner's gait—
knees too low, stance all wrong. Still, the gentleman in Lee forced upon
him a code of silence. So he watched the lonely months away, and the
years, until this boy qualified for the state championships in the 100, later
confiding to Lee that fear had driven him through every race, every qual-
ifying heat and every session of team practice—the terrible, deep-rooted
fear of someone's discovering, after all, that he was not really a runner but
only pretending.

Did Raina pretend? Or did she believe? In either case, did she actually
try to appear a certain way, or did she strive to *become* it?

Or was she that to begin with?

Back when she was Karlen, Kaz had pretended herself into and out of a
number of situations. Never, though, had she actually become what she
pretended to be. Not until she pretended to be Raina's lover, that is; she'd
woken up on a morning when snow mounded every window ledge, and felt
herself transformed. In a short space of time she'd actually become a lover,
become a new entity—*Kaz*—and while Karlen could use all manner of
pretense to her advantage, Kaz lacked the facility. With Raina, she could
no longer pretend. So in her presence she felt stripped. It would take her
a long time to discover where, with Raina, her own true source of power
lay.

At first, she'd attributed this nearly painful lack of pretense to the similarity between them. Both, after all, were women. And it's in the nature of love between two women that sensation given is also received, there are few obstacles of physical other-ness to overcome, boundaries can dissolve and time stretch long and leisurely in the realm between desire and satisfaction. But she soon realized that this physical sameness did not lead to lack of mystery. Raina was, to her, a secret. Sometimes she could feel herself wavering on the brink of the place where this secret was kept. She'd stop then, stop breathing; she would open her eyes and look into the face of this person who was now her lover and know that in there the secret waited; she'd try to look longer, search it out, prolong everything and make time stretch a little more, just a little—always, she had the feeling that if only she could wait those few seconds longer then, ah then, she'd seize it, know it, have it. But time never stopped long enough. She'd feel her eyelids flick shut and go into herself, roll in sensation, the search ended once more, the treasure hunt over.

Now, less than conscious, some part of her felt herself being set down on a dry, soft surface. Something whispered the word *feathers* to her; it was just like that, crushing against a bed of feathers here inside the earth. Kaz thought maybe she'd done it this time. Maybe she'd held concentration for that extra bit longer. Maybe she'd discovered the place, the core, where the secret lay. Maybe she had, and maybe that was why she felt a certain half-conscious ecstasy now, or triumph, and felt that—deep as she was under-ground—she was also flying.

Candles flickered from the walls. She wondered vaguely how they'd gotten hold of so many. The walls were colored, too, painted with figures she couldn't discern. She realized her eyes were open. She was awake. Candlelight brushed along the murals, distorted the ceiling of rock. For a second her sense of perspective was gone. So when she gazed across the room—because it was that, a large, circular room—she couldn't tell how far away the opposite wall was, couldn't tell how far it might be to the series of rocks inclining up, in crude replication of steps, to the flat-topped altar of stone, to the wood-framed thing behind the altar which was shrouded by another curtain that fluttered. Feathers. Feathers fluttering lightly in the occasional, gentle drafts that flowed through all the winding labyrinth from the night outside.

Kaz lay still. She couldn't regain her sense of perspective. She felt a kind of overriding calm, though. It occurred to her that maybe she was dying. But she let go of that idea with an ease bordering on resignation; it would have been too simple. No, she knew the pattern of her own life, was old enough to accept what it told her—she wouldn't be granted an easy, sudden death upon waking, wouldn't be allowed to just roll over and kick off like that. Things had gotten too complex, too out of hand. She began to feel better then, lay still and waited.

She was alone.

The loneliness of everything hit her suddenly with all the weight of its silence. It was as if each year of her life had rammed full into her, as if each moment she'd ever remembered had attacked now with its particular burden of pain. Kaz was sick, and tired. It was what she'd termed widow-walk sickness—that sickness stemming from sticking around at home waiting while a million Ahabs went off on the high seas to squeeze sperm out of whatnot—this sickness that had spurred her out of the city, the country, away from the earth's surface. And now that she'd come so far, right on target too, she'd been left alone again. Well, she for one was sick and tired of it. No more of this stuff. Not ever. She closed her eyes. The tears that squeezed out around the lids, dribbled down both cheeks and made crooked streams along the bridge of her nose were tears of frustration mixed with a sort of rage. Kaz could hear herself bitching out loud; the words rang senselessly along candle-flickering walls. All right, she said, she'd had it. No more hanging around the castle waiting for you-know-who to get back from the crusades, clanking along twenty years later in rust-laden armor with death clanking along a few steps behind. No, really, this was it. It was not for her. Not her cup of tea. Because she'd come at all costs—come to find Raina no matter what shape she was in, how damaged, how mad, how lost—she'd come to find her no matter what; and now, now if it meant that she'd come so far simply to be left alone again well, well, then she would go back the way she'd come, thank you. Yes. She'd had just about enough of this shit. And she would get up and leave if she had to. Just get up and leave.

"Don't."

She let the hands close around hers gently, gently wiggled free and with her own hands counted their fingers—one two three four, thumb, one through four and another thumb—without opening her eyes. Kaz pulled the hands up to cover her face. She covered the backs of both hands with her own, so there were four hands over her face and she didn't open her eyes. Sudden panic jumped through her: what if these were the wrong hands? What if she found nothing familiar in them, if she did not remember, after all? She waited, eyes shut, and the fear went away. Now fingers were moving lightly, slowly; they were tracing the path of her tears.

"Peekaboo."

She fought the urge to look.

"Peekaboo," the voice invited.

The face staring down at her was a zebra, a candy cane. It was something from a childhood fantasy of Halloween—the stripes applied in meticulous diagonals. Even the lips had been striped. Even the eyelids. Opening her eyes, Kaz gazed up from between the striped fingers that spread gently across her face, saw the flicker of candles on striped skin, saw the dark eyes that were not striped, the thick dark hair falling over striped ears. Hands shivering, she lifted the green and white fingers, saw the palms damply stained and breathed with relief. So it was paint after all, paint. Then a new terror moved in on her: what could the paint be hiding?

Peekaboo, the voice had said. Now the green and white lips parted to show white teeth, the mask was broken by a desolate grin. And the nursery rhyme finished:

"I see you."

Kaz moved the hands away. She held them quietly against her chest and could feel the chain slide under damp paint and sweat. Something cold blew across her face, then vanished.

"How have you been?"

"Tired, Kaz. I've been tired."

Sitting up from the pallet of feathers was easy. There was no more fever. She did it slowly, wanted to measure every movement, to somehow examine herself in the act of doing this: of sitting up slowly to press both arms around the camouflaged body crouching there beside her.

"Kazzy, I think I'm out of my mind."

"Don't you worry."

"I think that—oh, that I really am insane."

Green smeared her cheek. Kaz pulled back a little to see the stripes melting against another cheek. "What about this stuff?" she touched a stained cheek and smiled while tears still ran, tried to keep the shaking from her voice. "Does it come off with water?"

She moved closer and they hugged again, tiredly, firmly, white body swirling into the green-striped one.

"Don't," said Raina. "Please don't leave me."

The paint washed off slowly.

Steps led up to the altar, to the feather curtain behind the altar that opened the way to a chamber where more candles dripped, wax running free-form designs along the walls and stone floor. In this chamber was another altar on which was laid a large mattress of feather-stuffed animal skins, and blankets. Throughout this chamber rang a hushed bubbling, gurgling sound. Kaz saw the small pool of water echoing up to form a natural basin in the stone floor against one wall. Mountain springs, it was explained to her, underground streams that ran through various parts of the mountain. Originally it had been these streams that carved out labyrinths in the rock itself. Now, this small limb of the network bubbled out into the temple here. Yes, the *temple*. Raina smiled softly. It was their source of water. The perfect place for such a spring to be situated: in the Temple of the Moon.

She leaned down toward the bubbling cool liquid, dampened cloths.

She washed with great ceremony. Kaz wondered if it was for her benefit. Raina had always known how to put on a good show. Propped against the base of the stone altar, Kaz wrapped herself in a blanket for warmth, watched intently as the cloths were soaked and slightly wrung. The forearms were washed first. Then the upper arms, then the shoulders. She watched for signs of damage on the smooth skin; there were none. So far, so good. She watched Raina bending there in shadows, rinsing the cloths, standing straight again and elaborately applying cloth and water to every inch of skin—the front, the sides, ribs, thighs, down to the feet. She didn't wash her face or breasts. After a while she stood there dripping and Kaz stood too and approached a little tentatively, unsteady on her feet. It was a body she could recognize. Even in the half-shadow of mad candlelight; even with the changes forced on it by hard living, by time and life's increased toughness, it was a body she recognized as the body of her lover. A small indentation here. A tiny irregularity there. The things only a lover would know of or notice. But she approached with a certain fear now. She'd offer to help; offer to cleanse the back, the back of the thighs and back of the neck. She wanted desperately to reach out and wipe paint from the face, from the still-covered breasts. This desire also filled her with a kind of terror—perhaps she'd discover what she was afraid of. She reached out a hand anyway, let the blanket sift to the ground. Here, she heard herself say. Here, I will. The hand that reached was trembling. Raina hesitated. She was half Raina now, half some other thing. She handed a dripping cloth over and then immediately turned so her back faced Kaz, spread both arms like a bird and when the cold wetness crawled down her spine remained silent.

Terrified, Kaz sent the cloth in wide, careful sweeps along skin. With each sweep new flesh was revealed. She could make out no damage here, no deformation or sickness. Not anywhere along the back, the buttocks, the thighs. She washed the skin slowly, knelt through dizziness and growing relief to wash the backs of the legs. Everything strong. Everything stretched and lean and hard, very hard—a warrior's body. She stood again. She leaned against the long, damp back, rested her face there gladly. Still the terror called; she could feel it teasing her along, goading from inside.

"Turn around now," she whispered.

Raina did and the zebra mask loomed suddenly before her. She started with the forehead. Water dripped along the temples, the nose. She worked her way down over closed eyelids. The paint was dripping away now, flesh revealing itself, unmarred by anything except the growing reality of age and weariness. Down. The lips. Cheeks, and chin. Kaz rested a wet hand on each of Raina's shoulders, looked at Raina again full-face for the first time in more than two years and did not know what to do. She'd envisioned many meetings. Many embraces. Had played the limitless number of reunion scenes over and over in her head, until each blended into the other and there was only this—this looking at Raina, touching but holding herself slightly apart because without some separation there was no way to see fully. The face was hard, and fine. Dark. And it had aged. But it was nevertheless unmistakable—unmistakable, and there was on it no discernible injury.

"Here." Raina gestured toward her breasts.

They were swirled in lines of green and stark white. Kaz lifted the cloth to them. Raina's hand touched her wrist lightly.

"Careful."

The trembling started inside her again. Gently, hardly touching, she squeezed water over the breasts, watched paint drip, and wiped very softly from nipples to the base of each breast, cleaned everything away, and when she was done stepped back a little to see more clearly.

There was no change in shape or size; only a visible change in texture. It was by deep-running scars that the breasts had been mutilated. The scars criss-crossed, creased over one another. All healed, leaving pale scar tissue behind. There was barely an untouched surface left on either breast, and, pointing cleanly from the ruined flesh, each nipple seemed somehow incongruous.

Kaz touched the cloth thoughtlessly to her own face. She held it there a moment, then pressed it against her lips to stifle some sound that never came.

"Fertility," said Raina. "And honor in war. Blood from the breast of the Goddess—they take it, each season."

Kaz felt herself tilt forward, her tired head rest against Raina's neck, inch down until her lips brushed breasts. Poor breasts. The lips kissed very lightly—she was afraid to hurt them. And she felt tears spill soundlessly, run along the canals of scars slashed into those breasts. Raina's hands touched the sides of her face, lifted up until they were looking at each other.

"No Kazzy, don't. Don't feel this way. It's not so terrible—oh, not really." She smiled almost playfully. Her voice was calm, barely touched by sadness. "Everything has its price."

There was never complete darkness here. Candles or torches of wood burned always. So if daylight never seeped through, then it was just as true that nighttime never arrived. All life underground took place in an unchanging, timeless space.

On the feather-stuffed hide mattress Kaz stretched fully clothed. She'd envisioned this taking place in a nearly complete darkness and now, seeing that it would not be the case, she felt rattled and unreasonably shy.

Naked beside her, back turned toward her, the long candle-lit body of a goddess lay still and silent, demanding nothing. She was Goddess now, unquestionably. She'd had the marks of divinity carved into her flesh—the scars would never fade.

Oh. It was a small sigh Kaz breathed into the back of the Goddess, pressed her face against the smooth spine. She set a hand, just so, along the rib cage. She could feel the steady swell of each breath. She could tell that the Goddess did not sleep but must be wide-eyed, awake and silent, solitary in the midst of every tired thought.

"Raina."

The body didn't move. Kaz touched a shoulder gently, pulled and the body turned without protest but also without urgency, lay there looking up at her calmly. The eyes were bright with exhaustion. She guessed it was no easy job, being the Goddess. Poor breasts. They'd paid for their worship.

Kaz sat. She bent to kiss the forehead, the nose and chin. She touched lips to each eyelid, brushed lips against lips. There was a simple acceptance in the face of this—acceptance, but no response.

She held each hand up to her mouth in turn, stroked each finger, each knuckle. She pressed lips to palm. She touched each arm to the elbow and back, examined each inch of skin thoroughly. There was time, she told herself, time between now and the omnipresent then that had driven her underground, here at the center of things. Time to lay each arm gently against the feather-filled surface and to creep down, sit at the feet of the Goddess and lift each foot in turn as she had each hand, count every toe with a certain relief that there were ten after all, stroke the sole of each foot to the heel, around to the ankle. She kissed the feet of the Goddess, stroked up each leg to the knee. She shut her eyes to candlelight dancing on stone. Far, far in the background she heard a mountain spring bubbling up, heard gusts of breeze fading through labyrinths. She kept her eyes closed and now, in the darkness thus created she could see it all enacted just as she'd imagined, could feel her own hands doing what they'd planned on long ago before the light made them shy: removing her crumpled clothes in a quiet, leisurely way, letting them drop somewhere—she didn't see where; her eyes were still closed. In dark she could bend down again now, kissing the knees of the Goddess, palms touching lightly on thighs until she thought the thighs stirred, thighs moved; until she thought there was something anxious here in the dark, some clutching of hands on stone, fingers laid with a sudden, soft urgency against the back of her own neck, stroking through her hair. In the dark she moved up looking for Raina, up and up with open kisses to find her, rest against her, to stay a while. She thought for a second that this was what she'd come here for, just this: strange caress, played out in darkness; perhaps it was not the only way to find her, but it seemed the most intimate, the most immediate. Her lips moved, mouth rested, touched. Until the Goddess moaned, fell away altogether, and what was left was Raina, Raina asking her to stay, stay, don't leave yet. Her voice whispered somewhere above, insistent, sad.

"You know," breathed the voice. "Everything leads to death, Kazzy. That's the real truth. And it's okay. I still think you're beautiful."

There was hardly any more Goddess; only the breasts remained. Kaz eased up farther, rolled her face against mortal flesh, opened eyes to the stone-cold flicker of candlelight and fell into the place between mutilated breasts, kissed and kissed and then she cried.

In the chambers, light flared across rock, cut deep edges into each shadow, jumped higher and dimmed. Along the great twisting length of the stone corridor, guards stood silent and still, watching the darkness beyond each small circle of intermittent light. They stayed awake through every second of underground night, guarding the time and space along the way to morning. While in the farthest vestige of tunnel, wax dripped against stone, and in an innermost recess of earth a goddess slept, and loved, in love called out a single name.

SOLOMON STREET

Gabriel thought at first it was a scream that woke him. He thrust both hands flat out so they sliced through air, when he sat sweating and wide-eyed realized he was chopping away at nothing. There was only the room's comforting darkness, each smell familiar. An alarm clock ticked on the bed table next to Yael and he saw the green glow of numbers—twenty minutes to four in the morning—time passing, each second neatly marked and delineated. He felt the sweat subside, his breathing calm. But shut his eyes and he could hear it still: not the scream he'd thought it was, but a desolate sort of wail that was half human, half something else—he wasn't quite sure—half bird? It was long, began deep down in some imaginary throat and continued to a high, shrill pitch before withering slowly to one crying note that was inimitable, utterly alone. It made him think of a dying condor. Even though he'd never seen a condor. Shut his eyes and the echoes sounded. Shut eyes again and the echoes were fainter than before, like weakening ripples growing from the spot where a stone had dropped into water.

He turned to Yael. He'd jerked blankets away from them both in panic, and now her body was exposed. Five months pregnant; the belly beginning to round and stretch. She had to sleep on her back now. Her breasts were heavier, they'd ballooned and flattened slightly against her, the nipples dark brown. She got tired early these days. Now she slept entirely undisturbed.

His hand hovered over her. He wanted to rest a palm on the roundness but did not.

She came from a religious background and, though not religious herself, once in a while she'd revert to mildly mystical oriental customs. He'd hear her chanting some nights under her breath while she examined her own pregnant body from all angles in the mirror. He'd seen bright little charms scattered throughout her drawers and she'd smiled at him once when he held the miniature carvings out to her questioningly, then she'd blushed with embarrassment. They were very small—half a finger length at most—made of stone that had been intricately carved and smoothed by age, by the touch of many hands, each painted in warm, bright colors. At first he thought the little figures were female buddhas; they were plump bodies with large breasts, one stone hand vanishing beneath a breast while the other clutched a tiny sprig of something and held it out like a gift. On each bright-painted face, a close-lipped half smile. Each face was consumed by eyes that were enormous, and blank, turned up at the corners.

An old custom, she'd explained, her face burning red. For fertility and a healthy child. Her mother had done it, her mother's mother—all the mothers before them. She herself did it because, well, because she saw no harm in it. She lowered her eyes, took his hands between both of hers and kissed them many times. He'd laughed gently, after a while sat beside her on the bed and stroked her hair. It'll be okay, he whispered to her, it'll be okay. He didn't know why he said that. Maybe it was himself he was trying to assure—although he knew everything would be all right somehow—everything would be whatever it would be. His future was bright. It was. They were going to have plenty of children, he told her. And when she agreed he knew suddenly why he'd married her—because she would want plenty of children—so his melting feeling was because of this potential of children in her, in him, children she could bear because she was a woman. He loved her for what they'd propagate together. Yet he sensed her love for him was more generalized. She'd fit him into the sphere of her life; or, rather, the sphere of her life had encompassed him, too. And because she appreciated life's texture—something he had no time to do—she unwittingly served the function of making him feel his existence was complete. He'd fight for that feeling, and kill for it. He was willing to die for it.

Gabriel closed his eyes again. Faint echoes only, getting smaller each second. Something tickled his eyelids like a falling leaf. But he opened them to silence. A sleeping wife. Ticking clock.

He eased out of bed.

He was careful to cover her again. He folded the blanket back over her breasts and stepped quietly away. He walked through to the front room. He knew all the dark shapes of furniture here: sofa, two chairs, coffee table. Bookshelves. Opening to the kitchenette. Another closed bedroom door: Pablo's room. His brother slept a lot now. Sometimes they had trouble waking him.

Gabriel crossed to the window and opened it. He breathed deeply. The air was chilled, damp Jerusalem air in that time when winter was blending into spring. Below, Solomon Street and the street lamps still glowing. Through the yellowed light of one a figure passed—soldier, gun slung over a shoulder, boots scuffing the pavement and faint sound of whistling rising from him, disappearing in the air. Gabriel thought that in the entire world he was the only other man to hear it.

He shut his eyes.

Nothing. No bird cries. No screams. Just a full, dull silence in his mind and behind closed eyes he saw it stretch away infinitely, first black, then white. Gabriel reached blindly to wipe dew from the window ledge and without opening his eyes he brought the dew-sprinkled hand back in, pressed it to his face.

Thou holdest mine eyes waking. I am so troubled that I cannot speak.

He passed a hand over his body. Everything naked; the skin smooth here, curled with hair there; he touched mounds of old scar tissue. Wages of war.

I have considered the days of old. The years of ancient times.

Gabriel began rocking on his feet, hand over face, shoulders slightly bowed. He barely realized this; barely realized the words he spoke to himself. He felt nothing—no remorse, no pain or joy or comfort—just the physical sensation of rocking back and forth in darkness, the chill of nighttime breeze across his naked thighs and ribs.

I call to remembrance my song in the night. I commune with mine own heart.

Nothing. He waited for a sign, an echo. The bird cry that wailed through his dreams, tormenting him—he wanted it back and knew somehow it would not come again. A few months at most. Time up. Over now. Over.

The skies sent out a sound. Thine arrows also were sent abroad.

Time passed, more time gone. Over. Over and out. Wordless, soundless, he rocked back and forth and one hand reached to press against the wall. Yael chanted in the evenings for a healthy child. Gabriel hoped for a son. But sometimes, just before dawn, he'd wake praying that the child would not be male. He didn't know why; he'd lived thirty-four years determined to clean up certain dangers so no son of his would ever have to. But now, on another night, he knew he'd failed. He knew somehow he'd done worse than fail—he'd spread his own brand of poison, maybe—and knew he'd had no choice in the matter. It was done—all done. Too human, he'd dangled in the winds of history like everyone else, able to react effectively for short periods of time but never change the course of things in the long run. He would have sons and give them guns. In winter nights they'd stand high up on mountain ridges. They'd look down at stars. Lights of valley settlements. Lights of sleeping women, and children. So high up, they could not touch the light; so high up, they would die without touching this light, die leaving guns to their sons and grandsons. While on the other side of the border their enemy did the same. Gazed down at lights on a cold night in winter. Gazed up at the moon. Protected their power—like the king who stalked, sleepless, through the orchard wherein rested the golden branch of his rulership—until another king came to kill and replace him. Absolute solitude the price of power. No more bright futures. No more prophets.

Gabriel leaned forward, face against the wall.

Behind the morning you find the night.

Behind the darkness, light.

How can I eat while others starve?

How can I thrive while others fall?

No, no, no. Keep your mind on the one purpose. Keep your mind on the one true purpose. The clear purpose, limited, your own people and none other, flame burning all the more brightly because it is small. Clear white flame, burning in darkness. The one purpose, set your heart on it, leave no room in your heart for another purpose. Life is small. Life is brief, and finite. Without purpose, it is a breath in the night. A breath soon over. Leaving behind no stars, no children, no love. So keep yourself on the one path, the single purpose. Greatness recognizes its limitations. Greatness commits to one purpose. That one purpose is the world. That one path, all paths. And all paths lead to a single place: the end. All a matter of time, and of destiny. But all things arrive there, except perhaps time itself—arrive there—finish, climax, fulfillment—the end.

The bright, finite lines inside him stretched out, up, spread through him. Gabriel opened his eyes and for a minute thought the blinding white rays came from inside and had screamed out through his fingertips, boomeranged back. But he blinked and the black dots on his eyelids faded. He'd caught a glimpse of first sunlight edging over the rust-colored roof of a building, reflected off a metal antenna.

He hoisted the window up as far as he could and leaned out into the diminishing morning gray. The streets below still empty. But far off he could hear feet walking. He heard cars rumble to a stop several streets away. Close by, pigeons clucked.

Gabriel closed his eyes again and saw nothing. Darkness that was black, then shimmered to a red-tinged white. But nothing in it. No image. No sound.

When he looked down, then across the rooftops, he expected to see something different. He didn't quite know what; he wasn't even aware of this sense of expectancy until he realized his legs were trembling. He searched the rooftops with a kind of dread—what would he find?—and his eyes, which Pablo had sworn could see through the back of the head, slid everywhere with rapid thoroughness. Nothing. He sent his eyes searching again.

It'll be okay, he told himself.

It'll be okay.

Gabriel let air expand in his chest. Like eating or drinking something very sweet. This air was special: old yet fresh, cooled by the night. And now, in growing sunlight, the city was beginning to reveal itself—a desert, flesh-color, Jerusalem stone, orange metal rooftops broken here and there by church spires, mosque domes, strutting gray pigeons.

He thought he saw something fly by out of the corner of his eye. Something white, moving very swiftly. But he shook his head, forced a smile. It would be okay.

He looked out again and this time there was only city. Only Jerusalem, the morning brisk and clear.

ACKNOWLEDGMENTS

I'd like to acknowledge the help I received from a variety of sources in working on this book. Dr. Raphael Patai's magnificent *The Hebrew Goddess* was a source of both information and inspiration, as were sections of Sir James George Frazer's *The Golden Bough*. To say nothing of *Sportfishing for Sharks*, by Captain Frank Mundus and Bill Wisner. And Jonathan Katz's collection, *Gay American History*, from which I appropriated and reworked a Native American tale. For details of the life of artist Romaine Brooks, I'm indebted to Dolores Klaich's *Woman + Woman*; for details resulting in my fantasy version of the poet D'Annunzio, many thanks to Lady Una Troubridge's memoir *The Life of Radclyffe Hall*. The character of Dr. Porter was inspired in part by the real-life story of Mamphela Ramphele, colleague of the late, great Stephen Biko. At the time of this writing, Dr. Ramphele has just been released from banishment in South Africa.

Throughout the writing and editing process my family loved and encouraged me. They always have. Others did too, especially long-time friend Joyce Malo-Mikotowicz. And my dear Joan, squash and Ping-Pong player extraordinaire.

Finally, I want to acknowledge Ann E. Patty, best editor on earth, who worked with me through many difficult months of suffering and loss and rebirth.

Here goes, Ann. It'll be okay.

JENIFER LEVIN
New York
August 1983

ABOUT THE AUTHOR

This is Jenifer Levin's second novel. She has also written for *Rolling Stone* and *Ms. Magazine*. Ms. Levin lives in New York City.